THE VIKING'S HARMONY

A Bloodborn Fates Novel

C.P. Harrow

Copyright © 2026 by C.P. Harrow
All rights reserved.

No part of this publication may be reproduced, distributed, or transmitted in any form or by any means, including photocopying, recording, or other electronic or mechanical methods, without the prior written permission of the publisher, except as permitted by U.S. copyright law.

The story, all names, characters, and incidents portrayed in this production are fictitious. No identification with actual persons (living or deceased), places, buildings, and products is intended or should be inferred.

Book Cover by Muhammad Waqas
1st edition 2026

For the ones who lost their voice in the dark.
Who learned to survive, and to fight in silence.
This is for you.
May your heart one day remember its song, and the courage to let it sing again.
May you find your harmony.

Prologue

Winter, 879 AD. Somewhere in the North, lost to time and blood soaked snow.

The world was fire and screams when it ended. Ash drifted through the sky like blackened snow, and the wind carried the scent of burnt thatch and torn flesh. His village, his home, was nothing but smoke and bone. Longhouses, toppled. Warriors, gutted. Children…Gone.

He had fought, fought until his sword snapped, until his fists broke, until the claws of the monster of a man had ripped his body open and spilled him into the snow. Now, he lay dying in it. The same snow where he had once sworn to defend his brethren and their families, and to serve gratefully until the Gods had said otherwise. Blood pooled beneath him, steaming against the frost. His breath came in slow, freezing drags, crystalizing at the edges of his mouth. He couldn't move. He wouldn't scream or beg, but his body couldn't move a single muscle anymore. He could only listen as footsteps crunched through the snow.

Not many. Just one set. Slow. Deliberate. Then… a second. Quicker. Frenzied. A voice snarled through the trees.

"There are no more! I want more!"

A sickening *crack* followed. The other voice, colder, cut through the night. "Control yourself."

Silence again, and then, he saw the boots. Dark leather, perfectly clean despite the slaughter. They stopped inches from his head. A tall figure knelt beside him, shrouded in a black cloak, eyes aglow with unnatural calm. The man's face was unmarred, unreadable…ageless. He looked down at the dying warrior with something almost like respect.

"You fought well," the man said softly, in a language the warrior somehow understood. "Most scream. You did not. Your wounds are mortal. But your will... is not." He reached forward, fingers brushing through blood-soaked hair to tilt the warrior's face toward him. "What is your name?"

The dying man said nothing. His jaw clenched. His ice-blue eyes burned with fury. He would not give his name to the devil.

The figure smiled faintly. "So be it. Keep your name. Keep your silence, even in death. But strength like yours… it should not be wasted. Still, there is a price."

He leaned closer, voice turning to a whisper, *a sentence* handed down by a godless judge.

"Because you will not speak your name, the gods will never hear it. You will not rise with your brothers. You will not feast in Valhalla. The Einherjar will not know your face among them, warrior." A pause. "You will remain, nameless and alone. You will walk the earth forever. Strong, yet as silent as the death that is about to take you, and as forgotten as the heartbeat I will claim."

Then, darkness surged into him. Fire poured into his veins. He felt his throat burn with a sharp stabbing heat, his body seized and twitched under the endless agony. Every nerve screamed, and still he said nothing, still, he stayed silent, not even granting a scream through the pain. .

He clawed into the ice. Roared without breath. The snow beneath him turned black…and when he woke hours, or days, later, the men were gone. Only the wind remained.

Only the cold.

Chapter 1

Winter, present day. Thorne Ridge, Georgia.

Winter didn't just arrive at Thorne Manor, it descended. A slow, deliberate fall of snow buried the ridge in white, turning the towering pines into frozen sentinels and swallowing the usual sounds of the forest. Breath fogged in the air and drifted away like ghosts. Frost crawled across windowpanes, catching every scrap of light and scattering it back in fractured shimmer. Even the narrow road winding toward Thorne Ridge lay muted beneath the storm's quiet weight, as if the world had been momentarily suspended between heartbeats.

Snow could smother the woods, darken the sky, silence every last birdcall. Quiet even the most obnoxious of noises drifting in from the small town beyond the large manor hidden within the woods.

It did not, however, silence the twins.

Garin moved through the old house like a ghost. Massive, barefoot, shirtless, half feral and fully unbothered, he stalked down the upper hallway with only one destination in mind: Beau's study. Get his orders, then return to his solitude. Maybe have whiskey should the southern man offer.

He never made it. Not before he heard them.

"Careful, Rua," a low Irish voice murmured ahead, laced with mischief. "He's stompin' like a frost giant again."

"Aye, I hear it," came the redhead's response, utterly unrepentant. "Think if we run fast enough, we can trip him before he rips our arms off?"

Gods save him.

Rua and Cian O'Sullivan appeared at the end of the corridor like twin wraiths dressed in smug delight. Rua's copper hair tied back in a careless knot, Cian's blond waves a tousled halo of lies and impending violence. They were leaner than him, several inches shorter, wirier, but no less dangerous. But…infinitely more annoying.

They blocked the hall like the gremlins they were. Garin said nothing, hoping that perhaps this time, his silence would send them away.

False hope.

"See," Rua grinned, arms crossed. "That look right there? That's his I'm going to throw one of ye off the damn balcony face."

"I'd like to see him try," Cian added with a snort. "Break his silence long enough to grunt, maybe. Or bless us with a single syllable. Go on then, big lad. say 'good mornin'.'"

Still nothing. He stood motionless, blue eyes narrowed beneath thick brows, the runes inked across his chest and arms shifting faintly with tension. Not a man a sane being would ever test. He took one step forward, and the twins straightened like two feral cats ready to make a break for it. "He's glaring," Rua stage-whispered dramatically to his twin.

"That's just his face, brother."

"A face carved by the gods."

"From stone," Cian added. "Cold, emotionless stone."

Garin resumed walking. He was two seconds from gutting them, but nothing else was new. For the last century and a half, the two Irishmen had made it their personal mission every damned day to try and get a rise out of the Viking. He often wondered if Simon would ever make good on his constant threat to return the twins to Ireland to the dirt where he found them.

He'd have to find the Frenchman later.

"Wait, wait-don't go. Don't you want to hear about the incident in town?"

"It involved a llama, a banshee, and Addie's cafe," Rua offered helpfully, though Garin wasn't quite sure who it was supposed to help..

"No." It was the only word Garin had spoken all morning, the only one spoken for the last few days if he was being honest. Even then, his voice boomed in that low tone, his old Norse accent creeping in even with the single syllable.

It still did nothing to deter, nor scare away, the O'Sullivan brothers.

Cian clutched his chest, throwing himself back against the wall, blonde hair flying back as he whipped his head backwards. "Gods help us, he speaks."

Rua flung himself back just as dramatically into his brother's arms. "And I was starting to think he was mute again. Alert Mave, we won't need that speaking charm after all."

Garin reached the staircase. His hand curled around the banister. Ice-blue eyes fixed forward. If he ignored them long enough, maybe…just maybe…

"Simon says you've been brooding more than usual."

"We're worried," Cian added, utterly insincere. "You might freeze solid and shatter. Like an icicle."

"Again," Rua said mournfully, "Always."

Garin paused. Took a breath. Counted backwards from ten in Old Norse, then, slowly, like a man trudging through snow for a thousand years, he turned just enough to speak.

"Do you ever shut up long enough to grant the dead peace?"

The twins stared at him. Then at each other. Then burst out laughing, doubling over as they cackled.

"He's back," Rua said, waving his hand towards Garin in victory.

"Glory be, we've succeeded brother!" Cian replied.

"Long may he brood."

Garin continued toward the door, tuning them out, already regretting everything. Joining this coven, agreeing to stay. Letting the twins live as long as they have. He had fought in ancient wars. Survived the fall of kingdoms, massacre after massacre, even survived genocide.

But nothing, absolutely nothing, tested his will to live quite like the O'Sullivan twins on a snow-covered morning in Georgia.

They'd be back within the hour.

By the time the Vikings reached the wide double doors of Beau Thorne's study, the twin menaces had vanished down some dark hallway, more than likely to raid the kitchen or torment Mave again over her book collection.

He didn't knock, Beau already knew he was there. The study smelled like cigar smoke and pine. Golden lamplight flickered across worn wood, leather-bound books, and the blood-colored glass perched in Beau's hand like it belonged there. The Southern vampire leader leaned back in his chair, booted feet on the edge of the desk, his golden-brown eyes cutting through the dark like firelight in molasses.

"You're late, you know," Beau drawled, grinning over the rim of his glass. "Thought maybe Rua finally got brave enough to stab you."

Garin didn't entertain that with an answer. He stepped inside, bare feet near-silent on the hardwood, and closed the door behind him. In the soft light, he looked carved from something older than time.

Broad shoulders and arms thick with muscle, his body still glistened faintly from the walk in the snow. Tattoos, Nordic runes, coiled beasts, ancient knots, crawled over his chest and up his throat, marking him like scripture. His jaw was shadowed in stubble, lips full and unsmiling, and those piercing eyes, ice-blue and ancient, seemed to stare through stone.

He didn't sit, never did. Beau dropped his boots to the floor with a thump.

"Relax, big guy. Just need you to sign off on the new patrol schedule. Got some strange reports near Route 19 again. Figured you'd wanna head it off before Bobby sends us another 'stay off my crime scene' text."

Garin gave a low grunt and took the paper Beau slid across the desk.

"One day," Beau said, swirling his drink lazily, "I'm gonna get you to crack a smile. Hell, even a laugh. Maybe find yourself a pretty thing to warm that ice you call a heart."

Garin didn't bother looking up, this was nothing new. For centuries, Beau has tried to connect with him in more friendlier terms. He just wasn't interested.

"Control the Irishmen before I throw them to the wolves."

Beau blinked slowly, then laughed, rich and slow. "Well damn. A whole sentence. Someone done blessed me tonight. Now why would I torture the wolves like that?"

He finally looked at him. Cold. Flat. Still completely unamused.

"They're supposed to be grown men, almost two-hundred years old. Instead, they spend their days testing how long I can hold back before I snap their necks."

"Better you than them pissin' off Evangeline again," Beau said, smirking. "Last time they moved her hairbrush, she hexed the whole west wing with that sulfur stink for a week. Hell no, I ain't redirecting their chaos."

The vampire leader leaned forward, elbows on the desk, his smirk half crooked, "You, my friend, are the most dangerous blanket I've ever seen. Just thick, grumpy, and always there when it counts. We need that. But maybe, just maybe, you oughta let yourself live a little."

No answer.

Beau sighed, grabbed the schedule, and leaned back again. "Fine. Back to broodin'. See if I care. You'll thank me when some girl comes along who doesn't run from the growl. Maybe you'll find yourself a Leah, though maybe one less mean than mine."

Garin had already turned to leave, he didn't thank him, didn't even a grunt at the idea of finding a mate like Beau had just over a year prior.

Not yet.

He padded down the long, firelit corridor toward his room, the ancient hardwood cool beneath his feet. The walls trembled faintly with life, not from earthquakes, but from the chaos that came with housing the monsters who made Thorne Manor their home.

From one wing, he could hear them. The bastards, yet again.

"Rua, if you touch that bloody velvet one more time-"

"Oh come now, Mave, y'don't even wear half these things!"

"It's not for you to judge, you nosy little stray! Get out of my wardrobe."

A sharp slam. Laughter. Something shattering. Garin kept walking, because further down, past the central stairwell, two voices tangled like thorns on old stone. Simon's smooth French baritone, strained with weariness. Evangeline's sharper, clipped edge, fury wrapped in silk.

They were always arguing now. The once mythic lovers, the ancient Frenchman and his stolen queen, have been at odds ever since Beau had rescued and bonded to the mortal lawyer Leah Ricci, and the manor had fought against a rogue Dhampir.

"You do not listen, Simon."

"Non, I listen. You simply do not like what I say ma chère. I try to speak to you and you just-."

"You think I'm wrong! Always."

"I think you are angry, and I am tired of pretending not to see it and I am tired of you not telling me why."

Their voices faded behind closed doors and heavier secrets. Since Beau had found Leah, since the threat to the safety of the town and the Bloodborn had been burned to ash and Thorne Ridge restored…

The manor should have been at peace, but it wasn't.

It was restless. Like something had shifted deep in the bones of the place. Simon tried, Garin had watched every day for months how the Frenchman suffered and strained. But Evangeline slipped further each day, like frost melting into shadow. No one dared speak of it aloud. Not even the twins who ran their mouths constantly. Not even Mave, their seer who would normally interject on behalf of the coven's sanity.

Some didn't see it, such as Beau who remained in his happily mated bliss. Others saw too clearly and said nothing. Garin opened the heavy door to his room and stepped inside. Everything was clean as always, he kept it organized and tidy, and the mongrels away from it at all costs.

No portraits, no personal effects. Only his weapons on the wall, his coat folded at the foot of the bed, and the scent of cedar and steel. He moved without thought, pulling on his thick black coat, fastening the straps at his wrists. The leather was worn, marked by a hundred winters. He paused at the door, glancing back once. The room stared back, silent and still.

And for a single moment, as the wind howled outside…

Garin wondered if he would ever know peace in this death.

Chapter 2

The wind bit hard along the edges of the trees, sharp with ice and the metallic tang of oncoming snow. Garin moved like a shadow between trunks, black coat trailing behind him as his boots crunched over frozen pine needles. His breath steamed, but not from cold, really just force of habit. A leftover mimicry of life that the Viking held onto through the centuries..

He hated this stretch of patrol. Route 19.

It was too close to town, too close to the humans his coven swore to protect.

The old county road snaked along the edge of Thorne Ridge, just outside the deep woods the manor was buried in. Patrols were necessary, Beau had claimed, as part of their duty. Needed to make sure the dhampir hadn't left behind anyone to regroup after its destruction, needed to keep an eye on the occasional supernatural drifting too close to mortal lines.

He didn't care. This close to town, the air always smelled wrong, like diesel, old oil, too much light. He preferred the backwoods, where the silence was thicker, purer. The kind of stillness that made your bones hum, not like this.

He ducked under a low-hanging branch, scowling as headlights blinked briefly in the far-off distance on the road. The others didn't mind crossing into town. Rua and Cian couldn't be kept away from diners and late-night dive bars. Simon visited bookstores and Addie's cafe. Beau took Leah into town often enough that the locals had stopped questioning how little the man aged. Hell, even Mave had a favorite antique shop tucked behind the courthouse where she and Larazo indulged in curiosities.

Garin, as always, stayed away.

Humans were loud. Messy. Too curious, too fragile. All except Addie Whitmore, the only mortal who didn't grate on his last nerve. Mostly because she didn't *fear* him, probably because she'd seen worse. The old woman had a spine stronger than most warriors he had fought in his long afterlife. And Leah Ricci, when she wasn't barking orders like a five-foot mafia boss with a caffeine addiction, he respected her. Fiercely, not just as Beau's chosen, but because she had been thrown into their world and still had the nerve to sass every immortal she came across. But he still avoided town when he could.

And yet...

Tonight's route dragged him too close. Too far off his preferred path, and he was already turning to cut back into the deeper woods when he stopped.

Paused. Head tilted.

There.

A sound. Faint, unfurling like fog through the trees.

Music.

He went still, so utterly still that even the snow seemed to hush. The melody drifted from just beyond the tree line. Gentle. Imperfect. Played on keys older than the sound deserved. A piano? No...a keyboard. Slightly out of tune, mechanical, like whoever was playing didn't care much for perfection, just for the feeling.

And gods be, there was *feeling*. The notes wavered like breath in winter air. No rhythm. No discipline. But emotion, raw and soft and full.

Garin's eyes narrowed, and just ahead, nestled off the old county road, sat a small house. White siding faded by seasons. A porch light flickering, half-burnt, smoke curled from the chimney. A porch swing shifted slightly in the breeze, creaking once.

But the music, it came from inside. Or maybe just beyond? Closer to the porch than the hearth. A single light glowed behind the window. A shadow moved past it. Then...

A mistake in the melody. A missed key. A quick recovery.

Human. Definitely human. Garin stepped closer before he realized he'd moved at all. His body moved slow, cautious, though not for fear of being seen. But because something inside him said:

Do not startle this.

He reached the edge of the trees and crouched low behind a patch of winter-thin brush. Just enough to see. There, on the porch of the worn down little home, wrapped in a coat too big for her, fingers moving across an old keyboard perched on a table, sat a woman. And she was playing like the music was the only thing keeping her from breaking. Garin didn't move.

Couldn't.

The music drifted on the air, soft and strange. But it wasn't the notes that stopped him, no the melody was lovely, gentle, but it was her.

She sat alone on the porch, wrapped in an oversized coat that swallowed her small frame, a blanket tucked around her legs. An old keyboard rested across her lap, the back end propped against a crate, her long fingers moving across the worn keys like she didn't care who heard. Like this was for her, and no one else.

Her skin caught the glow of the porch light, pale, but not sickly, with a hint of soft pink I her cheeks. Warm, alive. Small freckles dusted her cheeks and nose, soft as starlight on snow. Her hair... gods, her hair. Long, loose waves of red that tumbled across her shoulders and down her back, tousled gently by the whispering wind.

She didn't look up, didn't glance around, didn't react like someone afraid of the dark pressing close as the night crept on.

She just kept playing. A small frown touched her lips when she missed a note. She adjusted, found her rhythm again. Her head tilted, and Garin caught the curve of her lashes, the faint glimmer of her eyes.

Green. Not dull or faded, but a rich, deep tone. Like moss and pine and something older than this world. Something ancient stirred inside the Viking. A pull. A weightless ache he hadn't felt in more than a thousand years. His fists clenched at his sides without realizing it. Not from aggression, but from restraint.

She looked like the goddesses his people once spoke of.

The ones who stood barefoot at the edge of battlefields, blood on their palms and stars in their eyes. The ones who waited to bless warriors before they crossed into glory after a death on the battlefield.

And here she was.

Sitting alone on a porch off Route 19, wrapped in blankets and playing an old keyboard like she didn't know she'd just torn a hole in his chest.

Garin's throat tightened. She was mortal, a human. Delicate in all the ways that made him dangerous to her mere existence. But right then…She was the only sound he wanted to hear. He shouldn't have moved, but his stance had shifted, just enough to adjust the weight of his body, a thoughtless recalibration, and beneath his boot, a small, frozen strip of bark cracked with a sharp *snap*.

The sound echoed louder than it should've. Garin froze like a giant Nordic statue in that snow.

Shit.

He hissed a curse in Old Norse, the words old and rough and ripped straight from the battlefield of his first life. But it was too late.

She stopped playing. Her fingers hovered above the keys. Her head turned slightly, brows pinching together, not in fear, but in focused curiosity. Then she called out.

"Hello? Is... someone there?"

Her voice was soft. Like the music. Low and clear and musical in its own right, slipping into the trees like a lullaby looking for someone to soothe.

He didn't move again, couldn't.

She stared straight ahead, but her eyes... they didn't follow the sound. Didn't scan the trees. They remained fixed and steady ahead, almost unfocused if hadn't thought better of it.

He realized, then. She couldn't see him. Thankfully he must've been too far back for her mortal eyes to catch him, and Garin had never thanked the gods for such a small favor before. A mortal woman, alone in the dark, and still, she asked the shadows if they meant harm, with calm in her voice and no fear in her limbs. Something in Garin's chest pulled taut.

He wanted to answer. For the first time in... gods, centuries... his mouth moved like it might shape words, and his body softened ever so slightly.

No sound came. He stayed there, barely breathing, as the woman tilted her head again, listening. Waiting. Then, with a small shrug and a faint smile, he could hear her murmur to herself, "Huh. Must've been a deer or something."

She went back to playing. Just like that. Like she hadn't just shaken something ancient loose inside a beast older than the soil where he house lay. The music resumed, slow and wandering, as if it had never stopped. As if he hadn't been there at all. And Garin, the silent Viking, the shield of the

Thorne coven, the man who had faced monsters and never flinched...stepped back.

Quietly. Carefully. Before he made another mistake, before he climbed those porch steps and ruined the peace that didn't belong to him, before he answered her call and let her know he meant her no harm. No, instead, he turned, and walked back toward the woods. Toward the shadows and toward the only world he had ever known. One that didn't include mortal goddesses who played melodies of peace.

The music helped her forget the cold, and her solitude.

Mira Cassidy sat curled on the porch with her keyboard across her lap, wrapped in a blanket that smelled faintly of cedar and something older, like the ghosts of autumn clinging to the fabric. Her coat sleeves were too long, covering half her hands as her fingers moved across the keys, searching for sound instead of perfection.

She didn't care if she played it right, she just wanted peace for the night.

The wind blew soft through the trees beyond her little property, carrying the smell of snow and bark and the distant hush of the road that curved along the back of the woods. Her breath clouded in the cold air, and she could feel the numb bite at her fingertips. Still, she smiled.

"Better than silence," she murmured to herself.

The melody she played was slow, simple, notes from her memory, pieced together from childhood and long-forgotten songs. Then-**snap.**

A sharp crack broke the rhythm. Mira's fingers halted, and the music cut off mid-note. She sat very still. The sound had come from the tree line?

She didn't tense. Didn't panic. She simply tilted her head slightly and listened, her brows drawing together with focus.

"Hello?" she called gently, voice soft but clear. No answer. She waited, the wind brushed her hair across her cheek, a long curl lifting briefly before settling again. Her eyes remained open, deep green irises catching the flicker of porch light, but they didn't move.

They didn't search the trees. They simply stared, unseeing, into the night.

Faint scarring curved from the corners of her eyes to the tops of her cheeks, nearly invisible unless someone was close. A faded testimony to a fire long past, the night that had taken her sight and left her with something else in return:

Stillness.

She gave it another breath. Then shrugged. "Deer, probably," she said aloud, half amused. "Or one of those fat raccoons again." She placed her fingers back on the keys and the music returned. Softer this time. Dreamlike. But something inside her whispered...

That wasn't an animal.

She didn't know how she knew. She'd stared straight ahead when it happened, listened for movement. Felt the air shift. There had been a presence, something just beyond reach. Watching. Listening.

But now... gone. Mira kept playing, letting the sound fill the quiet once more., and somewhere, in the forest beyond her little house, the snow took her melody and carried it into the dark. After a few more moments of gentle play, the song faded beneath her fingers. It wasn't finished, not really, but the wind had picked up and her hands were starting to go numb beneath the blanket. She sighed and slowly eased the keyboard off her lap, setting it carefully on the side table beside the porch swing.

The night was quiet again. Too quiet, as it always was in her day to day life.

Still, she moved with purpose, used to the steps, the edges, the feel of her space. Her coat sleeves dragged slightly behind her as she gathered the blanket and folded it neatly against her chest, fingers brushing over the soft worn fabric. She turned toward the front door and reached out, her fingertips sweeping across the porch railing until they landed on the worn metal handle.

She didn't hesitate. Mira had lived on her own for years. She didn't need light. She didn't need help, and tonight was no different than the others. The door clicked open and she stepped inside, the air warmer around her instantly, though it always took her a moment to adjust when switching worlds.

It door shut softly behind her as her hand found the switch near the door, not that she needed it, but she flipped it anyway. Habit. Routine. All things that had helped her find normalcy again after the accident. She listened for the familiar hum of electricity and let her other senses fill in the rest as she adjusted back to indoors.

The house was small. One story, a modest place for a single woman. A dark wood coffee table sat perfectly centered in front of an old leather couch, both anchored on a single bare floor she could cross barefoot without catching on anything. She didn't use rugs anymore, not after the last time she'd tripped and cracked her shin on the corner of the piano bench.

No framed photos, no shelves of trinkets. She didn't need to see memories to remember them. Everything had its place, and she liked it that way, or so she told the others. Simple, predictable, safe. But tonight? She paused halfway to the couch, the blanket still held in her arms. Something *had* made that noise. She kept telling herself it was a deer. Maybe a fox. One of the big raccoons that liked to tip over her compost bin if she accidentally packed it too full.

But. That presence, that *feeling*. The way the air had shifted. The silence that followed her question. Not cold, not dangerous. Just, present.

Like someone had been listening. Watching. She stood there in the center of her living room and tilted her head, just as she had outside. The hair on her arms rose slightly beneath her coat sleeves, not from fear, but from something else entirely.

"Whoever you were..." she murmured, voice barely above a whisper, "you didn't feel like a monster." She didn't know *why* she said it, there was no one here to hear her. Only that it felt true, and if someone *had* been out there...And if they ever came back?

Well. She hoped they'd find the courage to say something next time.

~~~

The snow crunched beneath his boots as Garin moved through the woods, his coat brushing along the edges of frozen pine. He hadn't realized how far he'd walked until the house, the woman, was well out of view. The road had curved off behind him, the trees were thicker now. Darker. He was heading back toward the manor's perimeter.

Good.

That's where he belonged. He tried to focus. Nothing had been out of place near Route 19. No odd scent. No rogue Bloodborn or restless Moonborn. Just tire tracks. A half-rotted deer carcass that looked more car-struck than claw-torn. Trash near the edge of the ditch. Human mess. Nothing Beau couldn't toss to Bobby. There'd been no threat tonight.

Nothing but...

No.

Garin clenched his jaw and pushed the thought down.

His steps quickened, boot falls harder now as if stomping out the ghost of the sound that still lingered in his ears.

It was just music. Just a woman. Sitting alone in the dark, playing like her soul was harmony itself.

He gritted his teeth so hard one could've swore they'd crack under the pressure. He didn't do this. He didn't *wonder*. He didn't *fawn*. He didn't walk through the damn woods replaying the sound of a voice like wind chimes made of breath and warmth.

He didn't remember freckles.

Or the way red hair had caught the porch light just right, like embers in motion. Or the fact that her voice had sounded like a melody trying not to break as she called out 'Hello'.

No.

He growled low in his throat and turned sharply at the split in the trail, moving back toward the manor's northern path. The wind picked up again, swirling flakes into his hair, catching on the edges of his braids. He didn't feel it. He didn't feel *anything*. He did patrols, he hunted threats. He fed when he needed and he protected his coven even when they pushed him to the brink of madness. That was all.

He wasn't like the others. Not soft like Simon could be. Not loud or obnoxious like the twins. Not foolishly in love like Beau with his sharp-tongued human mate. Garin was the blade that never dulled, he was the shield at the edge of war.

And yet…Why couldn't he stop hearing that damn music?

The manor loomed ahead, tall and ancient against the pale snow, its gables glowing with warm light that never quite reached the trees. Garin crossed the threshold without a sound, and inside, the house was quiet, but not peacefully so. It was the kind of hush that came after shouting. The kind of silence that pressed too hard against the walls.

He heard them before he saw them. A whisper of silk on wood. A breath that wasn't meant to be heard.

Evangeline.

She slipped down the stairs like a phantom, barefoot, wrapped in a long, pale robe that trailed behind her like fog.

Her eyes were forward but unseeing, her expression unreadable, blonde hair pulled away from a face that could charm most, yet radiated silent fury in her wake. She didn't speak, didn't glance at the door. Just drifted toward the east wing hall like a woman who didn't know whether she was leaving or returning.

From the shadowed hallway near the study, Simon watched her go.

He stood just beyond the doorway, fingers wrapped around the edge of the threshold like it was the only thing holding him still. His silver hair was tied back, his shirt half-unbuttoned, and his eyes, those ancient, weary dark eyes, were caught somewhere between *longing* and *resignation*.

He didn't follow her. He hadn't, in weeks. They would argue, then she would drift off alone for days on end, and Simon wouldn't give chase anymore.

Garin slowed. He wasn't close with the Simon. None of them really were besides the twins, who were more sons than not to him. The Frenchman kept to his books, his quiet corners, his too-gentle thoughts, but Garin had seen enough to know what it looked like when a man loved something that kept slipping further away.

Simon's jaw clenched. His gaze never left the place Evangeline had vanished into, and Garin stopped beside him. Said nothing. Just lifted one hand, that massive, scarred hand that had ended gods and monsters alike, and placed it once, briefly, on Simon's shoulder. A quiet weight. A silent acknowledgment.

Simon didn't flinch, and he didn't speak, but he nodded, almost imperceptibly, before letting his hand fall away from the doorway and stepping back into the shadows. Garin moved on. No words were needed. Because love between immortals... it never stayed simple. Centuries blurred what once felt eternal, and bonds frayed. Devotion turned brittle under the weight of time and change.

And Garin? He didn't want that. *This* was why he didn't take a mate, this was why he didn't chase softness. Why he didn't let warmth get close enough to cling. Even still now though, his mind betrayed him.

A red-haired woman. Freckles. Fingers dancing across old plastic keys. A voice that sounded like it had once belonged to the gods.

He clenched his jaw and turned the corner toward his wing of the manor, faster now than he had moved all night. He would forget her.

He had to. Because peace like that? It never lasted.

Chapter 3

The east wing was always the coldest part of the manor, and Garin preferred it that way. The stone stairwell creaked beneath his weight as he climbed, slow and steady, the quiet swallowing him whole once more. This wing was far from the hearths and noise of the others, no music from Rua's speakers, no laughter from Cian's chaos, no distant pages turning in Simon's library.

Just the cold.

His quarters were near the top, large, simple, spartan. Wood and stone. A rack of weapons, and blankets he never needed. A bed he barely used since he didn't sleep too often, however this night, he was exhausted in a new way.

He reached the top of the stairs and turned down the hall, boots soft against the rug less floorboards. It was perfect. Quiet. Unchanging.

Until it wasn't.

A presence stirred behind him, old, steady, not threatening. Just... inevitable.

Garin slowed. From the far corner of the hallway emerged **Larazo**. Broad-shouldered, still powerful despite the weight of time, the oldest vampire among them moved with the silent grace of something that had survived empires. His skin was a deep olive tone, sun-warmed in another life. His beard was salt-and-pepper, well-kept, matching the streaks through his long dark hair pulled back at the nape of his neck.

His eyes, though? They were timeless and they saw *everything*.

Larazo's accent carried the ghosts of ancient coastlines, Roman, perhaps. Greek. Maybe older still. None of them were certain. Mave said even she hadn't ever heard the full truth, and she was the only one he ever truly spoke to.

Except now.

"You walk heavier tonight, Viking," Larazo said softly, the words rolling smooth like sea-worn stone. "And your eyes..." He stepped closer, studying him with a gaze like molten metal beneath still water. "They are not so frozen as they were."

Garin didn't answer. Of course he didn't, he couldn't. Larazo stopped just beside him, looking out the window that overlooked the treeline below. His arms were crossed, his voice low.

"What could possibly have the beast of Thorne Manor looking less vicious than normal?" he murmured.

Silence.

Garin stood motionless. Blue eyes forward, jaw growing tight. But something must've flickered, *just enough*. Because Larazo's mouth curved slightly. Not mocking. Just... knowing.

"You saw something." Still no answer. "No. Not something..." he corrected himself. "Someone."

Garin exhaled slowly through his nose, a faint breath like wind through old stone. Larazo turned his head slightly, just enough to let the gold of his irises catch the hallway torchlight.

"Be careful, brother," he said quietly. "It does not take much to thaw a frozen heart. Only time... and music." And with that, Larazo turned and walked away, his steps echoing lightly down the hall, leaving Garin alone again. But now? The silence felt heavier. Like it had heard too much.

The door to his quarters creaked softly as it opened, the sound swallowed by the thick stone walls. Garin stepped inside and shut it behind him, the iron latch clicking into place like the seal of a tomb. The room was exactly as he'd left it. Always was, always the same.

Furs layered the floor and the edge of the bed, worn pelts from centuries past, bear and wolf, draped like forgotten trophies. His weapons lined the far wall in perfect formation, blades, axes, a single black-handled sword that had once sung in the snow.

Above the mantle, there were no portraits. No memories, but near the small table tucked in the far corner... sat books. Stacks of them. Quietly kept. Quietly read. None of the others knew. He never spoke of it. But over the centuries, he had collected them, histories, myths, even music theory bound in cracked leather and foreign scripts. He didn't need to read them. He *wanted* to.

They helped him remember, that once, he'd had lived.

He crossed the room and reached for the heavy curtain by the window, pulling it aside. Outside, the sky had begun to fade into the pale violet of approaching dawn. The mountains stood still in the distance, white-capped and eternal. The trees below didn't move.

And yet, **he could feel her.** Somewhere beyond the hills and frost and mortal fences...

She slept. Or maybe she played, maybe she wrote a new song. Maybe she forgot he'd ever passed through the trees, writing him ff as a wild animal, though she wouldn't be wrong.

He hoped so.

His hand tightened on the curtain, and in that quiet, in that sacred hush between night and sun, Garin did something he had not done in centuries.

He prayed.

Silently. Without words. But with *everything*. To the Valkyries who had not come for him. To the gods who no longer listened. To his fallen brothers, who knew silence the way he never would amongst the brave and fearless.

He asked them, with all of the might within his immortal body...

Do not let me fall.

Do not let me drag her into this cold.

Do not let her hear the echoes in me and mistake them for music.

She is light. She is sound.

I am what remains after the song ends.

He dropped the curtain after his prayer, the sun crept closer, and his body began that age old weariness that came with dawn.

Then, Garin, warrior, sword, beast of the Thorne coven, lay down alone once more. Sleep claimed him before the light could, though his mind, was still replaying a melody that didn't, and shouldn't, belong to him.

~~~~~~

Mornings were evil.

This was a truth Mira Cassidy accepted every day as she groaned into her pillow, her arm flung over her head like she was warding off a curse. Her bed was warm, her blanket soft, and her muscles long and loose with sleep. She had *no* desire to leave the cocoon she'd built in the corner of her modest bedroom. But her alarm, a faint classical piano, no violent beeping allowed here, chirped again from the table beside her.

"Alright, alright..." she muttered, her voice thick with sleep. "I'm up. You win."

She stretched her limbs out beneath the covers, long fingers flexing, toes pointing until she felt the joints pop in her ankles and back. Her red curls were a wild tangle, falling across her cheeks and sticking to the pillow in soft snarls. She shoved them back with both hands and finally swung her legs over the side of the bed. The floor was cold, as always, but it helped jolt her into a more awake state that way.

Her bare feet padded across the room with quiet certainty, every step was placed without hesitation. She didn't need to see, she had adjusted just fine over the years.

The shower knobs were simple, hot and cold marked by textured grooves she'd carved herself years ago with the guidance of her friend. The towels hung on the same rack, folded in the same order, the plush one on the left always her favorite.

The water hit her spine, hot and steady, and she let it run while she washed. The scent of her shampoo, lavender and cedar, was comforting, familiar. She never switched brands. She didn't need the risk of something feeling off, and she was a creature of habit.

Afterwards, her fingers brushed lightly along the edge of the wall as she made her way into the kitchen. Not hurried, but not cautious, just practiced. Her coffee pot sat in its rightful place on the counter, the exact same one she'd had since college, long before the fire took her sight. Its smooth knobs and satisfying click were muscle memory by now. No screens. No guesswork.

The smell began to bloom before the first pour. Rich and almost earthy, just a basic ground bean without a million added things. She had enough troubles with craving sugar as it was. The coffee grounded her more than the shower ever did. Dressing came next, jeans folded left side out, soft thermal top, wool-lined coat. Nothing fancy. Just layers for the cold outside and preparation for the work day. Her boots were easy to zip, the toes scuffed from years of use. She found her hair tie by touch on the counter, twisted her curls up into a loose bun, and fumbled for the final piece, damned curls never behaved.

The sunglasses.

Not for vanity, not for shame. Just for comfort. Protection, they blocked out the glare that still made her temples throb, even if she couldn't see it fully, but the way harsh lights sometimes glared too brightly in her face was too much.

She slipped them on, adjusted the fit, and exhaled softly, and cane in hand, she felt for the lock on her front door, found the latch by touch, and stepped outside into the cold.

Simple, routine, ease.

The wind kissed her cheeks with sharp fingers, and gave a large inhale. Smoke. Wood. Pine. The faint sweetness of frost, and something else...*something older,* buried deep in the snow. She couldn't name it. But it wasn't unpleasant.

She hummed softly to herself as she moved down the walkway, her cane tapping lightly ahead of her. A melody, something strange and new. It had been in her dream, a sound like nothing she'd ever heard before, something low in tone and almost ancient in the way it felt. Like a war horn echoing through time... or a lullaby sung by stone.

No words, no faces. Just a presence, vast and quiet and still. And the music. It wound around her now as she followed the edge of her property toward the old county road. The bus stop sat just past the woods, near the bend of Route 19. She'd made this walk a hundred times. Today though?

The air felt different. The cold didn't bite as sharply, and the wind carried that song again...She didn't know if someone had been there last night. Didn't know if she'd dreamed the presence, or imagined the warmth that pulsed just beyond her porch. But the song? It lingered. And part of her hoped she'd hear it again, perhaps soon, and even when she stepped onto the old bus as it arrived, she began humming it again.

Mira rose from her seat with her usual calm precision, offering a small smile to the driver as she passed by as the bus hissed to a stop, its brakes groaning beneath her feet after a short while.

"Have a good one, Ms. Cassidy," he called, as he always did, one of the sweetest men she's encountered.

"You too, Joe," she replied, stepping off the bottom stair and into the early morning air.

The sidewalk beneath her boots was familiar, paved with slightly uneven concrete near the third lamppost, where tree roots had pushed through from beneath. She adjusted her cane accordingly, humming that half-remembered melody from her dream as she made her way toward the front entrance of **Thorne Ridge Middle School**.

The security guard, Keith, gave her a cheerful "Morning, ma'am!" which she returned with a nod and a smile. The building greeted her with its usual blend of too-strong floor wax, faint teenage body spray, and the old book scent of a well-used school.

She'd taught here for seven years. Even after the fire, and even after her world went dark.

Because *music*, she'd told them, *doesn't require eyes, only ears.* And hers were sharp enough to catch the slightest hesitation in a student's fingers on the keys, a blessing she'd had since childhood. The faintest breath before a wrong note.

She still had her gift. Music has always been her life, and that hadn't changed in the last decade.

She reached the double doors of her classroom without help, her cane barely needed on the polished floor now that her feet knew every scuff and groove in the tile. Her hand found the knob and Mira entered her little sanctuary.

The music room was just as she'd left it, rows of chairs in precise formation, the old upright piano near the whiteboard, the shelves lined with battered flutes, dented trumpets, and hand drums. Each item had its place. Each one she could find by touch alone.

She moved through the room with ease, setting her bag on her desk, running her hand across the piano lid as she passed by. Thirty minutes until the bell. Thirty minutes until the noise began.

And oh how she welcomed it. She was halfway through organizing the braille sheet music for her sixth-grade class when the frantic click of heels echoed down the hall like a warning bell.

"Miraaa, good *morning!*" came the far-too-chipper voice of Mrs. Roberta Valdez, principal of Thorne Ridge Middle and the woman most likely to summon caffeine into existence by sheer will, the smell of strong coffee always following her. Mira turned toward the sound, one dainty brow rising beneath her sunglasses.

"Roberta. You're early."

"And you're here, as always. I swear, you'd show up during a blizzard with a broken leg and still tune the choir."

"Probably," Mira said flatly. "But I'd make them carry me."

The principal laughed and entered the room in a flurry of perfume and professionalism, heels tapping with urgency that Mira never understood before 9 a.m.

"I just wanted to check in, yes darling, again, about next year's contract," Roberta began, her voice lilting like she was trying not to pressure. "The kids adore you, and frankly, the district's more than willing to extend a raise if it means keeping you. I know it's early, but-"

"I haven't decided yet," Mira interrupted gently, turning back toward her desk. "You'll have my answer after winter break. Like always."

A beat of silence, then Roberta exhaled. "You're a very stubborn woman."

"So I've been told."

"We just don't want to lose you."

Mira nodded once, but didn't answer. Her fingers traced the edge of the piano as she sat. Roberta hovered a moment longer, then relented with a sigh, and Mira could hear the bracelets her boss wore jingling as she's sure she was waving her hand in a dramatic dismissal.

"Alright, alright. I'll leave you to it. But I'm bringing you a muffin later, and that's not up for debate."

Mira smirked. "Make it blueberry, and I might let you live after busting in on me so early. You know I'm not a morning person."

As the principal's footsteps faded down the hall, Mira let her hands settle on the piano keys, pressing one note softly. Then another...then a chord. Still that strange melody from her dream was haunting her. Still whispering something ancient she couldn't quite name. And as she played, her sunglasses hid the way her eyes drifted toward the window, toward the forest beyond the school, toward the shadows that had once stood still and silent, and listened.

The bell rang, shrill and slightly off-pitch, *she'd been telling the office for two years to have it recalibrated*, and like a dam breaking, the hallway outside her classroom erupted with the stampede of sneakers, giggles, and muffled shouts.

Then the door opened, and the first wave of seventh graders crashed into her life.

"Ms. Cassidy! I practiced the song, well, sort of, but my brother messed with my flute again-"

"Miss, I swear, the piano bench moved by itself, I think the music room is haunted!"

"Can we please do the Hamilton medley again? Please? Pleeeeease?"

"One at a time," Mira said, laughing despite herself. "And no, Marcus, the room isn't haunted. You just keep kicking the bench."

She stood beside the piano like a conductor before a ship full of feral birds. The noise didn't overwhelm her. It grounded her. Because in the noise, she *knew* where everything was. She knew Aaliyah would always sit on the second chair in the flute row, bouncing her foot even when the song didn't call for it. That Jeremy would try to sneak a bag of Takis in his trombone case. That the group by the percussion shelf would start tapping rhythms before she even gave them the signal.

She knew them.

They made her smile. They always had. However, as they began warming up, clattering instrument cases, laughing over reeds and buttons, tuning and arguing and settling in, something inside her remained still.

She walked through the room, checking chairs, handing out music, correcting posture with a tap on the shoulder. She corrected a clarinet grip by feel. Adjusted a pitch by ear. Caught a cough before it turned into a spit-valve catastrophe.

It was the same as yesterday. And the day before that.

And the one before that.

I love this, she told herself. *I love music. I love teaching. I love these kids.*

But even as she smiled and gave instructions, a part of her stayed back, adrift somewhere between the porch from last night when she heard that noise in the darkness and a melody she still couldn't name. She moved from student to student, but her soul felt like it had stayed outside.

Maybe it was the time of year. Winter always made her restless. Or maybe it was the dream. The song.

Or maybe it was the truth she hadn't wanted to say out loud…

Everything outside of this classroom had started to feel… hollow.

She still taught. Still played. Still gave every note, every breath, every memory to the music. But when the last bell rang and the halls emptied again? There was nothing waiting for her.

Just the hum of her coffee pot. The warmth of a worn blanket. The rhythm of another evening with no one to share it with.

And now... Now that she'd heard something in the trees, felt a presence that made the air feel *thicker*...

She wondered. What if she wasn't meant to keep doing this? What if her world, safe, predictable, silent, wasn't where she belonged anymore?

What if what was missing...

She shook the thought away as the class quieted. "Alright," she called out, clapping once. "Warm-up scales, top to bottom, then we're jumping into the winter concert medley. You've got two weeks to stop sounding like ducks in distress, so let's get to work."

Laughter. Instruments lifted, and the music began again. Mira? She played her part, but still... felt that missing piece.

~~~

The last bell had rung hours ago. The building had grown still, except for the faint hum of the air vents and the distant thump of sneakers echoing from the gym. Most of the other teachers had already gone home. Mira sat at her desk, fingers tracing the edge of a half-folded music sheet she'd been meaning to revise for the winter concert.

But she hadn't moved in ten minutes. Her cane leaned against the piano, and her sunglasses rested atop her music folder. Her red curls were half-fallen from their tie, a soft cloud over her shoulder.

She exhaled slowly, tilting her head toward the fading light behind the closed blinds. She couldn't see the sunset, not fully, but she could feel the shift in the air. The cooling of the room. The soft hush of light withdrawing.

Another day done.

She'd taught her classes. Tuned the out-of-key oboe, paced the room twice during her lunch break out of habit, not hunger.

She'd smiled. Laughed, even. But now? Now the stillness crept in, it always did after the day was done.

In her twenty-nine years, Mira Cassidy had always taught.

Even before the fire, before the smoke and flames had turned her world dark, she'd taught piano to neighbors' kids. Sang in choirs. Played in orchestras.

After the accident, she'd taught herself how to walk unfamiliar rooms with only her hands. Taught herself how to forgive a body that no longer worked the way it used to. Taught others how to be patient when they stumbled over her blindness with awkward apologies.

She had *always* taught. Because teaching was safe. Predictable. The one thing she could still do without needing to see the faces in front of her. Her hand fell to her lap, limp. The sheet music fluttered slightly from her breath.

"Would I even know how to be anything else?" she murmured aloud. Her voice didn't echo. The sound was swallowed by chairs and woodwinds and the memories that lingered in the walls.

Could she leave this behind?

The school, the classroom, the students who gave her purpose, even if lately, they were the only source of joy she still clung to. A job wasn't the same as a life. And maybe... just maybe... she was starting to feel the difference. The part of her that had always been content here...it felt hollow now. Like she'd outgrown her own skin and hadn't realized until the quiet pointed it out. And that melody from her dream? Still there. Still whispering something her life had never said before.

She stood slowly and reached for her cane, feeling the familiar weight settle into her palm. She knew the way home, knew that Joe would hold the bus for her just in case she was a little behind one day, but tonight, something in her heart tugged in another direction. For the first time in years... Mira

Cassidy wondered what it would mean to stop just surviving, and start *living*.

Chapter 4

The sun had dipped low enough behind the mountains that the shadows in the east wing began to shift. The light bled out, retreating in long fingers across stone and fur, disappearing like ghosts into the corners of his room.

Garin stirred. He woke the way he always did, without sound, without grogginess, his body rising like a blade being drawn from its sheath. But something was... wrong.

No, not wrong.

Different.

There was a sound in his mind. Faint. Lingering. A **melody**. Not the sound of battle, or the screams of the dying like he normally heard when his eyes closed for too long. Not the wet crack of bone or the rasp of a blade. This was something else. It played softly in the back of his skull, a piano, ancient and imperfect, the notes warm but wandering. As if someone were searching for something in every chord. It had followed him from sleep now even into his waking state.

His fists clenched in the blankets and he sat up slowly, dragging a hand down his face, his fingers rasping over the stubble on his jaw.

What the hell is this?

He didn't dream. Not truly. Not since the turning. His nights were full of instinct. Violence. The silent rituals of a creature built for patrol and protection. His mind didn't drift. It locked. Like iron. But now? Now he'd awoken with something soft echoing in his chest. And it hurt. Not pain. Not the good kind, either, the kind earned in battle.

This was *ache*. This was *yearning*. This was the sound he once thought the gods might welcome him with, if he had died on the snow beside his brothers, taken up by Valkyries, given peace at last. Only this wasn't divine. It was mortal. A piano…A woman. Red hair in the wind. Freckles like stars across winter skin. A voice that asked if someone was there and didn't tremble when no one answered.

Garin growled under his breath and shoved off the fur blanket. His bare feet hit the cold floor with force.

No.

He refused this.

He was not *that man*. Not some lovesick creature softening under the pull of human fragility. He was the shield. The sword. The silence after slaughter. He did not *ache* for melodies. He did not *crave* softness. He would not think of her.

He dressed in silence, pulling on his black shirt, leather coat, thick boots. The familiar weight steadied him. This was who he was. What he'd always been. Not some creature seduced by a whisper of music and a smile in the dark.

No.

And yet… As he fastened the last buckle at his wrist, his eyes flicked toward the frosted window. The forest beyond lay still, and somewhere in the back of his mind, the melody played again.

The stones were cold beneath his boots as Garin descended the tower steps, the fur-lined collar of his coat brushing against his neck like the edge of an old memory. The manor breathed softly around him, settling into the night, its walls steeped in shadow and old blood. He needed focus.

Clarity. Discipline.

Tonight he would report to Beau. Review the patrol schedule. Reassess any threats in the outer woods. Realign himself with the only purpose that ever truly kept the burning in his chest from consuming him. Protect the coven. Maintain the balance. Stand between the world and what might destroy it.

That was his job. His reason. His silence.

What *wasn't* his job...

"Ahhh, would ya look at that, Cian, the gods *have* answered! We've been graced with our favorite murderous ice cube."

...was *them*.

Garin hit the final stair and stopped cold. Rua stood dead center in the hall, one hip cocked like he thought he was charming, his wild red curls pulled back and his grin sharp enough to draw blood. Cian lounged against the opposite wall, arms crossed, golden blond hair falling into his eyes and a glint of shared devilry burning beneath them.

"He's lookin' moodier than usual," Rua observed, nudging his brother. "Think he finally got laid?"

"Doubt it," Cian snorted. "He still smells like a brooding monk. *Angry* celibacy, that one."

"Maybe he found a tree to scream at."

"Maybe he *is* the tree *Dearthái*r."

They laughed, they always did. It was ritual, by now, Simon's bastard sons, not by blood but by bond that the Frenchman still held, weaving chaos through the manor like feral songbirds with fangs.

And Garin?

He normally ignored them. Let them bark. Let them nip. It never touched him. But tonight... tonight, the melody still lingered in his head. Soft. Fragile. And their voices...*godsdamned Irish thunder*, cut through it like knives.

"Enough." The word came low. Rough, and both twins straightened in an instant out of the pure shock alone..

Rua blinked. "Well now…"

Cian raised a brow. "Did he just *speak*?"

Rua grinned wider. "Be still me heart."

"Out of my way," Garin growled, voice gravel and snow.

"Aye," Rua said, mockingly stepping aside with a dramatic bow. "The beast walks. Off to kill a squirrel, no doubt." Cian snorted behind his hand, but Garin didn't turn, didn't flinch. He just moved past them like a storm with nowhere left to go. But as he walked, his jaw tight and his hands flexing at his sides, he could still hear them laughing.

And worse. He could still hear the piano.

The door to the war room creaked open beneath his palm, the ancient oak groaning as Garin stepped inside. He expected Beau. What he did *not* expect…was the scent.

It hit him like a punch to the gut. Earth. Smoke. Pine needles and wild wind. A pure scent of wild animal filling the room where the Bloodborn coven held meetings of emergent matter. This scent…didn't belong here.

Moonborn.

His fangs punched down from his gums without hesitation, the snap of enamel meeting air loud in the quiet of the chamber. A low growl curled from his chest, beastly and ancient.

Unwelcome. Intrusion. Threat.

There were *two* others in the room with Beau. The first was Sheriff Bobby Schaffer, mid-forties, square-jawed, mustache hiding a scar on his lip, dressed in a denim button-down and a worn badge that had seen too much truth for a human. Bobby had been part of their unspoken alliance for years, just like Addie Whitmore down at the cafe. A rare man, but necessary one.

Garin did *not* growl at Bobby. He growled at **the other.**

Tall. Rugged. Light brown hair tousled like he'd ridden in on a storm. A green park ranger uniform clung to a frame built like it could wrestle mountains. And those *eyes*. Hazel. Bright. Sharp. And locked *directly* on him. Not in challenge, but in a ground stood without fear.

The Moonborn didn't flinch. Didn't drop his stare. He just stood there, broad shoulders squared, one thumb hooked in his belt loop, as if daring the vampire to make it physical.

"Why is there a mutt in this house," Garin growled, voice low and lethal. The tension snapped tight. But the moment he stepped forward, his coven leader moved. Beau stood slowly from behind the central table, his expression shifting from casual ease to something far colder.

The Southern King rose behind his eyes, jaw set, power radiating off him like heat. "Stand. Down." Beau's voice was steel and sin. "*Now.*"

Garin's jaw clenched. But he obeyed. Slowly, reluctantly, he retracted his fangs, though his eyes remained locked on the Moonborn.

Beau didn't move, didn't blink. "Sheriff Schaffer has something to share. And I expect you to listen."

Garin didn't respond. He didn't need to, but the room felt colder now, despite the heat simmering beneath his skin.

Bobby cleared his throat. "I know y'all don't usually entertain outsiders in this manor," he said, tone level. "But this here is Rafe Talbot, he's a Moonborn, though I'm sure you know that already. An alpha wolf to be exact. Works with the state police… unofficially. Handles certain matters that don't exactly make it into court records."

"Paranormal threats," Rafe added smoothly, his voice low and laced with Southern grit. Not from here, but further down south it sounded. "The kind of things that don't play nice with humans or vamps." He stepped forward just once, hands visible, movements nonthreatening, but confident. "I ain't here to piss in your territory," he said directly to Garin. "But we've got a shared problem on the borderlands. And I don't have the manpower to handle it alone."

Garin didn't speak still, didn't blink, however he did *assess*. The wolf stood his ground. Didn't lie. Didn't tremble. Didn't reek of fear. Only *truth*. And moonlight.

Beau folded his arms. "I trust Bobby. And Bobby trusts him. That's enough for now."

"Not for me," Garin said quietly.

Beau's gaze darkened. "It's going to have to be."

For the first time in *centuries*, Garin felt *off balance*. Because their species didn't mix, not unless something drastic was taking place. However, another step forward from the Moonborn. That was all it took to have Garin straighten again.

Another inch from Rafe and Garin's body reacted before thought could catch it, a low, guttural growl rolling from his throat, primal and unrelenting.

Beau's eyes **snapped** to him like thunder cracking across the room.

"Enough."

Garin didn't flinch. Didn't cower. But he did, slowly, tightly, clamp his jaw shut and let the silence reclaim the space.

Not of out fear for Beau, never that. But out of respect, order. Beau was king…and Garin his soldier, his sword. He stepped back and took his place against the wall, silent, motionless, carved from the stone itself. A sentinel. A shadow. But his gaze never wavered from the wolf.

Let the mutt speak.

Rafe exhaled, one hand running along the back of his neck as he stepped closer to the table and dropped a manila folder onto the worn wood. "I ain't here to start a turf war," he began,

Southern grit buried beneath layers of exhaustion. "But I don't make house calls like this unless something's real wrong."

He flipped open the folder, and several photos spilled out. Not of humans.

"These showed up over the past few weeks," Rafe said. "All of them found within a fifty-mile radius. All of them supernaturals."

The first photo was unmistakable. A Bloodborn male, head removed entirely. No sign of ash. Just a severed neck and runes branded into the chest.

Another.

A corpse so blistered and cracked it looked like it had been dragged through the sun, no not dragged.

Held there.

Even Garin's stomach turned at the scent soaked into the paper.

"Forced exposure," Rafe muttered. "We think they were restrained. And that ain't natural sunlight, it's **synthetic**. Military-grade UV, maybe. Weaponized. Burnt through that vamp before the sun ever even rose that mornin'."

Then…

"This one here's worse." A photograph of a Moonborn woman, her mouth foaming, veins darkened and twisted as she lay in a makeshift hospital bed. Rafe's voice dropped. "Poisoned. With aconitum laced in silver and ground wolfsbane. Only someone with access to *very* old hunter recipes would even *know* that combo."

He didn't stop there. A final photo slid forward. A wraithborn, a rare sight in the mortal realm as it was. Garin's gaze narrowed. The body had been burned and **exorcised**, salt rings visible even in the graveyard dirt, the remnants of purifying incense still scattered around the scorched bones.

"Wraithborn shouldn't even be *vulnerable* to traditional exorcisms," Bobby muttered. "But this one...he was branded. Marked."

Garin spoke then, hisvoice low and iron-wrought. "You're saying this wasn't an isolated attack."

Rafe shook his head. "No. I'm saying someone's organizing." He paused, eyes flicking between the three men before finally settling on the truth. "I think the LightBorne are resurfacing."

Silence. Heavy and ancient, yet filled with an immediate surge of rage from the two vampires in the room. Beau didn't speak. Bobby didn't breathe. But Garin... Garin felt the old ache return. The name alone was a wound that he had never wished to reopen in this time.

"Impossible," he growled. "They were purged."

Rafe lifted a brow. "So were vampires once upon a time. Didn't take."

Beau exhaled slowly. "You think these are the old bloodlines? The families that went underground?"

"Could be." Rafe nodded. "But this time they're smarter. They're not targeting humans. They're hitting *us*. Quietly. Cleanly. With surgical strikes." He met Garin's gaze again. "And you ain't gotta like me, vampire. But if we don't work together, this war'll be over before it starts."

The Viking didn't blink, and he didn't breathe, but something *stirred* behind his eyes. Not acceptance. Not yet. but a deep awareness. And in the back of his mind... the piano played again.

As if *she* knew. As if the melody had tried to warn him first.

For a moment, silence reigned. Even the snow storm outside the manor had gone still. Until Bobby, as stoic as ever, but human all the same, cleared his throat.

"Hold on now...who the hell *are* the LightBorne?" He looked between the three of them like a man suddenly aware that he'd stepped into a different war than the one he thought he'd signed up for.

Beau's jaw clenched, and he leaned forward, resting his elbows on the table like a king wearied by the weight of explaining ancient things to mortal ears.

"They're a cult," Beau said. "Human. Old. Older than most countries still standing. They came together centuries ago, born out of fear, of what we are. What we can do." His eyes flicked to Rafe, then Garin. "They believed the existence of supernaturals was a direct threat to the divine order. So they began hunting us. Calling it purification. Righteousness. A crusade."

Beau's voice darkened, and any sort of ease in his tone vanished completely. It was are to have the man like this. "They've burned villages. Massacred packs. Captured our kind, tortured them for information, techniques to destroy us. Experimented to find anything they could use. Weaknesses. They consider it holy work."

Bobby's brows drew together. "But I thought that was all over. Like witch trials, dusty, violent history. Not something brought into present day."

But Before Beau could continue, Garin spoke. "It's not history. It's nightmares come to life."

The room shifted, and all eyes turned to him. He didn't move from the wall. Didn't even blink. But his voice cut through the space like a blade honed on old grief.

"I saw them. Fought them." The flickering light of the overhead lanterns caught on the sharp angles of his face, cast shadows beneath his eyes, but didn't dim the storm behind them. "Germany. Long before I came to this land. Before I met Beau."

The word tasted like ash, but he kept going. "I had found a coven. Quiet ones. Young. They drank only what was given. Lived among the ruins of a monastery. No threat to the humans nearby. They'd even taken in some orphans from the war. Children. Kind souls, innocent." His jaw twitched. "That...was their mistake."

Beau didn't interrupt. No one did.

"Ignorance is nothing until it finds fear. And fear is what the LightBorne *sell*. They turned the town against them. Said the coven was grooming the children, drinking their blood, cursing the crops. None of it was true. But it didn't matter."

His voice dropped, quieter now, like ice along the ground as he dragged out the words from clenched teeth.

"I returned from patrol to find the gates of the monastery on fire. The walls soaked in holy water and salt. The coven, what was left of it, had been chained out front. One by one, their fangs had been torn out and nailed to the doors. As warning."

Rafe flinched. Bobby looked sick. Beau just bowed his head. He knew this story. He'd heard it once, long ago, but Garin rarely spoke it aloud.

"They didn't just kill them," the Viking murmured. "They made a *spectacle* of it. They left the youngest for last. A girl no older than fifteen. Burned her alive. Not to kill her...she would've survived the fire." His throat moved, like swallowing back a ghost. "They made sure her body could never rise again."

Silence. Not a soul in the room dared to speak.

"That," Garin said finally, eyes lifting to meet Bobby's, "is who the LightBorne are." His gaze drifted back to Rafe. "So don't call them a rumor, don't you dare call them history as if they mean a thing other than violence. Don't call them forgotten. And if you want my cooperation, Moonborn, don't speak their name like a theory." He stepped forward once.

"Speak it like the curse it is."

The silence still lingered like smoke in the war room, haunted by the shadow of Garin's words. But it didn't linger long. Because Beau rose, and just like that, the room snapped back into *order*. His chair scraped against the old wood, slow and deliberate. His hands braced the table. His jaw locked. And when he spoke, the drawl sharpened, roughened into something far older than the man in the tailored shirt standing before them.

"Garin." The Viking straightened. "You make your nightly patrol. Now."

There was no pause for agreement, just authority. Power cloaked in quiet Southern thunder.

"I want every goddamn corner of this territory checked. Ward stones, symbols, scent markers, every last boundary line from the Hollow to the western ridge. If a pine needle's out of place, you tell me."

Garin gave a single nod.

"If any sigil's wearin' thin, mark it down. You know which ones to reinforce. You always have." Beau's voice dipped low, the command pulsing beneath it like the hum of an old song that promised blood if ignored. "I'll alert the rest of the coven. We gather when you return. And *no one* leaves the manor grounds until then."

Then Beau turned. Slow. Measured. Those amber-gold eyes found Bobby first, respectful, but not deferent. Then…they locked onto Rafe Talbot.

Wolf.

Outsider.

Temporary ally.

"And you," Beau said, voice flat now, all drawl burned clean. "If you hear *even a whisper* of those LightBorne bastards sniffin' around your territory…" He took a step closer. "You come to me *first*."

Rafe didn't flinch, though Garin watched closely for any sign of rebellion.

"No lone wolf vengeance. No pack retaliation. You bring it to me. *We* handle it. Or you don't handle it at all."

His stare burned hotter than sunlight on a vampire's skin.

"Understood?"

Rafe gave a short nod. "Crystal clear."

Beau held his gaze for one beat longer than necessary, then turned his back like a king confident no one would dare strike.

"Good." He gestured toward the heavy map laid out across the table, the one labeled with their territory, and the town they guarded like family. "Because if the LightBorne *are* back, this ain't just about territory." His jaw tightened. "It's war."

Chapter 5

The war room doors creaked open, then shut with a heavy, final *thud* behind him. Garin moved like a glacier cutting through the manor. His boots struck the old stone floor, echoing down the hallway in slow, even rhythm. Each step bristled with restrained force, his jaw clenched tight, the leather of his coat brushing against his side as if even it knew not to make unnecessary noise.

He was **silent**, but not still. Not tonight. Tonight…he was *seething* beneath the surface. Glacial rage barely held in check. His duty came first, his orders and honor bound to Beau always. The only chains keeping the fury from ripping loose and turning these walls red, and the manor *felt* it.

The lights flickered as he passed, old enchantments reacting to the sudden pressure shift in the air. Somewhere, a portrait frame creaked in protest on the wall. Even the shadows *withdrew*, tucking tighter into the corners as if afraid of drawing his attention.

Then, he wasn't alone. Two voices rose, soft and low, from just ahead in the hallway. The unmistakable lilt of Mave, the ancient African priestess who served as both seer and sentinel of the coven. Her melodic accent carried warmth, wisdom, and magic in equal measure. And beside her…

Evangeline. Her voice, syrupy sweet and cold as a blade. She didn't speak so much as *pose*, every word meant to draw attention or remind someone she once held power none could challenge.

They were locked in conversation just beside the carved archway near the old library. Until, they *felt* him. The moment Garin stepped into view, the corridor dipped *ten degrees colder*. The warding candles along the baseboards flickered.

Both women turned.

Mave blinked once, slowly, her tone shifting from casual to concerned in an instant. Her eyes swept the towering figure of the Viking, shoulders taut, expression carved from stone, and *something* in his eyes that hadn't been there earlier. Something *lethal*.

"Garin," Mave said softly, dipping her head in acknowledgment, her accent rich and warm like the heartbeat of the continent that birthed her. "What has stirred the frost inside you tonight, my friend?"

But he didn't answer. Didn't even slow. Just kept walking, an icebound juggernaut, fury restrained only by discipline and duty. The silence might've passed unbroken...if not for her.

"Oh please," Evangeline drawled, her ruby lips curling around the words like smoke curling from a blade. She didn't bother to mask the condescension in her voice. "He's probably just upset the twins didn't bow to his bedtime schedule again. Or maybe Beau didn't say 'thank you' after a patrol."

Her eyes flicked to Mave, dramatic and sharp. "Honestly, these soldiers and their delicate egos..."

This time, Garin stopped. Mid-stride. Not turning. Not acknowledging. Just standing there, his back to them, like the executioner had just paused before raising the axe. The temperature dropped again, and the tension in the hallway coiled like a predator about to pounce.

And for one heartbeat too long, even Evangeline...forgot to breathe.

A heartbeat...then. He moved on. Never looking back, but the message had landed. Evangeline said nothing else, she didn't dare, because Garin never gave pause, but even the stillness of him was a clear warning not to continue whatever jest she had next.

Mave? She just watched him go, her head tilted slightly as if listening to something the others couldn't hear. "Whatever stirs," she murmured to herself, just above a whisper, "will not stay buried for long."

The manor doors groaned open on rusted hinges, and Garin stepped out into the night, his boots crunching over frost-slick stone, breath misting in the cold November air. Moonlight stretched across the rolling hills of Thorne Ridge, silvering the treetops like ghost light. The hour was late. The world hushed.

And yet, something in the air *thrummed*. Not with life, not with peace. With *warning*. Beau's orders echoed through him like a creed: Patrol the grounds. Check the wards. Reinforce every vulnerable inch of the territory. Protect the coven. Protect what is ours. And so he would, steel in hand, instincts sharp, mind *focused*.

Or...trying to be.

Because no matter how he tried to ground himself in strategy, in ritual, in the cold hard truth of threat.

That **song** kept bleeding into his thoughts.

A whisper of sound. A ghost of melody.

He paused at the tree line, towering between the oaks like some ancient sentinel carved from ice. His gaze swept the dark beyond the manor grounds, over the thickets and down the slope that led... To **Route 19**.

A lonely stretch of road that cut through the woods like a scar. And beyond it? The border. The edge of their territory. The place where the old protection spells began to thin, where ancient blood wards had grown weak over the years. Where *something* had begun to *watch* again.

Where she had been.

The Viking's Harmony

That *song*, it had come from that direction, he simply knew it. It called to him, that strange, otherworldly harmony that had stilled the monster in him for one brief moment the night before. A sound no predator should chase…but every part of him remembered.

Not because it made sense. But because it was *calm* in a world gone violent. It was soft in a world gone cruel. He should've ignored it. Buried it. Focused only on the threat ahead, the brutal deaths Rafe had described, the burned Bloodborn, the poisoned Moonborn, the desecrated Wraithborn.

And yet…

"Why now?" he muttered aloud, voice gravel-thick and low. "Why send *that*…in *this* time?"

He had faced monsters, fought wars under banners soaked in blood. He had felt what it was to be hunted and betrayed, had tasted ash on his tongue when good immortals were cut down for the crime of existing.

Still…that song. Was it a warning? A trap? A *gift*?

The gods were silent.

Only the wind answered, brushing past him like the exhale of something *watching* just beyond the trees. He tightened his grip on his blade. The frost around him thickened. And the cold in his chest, the one that had been rising ever since Rafe had spoken that cursed name, settled into something dangerously close to hope.

"No room for softness," he growled to himself, beginning his trek toward the outer wards. "Not now." But the melody followed. From memory… *fate*. He walked into the dark, because Route 19 waited.

~~~~~~~

The house was warm. Soft and still. Winter wrapped itself around her little home like a protective cocoon, the wind brushing against the windows in gentle whispers. Mira sat propped up in bed, her thick quilt pulled around her like armor, her hair let down to spill in unruly waves across her shoulders.

It *could* have been peaceful. Should have been peaceful.

If not for...

"Mira, honey, you *never* come home anymore, your father and I worry-"

Her mother's voice chirped through the phone, sharp, insistent, wobbling somewhere between guilt and smothering affection. Mira rested her temple in her hand, thumb rubbing slow circles to keep her patience intact.

"Mom, I'm fine," she said gently. "Really. Work's just...a lot right now."

"Then come stay with us over Christmas! We'll handle everything, you don't have to do a thing, sweetheart."

Mira's jaw ticked. She could hear it, the pity threaded beneath her mother's words like a stain no one wanted to acknowledge.

You're fragile, broken.

No matter how many years had passed since the fire, her parents still hadn't realized Mira didn't need to be *rescued*. She never had.

"I can't," Mira said, choosing her words carefully. "The school has scheduling conflicts, and I'm low on cash this month. Maybe in the spring."

There was a thick, disappointed silence.

"You always say that. We haven't seen you in a year."

Mira swallowed the ache that line always brought. "I know," she whispered. "I'm sorry. I just...can't this year."

There wasn't anger on the other end. Just defeat, and worse: *pity* softened into maternal sweetness.

"We just want what's best for you."

I know.

"We just want you happy."

I know.

"We just miss the old you."

Mira closed her eyes. Her throat tightened. "Mom," she said softly, "I have to go. It's late."

Her mother sighed. "Call us soon?"

"Of course."

She wouldn't. They both knew she wouldn't. Mira hung up, and for the first time that night, the house was *truly* quiet again. She let herself fall back onto the bed, the blankets puffing around her as she landed with a small, exhausted groan. The phone slid from her hand and landed beside her pillow while her fingers drifted over the thick woven blanket, following its texture to ground herself. Her breaths came slow, even. But her mind refused to settle.

It wandered To the melody she'd heard in her dream. The strange sense of being *watched* without fear and the feeling that the world outside her routines was shifting, pulling. Her mind began to wander further, to the question she had been avoiding for months.

What would her life look like if she didn't renew her contract?

She'd always taught. Because it was safe. Predictable, and routine. But...was she *happy*? Was she fulfilled? Or was she simply surviving in a life that had become too small for her? Her hand stilled on the blanket.

"What else is there?" she whispered into the dark.

No one answered. But something in the wind outside the window seemed to stir, like the first breath of a storm changing direction, and Mira decided there was no point in sitting there alone with her thoughts anymore. She moved quietly. The chill of the wooden floor met her toes as she slipped out of bed, wrapping the quilt tighter around her shoulders until it clung like a shawl. Her thick house shoes were right where she'd left them beside the dresser, lined with fleece, soft and scuffed at the toes from years of use.

A hum built in her throat as she padded through the hallway. Something quiet. Unfinished. Her fingers brushed against the doorframe, then the edge of the kitchen island. The piano keyboard was waiting on the counter. Always there. Always ready. But not tonight, not here.

Tonight she needed *air*. Needed *space*.

Mira scooped up the keyboard with practiced ease, tucking it under one arm as she used the other to crack the back door open. The cold bit at her cheeks instantly, but it was a welcome bite. Winter had always been her season. She could remember being six, running barefoot into the snowdrifts, arms wide, face turned to the sky. Her mother had screamed from the porch. Her father had wrapped her in a blanket so fast she never even got to feel the frostbite that could've come.

But *she* had loved it. Still did, even now. She stepped out onto the porch, breath blooming in the night like ghost flowers. The air smelled of pine, of frost, of woodsmoke drifting from somewhere far off. She smiled faintly.

"Can't see it," she whispered, "but I know it's beautiful."

She laid the keyboard gently atop the old wooden table just outside the door. Its legs were wobbly, but the surface was flat enough. She settled onto the porch swing with a soft sigh, quilt still wrapped around her, and adjusted the keyboard across her lap.

Her fingers hovered over the keys. Breathing and feeling. Searching. She didn't need her eyes, she had something better, *memory*. And tonight…something more.

That melody. The one from her dream. A harmony unlike anything she'd ever heard before. Cold and ancient and wild, but…tender. A single thread of sound woven through the shadows of her subconscious, and now, it teased the edge of her awareness again.

She pressed a key. Then another. Her hands began to move, uncertain at first. Searching for the notes like a blind woman searching for a lover in the dark. There. There it was.

Faint, and slippery, but real. The first line of the harmony unfolded beneath her fingers. Slow, haunting, broken in places. She followed it instinctively, her brows drawn in concentration, her head tilted as if trying to hear something *not* in the air, but inside her blood.

The music began to bloom, not perfect. Not yet, however it was close.

Close enough to feel like something she wasn't supposed to know. And somewhere, out past the porch, through the trees, over the rise of the hills, a pair of ancient blue eyes opened.

Silent. Still.

Listening.

***

At first, he dismissed it. A trick of memory, or a cruel echo left over from sleep.

Garin moved through the woods with steady purpose, boots crunching softly through snow-dusted pine needles, breath slow and controlled. The night was clear. Too clear. Moonlight filtered through bare branches, casting long skeletal shadows across the forest floor.

Nothing stirred. No threats, no trespassers, no sign of the LightBorne scum. Just silence. And yet...

He stopped.

Head tilting slightly, senses sharpening. There it was again. Faint, almost imperceptible.

No, he told himself. *You are imagining it.*

The melody brushed the edge of his hearing like a whisper through stone, so soft it could have been the wind threading through branches, or the echo of his own thoughts finally turning against him. He took another step. Then another. The sound strengthened. Not louder, but *clearer*.

Notes began to take shape, not perfect, a missed beat here and there.... Gods above, it was *close*. The same broken harmony that had wound through his dream. The same piano tones that had eased something deep and ancient in his chest, something he had sworn never to feel again. His jaw tightened.

"Impossible," he muttered.

Yet his feet betrayed him. Each step carried him forward, drawn not by command or duty, but by instinct older than blood or blade. The forest thinned. The slope eased.

Route 19.

The road cut through the land like a scar, its asphalt dark beneath moonlight, untouched at this hour. Snow clung to the edges, muffling the world, making everything feel... suspended. He knew this place. He had turned away from it last night.

Heart pounding now, not from exertion, but from something far more dangerous. The melody came from the left, from the small stretch of land just off the road. From the little house with the worn siding and quiet porch. And there, there she sat wrapped in blankets, red hair spilling loose around her shoulders, fingers moving gently across a keyboard balanced in her lap.

She played as if the night itself were listening, as if she belonged to it. Garin stopped at the edge of the trees, shadows swallowing his massive frame as he stared.

Gods...

She was real. Not a dream, nor a memory. Not a curse sent to test him. She was *there*. The music wasn't exact, no mortal hand could perfectly recreate what his ancient soul had remembered, but it was close enough to make his chest ache. Close enough to make him feel, for the first time in centuries, like he stood at the threshold of something sacred.

This is wrong, every instinct screamed. *This is dangerous. This is how gods punish warriors who forget their place.*

He still didn't move, didn't dare breathe, and didn't look away. Because the melody wasn't calling him to violence. It wasn't calling him to blood. It was calling him to **peace**. Garin, shield of the Thorne coven, slayer of monsters, survivor of centuries of war... Had no idea what to do with that.

Moments passed as the woman played, and...He did not move.

Not when her fingers danced across the keyboard in her lap, coaxing imperfect but haunting notes into the winter night. Not when she missed a chord and simply shook her head, laughing at herself beneath her breath like the error was an old friend. Not even when the wind shifted, brushing her scent toward him, soft, human, and laced with the faintest hint of cold cedar and lavender.

Garin remained stone-still beneath the shroud of the trees, hidden by the dark cloak he wore, his body half buried in shadow and snow, and yet, he felt like *glass.*

Cracked. Fragile

Every imperfect note scraped against a place in him he hadn't let breathe in centuries. The memory of the dream still lingered in his chest, and gods help him, this was *the song.* Or something close to it. Raw and hesitant in places. Almost fragile. But unmistakable.

You cannot be real, he thought. *You cannot have heard it too.*

He held his breath as she stopped playing. Fingers poised over the keys, her body very still. Her lips parted on a soft sigh. And into the frozen silence, she whispered;

"It sounded so much better in my dream."

Garin froze. No blade. No strike. No ancient curse could have hit harder. His heart, long since dead and still, felt like it seized in his chest.

She dreamed it too.

A chill licked down his spine, colder than the winter air around him. It wasn't coincidence. It wasn't mimicry. It wasn't madness on his part. The melody... the one he had buried so deep he dared not recall it aloud... *she had heard it too.* And not through him, not through contact, blood, or enchantment.

She had dreamt it.

How?

He watched her lower her hands, resting them gently in her lap. Her expression was unreadable to the world, but he could feel it, could sense the weight in her shoulders. The ache in her sigh. She was not afraid. She was not hunted.

She was *lonely.*

Somehow...somehow the song had found her too. He took one step backward. Then another. Retreating slowly, quietly, his presence never revealed. Because tonight, he didn't trust himself.

He didn't trust the way her voice curled inside him like it *belonged* there. Didn't trust the feeling unfurling beneath his ribs, and never trusted the gods not to strike him down for daring to believe that perhaps...after everything...he was being *called to something other than war.*

His boots crushed through the snow in slow, heavy steps. The further he walked from the little house, the more the silence clawed at him, no longer peaceful, but echoing with absence. Of music. Of fire-lit hair dancing in the breeze. Of the warmth he had no right to miss. He was a creature born in blood and baptized in shadow. There had never been softness left for him, not since the long winter that took everything.

And yet...

That melody had come from his dreams, and she...she had summoned it into the waking world like it belonged to her. His breath steamed in the frigid air, eyes narrowing as he reached the edge of the coven's northern perimeter. Beyond it, the trees thinned toward the old highway. Toward **her.** The silence thickened again. Even the trees seemed to lean in, as if the land itself held its breath with him.

He tilted his head toward the sky, that vast, ink-black void he had long stopped believing held gods or answers, but still, something ancient in him whispered to speak.

So he did.

A low rumble of voice cutting through the frostbitten stillness:

"What are you, little flame?" Yet…no answer would be given to him, and so, Garin moved, faster now.

The woods should have welcomed him as he all but fled, eased his mind with the trees and snow fallen like a blanket, the way they always had. But tonight…the quiet pressed. Not like an old cloak wrapped around his shoulders, but like a burden.

A **loss.**

The further he moved from the little house on Route 19, the heavier it became, as if every tree leaned inward to remind him of what he was leaving behind.

A woman with fire-kissed hair. Wrapped in blankets, playing a ghost of a song on a plastic keyboard like it could summon back warmth or answers or… peace. And her voice…gods.

"It sounded so much better in my dream."

Garin's jaw clenched, the leather of his gloves creaking as his hands fisted at his sides. He'd heard many things in his life. Screams. Cries. The last rattling breath of dying men. But nothing had ever haunted him quite like the softness of her voice saying those words.

She dreamt it too. She heard the song. My song.

He shoved the thought away, but it circled back with a vengeance, latching onto a part of himself long buried:

His hugr.

His spiritual essence. His soul's will. The part of him that wandered in dreams.

Long ago, when the snow still sang in the mountains of his homeland, his people had believed the hugr could travel in sleep. Could drift through realms, seek answers, find omens. He had abandoned such beliefs the day he was turned beneath a pale and frozen moon. Had buried them beside the gods who never answered his prayers.

Yet...She knew the melody. Knew it like it had lived in her ribcage since birth.

How? Why now? And why her?

Because she is not afraid of the dark. Because she plays to it like it might love her back. Because something inside you, something old and long-starved, saw her and did not run.

He slowed. Paused. The wind whistled through the trees behind him, carrying with it only the silence he hated now. The ache. Gods, the ache.

Why did the song live in her dreams too?

His hugr...his essence...had not stirred in centuries. Not until her. Not until that melody haunted his dream he night before after seeing her for the first time. And now it felt pulled.

Leashed. Not by blood. Not by magic. But by resonance. A thread between souls forged not by fate... but by harmony.

He turned his face toward the sky, his breath a ghost in the frozen air.

"Hugr minn...hvar ert þú núna?" *(My soul...where are you now?)*

And he swore...in the distant wind, the faintest echo of a piano answered.

Chapter 6

Garin stepped through the threshold of Thorne Manor just past midnight. His boots, soaked with snowmelt and shadow, somehow left no trace across the ancient floorboards but the weight of him filled the hall long before his presence was seen.

He should've gone back to the edge of Route 19. Should've turned toward the cedar-scented home with candlelight in the window and music in the air.

But he didn't.

Because she wasn't his to return to.

The pull still clawed at his gut, a thread of fire and memory tangled in his chest. But he shoved it down. Locked it away. Because duty came first. And tonight…the coven was already gathered, and he knew that tonight would be one where the Bloodborn faced a truth that most of them hoped would ever arise again.

The manor's grand hall was lit only by the fire and a few low sconces, casting gold and ash across the tension in the room. The twins were huddled together on the far velvet settee, identical murmurs slipping between them in Irish cadence. Cian's sharp jaw twitched with annoyance; Rua's boot tapped against the floor in restless rhythm. Simon stood just behind them, arms folded, his mouth set in that familiar disapproving line, the one reserved solely for the twins when they were being *utter menaces*.

Mave and Larazo sat side by side on the old brocade chaise. Hands entwined, posture always regal. Eyes too knowing. Whatever this meeting was about... they had likely seen it coming hours before the summons, perhaps even before Beau had summoned Garin earlier that same evening. The two ancients always seemed to be ten steps ahead of everyone else, and yet even they seemed uneasy.

And by the hearth... *Evangeline.*

Her posture was statuesque, her red-painted lips pursed in thought, her back to the rest of them. She watched the fire like it might offer her dominion over it. She hadn't greeted him, wasn't even facing or acknowledging the rest of the coven. She never did unless she had something to gain from it. But it was the figure standing at the heart of the room that made Garin's jaw tighten.

Beau.

The Southern titan stood tall, arms loose but unreadable, his dark eyes flicking toward Garin without surprise. He had *felt* the Viking approach long before the door had opened, and beside him?

Rafe.

That damned Moonborn wolf. Leaning one shoulder against the support beam like he owned the place, thumbs hooked in his belt, his expression unreadable, save for the ever-present scent of the wild that clung to him. Something about the way the others all held themselves, the rigid spines, the whispers cut short when Garin entered, told him this wasn't going to be an easy introduction into the night.

No, this was war council. Or prophecy. Or both. Garin stepped further into the room, and the door clicked shut behind him, sealing him in with centuries of secrets and one single thought screaming at the back of his skull...**Little flame.** He shoved it down again.

Beau turned to him fully now, voice low, steady, that southern tone deep with a seriousness Beau barely wore except in times of dire need. "Garin. You finish your patrol?"

The Viking nodded once. "Aye. All wards intact. But some are wearin' thin. I made a list."

Beau held out his hand, took the parchment without looking at it just yet. Then, he glanced to Rafe. Then to the rest of the coven, and finally back to Garin. "Good. Because we've got a problem. And it's got the scent of the LightBorne on it."

The hearth snapped softly behind Evangeline, and every creature in the room became as still as the statues outside the manor gates. Beau didn't raise his voice. He never needed to, but it cut through the hush like a blade nonetheless.

"Figured it's time the rest of y'all knew exactly *why* he's here." He didn't gesture to Rafe. Didn't need to.

Every immortal in the room was already *watching* the wolf like he was a spark too close to oil. Rafe didn't flinch, didn't smirk, didn't rise to meet any of their gazes. He just stayed leaning on that support beam, his stance deceptively lazy.

Beau's voice remained steady as he continued. "Rafe Talbot's been working with Bobby down in town for a while now. Tracks the kinds of things we don't always see. Things we *should've* been seein'."

That was when the twins moved. Rua sat forward first, eyes narrowed, tension lacing every line of his lean frame. "Why in *hell* would we need a wolf's eyes or nose for that?"

"We've got Rua," Cian added with a sneer. "And we don't invite mongrels into our home."

Simon didn't look up from where he stood behind them, but one sharply spoken word left his mouth like iron: "Enough."

It was a command, not a request. The twins stilled, but the heat between them and Rafe now hummed in the space like a live wire.

Simon folded his arms again, sharp eyes on Beau. "Go on."

Garin remained by the door, arms crossed, jaw set tight. But he said nothing. Because he had already heard it all, went through those damned territorial urges already and was silenced by their leader.

Beau's eyes moved across each member of the coven now, gaze sharp as glass. "We've got two Bloodborn dead. One found beheaded. The other burned to ash in a churchyard."

"A Moonborn," Rafe cut in lowly now, "poisoned. Drained of essence. Still barely alive."

"And a wraith," Beau added, "found stripped of its shadows. Left like an exorcism gone wrong."

Even Evangeline turned at that, and the former queen never flinched at a thing. The entire room felt colder. Beau let the silence stretch.

"All of them were found near our border. Within walking distance of the state line. Rafe found them all. Made sure every one of them were buried proper and looked after."

Mave leaned forward slightly now. Her voice was soft, dangerous. "You think it's them. The LightBorne."

Beau gave a single nod. "Too much coincidence. Too many patterns lining up just like before."

Larazo's hand clenched tighter around Mave's, the firelight catching the inked runes on his fingers.

Simon's brows drew low. "And you want to call a *truce*?" His French lit nearly sneering with the word, coming out as sharp as his gaze when it snapped to the wolf.

Beau didn't hesitate. "I already did son."

That made the room shudder. Rua surged to his feet. "*You what?* Without even-"

"Sit. Down." Garin rumbled lowly. For the first time since reentering, his voice filled the room, and when the Viking spoke, people listened.

Rua bristled, a low growl in his throat but sat. Garin's eyes went back to Beau, and gave a tight nod in return. Rua was on edge, they all were, but he knew that he wouldn't let the Irishman cause another problem, not when too many supernatural's were already dead so close to their home.

Beau finally looked back to Rafe. "He stays under my protection. So long as he reports what he finds, keeps our borders tight, and doesn't make this a pissin' match."

Rafe gave a single nod, arms still crossed. "I'm not here to fight you," he said quietly. "I'm here to help keep whatever's coming from burning down your entire damn ridge."

Garin's gaze never left the wolf. Not with suspicion, and not with hate. But with a warrior's calculation. Because *he* had seen the bodies the LightBorne once left behind, centuries ago. Knew what they were capable of. And now? He had watched that little woman play the song of his ancestors… and now, he was being told the world might be unraveling again just beyond her door.

No.

That thought was so deep in Garin's mind, that he barely registered the new voice speaking. The fire snapped behind her again, but this time, she finally turned to face them. Evangeline's voice, when it came, was low and cold, like winter's bite in a lace glove.

"What happens if they already know?"

That silence again. One that gripped the room with invisible claws. Because that was the fear *none* of them wanted to name. What if they were too late? What if this had already begun? But the one to answer wasn't Beau, or Simon, or Garin this time.

It was the wolf.

Rafe stepped forward, just once. Not to challenge. But to *declare*.

"If they *knew* about this place, really knew, " His gaze swept the room slowly, lingering on the velvet curtains, the polished wood floors, the vaulted ceilings, " then this manor would already be ash. And the whole damn town would've burned with it."

A chill slid through the gathered coven like fog over a grave. Even Cian didn't breathe.

"They don't know yet," Rafe continued. "But they're close. Close enough that I found those bodies no more than six miles out from the edge of the state border. "

He didn't look to Simon, or the twins, or even Beau this time. He looked to Garin, one warrior to another.

"You know I'm right."

And he was.

Garin didn't move, didn't blink, didn't *agree*, but the silence from him often spoke louder than words. Because Garin had *seen* what Rafe described. Had watched that unnatural stillness settle over the edge of the forest. Had tasted the metallic residue of something *wrong* in the air, even while being distracted by a melody he had no business craving. The others didn't know it yet, but the scent of sanctified ash had already crept too close to the ridge.

Rafe turned back to the rest of them now. "You've got the upper hand right now. But if you wait too long, if you keep pretending you can handle this alone, they *will* find you. And when they do, you won't get a second warning."

Simon's jaw was tight. But he remained still. Larazo looked at Beau, dark eyes heavy with concern. Mave, as always, was unreadable, but her hand moved to press against her abdomen, where old scars once burned.

Evangeline? She tilted her head slowly, eyes narrowing on Rafe. "And you're the one to save us? A wolf without a pack?"

The insult was sharp, and Garin expected the wolf to snarl or even bristle, but Rafe only smiled, bitter and tired.

"I'm not here to save you. I'm here to help you fight. If you're willing."

Garin finally exhaled, the sound coming sharp and fast. It wasn't consent. It wasn't refusal. But it was the first movement he'd made since entering the room.

Because the wolf was right, and Garin had too much *to lose* now. Even if the others didn't understand yet. He could still hear that melody. He could still hear her voice...

"It sounded so much better in my dream."

He clenched his jaw, letting the firelight flicker across the braided ink on his arm. There would be no burning of this ridge. No torch would touch her. Not while he still drew breath, or what passed for it.

~~~~~~

The coven began to fracture, not loudly, not dramatically, but in the subtle way only immortals did when something had gone wrong. Mave rose first, her movements smooth and deliberate. Larazo followed immediately, his hand never leaving hers, their fingers entwined as if they already shared the same thought. As they passed Garin, Mave inclined her head toward him, just slightly. A knowing gesture.

They were already calculating futures, including his.

Beau was next. The Southern king exhaled slowly, rubbing a hand over his jaw before turning toward the door.

"I'll make some calls," he muttered. "Bobby first. Then Leah." There was the faintest hint of something wry in his voice at that. "Because if I don't tell her what's happening," he added under his breath, "she'll be deadlier than any LightBorne bastard that comes sniffin' around." And then he was gone, already commanding a war beyond the walls, already managing protection of the town below them.

Evangeline didn't announce her departure. She simply turned from the hearth and glided toward the side corridor, her heels whispering against the stone. She never looked back, never did anymore...and never waited for her mate.

Garin watched her go. Not because she mattered to him, but because of the man she left behind.

Simon stood unmoving near the wall, his posture rigid, eyes fixed on the corridor where Evangeline had disappeared. A year ago, he would've followed her without hesitation. Would've reached for her wrist. Would've spoken her name.

Now?

He didn't move. The silence between them was louder than any argument. And when the Frenchman finally turned back toward the room, something in his expression had hardened, something old and lonely and unresolved.

Which left...

The twins.

Garin felt it before he saw it. Rua leaned forward slightly, red curls falling loose as his grin sharpened into something feral. Cian mirrored him from the opposite side, shoulders loose, stance casual, but his eyes were locked on the Moonborn like a predator sighting prey. Neither spoke, they didn't need to.

The air between them and Rafe tightened like a wire drawn too thin. Garin shifted his weight subtly, his body angling just enough that he could intercept either twin in a heartbeat if needed. He'd done it before. Would do it again.

Rua's gaze flicked to Garin for half a second.

Just enough. As if to say: *Relax, Viking. We're only considering murder.*

Rafe, for his part, didn't reach for a weapon. Didn't bare his teeth. Didn't shift. He just watched them with that same steady, infuriating calm.

"You two always stare like that," Rafe drawled lightly, "or is it just a 'welcome to the coven' thing?"

Cian's mouth curved. "Depends."

Rua cracked his neck once. "You tend to land on our bad side, wolf."

Garin didn't move yet. He stood there like a wall of ice and iron, every muscle coiled, every sense alert, not for the wolf, but for the twins. Because if one of them launched, he would end it before it started. Not for Rafe.

For Beau. For the coven. For the fragile balance already beginning to fracture, and somewhere, far beyond the manor walls…a melody still lingered in the back of Garin's mind, soft and dangerous.

Peace, he was learning, was far harder to defend than war…

Because the damned dog opened his mouth.

Rafe's mouth barely curved. Just a hint of humor, poorly timed, poorly chosen.

"Guess I'm flattered," the wolf drawled lightly. "Three of you starin' like you're decidin' who gets first bite. I know I'm pretty an all…"

He didn't finish the sentence.

Rua moved.

It wasn't a lunge so much as an *eruption,* red hair flashing, body coiling forward with feral speed, fangs snapping out in a white, lethal grin.

Garin was already in motion. He caught Rua mid-air. One massive hand closed around the Irishman's chest, the other locking into his shoulder as Garin pivoted, slamming Rua back against the stone wall hard enough to rattle the sconces.

"Enough," Garin growled low, *not loud,* but terrifyingly controlled.

Rua snarled, fangs fully bared, eyes blown wide and feral as he struggled against the Viking's iron grip.

"Get yer hands off me ye frostbitten bastard!"

Cian didn't move forward, but his fangs dropped instantly with a wet click, a low, dangerous snarl rolling out of his chest as his stance shifted, ready to spring if Garin faltered.

The room exploded with predator tension. Rafe stiffened, not backing down, not advancing either, but his shoulders squared, wolf instincts flaring in response to the sudden violence.

And then...

"ÇA SUFFIT."

Simon's voice cracked like a whip. It rose just a single octave, but it was enough, because he almost never spoke in such a way. It came out like a whip, sharp and commanding like few have heard from him. *Lethal*. The Frenchman stepped forward, fury burning clean and cold in his silver gaze as he snapped at the twins like a master disciplining beasts.

"Stand. Down. Or I will put you down myself."

Rua froze, still snarling, still straining, but he *stopped*. Cian's jaw clenched, his fangs still bared, but his feet rooted to the floor.

Simon didn't slow, didn't stutter, and didn't lower his voice.

"You will not attack a guest under this roof," he hissed. "You will not embarrass this coven, and you will not make me repeat myself."

His eyes flicked to Rua, still pinned by Garin. Silence fell hard and heavy.

Rua's chest heaved once. Twice. Then, slowly, his fangs retracted. Cian followed a heartbeat later, the snarl fading though the tension did not. Garin didn't release Rua immediately. He waited until the wildness bled out of the

Irishman's eyes, until the feral edge dulled just enough. He stepped back and let him go. Rua straightened, jaw tight, eyes burning, but he didn't move again.

Simon exhaled sharply through his nose, rubbing a hand over his mouth before looking to Rafe.

"Apologies mon loup," he said stiffly. "They are… emotional."

Rafe gave a tight nod. "Noted."

Garin turned his gaze on the wolf then, blue eyes cold, unreadable.

"Choose your words carefully," the Viking said quietly. "You are not prey here. But neither are you untouchable."

Rafe met his stare without flinching. "Fair enough."

The room remained tense, fractured, volatile, but the violence had been contained. Barely. And Garin knew, as he stood there between ancient predators and a lone wolf, that this fragile truce would not survive *much* more strain.

Not with the LightBorne closing in, not with the twins coiled tight as razors. And not with a little flame burning quietly at the edge of his soul, unaware of how many monsters were already preparing to fight for the right to protect her and the others around her.

Garin didn't relax. He shifted, subtle, controlled, but every muscle in his body stayed coiled, ready. He took half a step back, placing himself between the twins and Rafe without making it obvious.

Not because Simon couldn't handle them. But because someone had to be the wall if it broke again. For a few heartbeats, the room held.

Then Cian spoke. His voice was low, sharp, carrying every edge of Irish venom that normally hid behind charm and humor.

"We shouldn't have to be contained in our own home," he hissed, blue eyes cutting to Rafe. "If he's stayin', then let him stay *outside*. Like the dog he is."

The word landed like a slap. Rafe's jaw tightened, but he didn't move. Simon did. The Frenchman turned on Cian with a look so dark it could've curdled blood.

"Ta gueule."

Shut up.

The words were clipped. Dangerous. Then, without missing a beat, Simon snapped again, this time in Irish, his accent rough but unmistakable, the command carrying the weight of centuries and fury both.

The twins reacted instantly, snarling, bristling, snapping back in a heated mix of English and Irish that filled the room like sparks hitting dry tinder.

Rua surged half a step forward. "You don't get to talk to us like that!"

"You *always* do this," Cian bit out. "Like we're feral idiots!"

And then Rua lost what little restraint he had left. "You can't treat us like *children*, Simon!"

The words echoed. For a moment, no one moved. Not Garin. Not Rafe. Not even the fire dared crackle.

Simon stepped forward slowly, his expression no longer merely irritated, but *cold*. Controlled. Terrible.

"I absolutely can." His voice was quiet now. Lethal. "And I *will* treat you like children until you act like the men I raised you to be."

Rua recoiled as if struck. Cian's jaw clenched hard enough Garin could hear his teeth grind.

Simon didn't stop. "You are not wild animals. You are not entitled to violence because your pride is bruised. And you will not endanger this coven, *or this truce*, because you cannot control yourselves."

He looked between them, gaze sharp as broken glass.

"I did not drag you through famine, war, and bloodshed for centuries just so you could snarl like pups at the first inconvenience. I did not raise heathens!"

Silence crashed down again. Heavy. Suffocating.

Rua's chest heaved once. Twice. Then he turned away sharply, raking a hand through his hair. Cian looked anywhere but at Simon. Garin watched it all without comment. But something in his chest tightened, not with anger, not with approval, but with understanding.

Because discipline was the only thing standing between monsters and chaos, and tonight, the line was already too thin.

Chapter 7

The twins left like a storm. Rua was the first to shove through the doors, cursing in Irish loud enough to rattle the old glass panes, his insults flung back over his shoulder like thrown knives, aimed at Rafe, at Simon, at the very idea of restraint. Cian followed a heartbeat later, jaw tight, eyes burning, his voice sharp and cutting as he hurled his own venom into the hall before the doors slammed shut behind them.

The manor exhaled, and the tension didn't leave, but it settled.

Simon stood unmoving for a long moment, shoulders rigid, his hands clenched at his sides as if holding himself together by sheer will alone. When he finally turned, the firelight caught the silver in his hair and the exhaustion etched into his face.

"I apologize," he said quietly, the words meant for Rafe, but carrying far more weight than that. "They should not have spoken to you that way."

Rafe lifted a hand. "I get it. Families are… loud."

Simon gave a tight nod, then glanced once at Garin…just once. There was something unspoken there. Something old and shared and heavy.

"Bonne nuit," Simon murmured, and then he was gone, footsteps measured, controlled, retreating deeper into the manor where silence waited to swallow him whole.

The doors closed again. This time, they did not reopen. Rafe shifted on his feet, suddenly looking far less confident than he had moments ago. He rubbed the back of his neck, exhaling slowly.

"Well," he muttered, a deeper southern drawl slipping from his lips almost as if he were embarrassed, "that was... uncomfortable."

Garin didn't respond right away, just let his gaze drift to the wolf.

"Felt like I just watched a father one bad second away from beating his own sons on the front porch," Rafe added, voice low now, stripped of humor.

That made Garin turn. Slowly. Blue eyes fixed on the Moonborn with something sharp and ancient.

"That," Garin said, voice gravel-deep, "is exactly what you saw."

Rafe stilled.

Garin leaned back against the wall, folding his arms, not defensive, but grounded. When he spoke again, his words came measured. Rare.

"Simon found them during the Irish famine. They were children. Teenagers, barely. Starving, barely alive on the streets. He kept them alive. Taught them to fight, to read, to survive. When illness almost took one of them, he turned them rather than bury them."

Silence settled between them, and the Viking watched as Rafe's shoulders began to settle in realization of his words.

"He raised them into men," Garin continued. "And now they bicker like sons who do not know how to leave their father's shadow."

Rafe listened. Really listened. Then, quietly, carefully, he said the thing Garin did not expect.

"Then maybe that's the problem." The words landed like a stone dropped into still water.

Garin's gaze sharpened. "Explain."

Rafe shrugged slightly, but his eyes were serious. "Maybe Simon needs to let up. Let them prove themselves. You don't raise boys into men by reminding them they're children every time they bare their teeth."

For the first time since entering the room…Garin faltered. Not outwardly and not visibly, but something in his chest shifted. Because discipline was all he had ever known, because obedience had kept him alive. Because softness, to a warrior, was often a death sentence.

And yet…

He thought of Rua's fury. Cian's pride. Simon's tightening control as the years went by, and the twins became more restless with each passing season. He thought of a woman wrapped in blankets, laughing softly when she missed a note, playing a melody that lived in his dreams without ever knowing his name.

Strength did not always come from chains. Sometimes… it came from trust.

Garin didn't answer Rafe right away. But when he did, his voice was quieter than before.

"Be careful, wolf," he said. "You speak of things that change bloodlines."

Rafe met his gaze evenly. "War does that anyway."

Silence fell again between the two men, but this time, it was thoughtful.

The doors closed behind him with a sound far too loud for the way his head already throbbed. Simon walked down the corridor slowly, one hand lifting to pinch the bridge of his nose as the voices of the twins echoed ahead of him, raised, sharp, laced with fury and insult.

"Coward's choice, that's what it was brother."

"Should've let us handle it ourselves... and Simon always bloody chooses *them*"

"...and that Viking grabbing me like I'm-'"

"Enjoy your new pet wolf, *Père!*"

"Still playing king to bastards who never asked for a crown!"

The words blurred together. Irish curses. French insults hurled back in return. Footsteps storming away in opposite directions. Simon exhaled through his teeth with a hiss of frustration, and exasperation.

A migraine, sharp and merciless, pressed behind his eyes. Not from the noise alone, but from the *centuries* of it. The endless cycle of pride and rebellion and restraint. Of sons who did not understand that survival had once demanded obedience.

He stopped after a few more steps. Because he felt her before he saw her.

Evangeline stood farther down the hall, near one of the tall windows overlooking the dark grounds. Firelight from the sconces kissed her pale skin and caught in the red of her lips. She watched him openly now, no pretense of distraction.

"Why do you still allow them to speak to you like that?" she asked coolly.

Simon didn't look at her at first. "It is not your concern," he said, voice even. Controlled. "I handled it. There was no fight."

He started to move past her, but as she had done far too often lately, she got in the way. She stepped into his path.

"You *always* handle it," Evangeline said softly. "And yet nothing changes."

Simon stopped. Slowly, he lowered his hand from his face and looked down at her. Not with love, not with devotion. With more **exasperation**.

"Move," he said quietly.

She didn't. Instead, she tilted her head, studying him like something slightly disappointing.

"You should have leashed them," she continued. "Or better yet, left them human long ago. You created this problem."

The words landed cleanly, precise and cruel in way few could manage. Simon felt something in his chest go utterly still. The migraine vanished and the noise faded. And when his dark brown eyes lifted fully to hers, they were no longer warm.

They were ice.

"Do not," he said softly, "ever speak of them as mistakes."

Evangeline faltered, just a fraction. "You forget yourself," she snapped. "I am your mate-"

"You are overstepping." His voice was calm. Too calm.

"They are alive because I chose compassion over obedience. Because I would rather endure their anger than bury them beneath the soil of a starving country." He stepped closer now, his presence suddenly oppressive, the air thickening around them. "And you," he continued, eyes never leaving hers, "do not get to rewrite that choice because their grief inconveniences you."

"Yet they still act like feral dogs."

"And you speak like someone who has forgotten what love should look like," he murmured. "Or perhaps you never knew."

Her lips parted, sharp retort ready, but Simon was already turning away.

"This conversation is over." He walked past her without another glance, his footsteps measured, controlled. Behind him, Evangeline stood rigid and silent, the firelight no longer warming her face.

Simon walked on with the weight of fatherhood heavy in his chest, knowing, with a clarity that cut deeper than any insult…That some fractures did not heal.

They only widened.

Simon's footsteps echoed like a reprimand down the stone corridor. The twins' voices hadn't stopped. They bounced off the hall walls behind him like echoes of a battlefield, furious, foul, and far too familiar.

"Bloody bastard could've let me break his damn nose!"

"Should've let Garin break yours, Rua, runnin' your mouth like that!"

"Least I said what we were all thinkin'!"

The Frenchman's migraine returned as he walked away from the voices, only this time it was no longer just aggravation with the twins…it was the fact that for the first time since he had found Evangeline, and stolen her as his own mate…

Simon did not want to return to her arms.

And while the echoes of angry Irishmen carried, the huff the a forgotten queen faded, and the aches of a lover turned scorned grew… somewhere deep within Thorne Manor, something old and once unshakable cracked.

~~~~~~~~~~

Garin left the great hall without announcement. The manor had settled into a brittle quiet now, one that came not from peace, but from things left unsaid. He moved through the corridors like a shadow carved from stone, his boots soundless against the ancient floors.

And then, he felt it. Not a sound, not a scent. A **shift**. A fracture moving through the house like a tremor through old bones. He paused at the turn of the corridor, one hand resting briefly against the cold stone wall.

Simon.

He knew that kind of rupture. Had seen it before, centuries ago, in men who had held too tightly to what they loved, or what they feared losing. Garin did not turn toward it. Did not follow. That was not his way. Some battles were not meant for him.

Instead, he continued toward the east wing, toward the solitude he had always claimed as his own. But his mind would not still. Rafe's words echoed again, uninvited.

Let them prove themselves. You don't raise men by reminding them they're children.

Garin exhaled slowly through his nose. The twins were reckless. Loud. Sharp-edged chaos wrapped in charm and teeth. They tested patience like it was sport, treated danger like a joke. And yet...

They were more than trackers. More than glamours and grins used to disarm or deceive. They were warriors, undisciplined, yes, but powerful. Loyal. Fierce in a way that burned hot and fast. Deadly with their bodies and weapons more so than any others Garin had met through his long immortal life.

What would happen if Simon loosened the reins?

The thought lingered. What would happen if the coven stopped seeing the twins as tools, and started seeing them as men who had survived famine, war, and centuries of bloodshed? Would they grow into something steadier? Something sharper?

Something... *free*?

His steps slowed as another thought followed, colder and far more dangerous.

And what of you?

Garin stopped outside his door. The corridor was empty. Quiet. He stared at the iron handle, his reflection faintly visible in the darkened glass beside it, broad shoulders, scarred arms, eyes like winter ice holding back a storm.

He had leashed himself for over a thousand years. Wrapped duty around his throat and called it honor. Called it survival. Called it *control*. He did not dream. He did not wander. He did not want.

And yet...A melody had found him anyway.

A woman had played it without knowing his name. Without knowing *him*.

If the leash were loosened... If you allowed yourself more than duty...

The thought tightened something in his chest.

Could he change?

Or was he too old, too carved by blood and frost to become anything other than what he had always been? Garin opened the door and stepped into his room, the darkness swallowing him whole.

The silence did not comfort him, not tonight. And for the first time in centuries, the sword wondered what it would mean to lay himself down, not for a king, not for a battle, but for himself.

The room dimmed as the night bled toward dawn. Garin moved with the same careful ritual he had followed for centuries, unstrapping his weapons, placing them in their exact places, drawing the heavy furs over the stone floor where the cold crept upward. Outside, the world stilled beneath winter's breath.

He prepared for sleep. But his mind...His mind would not quiet.

How could I change?

The question settled into him, heavy and foreign. He had been forged for war. For silence. For obedience. His life, before and after the blood, had been shaped by duty, by restraint, by knowing when *not* to speak.

Change was for the young. For mortals. For those who still believed the world could soften.

Could he smile?

The thought almost startled him.

Could he speak, *not because he must,* but because he wanted to?

Could he allow himself moments that did not serve a purpose? Could he allow himself…

Her.

The red-haired woman with fingers that danced over keys like prayer. The one whose melody had found his hugr without permission. The one who had spoken aloud what he had only dared think.

"It sounded so much better in my dream."

He sat on the edge of the stone bed for a long moment, staring at nothing, his reflection faint in the darkened window. He had not approached her. Had not spoken. Had not allowed himself even the illusion of hope. And yet his soul, his ancient, battered hugr, had led him to her as surely as any battlefield instinct ever had.

Could I speak to her?

The thought was terrifying. Not because she might reject him. But because she might *see him*. Because she might accept him. Because peace, real true peace, was something he had never learned how to hold.

Garin lay back, the furs heavy over his chest, the stone cold beneath him. Outside, the first pale light of dawn crept over the snow-dusted Blue Ridge, painting the mountains in silver and frost.

As the sun rose, so did the thoughts covering the mind of the silent man, who had long given up a chance of anything kind, of anything real.

Garin the Viking made a decision.

Not a vow. Not a promise. Just a choice. The LightBorne would come, war would find them. Blood always did. But when night fell again, he would follow that melody. He would step closer. And for the first time in over a thousand years, as sleep claimed him and her voice echoed softly in his mind...

Garin allowed himself to hope.

"Ég get reynt."

I can try.

~~~

The alarm chimed at six-thirty on the dot. Mira groaned into her pillow, one arm flinging out until her fingers found the familiar shape of the clock and silenced it. For a long moment, she stayed there, wrapped in warmth, listening to the house breathe around her, the faint hum of the heater, the tick of cooling pipes, the muted hush of early morning.

Normal. Routine. Safe.

She rolled onto her back and sighed, red hair spilling messily across the pillow as she stretched, muscles protesting gently as they always did. Another day. Another class. Another bus ride down and back Route 19 from the school.

She frowned slightly. Because she'd dreamed again. Not just fragments this time. Not vague impressions or half-remembered melodies slipping through her fingers.

The music had been *clear*.

Full-bodied. Rich. Like something ancient and reverent, threading through her bones instead of just her ears. And beneath it, woven so gently she almost missed it...

A voice. A man's voice really, low and deep like the snow she loved. It hadn't spoken words she could remember. No name. No warning. No demand. Just presence. Steady and grounded, like standing near a mountain and knowing, somehow, that it was watching over you rather than looming.

Mira swung her legs over the side of the bed, bare feet finding the cold floor without hesitation. She moved through her morning by muscle memory, shower steam warming her skin, fingers tracing the grooves on the knobs to find the perfect temperature, towel exactly where it should be.

Coffee followed. The old machine hissed and gurgled, familiar and comforting, its smell anchoring her fully in the waking world. Still, the feeling lingered. Not fear and for sure not confusion.

Expectation.

She dressed carefully, pulled on her sweater, slipped her sunglasses into place before reaching for her cane. As she stood by the door, keys cool in her palm, she paused. Her chest felt… lighter. As if something unseen had shifted just enough to let air in.

Mira tilted her head slightly, listening, not for sound, but for intuition. For the quiet sense that had guided her for years now, sharper than sight had ever been.

Something is coming, it whispered.

Not like a storm, but like a door opening. She locked the house behind her, humming under her breath as she stepped into the crisp winter morning. The melody was the same one from her dreams, still imperfect, still searching, but she smiled faintly as she walked.

Change was frightening. But as the sun crested the snow-covered hills and warmed her face, Mira found she wasn't afraid of this one. She only hoped, that whatever was moving toward her was meant for the better.

Chapter 8

The sign passed beneath the headlights without ceremony, the black SUV rolling down the highway like a shadow made of shadow and rage.

WELCOME TO GEORGIA.

Alexander Weber's jaw tightened as the tires crossed the state line. His hands clenched harder around the steering wheel, knuckles whitening, tendons standing out beneath weathered skin. He did not slow. He never did.

In the back seat, Jonah Adams shifted, laptop balanced on his knees, dark eyes flicking between satellite feeds and handwritten notes scrawled in tight, precise script. He was young, too young, some would say, for this kind of work, but his instincts were sharp. Paranoid in the way good surveillance always was.

"Still nothing concrete," Jonah said finally. "No confirmed sightings. Just... patterns."

"Patterns are proof," Alexander snapped.

Beside Jonah, his sister Abigail leaned back against the seat, tablet glowing faintly in her hands. Where Jonah watched the present, Abigail combed the past, records, rumors, erased files that governments pretended never existed.

"They've been careful," she said calmly. "That's what bothers me. Power outages clustered around the same ridge. Missing persons reports that never quite line up. Old land deeds transferred under shell names going back over a century."

Alexander's mouth curved, not a smile, but something close to satisfaction. "*Parasites* always think they're clever," he said. "They forget humans write history."

Jonah glanced up. "Or erase it."

Abigail didn't look at either of them as she spoke. "There's a name that keeps surfacing. Thorne Ridge. Quiet town. Too quiet. No major incidents in decades."

"Which means," Alexander said, voice low and burning, "they've grown comfortable."

The SUV ate up the road, flanked by two others behind them, black, unmarked, identical. Each carried men and women trained from childhood to hunt what went bump in the dark. Silver sanctified under old rites. Ammunition etched with scripture. Knowledge passed down like inheritance.

Alexander Weber had been born into this war. His father had died screaming under fangs. His mother had burned in holy light to take a monster with her. And Alexander had sworn, standing in the ashes of their home, that no creature like them would ever be allowed to hide again.

He felt it now…pressure in his chest, heat behind his eyes. "They think Georgia's just another place to disappear," he muttered. "Another forest to rot in."

Abigail finally looked up. "We don't have confirmation of a coven yet."

Alexander's grip tightened until the wheel creaked. "If they're there," he said, voice ironclad, "we'll find them."

Jonah swallowed, unease curling in his gut as the trees thickened along the roadside. "And if they are… old, sir?" he asked quietly.

Alexander didn't hesitate, the clip in his voice heavy with decades of rage and burden. "Then they'll burn slower."

The vehicles pressed on, headlights slicing through the encroaching dark, unaware that something ancient had already felt the *disturbance*, that wards older than their faith had stirred, that a silent Viking had lifted his head somewhere deep in the woods, and an ancient group began to ready.

The hunt had begun.

~~~~~~~

The manor was quiet in that brittle, waiting way Garin knew too well. He stood near the rear entrance, fastening the final leather strap over his forearm, the weight of his weapons familiar, grounding. Outside, the woods waited, dark, snow-dusted, alive. He barely registered when Beau entered.

The Southern coven king moved with his usual easy confidence, broad shoulders filling the doorway, Larazo at his side like a shadow carved from older stone. The air smelled of oil, iron, and winter, comforting, familiar.

"Patrol?" Beau asked casually, though his sharp eyes missed nothing.

Garin inclined his head once. "As always."

It was true.

It was a lie.

Tonight, he had chosen something else along with his duties. One night. One moment of weakness. One step toward the melody his hugr had led him to.

Beau stood a few feet away now, coat already on, Southern calm wrapped tight around command as he spoke with Larazo in low tones. The Roman's posture was relaxed, but Garin knew better, Larazo was never truly at ease unless Mave was beside him.

Beau finally turned to Garin, that ease back in his expression as if nothing bothered the man. "Same route," he said. "Perimeter first. Check the wards near Route 19 and the ridge. If anythin' feels off-"

"I will know," Garin replied quietly.

Beau's mouth twitched. "I know you will."

Larazo studied him then, dark eyes sharp, ancient. "You are... unsettled tonight my brother." A ghost of a smile twitched on the ancient's mouth, even through the salt and peppered beard on his face, it was clear. He knew.

Garin didn't answer. He didn't need to, but as he reached for the door...

The world lurched.

Not sound. A violation. Like glass shattering through silence. The wards the coven had placed screamed. Not audibly, but violently, ripping through Garin's senses with brutal clarity. The air thickened, magic flaring sharp and acrid like burned metal and sanctified ash.

Beau stiffened instantly. His fangs snapped down from his gums with a harsh, involuntary sound, the air around him thickening with power. Larazo's chest vibrated with a low, rolling growl, deep, old, pulled from somewhere far beneath civilization. And Garin...

Garin knew. He went utterly still, blue eyes darkening as something ancient and merciless rose to the surface. Weapons and ritual magic. Hatred sharpened into purpose. The wards only cried out for one kind of threat.

LightBorne.

Beau straightened instantly, every trace of casual ease vanishing as command settled over him like a crown. His voice rang out, deep, Southern, and absolute, echoing down the stone corridors of Thorne Manor.

"Coven!" The word cracked like thunder. "On your feet. Gather! Now."

Doors opened. Footsteps thundered. Old power stirred as immortals rose from rest and ritual alike.

"They've crossed state lines," Beau continued, already moving. "That ain't an animal. That wasn't a fluke. That was intent."

Larazo turned toward Garin, eyes dark and knowing. "They come armed."

Garin's jaw set. "Yes." And somewhere, too close, far too close, the pull of Route 19 tugged at him like a wound reopened. The melody. The fragile thing he had *just* decided to reach for.

Beau's gaze snapped to him, sharp and unyielding. "You still leavin' the manor?"

Garin didn't hesitate. "Yes."

Beau held his stare for a heartbeat longer, then nodded once. "Then hunt," he said grimly. "And if you find anythin' out there before they do…" His fangs gleamed. "End it."

Garin turned toward the night, cloak settling over his shoulders, weapons humming with readiness. One night. That was all he'd wanted. But war, it seemed, had heard him choose something else…and answered with blood.

~~~

The manor had not felt this way since Leah Ricci had joined them, and the Dhampir had attacked. Heavy and alert in the most dangerous of ways.

Beau stood at the center of the great hall as Garin's presence vanished into the woods beyond the wards. The doors had barely settled before the coven gathered, drawn by instinct, by command, by the old pull that meant danger.

Rua and Cian were already there, coiled and bristling like storm-tossed blades, fury still simmering from earlier. Mave stood near the chaise, calm but watchful, until Larazo reached her, his arm wrapping around her waist without thought, pulling her into the solid shelter of his chest. She allowed it, resting her hand against his heart as if grounding them both.

Evangeline lingered near the edge of the room, arms crossed, expression unreadable but sharp. Simon remained in the doorway. Not inside the circle, but not outside it either.

Beau didn't waste time. "The wards at the northern state line were disturbed," he said, voice low but carrying. "Not tested. Not brushed." His gaze swept the room, lingering on each face. "Crossed."

That got their attention.

"They weren't subtle," Beau continued. "And they weren't careless. Whatever stepped over knew exactly what they were bringin' with them."

Cian scoffed. "Hunters don't last five minutes this close to-"

"Quiet," Beau snapped.

The blonde twin shut his mouth, but his jaw clenched.

"I've already called Bobby," Beau went on. "Rafe's headin' north to confirm and track. But I didn't need his nose to tell me what that was."

Larazo's growl rumbled low in agreement.

"I felt it," Beau said. "So did Garin. So did Larazo. The LightBorne are in Georgia."

Silence slammed down like a dropped blade. Beau straightened, shoulders squaring, not relaxed now, not casual. This was the coven king who had buried enemies and burned legends.

"Which brings us to my decree."

Rua opened his mouth. Beau cut him off without looking.

"No one leaves this manor."

That did it. "The hell we won't," Rua snapped. "What if we need to feed?"

"Already handled," Beau said flatly.

Cian stared. "You can't keep us penned in here Beau."

"Yes boy," Beau said, turning on them now. "I can." His voice didn't rise. It didn't need to. "I've already called Addie, she's going bring up some supplies. I've called our hospital contact. Blood bags will be brought in quiet, under cover, no questions asked." He stepped closer to the twins, gaze unflinching.

"You want to hunt? Fine. You can hunt the gym equipment and each other in the lower halls."

Rua snarled. "We're not fledglings."

"No," Beau agreed. "Which is why you'll listen."

The twins went rigid, anger warring with instinctive obedience. Beau turned back to the room, the weight of the enemies crossing the border weighing heavy on him now.

"Simon will be the only one allowed into town, and only for necessary supplies and check ins with Addie. No lingering. No social calls. Leah will remain in her apartment and in touch with state police and main point of contact with Bobby."

Simon inclined his head once, accepting without comment.

"Garin is already on patrol," Beau continued. "And he will remain out there until we know exactly what we're dealin' with. He will be the only one to patrol the territory and report back. Everyone else stays here." His eyes flicked briefly to the doors Garin had used. "If the LightBorne are huntin', they won't find soft targets."

Evangeline spoke at last, her tone cool. "And if they come here?"

Beau smiled. It wasn't kind, fangs dropped low, and his eyes burning that deep amber.

"Then they die on my land."

The room stilled. "Until this is handled," Beau finished, "Thorne Manor is sealed. No one in. No one out. We do this clean, quiet, and together." He looked at each of them in turn. "That ain't a suggestion."

The coven didn't argue again. Somewhere deep in the woods, Garin walked into the night, duty pulling one way, a melody pulling another, while behind him, the manor locked itself down for war. While somewhere far too close for comfort, the LightBorne readied to hunt shadows, unaware they had already stepped into a den of monsters who did not intend to run.

∽∽∽∽∽

Of course it would be tonight. Of all the nights in all the centuries he had walked this earth, it would be *this* one, the moment he allowed himself even the smallest fracture in his discipline, that the LightBorne chose to cross into Georgia.

Garin moved through the woods like a shadow cast by the moon itself, boots silent against frost-kissed leaves, breath misting in the cold. His senses were stretched wide, alert for the wrongness that came with sanctified steel and human hatred sharpened into ritual. Duty still guided his steps, always had.

But beneath it... something else pulled.

His unbeating heart ached, not with fear, not with rage, but with yearning so foreign it unsettled him far more than any threat ever could. Hope was dangerous.

Dreams were worse.

And yet, the melody came again. Soft at first. A whisper on the wind that slipped between the trees and into his chest like a blade made of silk. Familiar now. Intimate. Undeniable. Garin slowed. Then, without another thought, he turned. He still patrolled. Still scanned the shadows, tracked scents, marked paths and disturbances. But his feet carried him unerringly toward Route 19, toward the thin ribbon of road that cut too close to the edges of his control.

Toward her.

Garin stopped at the tree line, every instinct screaming at him to retreat, to remember what he was, what hunted the woods, what followed blood and sound and warmth.

The LightBorne were near. The risk was unforgivable. And still... he stepped closer. Snow crunched faintly beneath his boot. She didn't startle, not hearing him yet. She only smiled, small and private, and hummed a little louder, as if she could feel him there without ever seeing him.

Something in Garin's chest fractured completely then. The Viking who had survived fire and famine, steel and blood, stood rooted in place, undone by a woman humming a song she had dreamed of without knowing it belonged to an ancient soul watching her from the dark.

For the first time in centuries, he did not retreat. For the first time since he saw her, heard her, he let himself *stay*. Though the war crept closer with every passing mile, though hunters sharpened blades meant for his kind...

All Garin could hear was her voice. And for tonight? That was enough.

The snow drifted in lazy spirals around his broad shoulders, dusting the worn leather of his coat and clinging to the intricate Nordic braid woven down his back. Garin didn't feel the cold. He hadn't for centuries. Not since the night blood replaced breath in his lungs and silence became his only companion.

But now, the cold wasn't what pressed on him.

It was her.

That redheaded goddess on the porch.

Curled under a flannel blanket like a flame wrapped in softness, she sat cross-legged on the wooden swing, her fingers dancing over the keys of that old, slightly out-of-tune upright piano she'd dragged outside like it belonged in the snow. She hummed as she played, soft and untrained but achingly familiar, the exact same melody that haunted his dreams. The one he hadn't known before, not in this life, and yet knew in his bones all the same.

Garin stood beneath the shadows of the pine trees across the road, as he had for so many nights before. Only this time... this time, she laughed.

It was a small thing. A breath of joy. She'd missed a note and chuckled, soft, radiant, real. It lanced straight through the wall around his soul.

And then she spoke.

"I hope I dream it again," she whispered, voice curling up into the frostbitten air like a secret meant for the moon.

That was the moment when something shifted. When his feet, always rooted in duty and distance, betrayed him.

Garin moved.

One step forward from the trees. Then another. The crunch of snow beneath his boots was soft, careful, as if the ancient warrior feared waking a dream. The road stretched between them like the thread of fate, taut and gleaming beneath the ice-dappled stars. But his gaze never wavered from her. Not as her humming paused. Not as her head tilted curiously toward the dark woods, sensing him before seeing. Not even when her fingers hovered over the keys again, the notes waiting.

She was real, and tonight…He would not let her play alone. Garin stepped out from the tree line at last, each step deliberate, slow, as if the snow might shatter beneath his weight. Frost clung to his boots, the braided leather soaked in centuries of wandering. His shadow stretched long behind him under the pale moonlight, but his eyes, those cold, sharp, glacier-blue eyes, never left her.

She paused mid-note. The piano stilled beneath her hands, and her breath caught as if the air itself changed. Then, like a flame flaring against the dark, her head lifted.

Green eyes met him across the distance. Not frightened, but curious. Steady. As if somewhere deep in her bones… she already knew.

"Hello?" she called softly, her voice a winter hush over the snow. "Is someone there?"

He didn't answer at first. He didn't trust his voice. Not with her looking at him like that. Not with his name ready to burn through the frost on her lips if he spoke too loud. But still, her gaze held, unwavering and unafraid of what may lurk in the darkness.

Inviting.

Finally... he found it. The gravel of his voice scraped through the stillness, coated in the weight of the North, in a dialect older than the trees that lined the ridge.

"I didn't mean to startle you," he said lowly, that heavy Nordic accent curling like smoke through the syllables. "I... heard the music." His eyes dropped to the piano, then to her hands, then back to her face. "It was... familiar."

The woman smiled, soft and unbothered, as if his voice had melted right into the snow beneath her porch.

"I wondered if anyone else would recognize it," she said, those pale pink lips curving with quiet joy. "It's the silliest thing... I heard it in a dream."

She laughed lightly, the sound so gentle it nearly stopped his breath. No mockery. No fear. Just warmth. Then, still smiling, she gestured beside her on the bench, where a worn flannel blanket lay curled over the empty space.

"Would you like to sit?" she asked. "I'd like to keep playing, and... well, I wouldn't mind the company."

Garin froze.

Sit?

His boots remained planted where snow met gravel. The great wall of him, carved from battles and frostbitten winters, stood stiff as if the very idea might fracture him.

"Why..." he began, voice low, unsure, "why would you invite me?"

Her brows lifted slightly at the question, as if it were the strangest thing she's ever heard. "Why wouldn't I?"

He shifted, eyes lowering. "Most people…" he tried again, the words dragged from a place rarely disturbed, "they find me… intimidating."

It came out rougher than he meant. A truth laced with disappointment more than pride. A fact he'd accepted long ago.

She turned her head fully toward him, and with a faint wave of her hand across her own face, she gave a little shrug. "That doesn't matter to me," she said simply. "I can't see you."

For a long moment, Garin couldn't move. He'd faced men who screamed his name as they died, seen the world drown in war, and yet… nothing had ever struck him so utterly silent as this.

She was blind.

The woman before him, this pale, freckled creature who played the melody of his dreams, who laughed at missed notes as if the world hadn't hurt her, could not see him at all. And still… she smiled. Still, she offered kindness. Something ancient twisted inside his chest, a pull older than his second life, something he had buried beneath centuries of blood and silence. It hurt. Gods, it *hurt*.

"You can't see," he murmured, the words barely escaping him, half statement, half disbelief.

Her head tilted toward the sound, and she smiled again, gentle, unashamed.

"No. Haven't for years. But I hear plenty, stranger. You coming to sit or not?" That smile was soft… unguarded. It reached through the darkness and found him with ease, though her eyes never could.

Garin's throat tightened, a sound between a breath and a growl catching there. Before he could stop himself, before centuries of caution could lock him back into stillness, his boots met the first step of her porch. The wood creaked softly beneath his weight. Another step, and another, until he stood in front of her, towering, the snow sliding from his coat like frost melting under a flame.

Her hands rested on the keys still, fingers poised, patient, her green eyes, though ever so slightly clouded and unfocused, he noticed, now that he was near her, lifted toward where she felt him stand.

"See?" she whispered, that same faint humor threading her tone. "Wasn't so scary, was it?"

Garin didn't trust himself to speak. Not yet. He only stood there in the quiet, staring down at the woman who couldn't see him, but somehow, saw right through him anyway.

Chapter 9

Garin moved across the porch like a man stepping onto sacred ground. The boards creaked softly beneath his weight as he lowered himself onto the bench beside her, careful, so careful, as if the wrong movement might shatter whatever fragile thing had formed between them. Snow brushed his shoulders, melted against the heatless leather of his coat. He sat tall even now, instinct refusing to let him fully relax.

She turned her face toward him, smiling. Not tentative, not cautious. Just… warm. Then she did something that stole what little breath he had left. She held out her hand. The winter air kissed her open palm, pinkened her fingers, and she smiled like it was nothing at all.

"Hi," she said softly. "I'm Mira."

The name settled into him like a blessing.

Mira.

He had spoken the names of gods. Of kings. Of brothers lost to blood and fire. None of them had ever sounded like that, gentle and bright and impossibly alive.

He hesitated. Just a moment too long. She laughed again, that quiet, musical sound that made his chest ache.

"Oh," she teased lightly, "I don't bite. It's just a handshake."

Something in him gave way. Garin reached out and took her hand. His fingers engulfed hers easily, rough skin, scarred knuckles, the weight of centuries resting against her warmth. Her hand was soft. Warmer than the snow. Warmer than anything he remembered.

"Garin," he said at last, his voice low, heavy with that Nordic cadence he could never soften no matter how long he tried. "I'm...Garin." He felt the name leave him like an offering.

She squeezed once, gentle but sure, then withdrew her hand, too soon. Far too soon. Her smile lingered as she tilted her head, listening to him rather than looking.

"Your accent," she said thoughtfully. "It's... new."

He stilled.

"I've never heard one like it before," she continued, curiosity bright in her tone rather than suspicion. "Where are you from, Garin?"

The question hung there between them, light as falling snow. Garin stared out into the dark woods beyond her porch, jaw tightening just slightly. How could he answer that truthfully? That he was from somewhere forgotten. From a land that no longer existed. From a time she could never imagine, from a life soaked in blood and oaths and silence. And yet... for the first time in centuries, the answer didn't feel like a burden.

He turned back toward her, the porch light catching the pale blue of his eyes.

"The north," he rumbled. "Far from here. Overseas."

Mira smiled, like that answer was enough.

"Well, Garin from the north," she said, fingers returning to the keys with a soft chord. "I'm glad you found your way to my porch."

And for the first time in years, he *was too*.

The moment her fingers returned to the keyboard, something in the night seemed to ease. Mira tilted her head slightly toward him, listening for the shape of his presence rather than his face.

"Is there a song you'd like to hear?" she asked softly.

Garin didn't hesitate. Not this time.

"The one you were playin', when I came up." he said, that deep Nordic cadence steady now. "The one you said you heard in a dream."

The smile that bloomed across her lips was small, bright, and unguarded, and it made something unfamiliar flutter low in his chest, like a bird stirring after a long winter.

"That one?" she asked, almost delighted. "I was hoping you'd say that."

Her fingers settled, then began to move. The melody poured out again, soft, aching, intimate. Not perfect, not rigid. Alive. It curled through the cold air and wrapped itself around him like memory and promise tangled together.

As she played, she spoke, her voice weaving easily between the notes.

"I heard it a couple nights ago," she said. "And then again. Stronger. Like it didn't want me to forget it." She laughed quietly, shaking her head. "It's strange, isn't it? It's like... something calling to me. I don't even know from where."

Her giggle drifted into the night, light and unburdened, matching the melody in a way that made Garin's breath catch. Because it was the same. The same song that had followed him through dreams he did not allow himself to name. The same harmony that had led his hugr through the woods to her porch, and must have drifted into her own dreams.

"It probably sounds silly," she added, almost shyly. "Dreaming of music."

Garin turned his head toward her fully then, blue eyes fixed on the gentle curve of her smile, on the certainty in her hands.

"It's not silly," he said quietly. The words were simple. Honest. "It's beautiful."

Her fingers faltered for just a heartbeat, then continued, surer somehow, as if his words had anchored her. Snow fell

The Viking's Harmony

softly around them, and the war that Garin knew was coming crept closer in the dark.

But on a small porch along Route 19, a Viking and a blind musician shared a dream neither of them had ever meant to give voice to...until now.

~~~~~~~

Garin wasn't sure when it happened, when the rigid awareness of patrol routes and threat lines loosened its grip on him, but at some point, time slipped its leash. The snow had thickened, then thinned again. The moon climbed higher. Somewhere far off, an owl called once and then fell silent.

And still, he remained.

Mira played, her fingers wandering from melody to melody, sometimes pausing to hum, sometimes stopping altogether just to *talk*. She asked him questions the way one did when they were genuinely curious, not probing, not prying.

"You're very quiet," she teased at one point, glancing toward him though her eyes never quite focused. "You know, you're allowed to talk. It's good for the vocal cords."

A corner of his mouth had twitched before he could stop it. Normally, he would've answered with a grunt. Or not at all. Let the silence do the work for him. But with her, she couldn't see the warning look or scowl permanent on his face. Couldn't read the *leave me alone* carved into his posture. And worse...

He didn't want her to.

So he answered. Carefully. Simply. He told her he spent a lot of time outdoors. That he preferred quiet places, that he liked routine. He spoke of the woods without naming how long he'd walked them, of the cold without explaining how little it bothered him. And when he asked his own questions, hesitant at first, then steadier, she answered without reservation, sometimes even joy. But the one answer that she gave? Struck something in his chest again.

He'd asked her ; Why sit outside in the cold to play?

She laughed softly. "Because I love the snow," she said, tugging the blanket tighter around her legs. "I can't see it anymore, but I can hear it, feel it. The way it hushes everything. The way the air smells cleaner. Colder." Her fingers brushed the keys absently as she spoke. "This is the best way I can enjoy it now."

Something in Garin's chest tightened, not painfully, but deeply. She played other tunes after that. Familiar ones. Gentle ones. Some that made her sway slightly, others that made her grin when she messed up and started again without apology. Garin, warrior, sword, executioner, found himself leaning back slightly on the bench, hands resting loose on his thighs, shoulders no longer drawn tight.

Comfortable.

The word felt foreign. Dangerous. But it fit. He realized, distantly, that if Beau were to call for him now, if duty were to snap its fingers, he would answer. But a part of him would hesitate. Because on a quiet porch off, wrapped in snow and music and a woman who asked nothing of him except to *be there*, Garin had found something he hadn't felt in centuries.

Stillness. And he wasn't ready to leave it just yet. However, time was cruel to most, and she was still human. Still plagued by exhaustion.

Mira rose with a soft yawn, stretching her arms above her head as the night finally caught up to her. The motion was unguarded, easy, like she trusted the dark not to bite. Garin stood as well, instinctively straightening, and the difference between them became immediately apparent.

He towered over her, and yet, she wasn't small.

By mortal standards, she was tall. Long-limbed, sure-footed even in the snow, her height nearly matched Mave's if he had to guess. Around five foot ten, maybe. She carried herself with a quiet confidence that made her presence feel larger than it should have been. Her body held soft curves, and her stance was one of a gentleness, yet strength he hasn't seen in woman in centuries.

To Garin, she looked every bit the goddess he'd first mistaken her for. Only he wasn't sure he was mistaken now.

She gathered the flannel blanket, folding it with practiced ease, then tucked the keyboard beneath her arm, fingers finding the familiar edges without effort. Her movements were smooth, learned through repetition and trust in her own body.

She turned toward him, smiling.

"Thank you for keeping me company," she said softly. "It was... really nice. I don't get that very often."

The words landed heavier than she likely intended. Someone listening, someone staying.

Garin opened his mouth to respond, to say something polite, something distant, something that would let him retreat back into the woods and the armor of duty, instead, the truth escaped him.

"Would you mind..." His voice caught, just slightly.

Mira stilled, her head tilting toward him, attention sharpening. "Mind what?"

The snow seemed to hush around them, as if the world itself were waiting. Garin swallowed, hard. This was reckless. Dangerous and unwise in every way that mattered, and still...

"Would you mind," he continued, voice low, careful, "if I joined you again?"

Silence stretched, not uncomfortable, not sharp. Just... present. Then Mira smiled at him. Not polite, practiced or surprised. Just genuinely pleased.

"I'd like that," she said easily. "You're good company, Garin-from-the-north." She shifted the keyboard under her arm and added, almost as an afterthought, "Same time tomorrow?"

Something warm and unguarded stirred in his chest.

"Aye," he answered, before thinking better of it. "If that is acceptable."

She laughed softly at his formality, the sound brushing against him like snowfall.

"It is."

She turned toward her door then, careful steps carrying her inside. Before she crossed the threshold, she paused and glanced back toward where she knew he stood.

"Good night." she said.

"Good night…" Garin replied.

The door closed gently behind her, and Garin remained on the porch for a long moment after, snow settling on his shoulders, the woods waiting behind him, knowing, with a certainty that both thrilled and terrified him… He would be back tomorrow.

No matter the cost.

The door closed softly behind Mira, the click of the lock echoing louder than it should have in the quiet of her home. She didn't move at first. She simply leaned back against the wood, blanket slipping from her fingers to pool at her feet as a shaky breath left her lungs, one she hadn't realized she'd been holding.

Her heart *raced* like it hadn't in years, not from fear, but from *feeling*. That enormous presence, the towering shadow of a man who had come out of the cold night and into her quiet world, hadn't unnerved her.

He *centered* her.

Garin.

That was all he'd said when she asked his name in the softest, graveliest voice she had ever heard. She'd teased him gently when he didn't talk much, but oh, *when* he spoke… the sound of his voice settled into her ribs like a low hum from her piano. It was warm and grounded, a steady echo that had melted her usual calm into something she hadn't felt in a long, long time.

Something breathless. Something hopeful. He had stayed for hours. Just sat with her while she played, let the music guide the rhythm of their conversation. And gods, he listened. Not with nods or polite sounds. With full silence. With *attention*. Every time she shifted on the bench, she could feel his presence shift slightly too, never imposing, never restless.

Just... *there*. Solid and quiet like a large statue on her bench.

She didn't know what he looked like, but she *felt* him in ways that transcended sight. His hands were large, strong, but gentle when he took hers to help her sit again after she'd adjusted her keyboard. The way he did it... like she was something precious. Like he *saw* her, even without eyes. Like something ancient and unmovable had chosen to sit beside her. And all she'd felt was, safe.

Her fingers curled unconsciously, remembering the warmth of his grip, the way his rough skin had contrasted with hers. Steady. Anchoring. Mira wasn't someone who fawned over men. She'd learned long ago not to build castles out of strangers. She valued independence, routine, control. But Garin hadn't tried to impress her.

He hadn't filled the silence just to hear himself speak. Hadn't talked over her. Hadn't made the night about *him*. He had listened, asked questions. Let her answer at her own pace.

Stayed.

That alone set him apart from almost everyone she'd ever met.

And when he asked, so softly, so unexpected, if he could return? Her heart had leapt.

Now, inside, the warmth of her home wrapped around her, but it couldn't compete with the warmth she'd felt beside him. Mira pressed a hand to her chest, laughing softly to herself as she whispered to the quiet room. She rested her head back against the door, eyes closed, not that it changed much, and smiled softly to herself.

"What are you, Garin?"

Because she didn't know yet. But what she did know? Is that tonight... she felt seen. Heard. Cherished, even if only in passing. And tomorrow night? She hoped he would come back. Because the man with the quiet voice and the shadowed heart? He had just become the warmest thing in her winter.

Mira pushed herself up from the floor at last, the blanket nudged aside with her foot as she hummed again, the melody. Only this time it carried a little more *pep*. A little more confidence. Less searching, more certainty. As if the song itself had noticed something had changed.

She set the keyboard back in its familiar place on the counter, fingers lingering on the edge for a second longer than usual, before turning down the hall toward her bedroom. Her steps were light. Buoyant. And then, without ceremony, she flopped backward onto the bed with a soft laugh, arms spread wide, wild red hair fanning across the pillow.

"Get it together," she murmured to herself, amused.

She knew exactly how she was acting. Giddy. A little ridiculous. Like a girl half her age with a crush blooming where it absolutely shouldn't. But tonight, tonight was the first night in a long time she hadn't had to be *careful*. Or strong. Or composed. She hadn't been Mira-the-teacher, or Mira-the-blind-woman-who-has-it-together.

She'd just been... *Mira*. She stared up at the ceiling she couldn't really see anyway, smile tugging at her lips. Maybe she should have been more wary. A strange man with large callused hands, appearing out of the snow like he'd stepped out of a myth.

She *should* have questioned it.

But his voice... That same voice replayed in her mind again, low, rough, steady.

Her smile softened. She was almost certain now. It was the same one from her dream last night. The one woven into the melody. The one that had spoken softly, without threat or command. If it was him, if the dream had found its way into her waking life...

What if it really was him?

The thought made her stomach flutter.

Mira turned onto her side, curling slightly beneath the blankets, still humming the melody under her breath as sleep began to creep in. She had once heard a long time ago, that sometimes dreams were glimpses of the future. That maybe one could tell you where you were meant to go, or someone meant to be in your life. A guide.

If it had been his voice in her dream...

Well then.

I hope I dream of him tonight.

Outside, the snow continued to fall. And deep within her thoughts, one word continued to weave its way through her mind as her eyes fluttered shut for the final time that night.

Tomorrow.

Chapter 10

Garin did not remember the walk back to the manor. Not truly. His body moved on instinct, through trees, across snow, past ward lines he had helped reinforce a hundred times before…but his mind was somewhere else entirely. Tangled. Fractured.

Why had he asked? Why had she said *yes* so easily?

This had been meant to be one night. A single indulgence. A moment of weakness he would acknowledge, bury, and never repeat. That was how these things worked. That was how *he* worked.

And yet, it had been effortless. Sitting beside her, listening, answering. Just…talking. She had not flinched at his voice in the dark. Had not recoiled from the weight of him beside her. Had welcomed him as if strangers sitting together beneath falling snow was the most natural thing in the world. She could not see him, and still, she had not been afraid.

The realization unsettled him far more than any blade ever had.

She had asked about him. About where he came from. Why he liked quiet places. Why he stayed outside so much. She had listened when he spoke, even when his answers were few and careful. For a handful of stolen hours, Garin had known peace. True peace, that, perhaps, was the most dangerous thing of all.

The manor loomed ahead, lights glowing warm against the dark forest. The wards parted for him without protest, recognizing one of their own. He should've stayed gone longer...Because the moment his boot crossed the threshold...

Chaos.

Voices slammed into him like a physical force. Rua's voice, sharp and furious. Cian's, just as loud, cutting, relentless. Simon's, raised now, no longer controlled as if he were simply done and had exploded from rage.

"You do not get to decide that!"

"We're not your damned children!"

"I raised you from the dirt where I found you, merde-"

Garin stopped short in the entry hall. The great room was in disarray. Chairs slightly askew. The air thick with anger and old wounds ripped open. Rua paced like a caged animal, hands clenched, red curls wild. Cian stood opposite him, jaw tight, eyes blazing as he snapped back at Simon with no trace of humor left in him.

Simon stood rigid between them, every inch the furious patriarch, eyes dark, voice sharp, restraint cracking under the weight of centuries. His silver hair, normally pulled back and neat, now flowed slightly wild around his shoulders in disarray.

And to the side...

Evangeline. She did not intervene. She watched. Her arms were folded loosely, head tilted, red-painted lips curved ever so slightly, not in concern, not in alarm, but in something far uglier. Sick joy. As if this fracture pleased her, as if watching Simon unravel, watching the twins rebel, was exactly what she wanted.

Garin's jaw tightened. The peace he had carried back from Route 19 shattered completely. Duty surged back into place, heavy and familiar and whatever softness had taken root in him tonight would have to wait. Because Thorne Manor was coming apart at the seams.

Garin, sword of the coven, stepped forward into the storm, already knowing that the calm he had found on a snow-covered porch was something he would now have to fight to protect. Not just from the LightBorne, but from his own kind.

Garin stepped fully into the room, the doors closing behind him with a dull, final sound.

"Enough."

The word carried, not shouted, not barked, but weighted. Commanding in its own way. All eyes turned to him. Simon faced him first, exasperation written plainly across his features now, the polished scholar's composure finally frayed.

"Explain this. Now."

"Beau has locked down the coven," Simon said tightly. "No one leaves. And *they*", his gaze cut to the twins, "are throwing a fit because they believe themselves above restraint."

That alone would not have stopped Garin. But it was *how* Simon said it. Dismissive. Sharp. The same tone one used on reckless fledglings, not men who had survived centuries of blood and war.

Rua bristled instantly. "We're not reckless," he snapped. "And we're not children you get to cage-"

Cian surged a step forward as well, temper flaring hot and fast, fangs flashing. "You don't trust us, just say that!"

Simon turned on them again, anger snapping back into place, but Garin moved. Not with force and not with violence this time. He raised a single hand.

"Stop."

The twins froze, not because they feared him, but because they'd never heard *that* tone from him before. He turned, not to Rua or Cian, but to Simon, and then he said the thing no one expected. Not even himself.

"They're right."

The Viking's Harmony

The silence that followed was absolute. Rua blinked, Cian stared and Simon went utterly still. Even Evangeline's composed mask cracked, her eyes widening, breath catching as she turned sharply toward the Viking.

Garin didn't waver. "I spoke with the wolf earlier," he continued calmly. "Rafe."

Simon's jaw tightened, but he didn't interrupt.

"He said something worth considering." Garin's icy eyes held Simon's without challenge, but without submission either. "You leash them too tight."

The words landed heavy. Final, and the Frenchman took half a step back as if struck.

"You treat them like children," Garin went on, voice even, deliberate, "and then wonder why they bare their teeth."

Rua didn't interrupt. Neither did Cian. They were listening now, all of them were.

"They have survived famine. War. Centuries of bloodshed. They are not fledglings. And you are not allowin' them to prove that."

Simon's expression hardened.

"They are reckless-"

"They are *untrusted*," Garin corrected quietly.

That did it.

Simon's eyes flashed, fury and something wounded beneath it, but Garin wasn't finished.

"You're holdin' them back," he said. "And whether you mean to or not... you're teaching them that no matter what they do, they will never be enough."

The room felt like it might crack down the middle. Evangeline took an involuntary step back. Because this wasn't rebellion. This was **truth**. Garin shifted then, finally looking to the twins, who straightened the moment his gaze landed on them.

"You want to prove yourselves?" he asked. "Then do it. Be the men you claim to be."

Rua's breath hitched, Cian's jaw clenched, but not in anger this time.

Garin looked back to Simon. "Give them grace," he said. "Or lose them."

For the first time since the lockdown began, no one spoke. Because the Viking, silent, obedient, unyielding Garin, had chosen a side. And it wasn't the easy one. The silence lingered just long enough to sting.

Rua was the first to break it. He looked at Garin, not with challenge, not with humor, but with something like disbelief.

"Did the mutt really say that?" he asked, Irish accent thick, raw.

Garin didn't elaborate. Didn't soften it. He simply nodded once. That was enough.

Rua's mouth fell open just a fraction. Cian stared outright, blue eyes sharp but no longer blazing. Shock rippled through them both, real, unguarded.

Cian was the one to speak next, quieter now.

"Well..." he muttered, rubbing a hand along his jaw. "Maybe the dog isn't so bad after all."

The words sounded like they cost him something, and Rua snorted under his breath, but didn't argue. They exchanged a look, one of those wordless twin looks that spoke of shared history and instinct and blood-deep understanding. Something settled between them. Not peace. But possibility. Simon turned back to Garin then, and the anger was gone from his face. What remained was worse.

Hurt.

"And how," Simon asked quietly, "would *you* handle this?"

The question wasn't sharp. It was tired, maybe even a tad wounded. A father asking how he'd failed without quite saying it aloud.

"If I were to allow them more freedom."

Garin didn't answer immediately. He thought of discipline, of order. Of leashes tightened until they choked. And then, unbidden...

He thought of a snow-dusted porch. A blind woman humming his dream into the night. A choice he'd already made, and planned to make again. When he spoke, his voice was steady, betraying nothing.

"Ask Beau for permission," Garin said. "Let them patrol with me."

Rua stiffened, and Cian straightened.

Simon frowned. "Together?"

"No," Garin replied. "Separate." He gestured vaguely, already mapping the land in his mind. "I take one half of the territory. They take the other."

The twins exchanged another glance, this one sharper, excited, as if the idea of roaming the woods of the land were a gift handed to them.

"More ground covered," Garin continued. "Less time wasted. If the LightBorne cross paths with them...The Irishmen are deadly enough to handle it."

That earned a grin from Rua despite himself. Simon considered it, brows drawn low, mind racing. On the surface, it was sound and efficient. A way for the twins to prove themselves without chaos, a way for the coven to tighten its net. But beneath that, Garin knew the truth.

It would allow him to return to Route 19 without suspicion. Without breaking orders. Without abandoning his duty. Patrol, handled by three capable Bloodborn. He would continue his half. Just...with a different path.

Simon finally nodded once. "I'll speak with Beau," he grit out, jaw tight, and eyes still heavy with his frustration and anger.

Rua let out a breath he'd clearly been holding, and Cian rolled his shoulders, tension bleeding away, both turning to the Viking with looks of gratitude rather than mischief, for the first time ever possibly.

And from the edge of the room, Evangeline watched. Silent now. Calculating. Garin didn't look at her, he had said his piece, but he could feel her own rage wafting from her like a perfume. She wasn't pleased with this outcome, but he didn't care.

Because somewhere beyond the manor walls, snow still fell quietly on a small white house, where a melody waited, and a woman who could not see him had already welcomed him back. Tomorrow. He would walk that path again. Not as a deserter, but as a protector. Of both this coven…and Mira.

~~~

Friday mornings were supposed to feel the same as every other day. Routine. Predictable. Safe. Mira moved through her classroom by memory alone, fingertips brushing the edge of the piano bench, counting steps between desks, adjusting a music stand that had been bumped the day before. Everything was where it should be. Where it always was. The morning light was soft through the frosted windows, dappling across the floor of Mira's classroom like spilled milk. It was still early, the children wouldn't arrive for another half hour, but she was already there, moving through the room with her usual quiet precision.

Only today… She was humming.

She hadn't even realized it at first. Just a soft tune slipping from her lips as she crossed the room, light and unguarded. Not quite the melody from her dream. Not quite the one she'd played on the porch. Something new. Just a wandering tune, something born of the warmth she still felt lingering from the night before. From the deep voice that had unraveled in the cold beside her, smooth and heavy like aged oak. A voice that belonged to a man she hadn't seen, and yet somehow... trusted.

Her step had a little bounce to it today, and her hands moved from bookshelf to easel to bin, organizing without truly focusing. She was still in that dreamlike space, her steps lighter than usual, her lips tugging into a smile she didn't try to hide. A little joy she hadn't felt in... well, she couldn't remember the last time. Her thoughts drifted, uninvited, but not unwelcomed.

Would he really come back tonight?

Garin. The name alone made her smile. If he did come back, would he listen again? Would he sit beside her like he had, solid and quiet, letting the world fall away around them? What would they talk about this time? She adjusted the keyboard on its stand, humming a little louder now.

Tea? she mused. *No... cocoa.*

Cocoa was sweeter, warmer and basically comfort and a hug in a mug. She was so lost in the thought that she didn't hear the door open. Didn't hear the sharp *clack* of heels on linoleum. Didn't sense the presence behind her until...

"Well now," came a bright, sing-song voice far too close for comfort, "it sounds like someone is in a *verrryyy* good mood this morning!"

Mira startled, letting out a soft laugh as she turned toward the sound.

"Mrs. Valdez," she sighed, hand going to her chest. "You're going to give me a heart attack one of these days."

Roberta Valdez, principal, whirlwind, and professional interrupter, stood just inside the doorway, arms crossed, a knowing grin on her face.

She leaned in conspiratorially. "Oh don't you Mrs. Valdez me!" Mrs. Valdez continued, voice dropping into mock seriousness, "Is it a *man*?"

Mira felt her cheeks warm instantly. "No," she said too quickly. Then paused. "...I mean-maybe? No. I don't know."

The grin widened, she didn't need to see it, she just knew by the cocky tone in her voice now. "Ohhh," Mrs. Valdez hummed. "That's *exactly* what a woman with a man says."

Mira shook her head, laughing despite herself, but the hum didn't leave her lips...not entirely. "It's... complicated," Mira murmured, suddenly finding great interest in adjusting the alignment of her art supplies. "I don't even know his full name."

"Oh, honey," Roberta said, placing a hand on her hip and leaning in with the kind of glee only gossip or match-making could provide, "the best stories *always* start that way."

Mira let out a nervous laugh, rubbing the back of her neck. "I know it sounds silly. We didn't... talk that long. But something about him just felt..." she hesitated, cheeks warm, "safe. Like I've known that voice forever."

Roberta's expression softened, the teasing momentarily slipping into something gentler. She stepped fully into the room, closing the door behind her as if sealing the little sanctuary off from the rest of the world. "Tell me," she said, perching on the edge of Mira's desk, "what did he say that got you all in this state?"

She chuckled, her fingers skimming over the edge of the nearest table. "That's just it. He didn't say much. But he *listened*. Sat with me. Asked about my music. Didn't flinch when I told him I couldn't see him, he just... stayed."

Roberta's eyebrows rose, impressed. "A man who listens and doesn't run off the second things get real? That's a rare breed, darling. You might've found yourself a unicorn."

The Viking's Harmony

"I don't even know his full name," Mira admitted again, a sheepish smile tugging at her lips. "He could be a ghost for all I know."

"Well, if he is, he's got a hell of a voice for a phantom," Roberta quipped, leaning in with conspiratorial delight. "But let's be real, how do you *feel* about it?"

Mira's hands wrapped around the edge of the chair behind her, steadying the flurry in her chest. "Giddy," she whispered. "Like I'm back in high school and someone I never thought would notice me suddenly... did. And I know that's foolish. One meeting shouldn't do this much, but-"

"It's not foolish," Roberta interrupted gently. "It's human."

Mira turned her face toward her, expression quietly vulnerable. "Can I ask you something?"

"Always."

"If he does come back... what do I do? I don't want to scare him off by being too much."

Roberta reached across the table and took Mira's hand, squeezing it softly, "You never dim your light to make a man more comfortable. You hear me?" Her voice was low, firm in the way only a woman who'd lived through years of lessons could speak. "You may be blind, sweetheart, but you're still the only woman I know who can see straight through anyone's bullshit. Don't let a man in unless he's okay with that. Proud of that."

Mira's throat tightened, emotions prickling beneath her skin like music waiting to be played.

"You deserve someone who doesn't just sit with you in the dark," Roberta added, "but brings you warmth in it."

The bell rang then, distant but loud enough to break the moment. Mira smiled as she stood, brushing invisible dust off her dress. "I'll bring the cocoa tonight then."

Roberta grinned. "Bring the marshmallows too. He sounds like the type that needs a little sweet with his bitter." She gave one last grin as she turned for the door, her heels clicking softly against the tile. "Go get him, tiger," she tossed over her shoulder with a wink.

The door shut behind her with a soft *click*, and the classroom fell back into its gentle hush. Mira stood still in the center of the room, her fingers grazing the edge of her desk, the warmth of Roberta's words still lingering in her chest like an aftertaste of cinnamon.

She wasn't worried, not really. Not about being too much. Not about being a woman who refused to soften her edges for anyone. She had lost enough pretending to be smaller for the sake of comfort. Garin… he didn't seem like the kind of man who would want her to.

No, there was something in his voice, low and rough, like river stones beneath velvet. Something that didn't flinch at her directness, her calm control of her space despite the darkness she lived in. She had a feeling that, if anything, he respected it.

Possibly even *needed* it.

A small smile touched her lips. "Yeah," she murmured, adjusting one of the chairs with practiced ease. "You're more okay with it than most, aren't you?" The second bell rang, louder now, followed by the inevitable rise of children's voices flooding the hallway, laughter and shouting echoing like wind through the trees. Mira chuckled under her breath, turning toward the door.

"Definitely bringing marshmallows," she whispered, a playful lilt curling in her voice. "He seems like he could use some sweetness… for sure." She smoothed the hem of her cardigan, stepped into her role as Miss Cassidy once more, and waited with a smile as the door creaked open to greet her students.

Only a few more hours...then perhaps she'll learn something new about her mysterious man, and the voice drifting into her dreams.

Chapter 11

Mira sat on the porch bench, hands folded neatly in her lap, and told herself she wasn't checking the time again.

She was.

Not by clock, of course…she didn't need to see the hour to feel it in her bones, in the steady drip of cold air slipping beneath her cardigan sleeves. She strummed a few idle keys on her keyboard, the melody light and playful, trying to act as though she was patient.

She wasn't.

Two mugs of cocoa steamed gently on the small side table beside the bench, the rich chocolate scent curling into the cold air. She'd been careful with it, measured the milk, stirred slowly, added just enough sweetness. And, after this morning's conversation with Roberta, she'd gone a step further.

Mini marshmallows.

A ridiculous amount of them. She told herself it was practical. The cold demanded it. The snow demanded it. But her heart knew better when she had dropped a small handful into each mug. Her keyboard rested in her lap, fingers moving through familiar patterns as she played, trying to look nonchalant even though her thoughts refused to settle.

He'll come back…No, he won't.

He said he would. People say things all the time.

Her shoulders tensed beneath her coat.

Maybe he'd only been polite. Maybe he'd felt sorry for her, a blind woman alone on a porch, playing music into the night. Maybe he'd gone home and laughed at himself for indulging a lonely stranger. The thought tightened her chest. Her melody faltered.

That thought had started quiet. Just a whisper. But it had grown teeth. She hadn't seen his face, hell, she hadn't even *felt* him for long. One night. One conversation. One laugh, shared between strangers in the cold. Maybe it had been kindness. Or worse...pity.

She inhaled, steadying herself, just as doubt fully took hold, just as she decided Garin must've been nothing more than a figment of her imagination, a dream borrowing shape from loneliness...

Crunch.

Snow compressed beneath weight. Slow steps, deliberate. Her fingers froze over the keys.

Then...

"Mira."

Her name, wrapped in that deep voice. Earth and gravel and distance in it. A quiet reverence.

Her heart stuttered, and then... *relief.* So pure and sudden it nearly stole her breath.

Her lips curved upward, gentle and sure.

"Took you long enough," she said softly, the smile slipping into her voice like cream into cocoa. She didn't need to see him to know he was smiling too.

The boards creaked beneath his weight as Garin stepped fully onto the porch, the sound steadier now, less hesitant than the night before. Mira could hear the difference immediately. He was still careful, but there was intent in his stride this time.

"I'm sorry," he said, that deep voice rumbling low in his chest. "I didn't mean to keep you waitin'."

Mira laughed, soft and genuine, waving the apology away without ever lifting a hand. "I was only teasing," she said lightly. "I'm just glad you came back."

The words carried more truth than she let show. She shifted slightly on the bench and tapped her fingers against the small table beside her, then reached for one of the mugs. The ceramic was warm against her palms as she lifted it carefully and held it out toward where she'd last heard him stand.

"It would've been a shame if this cocoa went to waste," she said. "And not to brag, but I'm rather skilled at making it, for a blind lady."

The joke was easy, practiced. One she'd used before to disarm the awkwardness in others.

But Garin didn't laugh in the way people usually did. Instead, she felt it. Those large, callused hands reached for the mug, careful, deliberate. When his fingers brushed hers, it wasn't clumsy or rushed. He took the mug from her with a gentleness that didn't belong to hands that felt so rough, so worn by time and use.

His voice was quieter when he spoke.

"Being blind isn't a crutch," he said simply. "I think you're more skilled than most... even those with sight."

The words settled between them, warm as the cocoa steaming in the cold air.

"You...actually think so?"

He answered with no hesitation. "Aye. I've never met a soul who plays such music as you do, not even needing to see you instrument in front of you. In my eyes, you have more sight into what you do than most. More heart."

Mira stilled for a heartbeat, then smiled, not out of politeness, but because something in her chest had softened. That had been...unexpected. Her hear began to flutter again, but she quickly shook her head and gave a small grin, though she knew that a blush had crept onto her cheeks. She could blame the cold if he noticed...

"Well," she said, a teasing lilt returning, "then you're about to have the best cocoa of your life."

And as the snow fell softly around them, two mugs warmed cold hands, and something gentle and dangerous began again.

Garin lowered himself onto the bench beside her, the old wood creaking under his weight. The mug in his hands radiated warmth far deeper than it should have. Cocoa. Simple. Sweet. Mortal.

And gods help him, it felt like a gift. He watched her from the corner of his eye, every sense sharp. The way her shoulders relaxed now that he was seated. The way her lips curved just slightly, pleased despite herself. And then there it was, the faint bloom of color across her cheeks, a blush she couldn't hide even if she tried.

He hadn't meant to embarrass her, but the little smile that tugged at her lips, the tilt of her head when she teased him back? That told him everything. Mira wasn't afraid of him. She should've been. Any sane person would be. He was Bloodborn. Marked with violence and silence in equal measure. She wasn't scared, but her heart betrayed her anyway.

It fluttered, quick and light, a soft staccato he shouldn't have been listening for, but did of course. Always did. Bloodborn instincts were cruel like that. He heard the way it skipped when he took the mug from her. When he spoke. When he sat close enough that the heat of him bled into her space.

If his own heart still beat... He suspected it would be answering hers.

She had expected him, thought of him in the cold. That was the thought that unraveled him most. She had made cocoa. Set out two mugs. Added marshmallows. Sat in the cold and *waited*. Not out of fear. Not obligation. But because she believed he would return. For centuries, Garin had been a weapon. A shield. A beast others feared or revered from a distance.

But to her?

He was just... Garin.

No titles, no gore, no myths surrounding them, and he found, to his quiet shock, that he liked it.

He lifted the mug, the steam curling past his face, and took a careful sip. Sweet. Creamy. A little cinnamon on the edge. She had made it with care, and the moment settled deep in his chest like an anchor.

Comforting in a way he had no name for. He glanced sideways again, at those unseeing green eyes turned loosely in his direction, not focused, not searching. Simply present. She wasn't looking *at* him. She was with him. His grip tightened slightly around the mug, as if grounding himself, and when he spoke, his voice was low and careful. Not the voice of an enforcer. Not the growl of a monster.

Just a man asking something he genuinely wished to know.

"Mira," he began softly, then paused, giving her space to answer or not.

His voice was low when he spoke next. Not gravelly like usual, but quieter. Like he didn't want to disturb the peace they were wrapped in.

"Mira..." he said again, casting his eyes toward her as he watched the way the shadows caught in her long lashes, "May I ask something? I don't mean to pry, but...I've wondered."

He hesitated. Not because she frightened him, but because something about her felt...sacred, but she smiled again, tilting her head ever so at the sound of his voice.

"You can ask me anything, I don't have anything to hide."

The Viking's Harmony

He paused, turning the warm mug in his hands before adding, almost reverently, asked.

"How do you do that?"

He didn't mean just the cocoa. Or the smile. Or the way she teased a vampire like she wasn't a woman of soft edges and skin warmed by a human heart. He meant... How did she look at a man like him and not see the monster? How did she see *him* so clearly... when she could not see at all? And gods help him, he wasn't ready for the answer. But he needed it. Because Mira saw him better than anyone had in centuries. And in this quiet, flickering moment on a winter porch...

He wanted to see himself the way *she* did.

"How do you remain so kind, when something was taken from you? Even to a stranger in the snow."

Mira didn't answer right away.

She didn't rush to fill the silence like most did when confronted with something heavy. No, she simply sat there, her fingers wrapped gently around her mug, her head tilted slightly in thought, as if she were listening to something distant, something only she could hear. Maybe she was. Maybe that was the magic of her he thought, watching her carefully now.

The firelight from inside her little house flickered behind the lace-curtained windows. Snow whispered down around them, soft as ash. And finally, in her calm, honey-smooth voice, she answered.

"I was angry at first," she said simply. "So angry. Not at any one person. Just... at the world. At the unfairness of it all. One second I was teaching children in my first job, the next..." She gestured lightly to her face, to the opaque lenses covering the damaged eye and the other that still bore the faint green of what once was.

"Everything changed. My world went dark, literally. And for a while, I let that bitterness take root."

Her voice didn't tremble. She wasn't fishing for pity. She was just... telling the truth.

"But after a while, I realized something: I could carry all that hurt around and let it make me hard... or I could try and make the world a little softer instead. For myself. For the kids I teach. For anyone who crosses my path." Her smile was small. But it was real. "It doesn't change what happened. But being angry all the time... it didn't fix anything either."

She turned her face slightly toward him, unseeing eyes seemingly *seeing* him in ways that unsettled and comforted him all at once.

"As for strangers in the snow?" she said with a little laugh. "Well... now we're not strangers, right?"

And Garin...The ancient, battle-worn vampire who had torn through cities and outlived kingdoms.

He almost dropped his mug.

He stared at her like she'd just spoken an ancient spell meant only for him. His jaw clenched, and he looked down at the cocoa she made, the marshmallows now melting gently near the rim.

He didn't know what to say. So he said the only thing that felt true. Rough. Quiet. Honest in a way that cracked him open a little. Centuries of steel restraint, of silence, of violence, of emotional famine, and *that* was what unraveled him. Not fear. But the quiet certainty in a blind woman's voice as she welcomed him into her world.

"...You are truly... exceptional."

And gods help him, he meant it in every sense of the word.

His voice didn't waver, but something behind it did. And Mira, still smiling softly, didn't tease him this time. She just reached forward and lightly touched his forearm in thanks, one small hand resting over a limb marked by centuries of war. She didn't flinch at the cold of his skin, and she didn't pull away, neither did he. She just *stayed*. And for the first time in centuries...

So did he.

The night was quiet enough to hear meaning settle between breaths, and her hand...Her hand was still on his forearm.

Garin didn't move it away. He didn't *dare*. The heat of her skin seeped through leather and wool, through centuries of cold discipline, and lodged somewhere deep in him, someplace that hadn't been warm in a very long time. It felt... right. As if her hand has always known where to rest.

Snow drifted lazily past the porch light. Garin watched it fall, lifts the mug for another sip of cocoa, committing the taste to memory even though he'd never admit how much he cherishes it. Minutes pass like that, just her heartbeat echoing in his ear like a lullaby almost.

Then Mira breaks the silence with a soft chuckle.

"I know you're wondering," she said gently. "And it's okay to ask."

He stills. She can't see the way his jaw tightened, the way his shoulders shift as he wrestles with the question, but she knew him already. Gods help him, she *knew*. Garin nodded out of habit... then exhales when he realized the uselessness of it.

"How did it happen?" he asks instead, his voice low and careful. "Your sight."

She doesn't hesitate. "Eight years ago," Mira begins. "My first teaching job. A little town outside Atlanta." There's no tremor in her voice, just memory. "I'd just gotten my certification. I was so excited. The school wasn't much, but I didn't care. Music was music."

She smiles faintly, more to herself than to him, and yet he stilled anyway.

"They'd cut corners. Budget cuts. Faulty wiring. Halfway through the year, an electrical fire started in the building."

Her fingers tighten slightly against his arm as he was sure the memory began to surge.

"I was with a kindergarten music class. Five-year-olds. Little babies, really. We were almost out when the alarms went off... but one kid froze. Wouldn't move."

Garin's grip on the mug tightened in response, he knew full well what that child hd been experiencing.

"I got most of them out," she continues. "But when the ceiling started coming down, I still had him. I threw him through the doorway. Just...tossed him out and told him to run." She swallowed hard. "And then the ceiling collapsed."

Garin felt something old and violent coil in his chest at that, at the thought of Mira crushed under anything harmful, but he didn't interrupt her.

"I was buried. Debris everywhere. Something hit my face, glass, metal, I don't really know. By the time they got me out..." she shrugged lightly. "My eyes were too damaged."

The story ended there. No self-pity or dramatic sob of pain or defeat, not een a catch in her breath.

Just truth.

Garin was silent for a long moment. Then, slowly, deliberately, his large hand shifts. He covered hers where it rests on his arm, engulfing her fingers in his callused palm. The touch is steady. Certain.

When he speaks, there is no sorrow in his voice. No hollow sympathy.

Only reverence.

"I have fought in wars," he says quietly. "I have seen men flee in the face of death." His thumb presses gently against the back of her hand. "And I have never heard of anyone braver than you... for what you did for those children."

If she could see his face, she would know:

In that moment, Garin does not see a blind woman. He sees a warrior, and he truly…He felt…worthy. Of sitting here, with her hand in his, drinking cocoa he didn't want to admit he loved.

He watched her cheeks pinken again, and even saw how tears threatened the corners of her eyes, but she didn't let them fall. Rather, she gave his arm another squeeze in return, and those unfocused green eyes, so beautiful, so strong, finally found him dead on, and she simply whispered…

"Thank you."

Hours later, Garin finally turned away from Route 19. He had stayed far longer than he should have. Long enough for the snow to thicken, for the night to deepen, for time to lose all meaning entirely. Mira's touch had lingered, warm and gentle in a way he had never known, not in battle, not in blood, not in centuries of existence shaped by violence and restraint.

Her hand on his arm. Her laugh when he admitted, grudgingly of course, that the cocoa was good.

Sweet. Gods, it had been sweet. He didn't do sweet. Never had. And yet he had drained the mug without complaint, even as she teased him for the *excessive* number of marshmallows bobbing on top.

Far too many.

He would never tell her that. He would take the entire bag if she asked. Every last soft, ridiculous one of them.

The thought followed him all the way back through the woods. When Thorne Manor came into view, dark and imposing against the snow-covered ridge, Garin felt the familiar weight of duty settle back onto his shoulders, but it no longer crushed him the way it once had. Something had shifted. Something had *warmed*.

Inside, the manor was alive with sound. The twins, of course, though for once they weren't at each other's, or Simon's throat in rage.

Rua and Cian's voices echoed down the hall, animated, overlapping, infuriating in their usual way. But Beau's voice cut through them this time, low and tired, carrying the particular exhaustion of a man wrangling children rather than ancient predators. Southern, exhausted, sharp-edged with the patience of a man at the end of his rope.

Garin slowed as he passed the archway, listening.

"...I swear to God, boys," Beau drawled, rubbing at what Garin could only imagine was the bridge of his nose, "if you interrupt me one more time, I will personally chain you to the damn walls."

There was a beat. Then...

"Fine," Beau continued. "You want to prove yourselves? You patrol. Starting tomorrow night. Under Garin's command I swear to Christ, if you two set one more squirrel on fire, I will tan your hides. And he, unlike y'all damned pains in my ass, won't flirt with ghost deer or try to wrestle fog."

Garin's lips twitched. Just barely. Silence. Then stunned disbelief. Then poorly contained glee. Garin didn't stop walking, but something settled neatly into place inside him. Good.

Very good.

He would send them to the other side of the ridge. Deep into the mountains if necessary. Plenty of territory to cover. Plenty of room for them to burn off their reckless energy.

And plenty of time...for him to do what he needed to do. Because he had told Mira he would return the following night, she had offered to teach him to play piano. He had agreed once he saw how her face lit up when he admitted as well that he had never played an instrument before.

And the Viking was not a liar.

As Garin climbed the stairs toward his quarters, the echo of her laughter followed him like a promise, and for the first time in centuries, the night ahead did not feel like something to endure…

…but something to look forward to.

Chapter 12

Winter deepened quietly.

Not all at once, not with violence, but the way it always did, creeping into the hollows of Georgia where snow wasn't meant to linger, and the days passed like that first snowfall: slowly at first, then all at once.

By the end of January, Thorne Ridge was buried fully beneath winter's hush, and so too was the guarded heart of a Viking who once believed he'd known silence. But this silence was different. Not the cold, crushing kind that filled battlefields and bloodstained memories, but the kind that waited outside a warm little house with music spilling from its walls. The kind that curled around a mug of cocoa and listened to the sound of a woman's voice as if it were scripture.

For nearly two months now, he came to her.

Night after night, as soon as patrols were complete and the shadows safe for a few hours more, Garin's boots found her porch steps like they were carved for him. The twins, bless their reckless souls, took up the other half of the territory with *suspicious* enthusiasm that bordered on feral delight, racing off into the ridges as if Beau had finally unchained them. Garin didn't question it. He simply adjusted his route, efficient as ever, and arrived at Mira's just after the first stars came out, not even Simon dared question it. Especially not after Rua came back once with half a tree in his hair, claiming "forest combat training" and absolutely *no other context.*

Every night, Mira was waiting for him.

Sometimes with cocoa always with far too many marshmallows. Sometimes warm cider spiced just enough to make his undead senses hum when she was feeling festive around Christmas Eve and New Year's. Once, she poured him a mug of spiced wine gifted by her school principal.

"She said it was for luck," Mira smiled, handing it to him.

"Did it work?" he asked, eyeing the steaming mug.

"Well, you're here, aren't you?"

Garin had never taken a drink faster in his life.

The heat in his chest was not from the wine. She was warmth in every form it took. In her laughter, her teasing, her patience. Her music. Garin had not known music could touch something in him that centuries of violence hadn't already scarred, but Mira played it like a kind of healing.

And one night, when the wind howled and she claimed it was too cold to stay out, she invited him inside.

The house was modest. The furniture arranged with careful intention, the smooth paths through rooms, no obstacles to catch a toe. Buttons had carved notches to identify them. Light switches were marked with tiny braille labels. And when he hesitated near the door, she only smiled and said:

"Don't worry. I made this house blind-lady proof *and* guest friendly."

He didn't laugh. Not because it wasn't funny, but because something in his chest cracked open at her ease. Her resilience. The quiet confidence with which she moved through her space. Independence, earned and defended with the softest smile he had ever seen.

He adored that. He adored her patience even more. Her piano sat near the window, worn but tuned, as old as her home it seemed, but she still kept it in working condition. She guided him to it that night, fingers gliding over the keys like she was introducing him to something sacred.

He was *terrible*.

Sour notes followed him like ghosts. His fingers were clumsy at first, far better suited to weapons than keys, and when he hit a sour note, he'd scowl as if personally offended by the instrument. And Mira?

She had giggled.

"Try again," she whispered, placing her delicate hand over his and nudging it to the right chord. "You almost had it."

No one had ever said that to him before. Almost had it. He wanted to try again. And again. And again. He wanted her to smile, perhaps even praise his efforts again, when previously he had never needed anything from anyone regarding his actions.

She never pushed him to speak. Never asked for more than he could give.

Which, of course, made him want to give her *everything*.

He told her stories. Bits and pieces, not the whole truth, but enough. Tales of a snow-covered childhood, a family long buried by the years. Of chaos now, of a house filled with beings who bickered more than they bit, though he kindly kept that last part to himself. A present-day existence full of... *extended family*, as he called it.

"Chaotic," he admitted once, "Always loud, always pestering."

She'd smiled knowingly. "The ones who matter usually are. That just means they care."

In those weeks, he learned her as well. He learned the way her voice lifted when she spoke about her students, how the children adored her despite, or perhaps because of, her blindness. How they crowded around her piano bench, arguing over songs and clapping off-beat while she laughed and pretended not to notice.

He learned that she loved her principal fiercely and complained about her in equal measure.

"She means well," Mira would sigh. "But on God, the woman has the energy of five people and the volume of ten."

Garin had grunted in agreement. "Sounds familiar," he'd said dryly.

She'd laughed, unaware that his *boss* was a southern vampire king with a temper, a lockdown decree, and enough presence to command a battlefield. Still, exhaustion was universal, and they bonded over it. He spoke of a "boss" who yelled with a drawl and threw things when he was angry. Mira admitted hers did the same, except with cinnamon sticks instead of daggers.

"My boss once gave me a stress candle and said it was cheaper than therapy."

"Mine gave me a migraine and bourbon and said *'figure it out.'*"

They both agreed cinnamon was preferable.

At the manor, things shifted. Not in grand, dramatic ways, but in the quiet undertones of peace slipping in beneath the locked doors even in a time of war.

Rafe, the Texan-born Moonborn, took the dawn-to-dusk patrols, and would return to the manor and sleep in the guest wing after the coven awoke. Somehow, *somehow*, the twins warmed up to him. He believed it happened after he revealed how the wolf had been the first to suggest the O'Sullivans be trusted with more responsibility. Garin returned one morning to find the three of them in the kitchen mid-*whiskey war*, voices raised in brotherly fire.

"I'm telling you, y'all haven't *lived* until you've tried Pendleton."

"You shut your mouth, wolf. Irish whiskey built civilization."

"What Rua means is, you're wrong, and we're right. Sláinte."

The argument was loud, heated, and, for once, *not* about killing something, or someone, specifically the Moonborn. Garin quietly backed out and let them be.

Mave and Larazo had cloistered themselves in their wing, preferring solitude and meditation, being as mysterious and hidden as usual. Simon focused on surveillance and town whispers, avoiding both the twins, and Garin now it seemed. Sheriff Schaffer kept watch on the human front. And Evangeline? She hadn't shown her face since the night Garin stepped between Simon and the twins.

Good. Let the silence swallow her too.

The LightBorne remained unseen. No more bodies had turned up since that first night they crossed into Georgia and no other wards had been disturbed, but Beau maintained the lockdown regardless. He believed they were hunting, gathering sources and intelligence of their own, so he maintained his command of everyone staying within the home. Everyone remained on edge...

Everyone except Garin. Because for the first time in his long, blood-soaked life, he had found a rhythm.

A ritual.

He woke when the sun fell. Took his orders, walked the line. Checked the traps. Sent Rua and Cian to chase ghosts in the forest. And when it was safe...he went to *her*. To their stolen nights of peace and music, of laughter and even joy. He hadn't pushed her, and she never pushed him. It was...peace.

She became his calm, and her music, her music became something more. He swore, each time he returned to the manor, her songs echoed in his chest. If he had a heart still beating, it would've done so in perfect time with every note she played for him. And tonight?

Tonight would be no different...or so he thought.

The snow crunched beneath Garin's boots as he trudged toward the cabin, the deep cold of February sinking into the folds of his coat, not that it ever truly bothered him. What did make something stir beneath the ice...was the thought of her.

Mira.

She had said tonight she'd teach him a new song, one she swore would make even *him* laugh, if only for how badly he'd butcher it the first time. He already knew he would be terrible at it. He would miss notes, press the wrong keys, scowl at the piano as if it had personally insulted him though she wouldn't see it. And she would laugh, soft, musical, and gently correct him. Her pale hand would cover his, guiding him back to the right place with endless patience. He hadn't told her that he liked it when she corrected him. That her fingers, guiding his calloused ones with every gentle stroke along the keys or strings, made something heavy in his chest lighten. Gods help him... he liked when she did that.

No. He *loved* it.

He had even begun slipping up on purpose, just enough to earn that soft touch, that quiet encouragement. He would never admit it, not to her, not to anyone, but he found himself craving those moments more than blood, more than battle.

He let out a low chuckle at the realization, shaking his head with a muttered, "What have you made of me, little goddess..."

But that single sound, his deep voice, warm with amusement, shattered the quiet. It was followed by the unmistakable **crack** up above, branches shifting, snow shaking loose from high limbs. Garin froze mid-stride, every muscle locking into place. His breath stilled. His senses flared outward in a wide, brutal sweep.

There was a presence in the forest, and he was no longer alone. Garin froze mid-step, shoulders squaring, eyes narrowing. Something moved in the trees.

No...*two somethings.*

The wind wasn't right, the weight in the air shifted. The ancient instinct that lived in his blood began to rise, and his jaw clenched as a growl rumbled up from deep within his chest, a sound so guttural, it shook frost from the bark of a nearby pine.

"Show yourselves." His voice was thunder, calm but deadly.

A pause. Then movement again, this time not from above, but behind. Figures dropped from the trees with far too much ease, boots hitting the ground in near-unison. Red hair caught the moonlight first, followed by a blond head shaking loose snow from his shoulders. They didn't *smile* exactly, but their expressions weren't apologetic either.

"*Nice night for a walk,*" Rua said with a tilt of his head, green eyes glowing faintly in the dusk, his Irish lilt filled with a taunting he should know better than to give the Viking.

Cian added, fangs flashing in a deep amusement, "Or a secret rendezvous, hmm?"

The older vampire stared them down, unblinking, another growl slipping from deep within his chest.

"Well," Rua drawled, his voice now soaked in amusement, "that's no way to greet family, now is it?"

Garin's eyes burned ice-blue as his stare locked onto them. "You followed me," he said flatly.

Cian tilted his head. "Aye."

Rua shrugged. "Couldn't help ourselves."

The Viking's jaw clenched. This wasn't an enemy at his back, this was worse, far worse. Not enemies. No.

Nosy, meddling, chaos-drunk Irish twins.

"Go back," Garin ordered, voice dropping into the tone that had ended battles and silenced men twice their size. "This is not your patrol. You're out of bounds."

Normally, that would've been enough. Normally, the weight of him, the height, the stillness, the *promise* of violence, sent even the Irishmen thinking twice on a normal day. Tonight? It didn't.

Cian's grin spread slow and knowing, sharp as a blade. "We would," he said easily, "but we heard somethin'... strange."

Rua tilted his head, eyes glittering. "Thought we were losin' our minds, we did."

Garin's shoulders went rigid. "You heard nothing."

"Oh, but we did," Rua went on cheerfully. "Clear as day, right brother?"

Cian chuckled. "A laugh."

The word hit like a thrown stone.

Rua nodded. "A proper one, too. Not the 'I'm about to rip someone apart' kind."

Cian's eyes locked on Garin, bright with mischief and something more dangerous...curiosity. "Didn't think the deadly sword of Beau Thorne was capable of that."

Garin's jaw clenched. "You're imagining things."

"Are we?" Rua asked lightly. "Because we've been noticin' you, big man."

Cian stepped closer, boots crunching in the snow. "Slippin' off early. Comin' back late. Smellin' like cocoa and... music."

Garin's gaze snapped to him. "Leave," he said again. It was no longer a command. It was a warning.

Then Cian smiled wider, too sharp, too sure, and said the wrong thing.

"I'd smile too," he mused, "if I had a little redhead playin' music just for me."

Garin moved. There was no thought behind it, no restraint and no room left for any mercy. The breeze he made hadn't even settled when Garin's hand slammed into Cian's chest, pinning the grinning twin hard against the rough bark of the pine tree. Snow cascaded down in a glittering halo around them, dislodged by the sheer force of the move, and the sharp snap of a nearby branch cracking echoed through the cold silence.

Cian's eyes, bright green and mischief-laced, didn't dim with fear, but they did flare in surprise. Garin's ancient fangs had descended without hesitation, sharp and menacing, and his voice was a low, guttural snarl as his forearm crushed into the twin's throat, lifting him clear off the ground as ancient fangs snapped free, long and lethal and *furious*.

Rua swore, lunging forward, only to stop dead at the look in Garin's ice filled eyes. This wasn't discipline.

This was possession.

"This," Garin snarled, voice vibrating through the bark beneath Cian's back, "is your only warning."

Cian's grin was gone now, and his breath stuttered under Garin's arm.

"You do not speak of her," Garin continued, each word carved from ice and iron. "You do not follow me. You do not *look* in her direction." His fangs hovered inches from Cian's throat now. "Not now. Not ever."

The forest held its breath. Snow drifted down slowly around them, settling on shoulders and hair, as the Viking stood there, silent, deadly, and utterly unrecognizable from the man who had chuckled moments before.

Rua swallowed hard and nodded. Because whatever he had found out there on Route 19… It wasn't just a secret anymore. It was a line.

And Garin had just drawn it in blood.

The Viking's Harmony

"Speak of her again, and I will show you what silence truly means. She is not for your jokes. Not for your games. Not for your damn curiosity."

Rua shifted at the edge of the clearing, his resolve fading ever so slightly. The air was thick now, not just with frost, but with the weight of *Garin losing control*. That almost never happened. Garin was the fortress. The sword that never wavered. And yet here he was, fangs bared, chest heaving with protective rage...over *a woman*.

A mortal woman. The redhead who played music in the forest and smiled at him like she *could see him* anyway, and soothed the beast within him. And for the first time in a long while, the twins realized something: The quiet one doesn't stay quiet because he lacks words.

He stays quiet because when he speaks like this? The whole world *listens*.

Cian, ever the chaos-stirrer, let out a slow breath, his back pinned, but not afraid.

"Didn't know we'd find your weakness," he murmured with an amused tilt of his head, "but I gotta say, brother... it suits you."

Another growl rumbled from Garin's chest. "Leave."

Rua stepped closer this time, arms crossed casually but voice serious beneath the teasing tone. "We weren't mocking her, Garin, or you. Just... making sure you haven't lost your damn mind."

"Or your instincts," Cian added, though now with more caution in his voice. "Because if someone *else* saw her, if they figured out what she is to you..."

He didn't finish the sentence. He didn't need to. Garin's grip loosened. Only slightly. Because *that* was the danger. Not the twins' teasing, or even their discovery but the possibility that others were watching. And if they noticed Mira's place in his heart, they'd use her as a blade aimed straight at him.

He stepped back slowly, releasing Cian and staring him down. His fangs were still visible, his voice sharp as ice.

"She is none of your concern. Patrol your sector. And if you tell anyone back at the manor about her…"

Rua gave a small nod. Cian dusted off the snow but kept his eyes locked on Garin with a rare seriousness.

"Just be sure, Viking. We won't tell a soul, but you have to be careful. Because you might think she's your peace…but in this world? Peace gets hunted the fastest."

And with that, the twins faded back into the forest, leaving Garin alone in the snow, breath steaming, hands trembling not from cold, but from possession and now…resolve. He had no intention of ever letting anything, *or anyone*, threaten her. Even if it meant tearing down every damn tree in this forest to keep her safe, and every Bloodborn brother he had if necessary.

Garin stood in the snow long after the twins had vanished into the woods, their words still echoing like ghosts in his skull. His jaw ached from how tightly it clenched, his broad chest rising and falling with the effort of restraint. He could still smell the ink of their trail, feel the feral tension humming in the air, but he would not follow them. Not now.

Instead, he turned. The great beast of him, silent and scarred, shifted in the moonlight as he faced the gentle horizon. Smoke curled up from Mira's chimney in the distance, a soft plume against the darkening sky, like a beacon. She was home. She was waiting.

And she had left the door unlocked. Just for him.

His boots crushed the snow in steady, measured steps, but there was nothing soft about the man beneath them. Not tonight. Not after the clash with the twins. But even in his storm, he would not bring his rage to Mira's door. She didn't deserve that. She deserved warmth. Steadiness. Him…but not the wrath of him. Still… he wouldn't stay away. He *couldn't*.

As the wind shifted around him, Garin felt it in his bones, that something was about to change. The twins' discovery had stirred one truth. But the night… this night would stir another. Something would shift in the firelight of Mira's cottage, and the Viking would not walk out of that house the same way he entered.

Chapter 13

Garin stepped inside Mira's home without a word, though the silence he carried with him was far from heavy. It was reverent. He shut the door behind him with quiet precision, the old hinges barely whispering as he turned the handle. One by one, he unfastened his thick coat and hung it carefully on the little hook she had once told him she *hoped* was there, an empty space she had measured by hand. Then came the boots, large and snow-caked, set gently to the side on the mat so the melt wouldn't pool water into her careful path. Always mindful now. Always watching for the little things she shouldn't have to ask for, and never would have to with him.

Then, finally, he called out to her, not with a bark or a grunt like most would expect from a man like him. But with a word, one word. Soft, and almost unsure even given all this time.

"...Mira?"

Her response floated back like sunlight on snow. "In the kitchen," she *sang*, a light, off-key tune that barely reached past the doorway, but Garin felt it bloom in his chest anyway. And damn him, it nearly unraveled what restraint he had left. He moved through the house as if it were sacred ground, and when he stepped into the kitchen…he stilled completely.

She was facing the counter, back to him, her wild red curls tamed only slightly by a haphazard ponytail that had surrendered halfway down her neck. She wore possibly the baggiest and most unflattering set of matching sweats he had ever seen, soft gray fleece that swallowed her frame, hanging loose off one shoulder and pooling around her ankles. And yet, she had never looked more divine.

Because she wasn't trying to be anything for anyone. She *wasn't performing*. She was just...Mira. Real. Unvarnished. Bare in the way that mattered most. And the Viking? He couldn't look away.

She was feeling around the countertop with practiced ease, fingers moving with familiar patterns in search of something, something that now sat completely within the reach of those dainty fingers. The bag of marshmallows. The very same bag he'd *sworn* he had hidden this time.

"You're late," she teased, still not turning, fingers patting lightly around the breadbox and sugar jar. "Thought maybe you were avoiding your nightly ration of sugar."

His lip twitched. "...I was distracted, but I handled it." he rumbled, still watching her with the weight of a man who couldn't believe she was real. "And I hid those for a reason."

She smiled over her shoulder then, those green eyes bright even in their paleness.

"You forget," she said, "I've got ears sharper than your fancy boots, I heard you rustling around in here last night. And I *smelled* the bag where you tucked it behind the spice rack, you brute."

Garin exhaled through his nose in a quiet laugh, and just like that... the last thread of tension in his shoulders eased. He walked toward her, slow and measured. And when she found the bag, triumphant and beaming, he didn't scold her. No, never. He just stepped behind her, close enough for the heat of her body to reach his chest. And for the first time since that forest growl with the twins, his voice softened into something close to wonder.

"You're dangerous, little flame."

She leaned her body back against his chest with a soft sigh and murmured back, "Only to men who hoard marshmallows."

The Viking smiled. For real, this time, because gods help him, he was already hers.

She didn't flinch when he moved again, shifting so that she could lay against him easier, she never did. She simply settled back into him, like she belonged there. Like the vast, war-hardened wall of him was just another part of her kitchen. Another place she'd memorized and mapped out with trust.

He let her. He let her press her weight into his chest as she opened the crinkling bag, her fingertips working gently against the plastic, humming a simple tune as she did, soft and sweet, as if she were in her own little world. But Garin...Garin was drowning in it. The sound of her voice, so casual, so bright, *vibrated* where her back touched his chest, and he closed his eyes for just a second.

It was the most *wonderful* thing he'd ever felt.

The snow outside could howl, the night could darken, but right now... right here... she was warm, and soft, and utterly unafraid of him. She never had been. He didn't ask for more, never had. But somehow...they'd gotten closer. Inch by inch, night by night. Through song and cocoa, through laughter and quiet silences. She never forced it, never questioned it. Just welcomed him in her orbit until his world slowly began to spin around hers.

Tonight, his hands moved. He didn't think, he simply *placed* them, strong and gentle, on her waist, and when she didn't move away...when she *relaxed* into it... He set his chin softly atop her head.

"...What melody are you humming tonight?" he asked, his voice roughened by more than just the cold.

Mira smiled as she placed a few marshmallows into a little bowl, still humming, then answered easily, "Something simple. My class is learning it this week. A little winter piece." She paused, chuckling under her breath. "One of the girls keeps squeaking on her flute. Poor thing sounds like she's being attacked by the notes."

That made him huff, an almost-laugh, and he murmured, "You'll help her, though."

"Of course I will," she said, as if it was the most obvious thing in the world.

"You're extraordinary," he told her, with quiet finality. Not a compliment. A fact.

When she giggled, *truly* giggled, against him, the sound like starlight against his ribs, his eyes fluttered shut for real. This was so...human. So normal. So *good*. He never wanted it to change. But... The twins' words echoed in his mind. Her description on Cian's lips. The laughter. The teasing. The warning. His fingers tensed, just barely, where they rested on her waist.

She noticed. Of course she did. Mira always noticed. She tilted her head ever so slightly toward his chest, her temple brushing against him as she asked, not with alarm, not with fear, but in that gentle Mira way that peeled him open.

"...Are you alright?"

A simple question. But from her... It sounded like an anchor, like a lifeline. And Garin stood there, holding something he didn't understand yet. Something precious and fragile, and for the first time in centuries... He didn't know how to answer.

"Something bothered me tonight," Garin said at last, his voice low and rumbling, as if the words had been carved from stone before they were spoken. "And sometimes I wonder if this is..."

He didn't finish. Didn't need to. Mira turned in his arms. Her hands reached out, instinctively, as if guided not by sight but by *feel*, and Garin let her, his palms never once leaving her waist, just adjusting to her movements.

Their bodies remained close, heat shared in the hush of her kitchen. Her red curls, mussed and pulled into a sloppy ponytail, brushed his chest as she tilted her chin up to him, a soft smile tugging at her lips.

"I wonder that, too," she whispered. "If maybe I made this up somehow. You. Here. Like this." She smiled wider, a little laugh escaping, pure and breathy. "But then...there you are. Every night. Like some kind of dream."

And that...Gods, that *hit* him square in the chest. His heart, ancient and still, thudded once like a war drum in silence. He swallowed, hard.

"I'm not a dream," he said quietly. "Not to anyone." His brows furrowed, something almost haunted flickering behind his eyes. "There's so much I haven't told you, Mira. Things I've done...things I've *been*." He looked down at her, that firelight flickering gold in his irises now. "And I fear that when I do..."

His jaw clenched, voice tightening.

"You'll think I'm a nightmare."

But Mira, *his* Mira, did not step back. She didn't tremble. Didn't hesitate. Those hands, so *gentle*, so *sure*, the very ones that had played lullabies into the dark and soothed the monster that slept beneath his skin, rose. She found him by instinct, her fingers brushing the edge of his beard first. A tender sweep. Then her palm found his cheek. Garin...He leaned into her touch. Just the slightest, like it *hurt* not to. And then, her voice, soft and steady.

"No," she breathed. "You're not a nightmare." Her thumb brushed against his cheek, warm and patient and *kind*. "I think, in fact..." She smiled again, eyes soft and seeing *right through him*. "...you're the man of my dreams, come true."

And for a man who had endured war, and ice, and centuries without softness, that moment shattered him more than any blade ever had. Because *someone* had called him a dream, and *meant* it.

Garin moved before he could stop himself. He leaned in, slowly, as if drawn by a force older than language, older than fate itself. And Mira? She didn't flinch. Not even as his towering form curved toward her like a glacier shifting after centuries of stillness. Her hand remained steady on his chest, right over where his heart used to beat. Maybe, *just maybe*, it stirred for her now.

He paused when he was only a breath away, his lips so close that he could taste the sweetness of her breath, warm from cocoa and marshmallows he knew she had before he arrived. Still...he didn't close the distance. Because Garin would *always* ask. He would *always* give her the chance to say no.

"If you don't want this," he murmured, voice low and hoarse, barely a whisper, "tell me now. I'll stop."

Mira looked up at him, eyes luminous, and she *smiled*. The kind of smile that shattered walls and melted snow and reminded men like him, ancient, silent, battle-worn, that the world could still be kind.

"I'd never pull away from you," she whispered, and she didn't. Because it was *her*... Her, on her toes now, just the slightest shift, that small, instinctive motion. *She* closed the distance. Their lips met, and the moment exploded in silence. There were no fireworks. No fanfare. Just the stillness of *rightness*.

Of *finally*.

Her lips were soft and warm, and she kissed him like she'd known his mouth for a thousand lifetimes. Like she'd waited for this, too.

And Garin...

Gods, Garin swore he heard it. That ancient melody. The *hugr*, his soul, his fire, his forgotten voice, *sang*. The very song that had stirred the first night he saw her. The melody she played for him out in the snow. That soft beat that pulled him to her like frost to fire. And now, as their mouths met in this quiet place of marshmallows and melted snow and late-night music lessons...

He finally understood what the melody meant. It had never been a warning. It was a *promise*, and it was his promise to her. Garin kissed her like she was the only thing tethering him to the world, like if he let go, the weight of centuries would pull him under.

Mira matched him beat for beat. Her arms wrapped around his neck, pulling herself closer, and he gathered her to him with a reverence so tender it made his hands tremble. She was so small in his arms, yet she filled every fractured part of him, and as their lips moved in rhythm, the kiss deepened into something neither of them had dared name until now.

When she sighed softly against him, barely a breath, barely a sound, Garin broke. Not in violence, not in rage. But in *want*. Ancient, aching, a strangely mortal *want* for her. Because this woman, this mortal warrior who treated him with kindness like he's never known, leaned into him more, their kiss becoming more passionate with every breathe.

His fangs dropped, not out of hunger. Out of *desire*.

"Ah-!"

It wasn't until Mira gave the softest gasp and drew back just an inch, just far enough for the firelight to catch on something glinting red, that he realized what had happened. There on her bottom lip, just a pinprick of crimson, a single drop of blood bloomed. And his breath...stopped.

"Mira..." he breathed, horrified, the word nearly crumbling as it left his mouth.

But she blinked, fingers ghosting over her lip as she gave the tiniest laugh of confusion. "What...was that?"

Garin, gods help him, felt his entire body go still. As if his very being held its breath, waiting. Mira brought her fingers to her lips, confused, surprised, then looked up at him with wide eyes. She wasn't afraid, not yet, but she asked again, gently, curiously.

"...What was that, Garin?"

Garin...the sword of Beau Thorne, the warrior forged in snow and shadow, stood frozen. Because *this* was the moment, the one he feared. The one he knew would come. Where his truths would begin to unravel, not with a confession, but with a drop of blood on the lips of the only woman he'd ever let close. He...had hurt her.

~~~~~~~

Mira touched her lip, fingertips brushing over the spot where the tiniest drop of blood had bloomed. It hadn't hurt, not really.

She had been too wrapped up in him, in the kiss, in *him*, to feel anything but *warmth*. Garin tasted like winter, like snow and cedar and something older she couldn't name. His mouth had moved over hers with reverence and restraint, like she was something precious...something he wasn't sure he deserved to hold.

But God... the way he held her. He made her feel small, not in a way that made her shrink, but in a way that made her *safe*. It wasn't just his size, though she often teased that he could bench-press a building th first time she had felt his muscles. No. It was the way he wrapped around her like he was built for the singular purpose of holding her in his arms.

She hadn't needed to see him to *want* him, didn't need to know what he looked like. She *felt* him. Right down to her bones. So when that tiny, unexpected prick happened, barely a sting, she had only been surprised. But before she could say anything more, before she could even process the *how*, he moved.

His arms dropped, and the warmth and safety of him was gone.

"Garin?" she whispered, already reaching out, instinctively following the sound of his breath. Her fingers met only air.

"No," he said, further away now, firm, sharp. Distant.

She blinked, heart stumbling. "Garin, wait-"

"I'm sorry," he rasped. "I never meant to...Mira, I didn't mean to hurt you." His voice was rougher now, scraping over something raw. She took a slow step forward, hands gently searching.

"You didn't hurt me," she said softly. "It just surprised me, that's all."

"You have blood on your lip," he said, almost like a growl, but it wasn't anger. It was *fear*. "It shouldn't be there. I shouldn't have done this."

Mira froze, then pushed toward his voice, a small lunge, and she *found* him. She grabbed onto his arm, anchoring herself, holding tight. "*Stop it*," she said, louder now, chest rising with the swell of her emotions. "You didn't hurt me. I'm fine."

She felt it, he stiffened again. Under her fingers, his muscles were stone.

"You don't understand," he murmured, like a confession. "If I stay, I might... I might hurt you. I'm not... I'm not normal, Mira."

She went still and her fingers curled into his coat sleeve. Then she lifted her chin just a little, blind eyes searching toward his face.

"I *know*, Garin," she said quietly. "I've suspected for a while now. You're not normal." Her voice didn't tremble. "But I'm not scared of you," she added. "And I don't want you to leave. Please...don't go" The words filled the space between them like music. Soft, strong, and for the first time since that prick, she felt him *breathe*.

"You... know?" Garin breathed the words like they hurt.

Mira's hands tightened gently on his sleeve, grounding him, reminding him that she hadn't let go.

"I've suspected," she said softly. "For about a month now."

He didn't move, didn't speak. So she went on, because he needed her to. Because *she* needed to.

"I've felt your hands," she murmured, lifting one of hers to brush along the curve of his wrist. "Rough. Strong. Calloused like a man who's spent lifetimes building and breaking things. But they're never warm. Not really. Only when you've just come inside from the cold… or when you light the fire for me and let it burn."

Her fingers traveled slowly upward, past his elbow, seeking his chest, the place she always rested her head when he let her close. She placed her hand there now, over where a heartbeat *should* have been.

"I've leaned against you, Garin," she whispered. "You've held me before, and I'm always happy to lay my head here. I've listened. Waited. But there's no heartbeat."

He flinched, barely perceptible, but she felt it.

"And when I asked if maybe we could walk together one day," she continued, her voice barely above a hush, "in the snow, in the sunlight…you always had a reason not to. Always something that kept you away. And yet…you still came back. Every night. Like you couldn't stay away."

He swallowed hard. She felt the motion against her fingers.

"You never lied to me," she said. "Not once. You never made promises you didn't keep. You never hurt me, not even when you had the chance."

Her hand rose, found the edge of his jaw, felt the way his beard trembled beneath her touch and knew that his jaw was ever so slightly loosening with each word she assured him with.

"I figured… one day you'd tell me," she admitted. "And maybe part of me was scared to ask. But I've been so happy just *hearing* you come through that door every night. I didn't care what you were."

A pause, tthen, soft as a lullaby:

"Because you're Garin, right? That's who you are. Whatever else you've been… whatever you are now…you're still Garin."

That name, *his* name, spoken like it meant something holy on her lips… she knew. It nearly undid him. Someone knew, someone saw, and she didn't run, she didn't want to. She didn't scream.

She held him *closer*.

"Please don't run from me Garin. You don't have to tell me what you are, not if you don't want to. But please…don't take this dream away from me yet."

Chapter 14

"Don't take this dream away from me yet."

Her words echoed in his skull, over and over like a war drum against the inside of his ribcage, except there was nothing inside to beat with it, no heartbeat inside. Just her voice, breaking through centuries of silence he'd grown used to.

Still, she held on. Still, she begged him to stay.

Garin stood there in her tiny kitchen, every instinct screaming at him to vanish into shadow before she changed her mind, before reason caught up with whatever wild part of her had spoken such grace aloud. He could still taste the copper guilt from her blood on the tip of his fang, and it burned. *Gods*, it burned. Not from any hunger for her blood or even body now. From shame. From the terrible, soul-tearing truth that he'd slipped, even for a second.

And yet… She didn't run. She held onto him. It hit him, all of it, like a long-forgotten storm slamming into a worn-down shore. The way she always asked about the day, about the sun. The way she tilted her head ever so slightly when she leaned against him, as if searching for a heartbeat. The soft way she hummed, touching his skin like it wouldn't shatter beneath her hands. She knew. *She'd known.*

She still smiled each night, she still sang, still held his hand each time he missed a key. And now she begged him not to leave. He looked down at her, this woman who couldn't see, and yet saw *everything*. Those green eyes, fogged by the fire that had stolen her sight, still searched for him with a kind of desperate knowing that made something ancient in him shatter.

Garin, once a warrior of frost and fury, fell to his knees. One by one, they struck the floor of her kitchen with a soft, muffled *thud*, as if the world itself paused to witness it. He gathered her gently to him, arms wrapping around her like she was made of spun glass, like she was something fragile and holy and far too good for the ruined thing he was. He buried his face into her stomach, his massive frame curled around her middle like a man shielding something precious from a battlefield.

His voice was low, graveled and shaking. "I am a monster," he breathed. "From the deepest depths of whatever hell spawned my kind." Her fingers trembled in his hair, but she didn't pull away. Gods… she *never* pulled away. "But I swear to you…" he went on, voice cracking like old ice, "I will never allow another drop of blood to fall from you. Not by my hand. Not by *anyone's*."

Her hand cupped the back of his head now, gentle as falling snow.

"I don't know why you don't fear me," he whispered, barely able to say it aloud. "But I will never give you a reason to."

And there, on her kitchen floor, with the scent of hot cocoa still lingering in the air and marshmallows unopened on the counter, Garin vowed something no war had ever demanded of him before.

He vowed not to conquer…

…but to protect.

Heartbeats passed, hers against his ears now as he held her to him. He stayed there on the floor, clinging to her as though letting go would unravel something in him he couldn't stitch back together again. His head rested against her stomach, and he felt her fingers, small, gentle, unshaking, drift down the thick braid at the back of his head. She didn't flinch at the texture of it, didn't pause at the undercut where the hair was shaved close to the scalp. Her touch slowed over the rough ridges of scars that marked the sides of his head, souvenirs from battles long buried in snow and memory.

Scars she'd never see, and yet, she still touched them like they were holy.

She didn't speak at first. He wouldn't have minded if she never did. Her silence was reverent, anchoring. She simply touched him, and for the first time in centuries, Garin felt like a man again. Not a weapon. Not a monster. Just... *Garin*. But then she whispered, soft as falling ash.

"You're not a monster."

His arms tightened around her ever so slightly.

"I don't think so. And I never will."

He could've wept from it. Instead, he rasped low, "I am, Mira. I am. But I'll never be one to *you*."

Another heartbeat passed between them. Then she asked it, the question he'd feared since the first night he smelled her blood in the air and refused to take even a taste.

"...What are you?"

He shifted slowly, not to pull away, but to lift his head, so that when he answered, it would not be with shame.

"I am what your kind calls a vampire," he said, his voice calm. Steady. "But we are older than the stories. The truth is, we are *Bloodborn*. A race forged from the blood of the cursed. We walk this earth, bound by hunger, cursed to survive only on the blood of the living."

He waited. Waited for her to recoil. To step away. To treat him like every other creature of myth and shadow. But Mira... didn't move. She only exhaled quietly, and then, without hesitation, began to lower herself beside him. He caught her instantly, arms wrapping around her to guide her safely to the floor. She sank down gently onto his lap, letting him settle her across his legs, her head tilting toward his chest as though she could still feel the heartbeat that wasn't there.

She didn't run. She curled into him, when she finally spoke again, it was with a tone laced in awe.

"You're not just from the north, are you?"

His mouth tugged in the faintest, bittersweet smile. "No. I'm from what you now call Norway. It was my homeland, in ancient times."

Her brows lifted. "So…" she breathed, her lips curling upward, "you're a Viking?"

He chuckled, just once, a low, breathy sound almost lost in her sweater. "Yes," he murmured, a rare trace of amusement in his voice. "I was once a Viking." There was a beat of silence.

And then she laughed, soft and disbelieving and glowing like sunrise. "I just kissed a Viking," she said, grinning now. "And I *loved* it."

Garin's arms closed tighter around her, his head tipping forward to rest against hers. Gods forgive him. He was already hers, and he stayed holding her like she might vanish if he let go. The warmth of her body, so soft and alive against the cold of his own, grounded him, even as guilt churned in his chest where no heartbeat echoed.

"I'm sorry," he said quietly, his voice a low rumble against her temple. "That I lost control. It's been a long time since I've… touched anyone. And your kiss… the way you responded to me…" He trailed off, jaw tight. "It won't happen again."

Mira shifted slightly in his lap, tilting her face up toward him with steady hands. Her voice was gentle but sure when she said, "You really didn't hurt me. I was just surprised. That's all."

Her hand rose again, the fingers unshaking as they found his cheek and traced along the sharp angle of it. Then they moved, slowly, reverently, until they brushed against his lips.

"Can I feel them again?" she asked, almost in a whisper. "Your fangs."

Garin froze. His first instinct was to refuse. To protect her, even from himself. But then he saw the expression on her face…the curiosity, not fear. The trust. It undid something inside him. Slowly, cautiously, he parted his lips and allowed the shift to come. It was slow, deliberate, the kind of control forged from centuries of restraint. The fangs extended, gleaming ivory in the low light, elegant and deadly.

Her fingers found one.

Mira's touch was feather-light as she traced the curve of a fang, careful at the tip, and then slowly pulled away, not in fear or disgust. There was wonder in her movements. Quiet awe. Like she was touching a relic from some forgotten legend.

"They're… long," she said, breath catching slightly. Then, a beat later, "Do you really drink blood?"

He nodded against her hand when it returned to his cheek. "Yes. But not from living sources. Not anymore." He watched her expression shift, not with panic, but curiosity. "My coven," he continued, "the family I told you about… they work with certain donation networks. Hospitals, clinics. We receive the blood that's expired, or can't be used to treat patients for one reason or another."

Mira was quiet at that. Then her brows lifted again, still not in alarm, but this time amused almost.

"Coven?" she asked slowly. "There's more of you?"

Garin gave a low hum of confirmation. "Yes. A handful. They're… persistent. Loud. And often very annoying."

Mira laughed, a soft, breathy sound that made his chest ache. "I want to meet them someday," she murmured.

And Garin, sworn protector of his silence, almost smiled. Almost.

"One day," he murmured, his voice low and firm. "I'll introduce you to them. But not yet."

Mira tilted her head. "Why not?"

His jaw flexed. "Because," he said simply, "I don't wish to share you. Not right now. Life among them is... tense."

She giggled softly at that, oblivious to the weight behind his words, the tangled politics, the looming threats, the endless shadows that crept just beyond the Ridge and outside even her door. But he didn't explain further. Not tonight.

Instead, she teased lightly, "You greedy Viking."

And gods help him...he liked the sound of that.

Garin shifted, tucking her closer, one massive palm curling protectively around the back of her head. "I am," he admitted, the edge of a rare smile threatening his lips. "You've made me into a greedy man. With your cursed little drinks."

"My drinks?"

"Too many marshmallows," he said, deadpan.

She laughed again, the sound spilling into his chest, and Garin felt something shatter deeper inside him, some old, frozen part of his soul that had long since grown still. Mira pulled back just enough to find his face again, her fingers exploring the familiar terrain of his cheek, her smile dimming as she felt the tension still lingering there.

She cupped his jaw gently. "Can I kiss you again?" she asked, voice quiet but steady. "Fangs or no fangs... I'm not done with you yet."

Garin, who had survived war, famine, betrayal, and centuries of cold silence, felt himself unravel again beneath the soft plea of the one woman he never saw coming. His answer came in the form of his mouth finding hers. Starved now for the one who begged him not to leave, had asked the monster to stay. And this time, he didn't pull away.

He didn't stop to question it. Didn't dare. This time, the kiss didn't end in panic. It didn't snap off in fear or shame or regret. Because Mira knew now, **knew** what he was. She had felt the curve of his fangs with reverent fingers, had listened as he confessed to being born of blood and curse, had heard the word *vampire* and *monster* fall from his own lips, and still, *still*...she asked to kiss him again.

And gods...he kissed her like a man undone.

No longer gentle, no longer holding himself back, Garin poured everything into her mouth, centuries of silence, decades of restraint, years of pain...and the raw, bone-deep hunger to feel *alive* again. Mira met him breath for breath. Her lips parted beneath his, her fingers tangled in the braid at the nape of his neck, and she made the softest sound in her throat as he pressed her to him.

He could barely stand the way she clung to him, as if she *wanted* him. As if she *claimed* him in return. His hands slid beneath her thighs, lifting her effortlessly, and when she wrapped around him without hesitation, her long curvy body curling to his like it had always belonged there...that was when Garin truly lost the last of his composure.

Because her mouth brushed against his again, and she whispered it. That final shattering plea in a voice made of temptation and trust. Garin groaned low in his chest, the sound raw and reverent as Mira's whispered words ghosted across his lips.

"Take me to the bedroom, my Viking."

His eyes burned pure ice, only not from any seated rage like before. The ancient hunger roared in his body, but not for her blood.

For *her*.

Her warmth, and her trust. Her fire and her kiss. Garin didn't answer with words. He carried her, silent and reverent, toward the back of the home, toward the room he once thought would remain untouched forever. But not tonight. Tonight, it would become something new, a place not of solitude…but of devotion. As he crossed the threshold with Mira in his arms, he knew there was no going back. Not now, not ever, and he knew he would never want to.

"You don't know what you ask of me," he rasped, voice already thick with need as he moved through the room.

"Yes I do," she whispered against his jaw. "And I still want it."

He laid her down like she was sacred. Not fragile, *never* that. But *cherished*, as if this bed, this moment, this woman beneath him was something carved from fate itself.

Mira's back hit the mattress with a soft bounce, her red hair fanning around her like a halo of fire, and Garin followed, his mouth finding hers again in a kiss that no longer trembled with hesitation. No fear, no shame now between them Only her, only *this*.

His hand braced beside her head, the other cupping her cheek with a reverence that contradicted the raw power coiled in his frame, and when she arched up into him, her fingers already slipping beneath the hem of his shirt, he let out a soft growl of surprise into her mouth, half warning, half worship.

"You are a dangerous woman," he murmured, pressing his forehead to hers. "You make me forget the promises I swore to myself."

Mira smiled, her fingers finding the braid at the back of his head once more. "Then let me be the one thing you don't regret breaking them for."

Clothes didn't tear. They *melted* away…undone by hands that couldn't move fast enough, especially hers. She tugged at him with a mixture of eager desperation and blind certainty, and he, and gods, he tried to slow her.

"Impatient," he murmured against her lips, his voice thick with need and amusement, his fangs just brushing her bottom lip again.

Mira laughed, breathless and glowing beneath him, and it *shook* something loose in his chest.

"Maybe," she whispered, her hands skimming down the hard planes of his chest. "But I've waited long enough for a man who makes me feel like this..."

He kissed her again before she could say what *this* was, because he knew if she named it, if she gave it words, he might fall apart. Still, even as the fire built between them, he held back just enough, his control ironclad, even when every part of her was inviting him deeper, closer, *now*. But she felt it, his restraint, and she smiled against his mouth with maddening softness, trailing her fingers down his ribs to the inked marks he didn't think she knew were there.

"You don't have to hold back with me, Garin."

He stilled, eyes flickered open, and for a moment, he simply looked down at her, this woman with sightless eyes and a gaze that still *saw* him completely. A shaky breath left his chest. Then...

He let go.

Of the years. Of the fear. Of the solitude. Of the monster he thought he had to be, and Garin kissed her like she was the first woman he had ever touched... because in all the ways that mattered...**she was.**

He had known war, he had known cold and death hand in hand. He had known the weight of centuries pressing down on him like armor he could never remove. But *this*? This was something holy.

He moved over her with a kind of reverence he didn't know he was still capable of, like worship lived in the cradle of her thighs, in the shiver of her breath, in the way her body opened for him without fear, without flinching. Her hands slid along his shoulders, down the hard stretch of his arms, and as he finally pressed into her, slow, *achingly* slow, his lips parted on a sound that was not a growl or a moan...

It was a *prayer*.

"...Gods help me," he breathed, voice rough with awe as her warmth took him in. "Mira..."

She arched beneath him, a soft cry escaping her as their bodies met, and Garin had to *grip* the sheets beside her to keep from unraveling completely. His jaw clenched, muscles taut, the edge of his restraint like a blade against his spine, but not from fear. From *want*. From how deeply and fully he wanted to feel every inch of this, of *her*.

"Perfect," he whispered, unable to stop the words from falling from his mouth. "You're... *perfect*."

Her fingers found his face again, tracing his cheek, his jaw, his lips, and she smiled, soft and dizzy, as he began to move. Slowly. Deeply. Like he was learning her, like she was a language he was born to speak but had only just remembered. And he *praised* her.

Not like a man out of control. But like a man *home* at last.

"So soft... gods, how do you feel like this? I don't deserve you... You take me like you were *made* for me, my little flame..."

She pulled him closer at that, whispered his name, her legs locking around him like she never wanted to let go, and he buried his face in her neck with a sound that was half-broken, half-blessed.

There was no beast here. No Viking. No Bloodborn, only a man finally allowed to feel.

Finally *loved,* and he would savor every heartbeat she gave him of it. Garin didn't need breath, but Mira stole it from him anyway. Her hands clutched at him like she feared he'd vanish, like this was some dream her broken heart had conjured and she was clinging to the only proof it was real. Fingertips scraped across muscle, clung to his back, his arms, his braid, gripping him tighter with every deep, worshipful stroke of his hips. He moved like a man starved but savored her like she was the last thing in all the world he would *ever* consume.

And gods help him, maybe she was.

Below him, Mira gasped out his name like a plea and a vow in one breath, her voice breaking with soft, *needy* desperation, "Don't stop, Garin... please-don't you dare stop-"

He wasn't sure if it wrecked him or rebuilt him. His name, *his* name, on her lips as she begged him not to stop, like she truly believed he ever could. As if leaving her body, her arms, her *love,* was ever again an option in this life or the next.

He was already gone. "Never," he rasped, voice low, voice rough, *voice unholy* in its devotion. "You're mine, little flame. You hear me?"

She nodded beneath him, her legs trembling around his waist, her thighs pulling him in as he ground deeper with every thrust, and when her hands clawed at his back, desperate now, *close,* he dipped his head to her ear and whispered it. "Come for me. Let me feel it. Let me hear you, *light.*"

With a cry like a shattering prayer, Mira broke, her body arching, her breath catching, every nerve alight and undone as he kept moving, kept holding her through it like he *needed* to feel her fall apart on him.

And Garin? The ancient Viking, the cold warrior, the Bloodborn who had lived through centuries of silence, swore he had never heard anything more beautiful in all his cursed, immortal life. Not the chants of his old gods, the roar of battle. Not even the crackle of fire in her hearth... Nothing compared to the sound of Mira falling apart beneath him, gasping his name like it was holy.

He would never let her go.

She lay beneath him, gasping softly, her skin dewed with sweat and glowing in the low light of her bedroom. Her lashes fluttered as she tried to catch her breath, but the tremble of her thighs around his hips told him she wasn't quite done shivering just yet. And gods help him, the sight of her undone like this, her legs still wrapped tight around him, hands trembling where they clung to his shoulders, mouth parted in wonder and disbelief... *Garin was ruined.*

He let his head dip low, brushing the tip of his nose along her neck, his mouth following to kiss the thudding pulse there... not to feed. Just to *feel* her, warm and alive and his. But the moment his hips rolled forward again, slow and deep and sinful, Mira gasped, and her legs clamped tighter around his waist, drawing a dark, possessive chuckle from the Viking between kisses at her throat.

"That was beautiful," he rasped, his voice like gravel dipped in honey. "You'll do it again."

Her breath hitched, lips fumbling against his jaw as she murmured, dazed, "A-Again...?"

He smiled then, fangs flashing in the low light, and answered with another deep thrust of his hips, earning him the softest whimper of disbelief from her lips.

"Yes," he growled against her ear. "Again."

She moaned softly, helpless beneath the weight of him, the warmth of him, the *relentless worship* in every move he made.

"I am immortal," he whispered, nipping gently at the soft skin of her shoulder. "I have waited *centuries* for the touch of a goddess... and now that I've found paradise, little flame-"

His hips rocked again, slow and steady, until her hands clawed at his back once more, the sound of her moan catching between her teeth.

"I will stay right here... As long as you keep making those sounds for me."

Mira let out a soft, disbelieving sound that slipped between a laugh and a moan, her voice barely audible as she clung to him. "I-I don't know if I can do that again..."

Garin stilled above her. His dark brows drew together slowly, and then he leaned in, dragging his mouth to the shell of her ear as his hands gripped her hips with reverence... and intent.

"Ah," he murmured low, his voice a velvety threat. "Then this shall be... a *learning experience* for you."

She barely had time to gasp before he moved again, just enough to make her toes curl. His lips brushed her jaw, his voice a husky promise as he continued, "You don't yet understand what it means to be *worshipped* by a Viking, little flame."

He let his teeth graze her neck, not to frighten, but to tease, to remind her just what he was... and who she belonged to now.

"No one will ever adore you like I do. No one will ever *touch* you like I will," he growled, thrusting slow, deep, possessive. "And no one, Mira... will ever make you *come undone* as many times as I will tonight."

She whimpered beneath him, her hands sliding into his hair, her legs instinctively pulling him closer again.

Garin smiled darkly against her skin. "That's it," he praised, voice low and thick. "You're learning already."

And as her body arched into his once more, as her breath caught and her voice broke... The Viking set his pace, slow and damn near endless. Because it would be a long night, and he had centuries of restraint to *unlearn*.

Chapter 15

Mira couldn't move.

She wasn't sure if she ever would again. Her body was draped limply across Garin's massive form, one thigh slung over his hips, her cheek nestled in the crook of his neck where the scent of him…woodsmoke, winter wind, and something darker, wrapped around her like a drug. Her arm lay sloppily over his chest, hand fisted into the coarse hair there, her fingers too tired to do more than *hold on*.

And *God*, was she holding on.

She mumbled against his throat, her voice hoarse, spent, and dangerously close to a whimper. "Vikings… and their damn stamina… pretty sure I'll never walk again…"

Beneath her, Garin had the *audacity* to chuckle. That low, rumbling thing that vibrated straight through her poor overstimulated body like a wicked aftershock. She groaned, lifted one limp hand, and slapped his chest with absolutely zero threat.

"Don't sound so pleased with yourself."

Another laugh. Deeper this time. Smug. And utterly unrepentant. "I *am* pleased," he rumbled. "I'm very… very pleased."

She groaned again, this time sinking further into him with a huff of disbelief. "You're lucky I can't feel my legs, or I'd roll right off you."

He shifted, just enough to pull her tighter against him, and pressed a kiss to the top of her head.

"You won't fall, little flame. I've got you."

And *damn it*, she believed him. Even if her thighs were shaking, her body ached, and her soul felt like it had been kissed just as hard as her mouth had. She wouldn't fall. Not when this Viking held her like she was *everything* he'd waited for. She traced slow, sleepy circles into the center of his chest with the tips of her fingers, her breathing soft now, even if her muscles still hummed with exhaustion. There was no rush. Not in this quiet, in this warm cocoon of strength, arms still wound around her like armor made for her alone.

Her Viking.

The one who had just worshipped her body until it forgot its name. The one who, somehow, was **not** a man. Not truly. Not anymore. She had felt it, his fangs, the stillness of his chest where a heartbeat should have been, the unnatural *heat* of him when he'd moved inside her like a man possessed. Mira should've been scared. Every story said she should be. But all she felt was *safe*. Because she had gotten to know him. Piece by piece, and nothing about Garin frightened her.

Still…

"…Garin isn't a very Viking name, you know" she murmured softly, voice warm against the skin of his neck.

The hand that had been tracing lazy shapes down her back stilled. He was silent for a beat too long.

"No," he finally said, voice a quiet rumble. "It isn't."

She tipped her face slightly to him, her brows lifting with gentle curiosity.

"I abandoned the name of my people not long after I was turned," he said. "It… didn't feel right anymore. Didn't feel *mine*."

Mira's fingers paused, then resumed their soothing path against his chest. "So… where did Garin come from?"

Silence again. This one a little heavier. A little older. "I was in Germany," he said finally, voice low. "A long time ago. I found a coven of Bloodborn there. They... they were a family, of sorts. Took me in, and let me stay. Among them was a boy, a human. Lived with the coven after a time of war. They protected him."

She said nothing, only stroked his chest, encouraging him gently onward.

"One day, I saved him," Garin continued. "He'd wandered too far, and was attacked by a pack of rabid dogs. I pulled them off him, carried him back. And he looked up at me after, bleeding, shaking, and said he wanted to give me a name, since I never had one when I joined them."

Mira's hand stilled. "He named you?"

Garin gave the faintest nod beneath her cheek. "Garin. He said it meant *shelter*... or *guard*. Thought it suited me."

Her heart thudded, aching for the sweetness of it. "That boy must've adored you."

"...He did."

She hesitated, then asked gently, "What happened to him?"

And just like that, the shift was sharp. She felt it beneath her fingertips, the way his chest tensed, the way his jaw locked tight against the top of her head. His voice, when it came, was quieter. Rougher.

"Humans. A cult. They call themselves the LightBorne." His grip around her tightened almost imperceptibly. "They found the coven. Slaughtered them. All of them. The boy... was caught in the crossfire."

Her breath caught. "You couldn't save him?"

"I tried." Two words, but they bled with centuries of failure. "I wasn't fast enough. I...wasn't strong enough."

Mira, fragile, mortal Mira, pressed herself closer. Her lips found his collarbone, soft and reverent.

"You were his shelter," she whispered. "And now... you're mine."

Garin didn't answer right away. But the arm around her pulled her in tighter, and in the quiet, the ghosts of his past finally began to loosen their grip. Because this time...he had saved someone, and she was still right here.

"I'm so sorry you lost them," Mira whispered, her voice barely more than a breath as her fingers continued their slow movements across his chest, brushing lightly over the scars she couldn't see but somehow knew were there.

Garin didn't respond at first. Then, low and edged in a darker timbre, he said, "I got my revenge." That made her pause. She tilted her head, listening carefully. "But it wasn't enough."

She blinked up toward the shape of his face in the shadows. "What do you mean?"

That's when she felt it. The *shift*. Not outward or explosive. But inward, like something deep within him curled tighter, clenched in his soul. His arms wrapped tighter around her body, and the heat of him felt heavier now. Protective...and dangerous.

"The humans," he said slowly, like each word had teeth. "The ones who killed them... they passed it on. Their knowledge. Their training. They taught others how to hunt us. How to *kill* us."

Her heart beat louder now. Not from fear of *him*. Never that. But from what she heard *in* him.

"They still exist," Garin continued. "The LightBorne didn't die. They've just gone underground. Changed their tactics. But they're still out there."

Mira stilled completely against him, body frozen in the curl of his arms.

"And now..." His voice dropped lower. "It's believed they're here. In Georgia."

The silence that followed was so complete, Mira could hear her own breathing. Her fingers trembled slightly where they rested against his chest, but his grip never loosened.

"If they're here," he growled softly, "then let them come."

Mira opened her mouth, but he spoke first, voice fierce and certain, every word a vow written in blood and bone.

"I will *not* allow any harm to come to you. You hear me?" His hand splayed wide across her back. "You are *mine* now. And I am yours, if you'll have me." His voice turned to something darker, ancient. "And I will slaughter any creature, human or not, that dares come close to what is mine."

Mira didn't speak. She didn't need to. Instead, she leaned forward, lips finding his chest just above his heart, where it *should* beat, where it *might* have once, and where *she* now lived. She pressed the kiss there softly. Reverently. Then curled herself deeper into his embrace, one leg twining over his, one hand tightening in the wildness of his hair. Because she didn't doubt him. Not for a moment, and she would not run. Not from *him*, not from *this*, what they just found together in the snow those months ago. Let the world come. Her Viking was ready, and he was hers.

Rua slammed the door to their shared quarters harder than necessary. Not enough to break it. Just enough to make the walls shudder.

"Bloody *waste* of a patrol," he muttered, shrugging out of his coat and tossing it over the back of a chair. Snow dusted the floor where it fell, already melting. "Not a damn thing out there. Not a whisper."

Cian said nothing at first. He moved slower, jaw tight, one hand unconsciously rubbing the place on his shoulder where bark had scraped through fabric earlier that night. Pinned. Like a *fledgling*. Finally, Cian scoffed, accent thick with his irritation.

"Since when does Garin lose his temper like that?"

Rua stilled. That, now *that*, was the real question, wasn't it?

"Never," Rua answered slowly. "Not once. Not when Simon tore into him. Not when Beau ordered him into hell itself. Not even when we were at our worst."

Cian turned sharply. "He didn't just snap. He *moved*."

Rua nodded, expression dark. "Aye. Like we'd touched something sacred."

They stood there in the dim lamplight, the manor unusually quiet around them. No laughter. No arguments drifting through stone walls. Just the distant hum of something old holding its breath. Cian finally let out a humorless laugh.

"All I did was say *redheaded woman*. I didn't think he'd explode like that, brother."

"And he had you on a tree before I could blink," Rua finished.

Silence stretched. Then Rua exhaled slowly, something bitter and something aching tangled together in his chest.

"He's protective. Territorial, even."

Cian blinked. "What?"

Rua turned, eyes sharp now, not mocking, not teasing. Just... honest.

"He's protective because *he* found something. Someone." Rua gestured vaguely, frustration bleeding through. "Whatever that woman is to him, she's *his,* Cian. Something that isn't duty. Or blood. Or orders."

Cian swallowed. His voice came quieter. "And we're still treated like..." He stopped.

Rua finished it for him, softer now. "Like boys."

The word sat between them, heavy, like a shroud that held them down with the weight of any irresponsible action that would've been held over their heads.

"We do everything right," Cian said. "We patrol. We hunt. We bleed when needed. And still, Simon looks at us like we're waiting to fuck it all up."

Rua's jaw tightened. "And Garin?" He huffed. "The silent bastard gets to disappear every night, chuckle like he's lost his mind, and suddenly he's got something worth tearing trees out of the ground for."

Cian leaned back against the wall, staring up at the ceiling. "I don't even think he knows *what* he's got yet."

Rua snorted. "Oh, he knows." He paused, then added quietly, "And whatever it is…she's changed him."

Cian closed his eyes, the image replaying in his mind. Garin's eyes, not icy but blazing, bright with protective and territorial rage. "…Good luck to whoever tries to take it from him."

Rua let out a low, almost feral chuckle. "Aye," he agreed. "Because if our Viking's willing to bare fangs over a *name*…" He shook his head slowly. "…the rest of the world doesn't stand a chance."

For a few moments, the twins were silent. The realization of the night hitting them harder than anything truly ever had before.

Rua dropped onto the worn couch in their room with a low grunt, raking a hand through his wild curls as the door shut behind them. He looked tired, not in body, but in soul. In *spite*. The kind that festered too long without direction.

Cian leaned against the windowsill, arms crossed tightly over his chest. "He pinned me, Rua. Me."

Rua didn't need the reminder. He'd *felt* the snow shake from the impact. He'd *heard* Garin's growl, low, ancient, something that curled in the belly and made even *them* pause.

Cian scoffed. "All because I said the words *redheaded woman*."

Rua's brow twitched. "No, brother. Not just that."

Cian tilted his head, half-glare.

Rua sat forward now, elbows to knees. "It's *how* you said it. And maybe... maybe because you saw her."

Cian's silence was answer enough.

Rua's brow arched. "You saw her." He said far more firmly, eyes locked onto his twin.

Cian gave a sharp nod. "Few nights back. I followed him... wasn't trying to spy. Just...something was off. He walks different now. Carries something in his step that didn't used to be there."

Rua didn't interrupt, but he leaned forward, green eyes blazing in curiosity now.

"She was already outside when he got there. Just sitting there, legs tucked under her, all wrapped up in a blanket like winter didn't bother her at all. Playing a piano in her lap." He huffed. "Didn't even know those damn things *had* lap versions."

Rua stepped closer now, his voice low. "And what was she to him?"

Cian exhaled. "She smiled at him."

That made Rua blink.

"She smiled," Cian repeated, tone bitter, confused. "Like he wasn't a monster. Like he was just... a man. A man who came to listen to music in the snow."

Rua's mouth twitched, something caught between wonder and jealousy. "Our beast... got himself domesticated."

"No," Cian said. "He found something. Someone. And that scared him so bad he nearly broke my ribs because I *said* her hair color."

A beat of silence, and then Rua's voice turned low, introspective.

"How the hell did he find her?"

That question, soft and aching, hung in the room like smoke curling from a candle extinguished too soon.

"How does *he*," Rua went on, "the one who never leaves the manor, who barely *speaks*, the one Beau sends to terrify people...how does *he* find that kind of peace?"

Cian didn't answer. Because it had begun to gnaw at him too, and the blonde Irishman, didn't have an answer. Garin had done the unthinkable.

He'd *diverted*.

Slipped outside patrol, slipped outside routine. *Lied by omission.* The same silent weapon that had stood unmoving through centuries of war and silence and death... Now left each night, just for a song. And when he had turned on Simon, defended them, fought for them, got Beau to let them split patrol, it hadn't just been about duty.

It had been about *her*.

About covering his tracks, about buying himself the time and freedom to go to her, and that frozen ancient bastard... *he'd gotten it.*

Cian's voice came quiet, like a confession he almost didn't want to admit.

"...Do you think he did it for himself first? Or because he believed he finally *could*?"

Rua answered slowly. "Both."

Cian looked over, his voice a whisper. "Do you think...Rua, do you think there's a world outside this manor for us too?"

Rua didn't answer at first. The thought was dangerous. Treasonous, even. But damn it, watching Garin fall... watching him rise into *more* than what he'd been, how could they not ask? Rua's voice broke through, bitter but honest.

"Not while Simon keeps that leash on us."

Cian's lips pressed together, his gaze hardening. "Then maybe it's time we chew through it."

"We're still seen as Simon's boys, Cian. His little pets with fangs. Good for chasing down trails and playing nice at gatherings."

Cian's tone was venom. "He'll *never* see us as men."

"And that's the problem, isn't it?" Rua's voice was low now. Dangerous. "We *are* men. We're killers. Survivors. Warriors."

"...But not free," Cian added.

Rua's jaw ticked. "Not yet."

They didn't speak again after that. But the seed had been planted, and two Irish devils with centuries of chaos in their blood had just watched the silent Viking make himself a life worth bleeding for.

And now? Now they wanted *more* too. *They* wanted to know if there was something...or *someone*...waiting beyond the manor walls for them too. Because if there was?

Simon wouldn't stop them. *No one* would, not when the O'Sullivan twins had seen their brother in blood find happiness, something worth even attacking them over, and they began to crave a similar freedom themselves.

Outside the manor, back in the cold frozen world of winter...Somewhere beyond the manor's reach, beneath falling snow and flickering ward-light, Garin's choice was already reshaping the fate of them all, whether the rest of the coven knew it yet or not.

The hour had grown late, *dangerously* late, and Garin, still barefoot, fastened the last strap of his leathers with practiced ease. His shirt hung from his frame half-fastened, snow-damp cloak draped over the arm of the couch where he tossed it hours before. But his eyes?

They are on her.

Mira, curled under a throw blanket in her oversized sweater, sits at the edge of the bed with her hands folded neatly in her lap, head tilted toward the sound of his movements. Those unseeing green eyes somehow saw *everything*, and Garin...was terrified of what he was about to say. But he stepped toward her anyway.

"I'm going to tell Beau," he said, voice quiet but resolute.

Her head tilted ever so slightly, brows raising. "Tell him... about *me*?"

"Yes." He didn't hesitate. "He needs to know. Not because he'd be angry, he won't. Beau's many things, but cruel to the innocent is not one of them."

Mira was silent for a beat, fingers twitching where they rested atop the blanket. Garin moved closer, kneeling so she could feel him, always respectful, always present. "I have to. If the LightBorne grow bolder... if they ever come near this town, or near you..." His jaw clenched, voice dipping low. "You deserve protection, and Thorne Manor is the safest place I can offer."

Another beat passed, and Garin's hand found hers. "Say something, my flame" he murmured, rough but soft.

Mira inhaled slowly, and finally nodded. "I understand." Her voice was quiet, but steady. "I just... I do have a job. And, you know, *a life* during the day."

Garin chuckled under his breath. "I've already considered it."

That earned him a smirk. "Of course you have."

"We have allies in town. People who know what we are. They help us with transport, supply drops, occasionally food and hospital donations…" He squeezed her hand gently. "They'll help you too. I'll make sure of it."

Mira laughed lightly, some of the tension ebbing from her shoulders. "You've thought of *everything*, haven't you?"

He didn't deny it. Instead, Garin leaned forward, gathering her gently into his arms. It wasn't like earlier. There was no fire or rush in the kiss he gave her now, only reverence. A promise pressed to her lips. His hands were gentle at her back, anchoring her to him as if afraid the world might shift and take her away.

"I'll return tomorrow night," he said, forehead resting lightly to hers.

"You better," she whispered, then groaned playfully, "if I can even walk by then."

That made him grin against her lips, a rare and wicked thing. "If not," he murmured, deep and full of something close to *joy*, "I'll carry you, like the goddess you are." And with that, he kissed her once more, slow, lingering, like he could sear the taste of her into eternity, before finally slipping out the door into the snow-drenched night.

The cold did not touch him. But her warmth…followed him all the way home.

Chapter 16

The hush before sunrise, where the windows of Thorne Manor glowed faintly with the soft light of the dying moon, and the cold lingers like breath held too long. The front door creaked open just before dawn, and in Garin stepped without ceremony, his coat dusted in snow, boots near silent against the floorboards, but tension coiled tight through every inch of his towering frame.

He's late, and someone is waiting.

There, in the manor's grand foyer, stood Beau Thorne, every inch the Southern king he is. His arms are crossed over his broad chest, the muscles beneath his dark shirt shifting as he leans one shoulder casually against the polished banister, but there's nothing casual about the sharp glint in his eyes. The raised brow, the tightly held stillness, the way he watched Garin like a predator assessing whether the wolf has turned from the pack.

"You're cuttin' it close, Viking," Beau drawls, his voice low and even, laced with a Southern chill. "Sunrise don't wait for no man. Thought maybe somethin' happened."

Garin doesn't blink, or even flinch. He only moved forward, step by step until the two giants of the manor stand face to face, silent strength meeting Southern command.

"Something *has* happened," Garin says, voice like distant thunder rolling over ice. "And we need to speak."

Beau's brow lowered slowly, the mirth fading from his expression entirely.

"Privately," Garin added, gaze hard, tone absolute. For a moment, silence lingered between them, just the tick of the grandfather clock echoing through the hall like a heartbeat. Then Beau pushed off the banister, standing to his full height, and jerked his head toward the west wing.

"War room. Now."

No more words are spoken as the two most dangerous men in Thorne Manor disappeared down the hall, the door to the war room clicking shut behind them. And Garin knows…once he says her name, **everything** changes.

The room, lit only by the low amber glow of the sconces along the stone walls, carried the scent of firewood, leather, and ancient parchment. This is where strategy is born. Where hard truths are spoken. Where no lie survives.

Beau stood near the long central table, his hands braced on either side of it. Maps lie rolled and pinned beneath iron daggers, a decanter of aged whiskey sits untouched. His eyes, those piercing, shrewd eyes, locked onto Garin's the moment the Viking enters behind him. The tension between them sharpens like a drawn blade.

"What's happened?" Beau asked, voice still low, but no longer relaxed. "Is there trouble?"

Garin remained still for a heartbeat, then crossed the room in slow, deliberate steps. He didn't look at the maps, didn't glance at the weapons. His gaze is focused on Beau, steady and unwavering. But inside?

A war is raging.

He stopped a few feet from Beau, hands at his sides, shoulders taut. "There is no threat," he responded quietly. "Not to us. But I need…" He pauses, jaw tightening. "I need protection. For someone."

Beau straightens. "Protection?" His brow furrows. "You found someone out there? A witness? A survivor from the LightBorne?"

Garin shakes his head. "No. Not a witness. Not an asset." Then...he hesitated, and Beau saw it. The rare, raw flicker of something fragile in the Viking's normally unflinching expression. Something *human*.

"She's not a liability," Garin murmured, quieter now. "But she is human."

Beau narrowed his golden gaze. "Who is she, Garin?"

Another pause, and Garin knew, that *this* is the moment. Once he says her name aloud in this room, in the company of his coven's king, there will be no retreating from it. No slipping quietly back into the stolen nights of flannel blankets and hot cocoa. No pretending she's only a dream.

But she's *not* a dream. She is *everything*. So finally, with the weight of centuries pressing on his tongue, he says it.

"Her name is Mira." He looked down. Just for a breath, to catch himself if need be before continuing. "She's a music teacher. Blind." His voice softens slightly. "Human. And... I have fallen for her."

Silence stretched long between them, and Garin lifted his head again, steady now.

"I wish to bring her to the manor, Beau. For her safety. If the LightBorne draw closer, I will not have her caught in the crossfire, should they try to ambush us, or set traps. I will not lose her."

And with that, the blade has been drawn. Now all that remains is to see where Beau aimed it, now that the Viking has come clean. He isn't quite sure what to expect, mostly expecting silence. Expecting maybe a lecture, possibly even anger from Beau and his usual hot temper. What he doesn't expect...is laughter.

Low at first. A soft *chuff* of air through Beau's nose. Then the southern coven king straightened fully, crossing his arms over his chest...and lets out a full, deep-bellied laugh.

"Son of a bitch," Beau drawled once he caught his breath, a grin splitting across his face as he shook his head slowly. "The Viking found himself a woman."

Garin's brows drew together, his mouth tightening into something uncertain. "You're... not angry."

Beau barked another laugh, rubbing a hand across his jaw like he's trying to make sense of it. "Hell no, I ain't angry. Shocked? Sure. A little suspicious? Of course. But mad?" He looked back at Garin, and his smile turned a bit softer, more knowing. "Brother, I was beginning to think you didn't *have* a heart. Turns out it's just been sleepin' this whole damn time."

Garin doesn't respond immediately, but his fists unclenched, slowly. "I thought you might see her as a risk."

Beau sobered slightly, walking around the table until he stood in front of Garin, voice lowering to something more serious. "I ain't stupid, Garin. I know what we're dealin' with right now. LightBorne, unknown threats, coven tension and a god-damn wolf in my house." He paused. "But I also know you. If you're bringing this woman to me, if you're askin' for protection, then she's not just someone you like. She's someone you *won't lose*. That means something."

Garin nods once. "It does."

Beau studied him for another long moment before sighing and dragging a hand down his face. "Damn it. The twins are gonna lose their minds, so is damn Evangeline. They finally got used to having Leah around bossin' everyone. Now we'll have two human women. Lord save me."

That draws the smallest breath of amusement from Garin's chest.

"Alright," Beau said finally, slapping Garin's arm once. "You'll bring her tomorrow night. I'll make arrangements. She can stay in the east wing, close to your quarters, but you let me talk to Mave first, she'll want to check her over. Not for your sake, but for *hers*."

Garin's voice is quiet, low with a reverence he can't help anymore. "She's not sick. She's... brilliant. Her blindness doesn't change how she moves in this world, Beau. I do not wish to fix her."

Beau's grin faded into something warmer. "I don't doubt it. She must be somethin' real special, to crack *you*."

And for the first time in centuries, Garin actually smiles for someone other than Mira. Not because he's relieved, but because he's ready.

Tomorrow, he will bring Mira home.

The motel room was bathed in the muted blue light of the pre-dawn hour, the air stale from too many sleepless nights and bitter words. Alexander Weber stood near the curtained window, his spine rigid, hands clenched so tight at his sides that the leather of his gloves creaked in protest. The blinds were parted just enough for him to watch the sky bleed into morning.

His jaw worked in silence. Fury, contained...for now.

From the corner of the room, Jonah Adams ducked his head as he quietly closed his laptop, already sensing the storm brewing. Abigail, his sister, didn't even bother to look up from the stack of papers she was reviewing on the table, but her voice was clipped, dry.

"You're grinding your teeth again, sir."

Alexander's voice came like gravel sliding over steel.

"Two months. Two months, and we have nothing. Not one damned bloodsucker. Not a scrap of fur. No fae, no trace of energy, no drain victims. Nothing." His knuckles cracked as he finally turned from the window. "They're hiding *too* well. And that tells me something. That tells me they're here."

Jonah swallowed. He was the youngest of the three, barely thirty, more comfortable with tech than blades, but loyal, and smart. And unfortunately, stuck in the same room as a man whose rage could curdle blood.

"Sir, we've run multiple scans of the hospitals, blood centers, missing persons reports. We've chased every urban legend and haunted house from Valdosta to Dahlonega-"

"They're not in haunted houses," Alexander snapped, voice a growl. "They don't hide in graveyards anymore. They've adapted. They live *among* us."

Abigail finally looked up, eyes cool behind her wire-rimmed glasses. She was meticulous, analytical. The calm to Alexander's fire, until pushed too far.

"We've followed every sighting, every anomaly. But this state is *clean*, Alex. Whatever you felt crossing the line, maybe it was an echo. Maybe they *were* here. But if they are now? They're buried deep."

"I *know* they're here," he barked, stepping closer. "I've hunted these things longer than either of you have been out of diapers. The moment I crossed that border, I felt the stain. You don't forget the stench of death once it touches your soul."

Silence, and it was heavy. Jonah shifted behind Abigail slightly, like she might shield him if the chair went flying again like it had the week before. But instead, Alexander only moved back to the window. His voice low now, seething with a burning hatred far deeper then anything that could pierce the skin.

"They're here. And they've grown smart. Organized. This isn't the old way anymore. We're not hunting ferals. We're dealing with structure. With hierarchy. With...protection." He let the word hang in the air, bitter as poison. "Somewhere in these woods, in these towns...a coven sleeps. And when I find them?" His eyes narrowed on the faint light of the sunrise. "I will burn them from the inside out. Every last one of them."

From behind him, Jonah quietly whispered to Abigail:

"I liked it better when he was just angry about vending machines."

Abigail didn't look up. "Shut up, Jonah."

But even she...was starting to feel it. A shift, a dark whisper in the shadows. And Alexander Weber? She knew, wouldn't rest until the *source* was dragged into the light, and destroyed.

Abigail didn't look up right away as she spoke, flipping a page in the file she held between gloved fingers. Her voice was quieter than usual, like she wasn't sure if she wanted to open the door she'd just found.

"I may have something."

Alexander didn't turn. Not at first. But his shoulders tensed, just slightly, like a wolf who just scented movement in the brush.

Jonah looked between them. "...Please let it not be another missing housecat."

Abigail ignored him. "A name came up. Jude Lemir. Law intern, mid-twenties. Worked for a big-time law office out of Atlanta. About fifteen months ago, he up and quit out of nowhere. No formal resignation, no complaints filed. Just...gone."

Alexander finally turned now, sharp eyes cutting toward her. "And?"

She flipped to another sheet in the file. "He resurfaced, briefly. Tracked to a small town near the mountain ridge, a little place called Thorne Ridge, about two hours northeast of us. Took a job at a firm called Wexley & Ricci. After that? Nothing. No contact with his employers. No new leases, no bank activity, not even a coffee shop loyalty punch card."

Jonah frowned, brows furrowing. "Weird, but not exactly bloodsucker-level."

His sister gave him a flat look. "No family filed a missing person report. No one looked for him. Which means either someone told them not to, or they were paid off."

Alexander stepped forward now, taking the paper from her hands and scanning it. His eyes narrowed. "You said Thorne Ridge?"

"Quiet little place. Population under 5k. No crime spikes. No press. But…" She tapped another sheet she had clipped behind it. "There are anomalies. Ambulance reports showing high blood loss traumas with no listed cause. A girl who claimed she 'saw a shadow fly through the woods' before being dismissed as a sleepwalker. Not much, not enough to pin, but…"

"It's a *thread*," Alexander muttered.

His voice dropped low, quiet, and damn near almost reverent in its fury.

"Wexley & Ricci…they're connected to some political donors, aren't they?"

Abigail nodded. "Old money. They bankroll half the campaigns in the South. If a Bloodborn has someone in their pocket, that would be the place."

Jonah leaned in over Abigail's shoulder, eyes scanning the documents.

"So you're saying some intern walks into vampire territory, maybe learns too much…and gets claimed?"

She didn't answer that. But the look in her eyes? It said she was starting to think the same thing. Alexander folded the papers slowly, methodically, and tucked them into his coat. Then he turned to his team.

"Pack up, and tell the others to get the vans loaded. We leave in an hour. We'll start with Thorne Ridge."

Jonah opened his mouth, likely to ask if they could at least grab breakfast first, but Alexander's voice cracked out like a whip.

"If we've found a thread? I plan to pull it until it bleeds."

Jonah hesitated before speaking again, his usual levity gone, shoulders tight as he watched Alexander pace the length of the room like a caged animal.

"And if we do find them?" he asked carefully. "If there's a coven there, old ones, then that town's probably wrapped around their fangs already. Cops, doctors, politicians. People who won't talk. People who *protect* them."

Abigail stiffened beside him. She doesn't look at Alexander, but her fingers curl slowly into her palm. Alexander stops pacing and for just a moment, the silence is absolute.

Then he turned, and Jonah immediately wished he hadn't asked. The man's mouth twisted, not into a smile, not really, but into something *wrong*. Something satisfied. His eyes burned with a fevered certainty that has nothing to do with strategy and everything to do with vengeance long rotted and festering.

"What will we do?" Alexander repeated softly. He stepped closer, boots heavy against the thin motel carpet. "We'll do exactly what was done to *our* families, Jonah."

Abigail's breath caught despite herself and Jonah's jaw tightened, a muscle jumping in his cheek.

Alexander's voice dropped lower, steadier now, almost calm. "But we won't show mercy." His gaze flicked between them, sharp and unyielding. "That rogue Bloodborn who slaughtered your mother and father?" he continues. "He killed quickly. Efficiently. Like an animal protecting territory."

A slow, sick grin spread across his face. "I won't make that mistake."

He leaned forward slightly, hands braced on the edge of the table as he stared down the siblings now, a sick gleam in his eyes.

"I want them afraid. I want them to *understand* what it feels like to be hunted. To watch their family die one by one. To beg."

Jonah swallowed hard, and Abigail looked away, unable to even keep her gaze level with either of them now.

"And if it's a coven?" Alexander finished, straightening again. "Then that just means more fangs to hang on my wall."

The room felt colder after that. Abigail looked down at her papers, jaw clenched so tight it ached. Jonah said nothing more…he learned long ago when Alexander reached this point, words were useless. Outside, the sun finally crested over the horizon, and somewhere far north, in a quiet town tucked against the mountains, a Viking vampire is preparing to bring the woman he loves home…

Unaware that the first blade has already been sharpened, and drawn.

~~~~~~~~~~

The eastern wing of the manor was quiet as Garin closed the heavy wooden door behind him. The weight of the hour pressed against his shoulders, but not from exhaustion. Not tonight. Not after her.

He moved through the dim chamber, the familiar scent of leather, snow, and ancient stone settling around him like a second skin. Furs draped across the massive bed welcomed him, and he slowly removed his coat, setting it on the carved trunk at the foot of the frame. The room still carried the chill of the Georgia mountains, but it was nothing compared to the warmth he had just left behind. **Mira.**

His Mira, his little flame, and goddess of his soul's song. The blind woman with fire in her hair and music in her heart. The one who kissed him despite his fangs, who touched his face and whispered promises against his chest. The one who didn't flinch when he told her what he was.

Tonight, he had loved her, took her as his, and would again, and tomorrow night, he would bring her home. Garin sank onto the edge of the bed, exhaling a slow breath as he tugged off his boots, setting them beside the others she'd teased him for always lining up so precisely. She'd laughed at that. He found he liked her laughter more than the silence he once worshipped.

Beau would welcome her. That much, he knew now, that damned laugh of his being obvious on how the Southern man felt about her already. The others? The coven would adjust. Mira was strong in ways they hadn't seen before. Not loud like Leah, not mystical like Mave, but quiet strength, patient, warm, clever. She would be safe at Thorne Manor. He would ensure it. If any LightBorne threat did rise, they'd have to go through him.

But as he lay back onto the pelts, letting the cold silk of the pillowcases cool his skin, something in the back of his mind still stirred, like wind over an old battlefield. A prickling down his spine.

He didn't feel fear often. But Mira... she made him dream again, and the gods never let a warrior dream without a price.

Still... Garin the Viking closed his eyes. And for a few hours, he would allow himself to believe that everything would go as planned. Unaware that just beyond the horizon, steel was being sharpened... And Mira Cassidy would change everything once she stepped across Thorne Manor's threshold.

There is no worry in his heart, not for how the coven will treat her. Not for Beau's acceptance. Not even for the storm of chaos that is surely coming once Rua and Cian realize someone else now shares Garin's silence.

No, his thoughts drifted to Mira yet again as memories began to take him, and how she had curled into his chest and whispered against his skin that she didn't care what he was. Only who he was. And as the Viking finally surrendered to sleep, the first beams of sunlight rising over the distant mountains of Georgia…

He remained utterly unaware that his next battle will not be with the LightBorne alone, a battle that he surely could withstand if need be. Because Mira's presence at Thorne Manor? It will awaken more than just suspicion. It will awaken the one thing Garin feared far more than death, and what has destroyed entire nations under its cruel hand:

Jealousy.

Chapter 17

Mira paced in slow, practiced steps across her small living room, bare feet brushing along the hardwood she'd memorized long ago. Her fingers twisted and twined before her chest, nervously fidgeting as her thoughts ran wild, circling, darting, doubling back.

She wasn't *scared*, not exactly. Not of Garin, never of him. But of what came *next*? That was another story. A *house* of vampires. His coven. A manor full of ancient, blood-drinking creatures…some of whom might even be centuries older than the Viking who had kissed her breathless only the night before.

Her mind spiraled.

Would they hate her? Would they judge her? Could they smell the fact that she loved him already? Would she be welcome…or would she be treated like prey?

She groaned aloud, pausing near the coffee table to press her fingers into her forehead.

"He said they wouldn't bite me," she muttered to the empty room, mostly to soothe herself. "He said it's just for protection. He wouldn't let them hurt me…"

But then her thoughts *drifted* again.

Would he ever bite her?

That was…

That was a very different question entirely.

Her hands fumbled mid-thought, flustering at her own wandering mind, and she turned back toward the center of the room, still mumbling. "I mean... if he *did* bite me, it'd be on my terms, right? If I *asked* him to-"

"Your forehead is furrowed too hard, little one" that deep, silken voice interrupted from behind her, laced with warmth and unmistakable amusement. "And I would only bite you... if you *asked* me to."

Mira yelped, startled half out of her skin as she spun instinctively, nearly tripping over the corner of her couch in the process. But she didn't fall, because in the next second, Garin's arms were around her, strong and steady, pulling her into his chest with a low chuckle.

"Garin! I swear," she breathed, voice half-laughing, half-scolding, her hand over her racing heart. "One day you *are* going to give me a heart attack."

"I would never allow that," Garin rumbled, the words brushing against the shell of her ear like a promise. "I need that heart far too much."

Mira exhaled shakily into his chest, then smacked his arm lightly. "Vampire," she muttered, arms crossing with a soft huff.

"Goddess," he countered.

She melted, and just like that, her nerves softened. Because whatever came next, she wouldn't face it alone. She had *him*, and he was here... to take her *home*.

Garin's arms remained firm around her, steadying her even as her heart slowly climbed down from where it had nearly leapt into her throat. She didn't know how such a hulking, ancient warrior could make her feel so safe, but he did. Every single time.

He pulled back just enough to brush a strand of her red hair away from her cheek, his hand warm only from proximity to the fire, not from his skin itself. "Are you ready to go?" he asked, voice low and steady, but with something else beneath it. Something *solemn*. The weight of this next step, for both of them, hung heavy in that question.

Mira nodded, then remembered and said softly, "Yes. I-I spent a little while packing. Just the essentials. Clothes. My cane. A few things I need."

She hesitated, her fingers curling lightly into his sleeve.

"I was wondering if I should bring the keyboard. The little one I play outside." Her lips curled slightly. "It's not fancy, but it's... it's part of my routine, you know?"

Before her nerves could build again, she felt it, that shift in him. Garin's hand slid down and gently lifted hers, bringing it up until her knuckles brushed his lips. The kiss he placed there was softer than anything he'd ever done. Like she was made of music itself.

"You can bring it, if you wish, my goddess of song, " he said quietly against her skin. "But at Thorne Manor... there is a piano. A real one. Simon brought it in from France a long time ago. Still says the tuning isn't up to standard, though none of us would know."

Mira blinked, surprised, and yet charmed. "Simon...?"

"One of the leaders, second to Beau," Garin murmured. "He'll be curious about you, I imagine. He's a scholar... and a musician when the feeling suits him. It hasn't in some time."

She smiled, her heart skipping.

"And Mave," he continued, brushing his thumb over the back of her hand. "Our high priestess, though seer now. She plays the violin when the occasion suits her, or if the twins pester her enough. The manor has gathered music for centuries. You'll have more than enough songs to learn... or to teach."

Mira felt her breath catch again, not in fear, but wonder. The idea that this place...this *coven*, could hold space for music, for beauty, for her... It felt surreal. She squeezed his hand.

"Then I think I'll leave the keyboard. It's had enough snow for one winter anyway."

Garin chuckled, the sound vibrating through her where they touched, and just like that, she was ready. Because she wasn't scared, and because she wasn't alone. Tonight, she would walk into a house of vampires. But she would do it with her Viking, hand in hand, for the first time in a very long time...

Mira Cassidy felt like she was going home.

~~~~~~~~

He hadn't walked tonight. He couldn't, wouldn't really. Not with Mira beside him. The snow was too thick, the woods too long, and despite her insistence that she was perfectly capable, *and he believed her*, he refused to make her trudge through winter just because he was too stubborn to use modern vehicles.

So he borrowed the old pickup truck Beau kept around for town errands. He *hated* the thing. It was boxy, temperamental, and smelled vaguely of leather, cedar, and... Leah's perfume. But it worked. Mostly. His fingers tightened around the steering wheel as he turned onto the winding road that would eventually bring them to the manor gates, the headlights cutting through the icy fog.

Mira sat beside him, bundled in her coat, her hand resting atop his on the gearshift like it belonged there. Like *she* belonged there. He swallowed the emotion rising in his throat and focused on her voice. She had asked about the others in the manor, and he would tell her.

"Mave," he began, his voice low, careful not to jostle the peace she always made him feel. "Our seer. High priestess, once, long ago. From a bloodline older than most can recall, deep within the mountains of Africa." He flicked his eyes toward her. She was listening, rapt, the gentle curve of her lips tilted in curiosity.

"She was worshipped in her village," he continued. "Still *is*, by some, I think. They called her goddess. Sometimes...I think they were right."

"And Larazo?" Mira asked softly.

Garin huffed a breath of amusement, always impatient, his flame. "Her mate. Quiet, ancient, terrifying at times. He rarely speaks unless he has something worth saying. No one knows how old he is, not even Beau. But I suspect...older than Rome."

Mira let out a breath of surprise. "That old?"

Garin nodded. "His accent alone shifts between dialects I can't even place. But Mave tames him. The same way you..." He trailed off, unsure if he was brave enough to finish that sentence. But her hand squeezed his just enough. So he kept going.

"Then there are the *twins*," he said, exasperation creeping into his voice.

Mira grinned immediately. "The ones you warned me about?"

He groaned, and she *laughed*. That sound, he'd walk barefoot through fire for it.

"They are... chaos. Rua and Cian O'Sullivan. Simon found them during the famine in Ireland, centuries ago. Took them in. Raised them. Turned them when illness came. And ever since, they've been the biggest thorns in my side, the moment Beau allowed that trio to join us."

Mira giggled again, her voice dancing with mischief. "They sound charming."

"They are nightmares," Garin muttered.

She just laughed harder.

"Then there's Beau Thorne," he said, softening slightly. "Our coven king. Southern-living now. Charismatic, but brutal when needed. And completely at the mercy of his mate."

Mira perked up. "Mate? Is she human?"

"Yes," Garin confirmed. "Her name is Leah Ricci. She owns part of the law firm in town."

There was a beat of silence, and then Mira gasped. "Wait. *The Leah Ricci?* From Wexley & Ricci?"

Garin gave her a sidelong look, and he swears…maybe a tad of fear. "You know of her?" he asked gently, because if she knew Leah personally…

"Know of her?" Mira snorted. "She once cross-examined a principal on behalf of a substitute teacher and got half the school board replaced. She's a legend."

Garin chuckled, that deep, rolling sound only she ever got to hear, just about in relief. "That sounds like her. She came to town a little over a year ago. Beau and she… well, they fought like wolves until they fell in love. Deeply."

Mira was quiet a moment, then teased, "And she lives at the manor?"

He paused. "No," he admitted. "She refuses. Says she likes her own space. And…" He cleared his throat. "I think she enjoys watching Beau beg every few months."

Mira's laughter filled the cab, rich and unrestrained, and it lit something inside him. Not hunger. Not need.

But peace, and a warmth he's come to expect being with her. And when her hand slipped fully into his, fingers threading with his own as they crested the final hill leading to the faint silhouette of Thorne Manor beneath the winter moon… Garin knew he'd never be the same again. He had brought war home before. Tonight, he was bringing music.

Garin's gaze stayed on the road, but his thoughts lingered on the threads of truth Mira deserved to know, especially before she crossed the threshold of the manor, and into their world completely. He had already told her of Beau and of Leah. Of Mave and Larazo. Of the twins and their chaos. But there were *two more names* she needed to hear.

"Simon Lenoir," Garin said at last, his voice low, like a memory half-whispered through a tomb. "The Frenchman."

Mira tilted her head gently. "Another vampire?"

Garin nodded once. "Turned during the Fronde, back in France. He was a scholar before he was Bloodborn. He still is. Collects knowledge like some hoard gold. There is no ancient tongue he can't read, no forgotten war he hasn't studied. His mind is a library."

Mira smiled softly. "He sounds...kind?"

Garin let out a breath that wasn't quite a laugh. "*Most* of the time," he said. "He can be... difficult to label. Detached, sharp-tongued, cold. Other nights? Gentle. Protective. He's the only one the twins ever really listened to. He raised them."

Mira absorbed that, quiet again, and Garin hesitated, before saying the next name.

"Evangeline," he said, the word like glass against his tongue. "The former queen of the Bloodborn."

Her brows lifted in surprise. "*Queen?*"

"She was once mated to someone older than time, the god of our race in most terms, " Garin said vaguely, "But she ran. Came here. Chose Simon instead."

"And they're together now?" Mira asked.

He exhaled slowly, grip tightening slightly on the wheel.

"No," he said. "Not anymore. They're...at war, I'd say. Quietly. Coldly. Simon barely speaks to her, and she spends most of her time haunting the north wing."

"Why?" Mira asked, voice gentle, curious.

He struggled for a moment before answering.

"There are theories, between the coven" he admitted. "But I believe...it's because Evangeline is used to being *worshipped*. Revered. And when Beau brought Leah into the manor, when the attention shifted from Evangeline's perfection to someone *human*... she unraveled."

Mira was quiet, then asked in a smaller voice, "Will she cause trouble...because of me?"

That snapped something in him. Garin's hand left the wheel, found hers where it rested in her lap, and he brought it to his lips again. A soft, reverent kiss.

"No," he said, firmly. "You are *not* trouble, Mira. You are peace. You are... everything soft I never thought I could have. And the others?" He smiled slightly. "They'll adore you. Even the twins, though they'll never admit it."

Her lips tilted up. But Garin wasn't finished. He gave her hand a gentle squeeze, just enough to ground her before saying, "There is...another."

Mira blinked. "Another vampire?"

"No," Garin muttered, tone shifting. "Not like us. A wolf."

She straightened a little. "A werewolf?"

He sighed through his nose. "Moonborn, technically, they refuse to acknowledge being called werewolves, since they vary in species. From *Texas*."

There was a beat, and Mira *laughed*. A bright, musical sound that bounced through the cab. "A *Texas* wolf?" she echoed. "Why did you say it like that?"

Garin groaned, dragging a palm over his face. "Because," he grumbled, "I already have one southern bastard in my home with too much charm and too many sayings. I didn't need another."

She *giggled* again, and he could feel it in his chest this time, vibrating against the ribs that hadn't moved in centuries.

"And now," he continued with mock despair, "the wolf has befriended the twins. They've started sparring together. Wrestling. Sparking chaos."

Her grin was radiant now. "So it's louder."

"It is *always* louder," he muttered, but the truth was...he didn't really mind. Not anymore. Especially not with *her* by his side now. As Thorne Manor loomed into full view, Mira's hand still warm in his own, Garin knew: His world was about to change.

And this time? He *welcomed it.*

The engine cut as Garin settled the truck in the driveway before the manor, and silence followed. Then motion. He was out of the truck in an instant, boots crunching against frostbitten gravel, his long dark braid thumping once against his spine as he strode around the vehicle, not with urgency, but with something older, deeper.

Protective pride.

Because this moment...was *everything*. This wasn't just a visit. This was *her arrival*. Her crossing into his world. Her first step into the place that would, from tonight on, be her *home*...should she choose to stay here longer after the threats have passed.

He reached the passenger side just as Mira opened the door slowly, her fingers trailing along the edge as though feeling the shift in the air. Garin was there to take her hand, steady and silent as always, but there was warmth in his grip. Reassurance. Devotion.

And then...**the doors opened.**

Of course they did.

The great dark oak doors of Thorne Manor swung wide like some damn gothic stage play and-

"Well I'll be damned!"

That southern drawl cut through the dusk like a whipcrack wrapped in honey.

Beau Thorne, the king of dramatics himself, stepped out into the cold with his usual flair, coat unbuttoned, boots gleaming, that infuriating grin already curling across his face as if he'd been *waiting* for the moment Garin brought a woman home.

"You bringin' me a gift, Viking? 'Cause she's just too damn pretty for a brute like you."

Garin *groaned* under his breath and Mira startled for half a heartbeat, then let out a bright, delighted *laugh*, her cheeks instantly blooming pink. Garin tightened his jaw. Her laughter was everything.

Beau's *comment* was not.

He debated it...briefly. There was a good-sized stone half-buried in the dirt just by the path. He could throw it. Clip the Bloodborn leader right in the shoulder. Nothing fatal. But Mira was still laughing, and Garin...couldn't bring himself to interrupt that sound. Not even to get revenge on Beau's mouth.

Yet.

So instead, he just muttered low enough for Mira to hear, "If I kill him, I want you to look shocked when the others ask what happened."

She giggled again, and the blush remained, "Well...not like I would see it happen."

With her fingers still wrapped in his, the Viking led her up the path, toward the manor, toward the coven, toward the place that would never be the same now that his little flame had arrived.

Garin led her up the stone steps, her small hand nestled in his, their joined fingers a grounding weight as the cold crept around them. The manor loomed ahead, gothic and regal, its sharp lines softened by a kiss of moonlight, but he didn't look at the house.

He looked at *her*.

The way her lips parted in awe as she felt her new surroundings, the way her free hand brushed over the textured iron railing like she could *feel* the history through her fingertips. She was nervous, yes...but brave. And utterly his.

They reached the last step when Beau's voice rang out again, infuriatingly smug.

"I heard that little mutter, Viking."

Garin exhaled slowly through his nose.

"Lucky for you," Beau drawled on, "your lady don't have any sight. Otherwise she'd have to watch me whoop your big ass back into place."

Mira giggled, again. That same bright, impossible sound that cracked through the tension like a sunbeam through storm clouds. Garin growled this time, *loudly*, a sound like rolling thunder from deep in his chest. But he didn't lunge for the southern bastard.

Not yet.

Because Beau, dramatic, frustrating, loud-mouthed Beau, *softened* the moment Mira stepped within arm's reach. Gone was the cocky smirk. In its place: something warmer. Gentler. He reached out, not too fast, not too bold, and took Mira's hand in his rough, calloused fingers brushing over hers with surprising care.

"Welcome," Beau said, voice low now, soft with southern charm. "I'm Beau Thorne, sugar. This old place is mine...which means for as long as you're here, it's yours too."

Mira smiled, cheeks pink again as she answered, her voice clear but tinged with a polite shyness. "I'm Mira Cassidy. It's...nice to meet you."

Garin watched it all, protective, *watchful*. The moment the handshake ended, he reached out, slow but firm, and tugged her gently back into his arms. Not possessive, just certain. He kept his chest close to her back, one hand resting protectively at her waist. **His.**

Beau, of course, noticed. Smirked like the bastard he was. Then gestured toward the open door behind him.

"The others are inside," he said. "Been waitin' to meet the lovely lady you brought home. Though if any of 'em get too close...feel free to growl again. I'll let you have that one."

Garin didn't dignify it with a reply. He simply led Mira forward, past the threshold, past the old wood doors, and into the coven's lair where shadows, history, and family awaited.

Chapter 18

Garin followed Beau through the wide double doors of the main hall, Mira's small hand still cradled in his own. He felt the subtle shift in the manor's air immediately, warmth laced with anticipation. A hush not of silence, but of *watching*.

Just like Beau promised, the coven lay in wait. The first sight that met him was exactly what he'd expected: the twins, tangled in each other's limbs on the velvet settee like overgrown cats. Rua was grinning ear to ear, his green eyes sparking with mischief as he lounged sideways, booted feet kicked up over the armrest like a throne made just for him.

Cian…gods help them…was upside down, head dangling off the back of the couch like a golden bat, his white-blonde hair nearly brushing the floor.

"Oi!" Cian called, spotting them the second they entered. "So that's your little flame then, Garin? You didn't say she was adorable. Looks like a fairy wandered into a den of monsters ready to be snacked-"

SMACK.

Rafe's hand connected with the back of Cian's head before Garin could blink, let alone react in his own violence.

"Have some damn manners, Irish," the Texan said, calm but firm, not even looking up from where he sat in a nearby chair, legs spread wide, hat perched on one knee, smile polite and *decidedly less feral* than the twins'. "You don't talk in front of a lady like that."

Cian winced, rubbing his scalp as Rua barked a laugh beside him. "Ah screw you, ye damn flea bag."

Garin leaned down just enough to murmur into Mira's ear, voice low and wry. "Ignore them. They were feral before they were fanged."

She giggled, soft but real, and it warmed something deep in his chest. But before he could guide her further into the room, another voice, this one gentle, rich, and unmistakably *female*, rose above the noise like a balm.

"Oh thank the old gods, *finally*."

Mave.

She stepped forward from her usual place by the fireplace, her tall frame moving with an elegance Mira could *feel* rather than see. Her long braids were laced in copper threads tonight, and her eyes, dark and ancient, held a spark of joy. She didn't hesitate. Didn't hover or ask permission. She reached for Mira's hands and took them in her own, warmth radiating from her like the hearth she stood beside.

"Welcome, sweet girl," Mave said, her African accent curling around each syllable like a soft hymn. "It's about damn time another woman joined us in this house. Without Leah here, I've been stuck with nothing but these foolish men and their never-ending idiocy."

Rua gasped with mock offense, hand on his chest. "Mave, are you including your own mate in that slander?"

Mave didn't miss a beat. She leaned closer to Mira with a dramatic whisper, just loud enough for all of them to hear.

"Of course I am, darling. Ancient doesn't always mean *sane*."

Garin barely stifled a smirk as the room filled with laughter, light, bright, rolling through stone and shadow like a welcome all its own.

And Mira?

She laughed too. A little breathless, a little shy, but she didn't flinch or step back. She *stood* there. In the middle of the manor, in the arms of a Viking, and in the heart of a coven older than kings. And Garin?

He had never seen anything braver in his long, brutal life. The warmth lingered as the laughter from Mave's jab settled into contented hums. Garin stood still, letting Mira soak it in, letting the rhythm of the room wrap around her like a new skin. But then…movement.

From the shadows of the hearth, Larazo emerged. Towering, eternal in ways none of them will ever understand. He moved like a myth, shadow and flame flickering across his dark skin, his greyed hair pulled back from his bearded face, and rested one calloused hand on Mave's shoulder with a reverence that spoke of centuries. His molten-gold eyes, quiet where hers were fire, settled on Mira.

"My queen speaks of you often, little one," he said, his voice like iron dragged through silk. "In her sleep, in her trances. She saw your coming before you did."

Garin felt Mira tense ever so slightly in his hold. She tilted her head, brows knitting in surprise.

"But… how?" she asked, gently. "How could she know? I've never met her before."

Mave gave a knowing hum, her rich laugh a soft drumbeat of secrets kept. She squeezed Mira's hands and leaned in once more.

"Because my eyes," she whispered, "see far more than anyone else's. Much like yours."

Mira's brows lifted in confusion, her green eyes shimmering though they held no vision. She gave a weak chuckle, brushing a red curl behind her ear.

"I don't see anything at all anymore."

But Mave shook her head, firm but kind. "No, child. You see with more than your eyes. You see with your heart. Your soul. How else do you think you and Garin found each other, hmm?" Her eyes flicked briefly toward the Viking. "That song between you two? That didn't come from nowhere."

And Mira, his sweet Mira, blushed so fiercely Garin could feel the heat rise against his skin. Her lashes fluttered. Her lips parted, trembling with the weight of a truth too large to carry all at once.

But before Garin could pull her into his arms, before he could claim her in the safety of his home, of his coven...

It broke.

The spell, the softness. Shattered like ice beneath a heel. From the far corner, where shadows gathered like courtiers waiting for their queen, a voice lilted out, sweet on the surface, but laced with vinegar.

"We must be truly desperate..." came the drawl. "Taking in another stray human. Only this one's broken."

The room froze. Even the twins stopped moving. Mira's hand curled tighter around Garin's, but she didn't speak, not yet. Not when the air was suddenly thick with tension, not when the woman who had once worn the title *queen* stood with her arms crossed, half-lit by firelight like the ghost of some throne long since abandoned.

Evangeline.

Garin's jaw flexed, slow and silent. He didn't move yet. He didn't need to. Because the silence itself began to bristle, and Mira's presence in the manor, barely ten minutes old, had already shaken the nest.

The coven turned as one. Eyes found Evangeline as she stepped forward from the shadows, firelight dancing along the hem of her gown like it remembered the blood she once wore like perfume. She was elegance carved in ice, lips curled in amusement, gaze sharp as broken glass.

Garin shifted the moment she moved, his massive frame instinctively stepping in front of Mira. One arm looped protectively around her waist as he bared his teeth in a low, guttural growl, a sound that turned heads, even from the twins.

"Watch your tongue," he warned, voice like distant thunder. The promise of violence lingered behind every syllable.

But Evangeline? She laughed.

"Please, Viking," she said, waving a hand with mocking ease. "I only tease." Her smile tightened. "She must be something special... if she managed to tame *you*."

Then her gaze slithered to Mira, all pretense of jest curdling into something darker.

"But tell me, little human, " she purred, circling ever so slightly, "do you truly understand the brutality of the world you've stepped into? Of our kind? You may find out... sooner than you'd like."

The room held its breath. Garin's muscles coiled, ready to lunge. His eyes began to glow faintly, the ancient fury behind them rippling forward, but he didn't move.

Because Mira did.

She didn't shout. She didn't posture. She didn't even flinch. She simply placed a hand on Garin's chest, soft and calm, grounding him like her touch was the only thing that tethered the old god of war to this moment. Then she turned her head just enough to face the voice that tried to shatter her. Her voice was quiet and measured, and Garin only assumed this is how she spoke to wayward students of hers.

"Seems to me," Mira said softly, "the only brutal thing here... is your attitude." There was a beat of silence. A flicker of shock. "You'd catch more flies with honey than vinegar, you know. You don't have to be rude just because you're jealous."

The room *snapped* with laughter. Rua let out a bark of delight, and Cian had rolled from the couch to the floor in a flurry of chuckles, even Mave smothered a grin behind her hand.

Garin?

He looked down at the woman in his arms, the blind, delicate pianist the world might have called broken, and felt something in his chest ache with pride. Because Mira hadn't just walked into Thorne Manor. She had *arrived*.

Evangeline staggered back a step, like Mira's calm retort had landed a slap across her flawless cheek. Her mouth opened, then closed. Then opened again, her poise unraveling just enough to show the petty child still lurking behind the former queen's eyes.

"You dare!" she hissed, voice rising, "You *dare* speak to me like that? Like I'm some child?" She stepped forward again, a sudden spark of supernatural energy flaring behind her, as if she meant to lash out.

Garin shifted instantly, Mira tucked behind him as he bared his fangs now. His body went rigid, eyes glowing that icy blue, rage a hair's breadth from breaking free. He was prepared to strike. But before anyone could move, a voice, smooth as silk and sharp as a scalpel, sliced through the moment.

"Evangeline."

The name, spoken with that familiar French lilt, landed like a thunderclap. The coven turned again, and Garin, along with everyone else, watched as Simon Lenoir stepped through the archway.

Late, as always, but yet precisely on time.

The scholar's long coat drifted around his legs, dark silver curls pushed back, and his brown eyes, usually warm, if distracted, now blazed with focused fury that has become dominant as of late. Not wild. Not loud. But the kind of fury that came from an immortal who had long mastered the art of control... except when he chose not to.

He leveled that searing gaze on Evangeline. "If you do not wish to be treated like a child," he said calmly, voice dipped in warning, "then do not throw tantrums in front of our guests."

Evangeline stiffened. Her lips parted to argue again, but Simon stepped closer. He towered over her, not with physical threat, but the sheer force of presence. His words were colder now.

"Go back to the north wing, mon cœur. If you insist on haunting this house like a banshee... you may even find one up there willing to keep you company."

A long, tense silence, and Garin... Garin couldn't help but feel the corner of his mouth tug, just slightly, at the dry venom in Simon's tone. Behind him, he could feel Mira's pulse calming again. With one last venomous glance at Mira, Evangeline turned sharply, heels clicking on the manor floor, and disappeared down the hallway with a whirl of lace and spite.

Garin exhaled slowly, his hand reaching back to rest against Mira's spine in reassurance. Simon caught his gaze briefly, and gave a subtle nod. Order restored.

For now.

Garin's eyes narrowed as Simon moved forward, the elegant lines of his coat catching faint light from the chandelier above. The Frenchman always moved like he had all the time in the world, a fact Garin sometimes found irritating. But tonight, there was a softness beneath his precision.

Simon stopped before Mira, hands loosely folded behind his back, and bowed his head slightly.

"Mademoiselle," he began, "permit me to offer a formal apology." His voice was low and smooth, tinged with apology but never weakness. "Evangeline's behavior was...

unbecoming. Eternity does not agree with all creatures. I hope she did not frighten you away."

Mira tilted her face up toward the voice, smiling softly. "She didn't scare me," she said simply. "But I'm not a fan of bullies like that. Everyone else has been wonderfully kind."

Garin caught it then, that rare shift in Simon's expression. The faint crinkling at the corners of his eyes, the fleeting softness that tugged at the edge of his mouth.

A smile.

"Vous avez une lumière calme, douce et ancienne," Simon murmured in his native tongue, quiet enough Garin only caught the rhythm, not the meaning. But Mira smiled again, and that was enough. *"You have a calm, gentle, and ancient light."*

Then came the flurry of chaos.

"Oi, Viking!" Rua's voice rang out like a cannon, followed by Cian tumbling over the back of the couch like a cat landing on its feet. "You didn't tell us she was this pretty," Rua grinned, eyes twinkling.

"What in the hells did you do to make a sweet redheaded lass like this fall for *you*, Garin?" Cian added, absolutely unbothered by the growl that rumbled low in Garin's chest.

"Are you sure you don't want to trade up for an Irishman, love?" Rua added with a wink, waggling his brows.

Garin's snarl deepened, and he took a step forward, ice-blue eyes glowing faintly now, but before he could act...

"All right, all right!" Mira giggled, placing a hand gently on his arm as if reining in a storm. Her other hand found Cian's shoulder, her laughter soft but open. "Don't pick a fight, please."

It worked. The sound of her amusement, the way she *touched* Cian without flinching, stilled Garin's instinct just enough. Though his jaw clenched as she was swept away from his side, pulled toward the couch by the chaotic pair.

"Wait, wait," Rua said, helping her sit as if they were perfect gentlemen, which they weren't. "We've got questions."

"Real ones," Cian added. "Can you, y'know, taste things better? Smell things better? Is that a thing?"

"You can *definitely* hear better, can't you?" Rua asked, pulling out a box from behind the couch that absolutely hadn't been there before.

"They manifest snacks when bored," Beau drawled behind Garin, slapping a palm onto the Viking's shoulder before he could move himself and snatch Mira back. Garin didn't flinch, but he didn't look away from Mira, still watching like a soldier watching the door.

"Relax, big guy," Beau said with a crooked grin. "They're not trying to steal your woman." A pause. "Well, not *seriously*, anyway."

Garin growled again, but Beau just chuckled.

"They're bored, curious, and she's sweet as hell. Let them get it out of their system."

Garin grunted in reluctant agreement... mostly because at that exact moment, Rua held out a piece of chocolate and asked Mira, "Bet you can tell what flavor it is without even tasting it, can't ya lass?"

And Mira? She leaned forward, smiling still, wrinkling her nose slightly as she took a soft breath.

"Is it hazelnut? That's my favorite!"

The twins gasped like they'd witnessed witchcraft before moving on to yet another piece of the candy stash.

Garin still didn't move, and he still didn't sit down. But some small part of him finally let go of the tension, if only for a moment. She was smiling. And that was all that mattered.

In the shadowed halls of the north wing, the air crackled with fury. Glass shattered. A perfume bottle exploded against the stone wall. Evangeline stood trembling, nostrils flared, eyes glowing with rage…**and humiliation.**

That girl. *That* mortal girl had dared to speak to her like a wayward child, and the coven, those ungrateful fools, had *laughed*.

Her fingers clenched into white-knuckled fists, her nails digging crescents into her palms as she snarled beneath her breath. "She's blind. Blind. And yet they all looked at *her*."

She paced now, her silk gown dragging behind her like spilled moonlight as she whirled toward her vanity, now shattered. The broken fragments of crystal, glass, and gemstone glinted like scattered teeth across the floor.

"Simon…" she hissed aloud, voice trembling not from weakness, but from betrayal. He had stood there. Watched, and called her a banshee.

"He used to *worship* me. They all did."

She turned to the mirror, or rather, what was left of it, and stared at her fractured reflection. Dozens of her stared back, all distorted. All broken. Just like her place in this house.

"He once said I was the reason stars envied earth." Her voice cracked, soft and furious. "Now he looks at me like I'm… like I'm some shrieking ghost haunting the corners of a home that *should* be mine."

Her fingers reached toward the mirror, hovering just over a jagged edge, before curling back into a fist and slamming down, cracking the shard into even smaller pieces.

This was happening again. Just like when Beau brought his brat into the manor. That *lawyer* who barked orders and strutted about like she owned the place and the coven let her. Simon let her.

And now? Another mortal. Sweet and soft-spoken, oh yes, but beneath that? There was strength, there was *danger*. Evangeline saw it, and worse, so had Garin.

Garin, who had never looked at anyone. Garin, the beast of the manor... was soft for her. He had never once even looked her way, not when she first came here so long ago with Simon, but now he worshipped a fragile human like a goddess.

Evangeline let out another scream, one that rattled the chandelier above her head. "I *will not* be made a fool again. Not by them. Not by some blind girl who doesn't know the monsters she walks along."

She moved to the wardrobe, flinging it open, pulling cloth aside as her mind spiraled. This girl...this Mira...would not stay sweet. No mortal ever did.

And Evangeline? She would not be pushed aside again. Not in *her* home. Not when she still remembered the weight of every worshipful gaze.

Her lip curled. "Let's see what your sweetness is made of, girl," she whispered to the night. "Let's see how long it lasts... when you start bleeding."

Chapter 19

The halls of Thorne Manor whispered beneath her steps, polished wood humming under her heels as she was, gently, dragged through the corridors by one very large, very possessive Viking.

Mira giggled again, unable to help herself. "You're sulking," she accused playfully, letting his much larger hand envelope hers as he all but hauled her along. He didn't say anything, but she could feel it in the way his grip tensed just slightly. In the way the air around him buzzed with low, smoldering frustration.

She was nearly breathless from laughter by the time they rounded a corner. "Garin," she said again, still breathy, still amused, "they weren't bothering me at all, I promise. I *liked it*, actually."

He grunted, a sharp and disgruntled sound that vibrated through his chest. Mira only smiled in response.

"I mean it," she said, bumping her shoulder gently into his arm as they walked. "Do you know how rare that is? People asking questions out of genuine curiosity instead of pity? Instead of that quiet, awkward tone where they assume I'm one breath away from breaking?"

He stopped then, which surprised her. She felt the subtle shift in the air. The way his body stilled beside hers. The way his fingers curled just slightly tighter around her hand, not to confine, but to anchor.

His voice rumbled out low. "May be..." And that was all he gave her for a beat. Until...

"...However." That word came heavier, a growl more than a breath. "I am *not* a fan of how Cian laid his head in your lap."

Mira let out a snort of laughter. "*That's* what this is about?" The low, warning sound he made only made her grin grow wider. "His hair was *soft*, Garin! Like velvet. Honestly, I think he uses better conditioner than I do."

He started walking again, faster this time, and she had to pick up her pace, her free hand brushing the stone walls as she moved beside him. Still smiling.

"You're impossible," she said fondly.

"And you're too kind to chaos in Irish form."

"He meant no harm."

"He meant *charm*," Garin muttered darkly.

That made her laugh again, soft and bright in the hush before dawn. Gods, he was brooding and massive and utterly ridiculous. But she could feel the tension behind it. Not anger. Not jealousy. Possessiveness, yes. But not just of her attention. He had brought her into his world tonight, **his** home, **his** family, and she had been taken from his arms, teased, passed between them with curiosity and affection.

And though she hadn't minded one bit, she realized now...

He had.

She squeezed his hand and tugged lightly, pulling him to a stop again. "I'm yours," she said softly, turning her face toward him. "You don't need to growl at anyone to remind me."

Garin didn't speak, But he leaned down a moment later and kissed the top of her head, a low rumble in his chest that she felt more than heard. He started walking again, slower this time, and this time, she followed without laughing.

Mira heard the door creak open moments later, followed by the soft whisper of hinges as Garin's hand moved with careful pressure to her lower back. That touch again, protective, steady, **home**. He said nothing at first, simply guiding her across the threshold as though this space had been waiting for her.

Then his voice rumbled close to her ear, low and rough with affection. "I've brought you to my room. It will be safer this way." A pause. Then a dry edge. "...And the twins know better than to enter here."

Mira laughed softly, the sound dancing in the stillness. "You make it sound like they're the wolves instead of Rafe."

"They are," he muttered, though she could hear the reluctant fondness beneath the grumble.

She reached for his arm again, grounding herself in his presence as he led her deeper into the room. The air changed, it was warmer, thicker with the scent of him: smoke, pine, iron, and something darker she hadn't yet placed but already found comforting.

Her fingers brushed over something soft. She let them trail down, then sink in. "Is this...?"

"My bed," he confirmed.

"Oh my God," she breathed, her hands pressing deeper into what had to be layers of thick furs. "This is *decadent*. What is this? Cloud?"

"Fur," he answered, amused now. "Good fur."

She chuckled again, until she felt a shift in the air. Heard the quiet bend of knees. Then his voice, closer now, lower, came from in front of her.

"Mira." She tilted her head toward him, heartbeat slowing. "Are you alright?" he asked. "After...everything. Evangeline. The twins. All of this."

The way he said it...*all of this*...carried more weight than the rest. As if he knew just how strange this world must be to someone like her. As if he knew that bringing her into it meant placing a fragile flame into a den of shadows.

But Mira only smiled, soft and sure. "I'm okay, Garin." She reached for him instinctively, her fingers brushing his shoulder as he knelt before her. "Evangeline was...moody, sure. But I've met worse. She's not the end of the world."

His growl was quiet but present.

"And everyone else has been so kind," she continued, her tone turning light again. "Beau is funny in that Southern scoundrel kind of way. And the twins? They're adorable, honestly. A little chaotic, but I think they mean well. I didn't mind their questions."

She hesitated, then added in a quieter voice, "Though... I really like Mave. She's so kind, and there's something steady about her." A pause. "...But she scares me. Just a little."

She heard Garin exhale, and the warmth of it ghosted across her knee.

"Mave scares most," he said. "Because she knows too much."

That made Mira smile again. "Like she sees through you."

"She does."

Another silence settled between them. Not tense. Not uncertain. Just *full*. Full of things unsaid. Full of questions waiting to be asked and touches not yet made, and yet... it felt like the safest place in the world. With him kneeling in front of her like that, with his voice as her anchor. With the wild weight of the night finally beginning to fade... just in time for the sun to rise.

She felt the weight of the moment before he spoke, the careful tension in the air, like the last breath before morning.

"You should rest," Garin said softly. "The sun's nearly risen. I'll arrange for someone to get you to work in a few hours."

Mira let out a soft laugh and reached for his hand again, large, calloused, and warm in a way that made her chest ache. She wrapped both her smaller hands around his, her smile blooming wide across her face.

"Garin," she said with teasing affection, "today is Saturday."

He stilled.

"I don't work on Saturdays," she added, her voice a hushed lilt of mischief. "So I'm all yours for the next two days."

The silence that followed wasn't awkward. It was electric. She could feel it, the shift in the air, the change in him. Even without eyes, she could *see* it through the bond they were developing and she was beginning to understand.

He didn't say a word. He didn't have to. She knew the exact moment that wicked grin spread across his bearded face. Because in the next breath, Mira was suddenly flat on her back, sinking into the decadent warmth of the bed, a breathless yelp left her lips as her back hit the furs, a rush of warmth and spice enveloping her as Garin surged over her. The bed gave slightly beneath his weight, but the furs caught her like snowdrift, soft and cool against the fever his body poured over her.

"Garin!" she laughed, half-scolding, half-delighted.

He growled low, the sound vibrating against her skin as he lowered himself closer, his breath brushing against her jaw. His voice was rough silk, barely leashed.

"All mine?"

She nodded, breath hitching. "All yours."

Another beat passed. Then his mouth found hers, not soft, not tentative. But *devouring*. Like a man starved of touch, of comfort, of *her*. The kiss pulled a sound from her throat she hadn't meant to make, and his weight shifted just enough to press her deeper into the bed.

Mira? She didn't need sight to know exactly what kind of look was in his eyes. Because she could *feel* it. The heat, the hunger. The possessive delight of a Viking who had just been given permission to keep what he'd found.

And the furs whispered around them, as the first light of dawn dared to peek beyond the windows, finding no audience in that room but two shadows tangled together, a silent promise unfurling between each breath.

She had given him two days, and she knew he was going to make them count.

He moved over her like a wave crashing to shore, nothing hesitant in him now. The soft reverence from before, the careful touches, the patient worship, no it was still there... but buried beneath something deeper.

Ravenous.

This wasn't the composed, silent man who had once touched her like she was a secret he feared breaking. No. This was her *Viking*, starving, growling low in his throat as he pressed kiss after kiss down her throat, her collarbone, her chest.

And God, she *giggled*. Giggled like a woman already breathless, her hands tangling in his thick hair as he shoved her dress up, baring her inch by inch to the cool air and his hot mouth.

"Garin, " she laughed, squirming under him, "you don't have to rush. We have all morning, if you-"

But then she went still. Because he moved again. Her breath caught as her underwear was slipped down her legs in one smooth, practiced pull, like the man had done it a thousand times. Like he'd been *waiting* to do it again, and then his voice, that voice, dropped like velvet-draped thunder as he growled into her skin.

"This isn't rushing...my little flame" Another kiss lower, his hands gripping her thighs gently, yet firm. "...this is worship."

And before she could say a word more, before her heart could steady, Mira gasped,

Because he pulled her down onto his mouth, with a hunger that shattered breath and thought alike.

She could feel everything too well. Every flick of his tongue, every drag of his mouth against her, every slow, deliberate stroke of his fingers working in tandem with the heat of his mouth. Her back arched against the furs, her breath catching in a gasp that barely escaped before another wave hit her as he added another fingers to his torment against her body.

Garin wasn't gentle, no, not now. He was *thorough*. Devastating in his devotion, methodical in the way he tore her apart, only to build her back up again with the next pass of his tongue.

She gripped the furs, knuckles white, her thighs trembling as his hand held her open, possessive, protective, his.

And he never stopped. Not when she whimpered, not when her hips tried to rise off the bed, and his other hand gripped her and held her steady against his assault. Not even when she gasped his name like a prayer...

"Garin!"

A growl vibrated against her, as if her voice alone stoked the fire in him further. She couldn't see him, but she didn't have to. She felt the way he looked at her, could hear it in the way he groaned like a man tasting heaven.

And then his voice, low and ruined and reverent, broke against her inner thigh:

"I will spend all morning worshipping you like the goddess you are." Another stroke of his tongue. "You'll forget every name but mine." A curl of his fingers inside her, coaxing more broken sounds from her lips. "You'll know you were made for this. For me, only me, my little flame. My song."

Mira shattered like glass under his mouth, her body nothing but sound and sensation and the anchoring grip of his hands. She cried his name again, thighs clenching against his head, and she could feel it...just like before. That sinister smile of his against her thigh as he groaned out:

"Again."

And Garin, her Viking, kept worshipping, mouth returning to her yet again, and her cries faded into the sun that rose outside of that darkly covered window.

～～～～

Elsewhere now, down the quiet corridors of Thorne Manor, where old stone whispered and stained-glass windows glow soft in the breaking light. Where shadows stretched long in the hush of early morning...and where one Frenchman walked with purpose.

His footsteps echoed in perfect rhythm, each step punctuated by the sharp flick of his coat behind him. The manor slept around him...except for *him*. Always him. Restless, tense, and too sharp for peace. He descended the grand staircase with a tension coiled in his jaw, and there, near the front door, stood the wolf.

Rafe, bent at the waist, boots in hand, pulling them on before his patrol. He glanced up as Simon approached, offering that usual, casual drawl:

"Well good mornin' to you too, Frenchie. Can't sleep either?"

Simon didn't smile. He stopped just a few feet away, arms crossed over his chest, dark eyes narrowed like storm clouds sharpening to a point.

"What is your game, *loup*?" he asked softly.

Rafe paused, boot halfway on, brow raising. "...Come again?"

Simon didn't flinch. "You arrive just as the LightBorne stir again, after centuries of silence. Coincidence? Perhaps." He moved closer. "Then, you speak to Garin behind my back. Suggest I am too hard on the twins. That I should *free the leashes* on them. You, who have been here what, months? And now you befriend them, after they nearly tore you apart when you arrived."

He stepped in, almost nose to nose with the wolf, voice low and laced with that cold French bite.

"What is your goal here, *monsieur* Talbot? To drive a wedge into this coven? To play some Moonborn game of conquest and fracture us from within? I will not have it, not in my home."

Rafe straightened to his full height, taller than Simon by inches, jaw ticking now. But he didn't back down. Not an inch.

"Y'know," Rafe drawled, his Southern voice low and steel-edged now, "for someone accusing me of stirring the pot, you sure sound like the one doing all the stirrin'."

Simon's eyes narrowed further.

"You think I ain't seen it?" Rafe continued. "Your mate throwin' tantrums like a high school drama queen. Damn near puttin' hands on guests. Snapping at humans nonstop just for existing. And the second someone doesn't bow to her? You act like *they're* the ones tearing the coven apart."

A flicker of fury crossed Simon's face, but Rafe leaned in before he could speak.

"Maybe you ought ask yourself if the cracks you see in this place didn't start long before I showed up."

Silence. Simon's fingers curled at his side, but he didn't strike. Didn't speak. The tension between them burned, thick as oil. Then Rafe finished slipping on his boots, stood, and tipped his head just slightly.

"I'm goin' on patrol. I'll be back by noon."

And with that, the wolf opened the door and stepped out into the morning mist. Leaving the Frenchman alone in the stillness. To brood, to think, and for the first time in a long while…maybe to doubt. But that silence didn't last long.

"Aye. That was cute."

The voice came from behind him, dry and filled with Irish drawl.

Simon closed his eyes with a slow, exasperated sigh. Of course. He turned, already knowing who it was. Rua O'Sullivan stood in the archway to the main hall, arms folded over his chest, green eyes sharp and narrowed. The ever-unruly curls looked more like fire in the pale morning light, and his expression held no amusement this time.

"Wanna tell me what the point of that was?" Rua asked, one eyebrow cocked up in more of a demand than question.

Simon's voice was clipped. "It's none of your concern."

But Rua didn't move. Didn't back off, instead his gaze stayed locked on his sire, expression hardening.

"Non." Simon added more coldly. "Walk away, *fils*."

Rua did the opposite. He stepped forward, and now they stood face to face. Simon still had a few inches on him, but Rua didn't flinch. Not even a little. That stubborn streak, that fire in his blood, it burned hotter than pride or fear. And Simon, for all his age and command, knew better than to dismiss it.

"Maybe you oughta listen to the wolf," Rua said, voice tight now. "You've been on edge ever since the dhampir attack. Since Beau found his mate. Since all this *shifted*. And you think you're the only one who notices it?"

Simon's jaw ticked, but Rua kept going.

"We all know Evangeline's been a bloody nightmare lately. And not because of Rafe. Not even because of Mira. But because she's losing the game she thinks she owns." He stepped in closer now, green eyes glinting with something darker. "But accusing Rafe of some grand scheme? Of *manipulation*? That's not the scholar I know."

Simon's voice dropped dangerously. "Watch yourself when you speak of her."

But Rua didn't back down. In fact, he *snapped*. "*Why?* Because you mated her?" he growled. "Cian and I were here long before she walked her frozen ass into this manor. And maybe it's about damn time you looked at your own house before throwing stones."

Simon's eyes narrowed. "That does not give you the right-"

"It gives me the right to remind you what this coven used to be before she got her claws in it."

Silence rang like a bell. Rua's chest rose and fell with sharp breaths. And then, softer...but no less pointed continued on.

"Maybe instead of trying to 'save' something that's already cracked, you oughta take a look at your *real* family. The ones still here. Still loyal. Still waiting for you to remember what the hell that used to mean."

Simon's jaw clenched, his expression unreadable. The words landed hard. Simon's breath caught ever so slightly, but his face didn't shift. He didn't strike. Didn't shout. But something in him *fractured*, quietly, and Rua saw it.

He exhaled, softer now. "We love ya, y'know. Even when you make it hard. But don't protect a lie, Simon. Don't lose the whole coven over somethin' that was never real."

Simon opened his mouth to respond. Maybe yell, maybe...apologize, but Rua just turned and walked off without waiting for a response, leaving the Frenchman in a hall full of ghosts. And the echo of truths he didn't want to face.

Chapter 20

Two weeks.

That was all it had been. Two weeks since she'd arrived at the manor, two weeks since the earth beneath his feet shifted. Since the shadows that had once been his only companions began to glow with color, with laughter, with *her*.

She had moved through his world like a soft flame, gentle, warm, but impossible to ignore. Mira hadn't just *settled in* to the coven. She had rooted herself there, like she had always belonged.

On weekdays, she left him in the mornings with a kiss and returned each afternoon wrapped in the voices of others who had come to love her too. Addie Whitmore, who had declared Mira her "new favorite person" within five minutes of meeting her, and Leah, Beau's sharp-tongued, stiletto-heeled mate who had once scowled at him for existing wrong, now smiled like Mira had softened even her. They escorted her to and from the school where she taught music, as if the entire coven had collectively decided Mira was the most precious cargo to exist.

And each time she came back, each time Garin felt her hands find him, her voice whisper his name, he breathed again.

The manor had changed as well. Joy had managed to find its way back in.

Nights were filled with sound now. Rua and Cian dragging her to the sitting room or the music library, challenging her to games of sound and scent, testing her heightened senses, asking her questions about songs she'd loved since childhood. Mira never tired of them. She clapped for their teasing songs, hummed along to old folk melodies, laughed when Rua made wild claims about who had the better voice. Even on their most chaotic of nights, she never once turned them away…and Garin swore, he saw a change in the Irishmen.

Simon, too, seemed steadier with her near. He'd begun reading to her at night, passages about their kind, their histories, philosophies she devoured with awe. Mira would listen, head tilted, and then ask questions that made the Frenchman pause and actually *smile* before launching into a full lecture. Garin watched those moments from the shadows, quiet and still, never interrupting her curiosity.

She was healing something in all of them. But it was the nights just before sunrise that belonged to him, where Mira's soft hands sought him. Nights where her laughter tangled with his deep voice, and where she curled into his chest with a sigh so sweet it soothed the battle-scarred pieces of his soul. Where he fell asleep with one hand in her curls, the other wrapped around her waist. *Their* bed now.

Their space.

And still…Evangeline watched.

He always saw her. Lingering like a phantom in the corners, and each time Garin felt her eyes on them, he met her gaze with the full, quiet weight of his disapproval.

Leave her alone. She is not yours to ruin.

The glint in Evangeline's eyes faded, and she would vanish back into the dark halls like smoke. But danger stirred outside those walls, too.

Rafe had picked up a scent…magicked weapons, likely LightBorne-forged. Enough of a trail to warrant tighter patrols. Deliveries were cut to once a week. No guests. No outsiders. The manor was locked down once more, its residents alert beneath their surface routines.

And yet tonight…

In the low-lit grand salon, where the fireplaces cracked and flickered against ancient stone walls, Garin stood silent, watching something he had never seen before.

Joy.

Real, raucous, *ridiculous* joy. Mave, usually so guarded, stood with her back straight, chin lifted as she played a hauntingly beautiful Irish folk tune on her violin. Her eyes were half-lidded, but her fingers danced like fire on the strings. And in front of her?

Rua and Cian were spinning like lunatics. Shouting verses in Irish, harmonizing wildly, dancing in a way that could hardly be called graceful, but was *infectious*. Cian's voice cracked mid-verse from laughing too hard, and Rafe, seated on the stone ledge of the hearth, caught the empty beer Rua tossed and threw a fresh one back across the room.

Mira sat between them all. Laughing, her hands clapping to the beat, her smile wide and open as her hair tumbled free from its clip. She didn't see the chaos, oh but she *felt* it. She *lived* in it, and she was *loved* in it.

Garin's heart…beat, maybe. Just once, hard. *Like a war drum.* He watched her laugh again. Watched as her hands reached out and caught Cian's arm mid-spin, and he twirled her with mock drama before falling to his knees in a bow that earned another ripple of laughter from everyone in the room.

And that was when the Viking made his decision. *Tonight*, as the sun fled and the moon rose, he would ask her to stay. Not just for the next weekend. Not just for another week, or until the threat was gone. But **for good**.

Because the warrior had known many homes, and lost them all. But this one, the one curled in soft laughter and sweet music and Mira's clapping hands?

This one, he would fight to keep, and this one, he would ask to build…with her. An eternity…with his little flame.

The moment settled like stone in his chest. A choice no longer brewing... But *forged*. She would stay. Not because he demanded it, but because she *belonged*. Here. With him, and the longer he waited... The more he risked her not knowing just how fiercely he intended to keep her.

So the Viking moved.

He waited with his usual patience, standing like a mountain in the back of the room as Mave's bow finally slowed, her final note trembling through the warm air like the echo of a heartbeat. The moment it did, Garin stepped forward. Not rushed. Not hesitant. But steady. His entire purpose now stripped down to one thing.

Get his woman.

Mira sat just ahead, still breathless from laughter. Her face was flushed, curls falling wildly around her face, cheeks flushed pink. Her lips moved quickly as she chattered between breaths, the sound of her joy like a sacred hymn that pulled him closer with every step. Her green eyes, clouded by blindness but sparkling with life, turned instinctively toward the sound of his approach, and before he could even speak, her hand found his. Like it always did, like it *knew* him.

She leaned instinctively into his side, her body fitting beneath his arm like it had been made for the space.

"God above," she panted playfully, resting her head briefly against his chest, "I don't know what kind of supernatural stamina those twins have, but I've wrangled thirty sixth graders on a sugar high and it was *less chaotic* than Rua and Cian on beer and folk music."

That earned a howl from Rua, who spun on the heel of his boot with an exaggerated bow. "You hear that, Cian? We're more exhausting than hyper children. *Praise from a true warrior.*"

"We've peaked, brother!" Cian grinned, shoving Rua playfully before reaching for another drink.

But Rafe, lounging with boots up and beer in hand, snorted through a crooked grin. "Probably because the two of you *act like middle schoolers*, not grown-ass men."

Without pause, Rua hurled an empty beer bottle at him with perfect aim, Rafe ducked, cackling, and Mira startled at the sound of the glass clattering across the hearth floor.

"Hey, watch it Irish! I'm sittin' here!"

"Oh shut it, ye damn mutt!"

The room *exploded* in laughter again, but Garin didn't laugh. He only looked at her. Her cheeks pink with her joy at the antics of his immortal brethren. The way her nose scrunched when she laughed. The way she tilted her head toward chaos like it was music she could read.

So bright. So *alive*. And yet…so unaware that her happiness had become his anchor. That her presence in his life had stilled every war still howling in his blood. He let her laugh. Let her finish soaking in the chaos. And when her giggles finally faded into soft sighs and that soft smile lingered on her lips, Garin lowered his head and pressed a kiss into her curls, *a vow in touch, not words.*

Then, deep and low against her ear, he murmured, "Come with me, please."

She tilted her head, sensing something in his tone. Her fingers curled tighter into his.

"What is it?" she asked gently, already trusting him enough to follow.

"There's something I want to speak to you about," he said. "In private."

And just like that, her laughter quieted. But her smile never faded. She rose to her feet, fingers sliding fully into his hand.

"Lead the way, my Viking."

With no hesitation and no backward glance, Garin did so, taking her and leading her back towards their room. Because, he would ask, and *no part of him* would let her go.

The door closed softly behind them, sealing out the laughter, the music, the chaos of the manor. The room they shared welcomed them back the way it always did, quiet, dim, heavy with the scent of furs and old wood and *her*. His room no longer felt like a place of solitude. It felt…lived in. Warm. Claimed. Theirs.

He guided Mira to the bed with a hand at her lower back, steady and familiar. She sat easily on the edge of the furs, tugging her cardigan back into place as she tilted her head toward him, that knowing smile already forming.

"You've got that look," she teased lightly. "The brooding one, I can feel it. Should I be worried?"

"No," he said at once, too quickly. He knelt in front of her, large hands settling on her knees, grounding himself as much as her. "Nothing is wrong."

Her smile softened, but she could feel the seriousness in him now. Mira always could. "…Alright," she said gently. "Then what is it?"

Garin didn't circle it. He never had patience for that. He drew in a breath he didn't need.

"I have fallen for you," he said, his voice low, steady, stripped bare of armor. "More deeply than I believed possible. You are the song in my chest, Mira. The one my heart no longer has…and yet somehow still follows. My *hugr*… the part of me I thought long dead… it led me to you."

Her breath caught. He could hear it. Could hear her heart stumble, then race.

"I do not wish to wake another evening without you," he continued, thumbs brushing slow, reverent circles over her knees. "I do not wish to return from patrol and not find you in my arms. I want you here. With me. Always."

Her smile bloomed, wide and trembling, and he felt moisture gather at the edges of those unseeing green eyes. Tears, not of fear, but of feeling.

"Mira, " he said softly, but he wasn't finished. "There is more," he added, and this time there was no mistaking the weight of it.

He lifted one hand, gently cupping her cheek, his thumb brushing beneath her eye as if he could see every freckle she could not see on him.

"I do not only want you to stay," he said. "I want you to *join* me."

She stilled, but Grain continued on, before even he lost his own nerve.

"I want you to stand beside me in eternity," he went on, voice rough now, raw with truth. "As my equal. As my chosen. As one of us." Her lips parted slightly. "As Bloodborn."

The word settled between them, heavy, sacred, terrifying, *honest*. Garin did not rush her. He never would. He stayed where he was, steady and open, his forehead resting briefly against her knee as if bracing himself, not for rejection, but for the gravity of the choice he had just placed in her hands.

"You would never be forced," he said quietly. "Not now. Not ever. I will love you whether you choose this path or not." He lifted his head to face her again. "But I would walk eternity at your side," he finished, simply. "If you would have me."

And then...he waited. He watched it all play across her face. The way her brows knit softly, freckles shifting as her nose twitched in thought. The way her lips parted, then pressed together again as if she were trying to find the *right* words and realizing there might not be any.

"I-I" she stammered, a small breathy laugh escaping her. "I never thought you would ask me that."

"I have thought of little else," he answered gently. He shifted closer, still kneeling, still giving her space even as every part of him wanted to gather her into his chest and never let go.

"These last two weeks," he said quietly, "I have watched you become part of my world as if you were always meant to be here." Her head tilted, listening.

"You settle Simon," he continued. "He is calmer with you. Focused. He remembers why he loves to teach." A faint smile tugged at his mouth. "Leah and Mave flock to you like sisters. Even Larazo listens when you speak. And the twins," he added, voice softening further. "They adore you. You ground them. They listen to you in ways they rarely do anyone else."

His thumb brushed lightly over her knee again. "You belong here, my flame. I know it. And they would welcome you, not because you are mine, but because you are *you*."

She swallowed.

"And I remember," he went on, "those nights at your home. The cocoa that was far too sweet."

Her lips twitched despite herself, a breathless laugh escaping her.

"You spoke of the school. Of how you were unsure if it was still where your heart lay." He inhaled slowly. "If you say yes," he said, "I will help you find what fulfills you. Whatever that looks like. You could continue to teach. Or travel with me, if you wish. See the world in the ways you see best, through sound, touch, memory. You could teach *me*. The twins. Anyone who would listen. Music belongs to you."

His voice lowered, rough with truth.

"I would move the world to make you happy." Then, firm, unwavering, Garin added in, "But if you say no… I will still do so. I will stay with you for as long as this earth allows. I will love you fully, fiercely, without resentment or regret until your last days." He lifted his hand to her cheek again, reverent.

"There is no wrong choice here," he said. "Only *your* choice."

The silence stretches, thin, fragile, sacred. Garin doesn't breathe, though his chest feels like it *should* be rising and falling. He watches the tears trace warm paths down Mira's pale cheeks, watches the way her mouth trembles as she tries to hold herself together.

For the first time in centuries...

He is afraid.

Afraid that he has asked too much, that eternity is a weight no mortal heart should have to carry. Afraid that loving her means letting her go one day.

Then, her head lifts. Those green eyes turn toward him, not wandering, not uncertain, but *fixed*, as if she sees him clearer now than she ever has. Her hands rise, gentle and sure, finding his face by memory alone. Her thumbs brush his beard, her palms warm against his cold skin.

"Yes."

It comes out choked, breathless, trembling, but unwavering.

Garin's world tilts.

"Yes," she repeats, stronger now. "To you. To... to eternity. To *us*."

He makes a sound, a low, broken, almost a sob, and if he still had knees strong enough for pride alone, he would have fallen anyway.

"I'm scared," she admits softly, her forehead resting against his. "I'd be lying if I said I wasn't. But I've thought about it too. About what it would mean to stay. To become one of you." Her fingers tighten in his beard. "I don't want a life where you grow distant while I fade away," she whispers. "I don't want borrowed time. I want *you*."

Then, quieter, braver than anything he has ever faced:

"I love you, Garin."

The words strike him like a blade straight through the chest. Love. Not worship. Not fear. Not fascination.

Love.

Garin gathers her to him in a single, reverent motion, pressing his forehead to hers as his arms wrap around her like a vow made flesh.

"I will honor that choice," he vows, voice thick and raw. "Every night. Every century. I will guard you with my life, my blood, my soul." He kisses her brow, her cheeks, her trembling lips, slow, grounding, worshipful. "You will never face eternity alone," he murmurs. "You will walk it with me."

He can feel her trembling in his arms, her tears soaked his shirt, but he didn't care.

"You are the song in my silence. The fire I thought long cold. You are my hugr, Mira. My soul's echo. I was born of ice and vengeance… but I will spend eternity learning the shape of your love."

And for the first time since snow soaked his blood into a long-dead battlefield, the Viking knows, this is not a curse. This is salvation.

She didn't know how long she stayed in Garin's arms, wrapped so tightly in his warmth and quiet strength that her trembling eventually stilled. The tears that had once streamed from fear and uncertainty now slid down her cheeks for a very different reason. Joy. Joy so sharp it ached.

A laugh slipped from her throat, broken and breathless, muffled against the broad plane of his chest.

"This is so much better than any human proposal," she whispered, voice thick and trembling with wonder.

She felt the deep rumble of his chuckle vibrate through her ribs, and when he pulled back, his calloused fingers were surprisingly gentle as they wiped the tears from her cheeks.

"If you want a ring, Mira," he said, voice low and steady, "I will get you one. Or any other tradition you'd like before you join me. Whatever makes you happy, my light."

She could feel the smile on his face when he said it, pressed so close to hers. And God help her, she knew without a shadow of a doubt he meant every single word. Whatever would make her happy, he would do it. Even if it had nothing to do with Viking rites or immortal rituals. He would learn it. He would give it.

Her hands gripped the collar of his shirt, anchoring herself against the rush of emotion flooding her heart. "When?" she asked, barely more than a breath. "When will we... do it?"

Garin didn't hesitate.

"Tonight, I'll speak to Beau. Get his blessing. I must gain his permission to have you join the coven, but I know he will be overjoyed. We'll plan it after the school year ends, when the children no longer need their teacher for the summer." He leaned down, pressing his forehead to hers. "I want your transition to be peaceful. Unrushed."

Mira nodded against him, chest swelling with emotion so fierce it almost overwhelmed her. But a new question bubbled up, fragile and honest.

"Will it hurt?"

There it was. He could've lied. Told her no. But he never had. Not once.

Garin drew back just enough to meet her gaze fully, his hands cupping her face so she knew where he was at all times in this moment.

"Yes," he said quietly. "It will hurt. But not like it once did. The world is different now, Mira. There are new ways.

Medicines. Remedies. Simon and Mave will help us. And I will do anything, *anything*, to ease it for you. I swear it."

She took that in, and despite the tremble in her lips, her eyes never wavered. And then she smiled. A strong, beautiful, *blinding* smile.

"Then you better get ready," she whispered, fingers curling into his shirt. "Because you just bought yourself forever with me. I hope you like marshmallows."

Garin exhaled like the earth had finally settled beneath him. His arms crushed her to his chest again, and this time she knew, this wasn't a dream. It wasn't a fragile hope whispered into the wind.

It was a vow.

And she'd never felt more alive, than knowing soon, she'd be dying.

Chapter 21

If his heart could still race, it would've thundered like a war drum in his chest.

He had barely torn himself away from Mira, her warmth, her laughter still echoing in his memory, her body and soul still wrapped around his in ways he would never recover from. Her scent lingered on his skin. Her tears, those tears of joy, had dampened his chest when she whispered that no human proposal could ever compare to the vow he'd made.

She said *yes*.

Now came the next part. The ancient rite of respect, of loyalty. He made his way through the halls of Thorne Manor, each step carrying the weight of centuries. He wasn't just asking to turn her, he was asking to bring her into their coven. Into *their family*. That meant facing the Southern Coven King himself.

The wooden door to Beau's study loomed ahead. Garin lifted his hand and gave a single knock.

"Come in," Beau's drawl rang out lazily, laced with charm.

Garin opened the door, stepping into the study, and immediately halted. Beau was reclining in his leather chair, feet propped up on the desk like the picture of relaxed authority... and cradling an old flip phone to his ear.

"Darlin', I *heard* you, y'ain't gotta keep snappin' at me. I'll handle it." Beau was saying, drawl heavier than usual, clearly trying to mollify whoever was on the other end.

From the phone speaker, a sharp Italian accent fired back like a bullet, definitely not in English...and definitely not amused. Garin didn't catch every word, but he heard enough to know the voice belonged to none other than Leah.

Beau winced, side-eying Garin with the guilt of a man caught halfway through a scolding. "Baby, I gotta go. Someone just walked in."

A harsher curse came through the phone.

Beau flinched. "Yes, I know you told me. Yes, I know I didn't listen. No, you don't have to bring up the coffee incident again...*baby please-*"

Another snap, sharper than before.

With a sheepish grin and a sigh of resignation, Beau closed the flip phone with a soft *snap*. "She said I'd better call her back before sunrise or she's gonna make me regret it."

Garin arched a brow. "I assume she will."

"Oh, she will," Beau muttered, dragging a hand down his face before sitting upright. "Alright then, Viking. What's got you down here instead of upstairs with that woman you can't stop hovering around?"

Garin stepped forward, voice steady but low. "I need to speak to you. I have something to ask."

Beau's amusement faded. The Southern King leaned forward, arms on the desk now, expression sharpening. "Go on."

Garin hesitated. Not out of fear. Not ever that. But because Beau Thorne was unpredictable at best, dangerous at worst. No matter how many decades had passed, Garin never took the man lightly, not when it came to matters of the coven. Especially not when it came to eternity.

Beau noticed it instantly. Those sharp dark eyes cut through the stillness, and he let out a breath that was half amusement, half challenge.

"You never ask for a damn thing," Beau said, folding his arms across his chest. "So go ahead, Viking. Let me have it."

The words struck like a match. Garin took one more breath, and stepped into it.

"I've asked Mira to stay with me," he said, voice low but sure. "Not just for the summer. Not just until her mortality runs out."

Beau's gaze narrowed, but he didn't interrupt.

"I've asked her to join me. In eternity." Garin met his leader's eyes without flinching. "I would like your permission to turn her. And to bring her into this coven. As one of us."

Silence. Not even the grandfather clock ticked. It was a dead, ancient kind of quiet that blanketed the room like fog. Neither of them moved. Neither of them showed an ounce of emotion. Two apex predators locked in ritual, waiting to see who would shift first.

Finally, Beau spoke.

"Did you explain to her what this means?" he asked, voice unreadable. "That she won't be able to keep her job at the school? That she can't go back to her family, not ever?"

Garin gave a single nod. "She plans to resign at the end of the school year. She's already made the choice."

"And the family?"

"The relationship with her parents is... strained. Mira sees them once a year at best. She said goodbye in her heart a long time ago."

Beau drummed his fingers once against the desk. Still not giving anything away.

"Alright," he said at last. "Then let me ask you this." His eyes locked on Garin, sharper than blades. "Are *you* ready?"

Garin tilted his head slightly in question, because this he didn't fully understand.

"You've seen fledglings," Beau went on. "You know what it's like. They can be unstable. Loud. Starvin'. Wild. Mira's not like us, son, not yet. Are you ready to see her suffer? To watch her cry out in pain while the turn takes hold and not be able to stop it?"

Garin felt something twist behind his ribs. Not fear or doubt, but a depth of protective instinct he hadn't known he was still capable of.

"I will be responsible," Garin said, voice iron. "I will handle her hunger. Her training. Her care."

Beau raised a brow, but didn't interrupt again.

"I will ask Simon and Mave to assist with the pain. We have medicines now. Rituals. I will do whatever I must...*whatever it takes*...to keep her safe."

Beau leaned back in his chair. Studying him now. Weighing not just the words, but the man beneath them. He was quiet again. That damn silence wrapped around them like smoke, interrupted only by the slow, rhythmic tap of the Southern king's fingers on the polished mahogany of his desk.

After a moment, he stopped tapping. Pointed a finger toward Garin.

"You talk to Simon." His voice was sharp, but not unkind. Just final. "You ain't turned anyone before, Viking. So educate yourself. Learn the full ritual. What needs to be done, what could go wrong. Let the scholar fill in the blanks. Then..."

Beau stood. Walked around the desk with the slow, heavy gait of a man used to others parting for him.

"...you ask Mira again," he said, eyes meeting Garin's without a trace of doubt. "After *both* of you speak with Simon. After she fully understands what the turnin' means. And if she still says yes..."

Beau's mouth twitched, the ghost of a grin.

"Then I'll be proud to welcome her into this coven."

Garin nodded once. A gesture of immense weight. "Thank you," he said, the words gravel in his throat. "For giving me my mate."

Beau's grin spread just enough to flash a hint of fang. "Don't thank me yet."

He stepped forward, until only a breath separated them. Only an inch divided their height, but the weight of history behind both men made them equals now. Not just vampires. Not just warriors.

But mates. And soon, partners to fledglings.

Beau clapped a strong hand on Garin's shoulder. "Let her get through her fledgling phase first," he said, wry amusement lighting his tone. "That's gonna be a whole lot of hell." Then that grin turned wicked. "But congrats, Viking. At least your girl's willin' to be turned." He let out a dry, theatrical sigh. "Leah's stubborn ass is still holding out. Says she wants to *live a little* first."

Garin grunted. A low, amused sound.

Then...

BZZZZT!

The little flip phone on Beau's desk vibrated to life. Beau groaned like a man who already knew what was waiting on the other end. "Used to be me they summoned when someone said 'speak of the devil,'" he muttered, snatching the phone off the desk.

"I WASN'T DONE TALKING TO YOU, BEAU THORNE-"

Leah's furious voice barked through the speaker before Beau could even say hello. Garin turned away with a low rumble of approval, letting his leader handle the fire he had chosen.

Because for Garin?

It was done. He would return to Mira now. Tell her the next steps. Speak to Simon. And prepare the life they would soon begin together. She would join him in eternity. His woman. His light. His *wife*.

Forever.

What he didn't see...

What he *couldn't* have seen...

Was the shadow down the hallway. A figure draped in silk and fury. Blonde hair catching the warm flicker of the sconces as she turned. Red lips twisted in a snarl. Pale eyes burning. She had heard *everything*. And as she slipped back down the corridor like a wraith, fury curling around her spine like a serpent, she began to plot.

Garin might have claimed a future. But she? She still had claws, and she *would* use them.

~~~~~~

Somewhere just outside Thorne Ridge...

The motel was a rotting husk of a place.

Peeling paint. Buzzing overhead lights that never stopped flickering. Cheap brown curtains drawn tight against the early morning light. And just beyond the edge of the parking lot, where the gravel met the woods, two men stood, the air taut with simmering irritation.

Alexander adjusted the cuffs of his sleeves. His clothing was crisp, pressed. Too fine for this place. But everything about Alexander was curated like a blade, always clean, sharp, and made for precise cutting.

Beside him, Jonah paced. The younger man's jacket was scuffed, boots muddy from their last patrol. He rubbed the back of his neck like the silence itched.

"They're hiding something," Jonah muttered, breaking it. "The town. The people. All of it."

Alexander didn't look at him. Just stared across the road, eyes narrowed. "They always are," he said, voice low. "It's how these places work. These...*nests.*"

Jonah stopped pacing. "Scouts couldn't find shit. One of them said he heard a woman talking about a 'town benefactor', some legacy heir from the original founders. Another heard whispers about a 'professor' who volunteers at the clinic and library."

Alexander finally turned. "Names?"

"None confirmed. Locals clammed up the second our scouts pressed them. They either *know* something or..." Jonah shrugged. "They've been glamoured."

Alexander's jaw clenched. He hated this kind of hunt. The ones steeped in charm and subtlety. He preferred monsters who bared their teeth. Who could be put down with silver or fire. But this? This was worse.

"They're nesting," he hissed. "Feeding slowly. Quietly. Like they always do when they want to infect a town from the inside out. They build roots. Influence. *Control.*" His gaze swept over the woods again. "And the moment they find someone worth keeping, they turn them. That's when the town truly becomes theirs."

Jonah looked back toward the motel, unease tightening his shoulders. "You think someone's been chosen already?"

"I think," Alexander said coldly, "that they've already begun."

He reached into his coat, pulling a folded map from the inside pocket. Not digital. Not traceable. Paper marked with symbols and etched lines, warding points they had laid. Places salted. Cross-checks where vampires might be vulnerable.

But still...nothing. No scent of death. No surge of power. Just that...*wrongness.* That sense of something vast and old sleeping just beneath the surface. Alexander tapped the map, marking their next perimeter.

"Send two more scouts tonight. But not into the town this time. I want eyes on the forest. The lake. The old chapel." He paused. "And the library."

Jonah raised a brow. "The professor?"

"If he's educating the medical staff, he's already embedded. And that means he's powerful enough to pass among humans unnoticed." His voice dropped a degree colder. "We find him, then we find the nest."

Jonah nodded once and turned back toward the motel, but Alexander lingered. Watching the trees sway. The wind shift. He hated this quiet, hated the taste of magic in the air that didn't *belong* to them. But most of all?

He hated the thought that they were already too late. But as soon as he turned to follow Jonah…

The wind shifted. Not enough to carry scent, just enough to disturb the quiet.

Alexander felt it first. His spine straightened, every instinct sharpening as his hand drifted toward the weapon hidden beneath his coat. Jonah stiffened beside him a half-second later, boots grinding softly against the gravel.

A voice.

Soft. Feminine. Trembling like it had been rehearsed and feared in equal measure.

"E-excuse me…"

Both men turned. From the edge of the tree line, a petite woman stepped into the spill of the motel's sickly yellow light. She wore a long black skirt and an oversized hoodie pulled low, sleeves hiding her hands. She moved slowly, almost deliberately, like someone approaching predators and fully aware of it.

Alexander's eyes narrowed to slits and Jonah shifted his stance, placing himself half a step back and to the side, ready.

The woman swallowed hard. "Are you... are you the ones asking questions? About the... creatures in town?"

Alexander stepped forward at once, boots crunching loud in the silence. "What do *you* know about that?" he snapped.

The woman flinched. Up close now, the motel light caught her features, which were far too pale. Lips drained of color. Blonde hair striking against the darkness of her clothes. Her eyes were wide, glassy, darting between the two men like a trapped animal's.

"I-I have information," she said quickly, voice shaking harder now. "I heard you were looking. That you're trying to stop them."

He studied her like a specimen. "Why come to us?" he asked coldly. "Why not the police?"

She gave a weak, almost hysterical laugh. "Because the police won't listen, they won't believe me. And because they can't help." Her gaze dropped, then lifted again, glossy with something dangerously close to tears. "There's a group of monsters in Thorne Ridge," she whispered. "Old ones. Powerful ones. And they're hiding in plain sight."

Jonah's jaw tightened. "And how exactly would *you* know that?"

The woman's hands clenched beneath her sleeves.

"Because I live there," she said. "And because I've seen what they can do."

Alexander leaned in, his shadow swallowing her whole. "You'd better be very careful with your next words," he warned. "People lie to us all the time."

Her voice broke, but she didn't back away.

"I-I'm scared," she said. "Not for myself." She hesitated. Just a beat too long. "There's a woman," she continued. "Human. She doesn't belong to them. She doesn't understand what she's been pulled into."

Both men went very still. "What woman?"

The blonde swallowed. "They're planning something," she said. "Something permanent. And if you don't stop them-" Her eyes lifted, locking onto Alexander's with desperate intensity. "They're going to turn her into a monster."

Silence slammed down between them. Alexander straightened slowly, a thin, dangerous smile beginning to curl at the edges of his mouth.

"Now," he said softly, *"that...* is interesting."

Behind him, Jonah felt the air change, felt the hunt finally take shape. And the blonde woman? She stood there trembling in the light, fear and fury twisting together beneath her calm exterior, having just set something catastrophic into motion.

The woman's voice trembled again, faint, almost lost beneath the hum of the sodium lamps above them, but it's enough. Her fingers twisted the hem of her long sleeve. She never quite looked up. That hood shadowed half her face, but Alexander didn't miss the important things: the pale lips, the too-fair skin, the long striking blonde hair. She could've been beautiful once, but fear has hollowed her.

"I heard talk," she whispered, "of a woman. A teacher. Blind. She works with kids, I think. People say she fell for a man no one has ever seen before... and now... she's not the same."

Jonah stiffened beside him, jaw ticking. Alexander didn't speak, no, he stared, eyes like steel, reading her body language like scripture. Lies show in the hands, the eyes. But this woman? She's shaking. Either she's scared out of her mind... or she's telling the truth.

"She still goes to work," the woman adds, "but she's never home at night. They say the man visits her, or maybe... maybe takes her somewhere. I don't know. But then I heard one of them. One of those things. I swear, I heard him say they were going to *turn* her. Make her one of them."

A gust of wind picked up the edge of her skirt, brushing grit across the pavement.

"She doesn't know," she finally said, breath catching. "I don't think she knows what's happening. She thinks he loves her. But it's not love. They don't love. They *feed*, they *change* you. They drain what you need and leave you hollow, haunted by what you used to be." The way she said it...her voice so full of disdain, hatred. Like she had lived through it, experienced herself with that tone full of venom, hissing out that last line.

And that's when Alexander stepped forward, silent and methodical. The way only a hunter does when he thinks he's found the scent.

"Do you know her name?"

The woman flinched again at his approach and backed away half a step, looking down.

"No. I-I only heard bits. Just that she's blind. And she sings sometimes... maybe teaches music. That's all I know."

"Why come to us?"

"Because no one else will. The people here... they *protect* the monsters. Like they're part of the town. But they're not. They're dangerous. And if you're really here to stop them... then please... please help her."

Alexander turned slowly to Jonah, the tension crackling between them like a live wire, exposed to too much too soon.

They finally had their first real lead since coming close to Thorne Ridge. A name isn't needed. A blind teacher who sings? That will narrow it down quickly enough. And now, they aren't just looking for monsters. They're looking to save a woman who might not even realize she needs saving.

Jonah's jaw was clenched, his hand flexing at his side like he wished it held a weapon. "A blind woman," he muttered, voice thick with anger and pity. "A human...*blind*...and they still went after her? Sick bastards."

Alexander's face twisted, but not in shock. No, he looked furious, like something long dormant had been confirmed. "They don't care who they hurt. The softer the target, the easier the manipulation. Seen it too many times before." He looked toward the direction the woman had disappeared into. "We go to the school tomorrow. Find out who on staff's blind. We'll ask questions."

Jonah nodded grimly. "I'll get Abigail on it too. She's good at digging through records without making waves."

But as both men turned, ready to thank the woman, to press her for more...

She was gone.

Vanished.

No footfalls fading, no perfume scent lingering in the night air. Just cold breeze and vacant sidewalk where she'd stood wrapped in her black skirt and hoodie.

Jonah froze. His brows furrowed. "Wait-what the hell?" He stepped forward fast, scanning, calling out, "Miss? Hello? Ma'am?"

Nothing. Only the distant creak of an old sign in the wind and the flutter of dry leaves across the pavement.

"Jonah..." Alexander's tone was flat, like he wasn't even surprised. "She must've bolted. Didn't want to be caught helping us, maybe. Bloodborn are nasty like that, use 'em up and spit 'em out."

Jonah's suspicion only grew, eyes narrowing as he scanned the edges of the street again. "Or she wasn't scared at all."

But Alexander had already turned away, shaking his head. "Come morning, we help that poor blind woman get away from those monsters before they ruin her too."

He said it with conviction, like a man on a mission, disgust so deep in his marrow it refused to let doubt take root.

And behind them... the night held its breath. Because now, The LightBorne would move...believing they were saving an unfortunate disabled woman, from the clutches of bloodthirsty beasts.

Chapter 22

The sun had barely crested the horizon, soft morning light spilling like gold across the stone walls of his room. He should've still been sleeping, should've been wrapped in the comfort of darkness, in the quiet stillness of day rest. But he wasn't. Not when she was beside him. Not when her warmth was nestled beneath the pelts, hair strewn across his chest like the aftermath of a storm.

Mira.

His light. His flame. His soon-to-be immortal mate.

She was curled against him, lips parted in the softest breath, the fall of her chest even and slow beneath the covers. She always slept hard after nights like theirs, nights full of whispered promises, soul-deep laughter, and the kind of touch that made even immortality feel too short. But now, it was morning, and Mira had a job to do. Children to teach. Lives to shape. And he? He had a promise to keep.

No alarm clocks in his chamber. He hated the shrill artificial noise of them. Mira had teased him at first, but agreed in time, especially when Garin offered himself as her personal wake-up service.

And he *loved* waking her, because this was a side to his loving, and sweet mortal that no one else ever got to see.

He leaned in, his beard brushing the curve of her shoulder as he began to place lazy kisses along her bare skin. "Light..." he rumbled, low and warm. "Time to rise."

Mira groaned, tugging the furs up further, burying her face. "Go swing an axe or something," she mumbled, voice thick with sleep and disapproval. "Damn Vikings…waking people up at dawn like it's still 1200 BC."

Garin bit back a laugh, chest shaking beneath her. "You agreed to this, little flame."

"I agreed to *you*, not your Neanderthal sleep schedule," she grumbled again, one delicate hand swatting blindly toward him.

He caught it easily, pressing a kiss to her knuckles. "Neanderthals didn't build ships."

"You probably *punched* trees until a boat fell out," she muttered.

Garin's grin grew. Gods, he loved her like this. Grouchy, grumpy with her sleep and disheveled. Mouthy. Mortal still, for now. But soon…she would be his in every way.

He pressed his forehead gently to her shoulder, his voice a rumble against her skin. "Come now, wife. The children will miss you."

"They won't if you write me a note saying I was kidnapped by my Viking," she sighed dramatically, finally cracking open one eye.

"Tempting," he admitted, hand sweeping over her waist. "But Addie already suspects I'm the reason you're late most days, she does yell at me each time."

"You *are* the reason."

And still, she didn't move. Not yet, and he didn't push. Not yet. Because this? This moment, where she was still soft and warm and real in his bed, with her scent all around him and sleep still clinging to her cheeks?

This was his favorite part of the day, and he'd wake her this way every morning…for the rest of their forever.

Garin's lips dragged over her shoulder again, his fangs tucked away for now, though a part of him always stirred when she was like this, half-awake and tucked into him, full of sass and heat and sleepy complaints. But he focused on her warmth, the way it bled into his chest, her mortal heartbeat steady against his ribs like a war drum he never wanted to silence.

He nuzzled behind her ear, his voice like thunder smoothed by affection. "Leah's takin' you to work this morning."

A soft groan vibrated in her throat, and she rolled into him, pressing her face right into the coarse hair on his chest like it was her own personal pillow. Her hand slid over his ribs and curled possessively, and Garin…Gods help him, shut his eyes for a moment just to feel it.

"And don't forget your cane this time," he added, barely hiding the smile tugging at his mouth.

That earned him a low, exasperated groan.

"I forget it *one time,* and you *never* let it go."

Garin huffed a laugh and kissed the crown of her head. "You walked into a *bike rack,* Mira. You nearly flattened it according to Addie."

"It shouldn't have been there."

"It was *bolted* to the sidewalk."

"Still shouldn't have been there," she mumbled stubbornly, her voice muffled against him as she continued to nuzzle. "It's a hostile obstacle."

Garin's broad chest rumbled beneath her ear, his arms locking tight around her now, one hand sweeping slow over her bare back.

"You're a menace in the mornings," he murmured, pressing another kiss to her temple. "But you're *my* menace."

She sighed, content now despite the inevitable crawl of the day ahead. And Garin just held her there, her softness melting into the unyielding wall of his body, her scent steeped into every inch of the bed, and her heartbeat, the last mortal echo he'd ever get from her, thudding gently against his chest.

He'd let her sleep just a minute more. Just one. But the cane was *not* negotiable.

After another few minutes, Mira finally lifted her head from the warm cradle of his chest, red curls a wild mess, her lashes still heavy with sleep. Her green eyes, the ones he loved so dearly, still managed to narrow in his direction with lethal intent, as if sheer willpower could glare him into submission.

Garin didn't flinch. He never did. But he knew that look. He *felt* it.

"You," she muttered, voice still rough with sleep, "are *not* allowed to be all sweet in the mornings. It's cheating."

The corner of Garin's mouth curled in silent amusement, the low rumble of his laugh vibrating through her hands as they pressed to his chest. His fingers moved gently, brushing those chaotic red curls from her face with reverence that should have belonged to a god worshipping his flame.

"I will be sweet as I damn well please," he said softly, leaning down to kiss her forehead, then the bridge of her nose. "You've only so many sunrises left, *goddess,* and I intend to enjoy every single one."

He watched her, watched how the words hit her. How they stirred something deep in that tender heart she tried so hard to guard. Emotion flickered across her face like sunlight behind storm clouds, soft, flickering, real. And then she groaned dramatically, flopping back into his chest like she was defeated in battle, her arm draped across his ribs as if that alone might chain him there.

"Fine," she muttered into his skin. "You win. You can be sweet. And I'll get up."

He smirked, not moving yet, not letting her go. But inside? He already had. Let her go win the day. Because come nightfall, she'd come back to him, back to his arms, and the beginning of their chaotic routine each evening. Soon though, one day soon, there'd be no more sunrises left.

Only eternity.

Finally, half an hour later, they managed to emerge from the den of furs of his room, and made their way out, together.

Garin's heavy boots made soft thuds on the wood as he descended the staircase, Mira tucked against his side, her hand looped through the crook of his bicep with casual trust that still made something shift in his chest. She matched his steps perfectly, coffee mug in one hand, the other absently stroking the fabric of his shirt where it clung to his arm.

"...they're all so excited," she was saying with a sleepy smile, voice light as sunlight through curtains now that she had been properly caffeinated. "We've got the spring recital in a few weeks, and if little Melody sings 'Somewhere Over the Rainbow' one more time in rehearsal I might *actually* cry."

Garin's lips twitched. "You'll cry anyway."

She elbowed him gently. "Maybe. But this time it'll be because it's my last recital. I'm going all out for them! Ribbons. Spotlights. Maybe even glitter if Roberta doesn't have a heart attack."

He made a low noise of agreement as they reached the bottom of the steps, his hand steady on her back. "Roberta will survive. And they'll find someone to take your place."

Mira sighed, sipping her coffee. "She was pretty upset when I told her I wouldn't renew my contract. But...someone else will come in. They always do."

Garin turned his head slightly, letting his voice drop just enough that she'd feel it rumble through her bones.

"No one will ever be as good as you."

Her steps faltered slightly, just a hitch, and when he glanced down, the blush on her cheeks nearly matched the vivid red of her curls.

"But," he added, softer now, "I can't wait to introduce you to the music of forever."

That earned him a stunned silence. The kind that filled the air like held breath. Right up until the sharp *click* of stilettos on marble and a theatrical sigh cut through it all like a courtroom objection.

Leah Ricci stood by the front door, arms crossed, dark lipstick and long brown hair pulled into a bun, flawless despite the early hour, and her pointed-toe heels tapping against the floor like the countdown to a trial. All 4'11 of the fiery Italian woman was still, watching them with a mix of impatience, and fond amusement.

"Oh my god," she said dryly, tossing her long dark waves over one shoulder. "Can you two *not* be adorable for five minutes? Some of us have court this morning, and I refuse to be late because the Viking got *sentimental*."

Mira bit back a laugh, pressing her face into Garin's arm with a muffled giggle. Garin, however, just grunted, nonplussed, unmoving.

"You're early," he said plainly.

Leah smirked. "You're slow. Move it, Furball, let the lady get to work on time for once."

But there was no real venom in it, just the usual thorn-laced banter. Garin stepped aside, placing a kiss to Mira's temple before she slid toward Leah, already teasing the lawyer about her signature heels and how she swore they had to be enchanted for her to survive in all day long.

Garin watched them walk out the door, Mira's curls bouncing as she laughed, her warmth trailing behind her like a soft flame. And when the door finally shut? He stood still for just a breath longer...

Until the first scent of something wrong drifted in. Faint, and slightly familiar. But dark. The peace wouldn't last. It never did.

~~~~~~~

The school hallway buzzed with its usual end-of-day rhythm, distant slams of lockers, shoes squeaking on linoleum, the faint echo of laughter trailing from the gymnasium. Mira kept pace beside Roberta, her cane sweeping rhythmically in front of her, coffee long since traded for a water bottle tucked under her arm.

Roberta was mid-rant. Again.

"Okay, hear me out," she said, with the manic energy only an overworked vice principal possessed. "What if-just *what if*-I give you a *ten percent* raise, a new digital Braille display system *and* I throw in that antique Steinway I've been hoarding in the band room since '07? Huh? Tempted?"

Mira laughed, head tipping back as her curls bounced with the movement. "Tempting? Roberta, that's practically obscene bribery."

"It *is* obscene, to my budget," Roberta huffed. "But you're worth it, and I'm desperate."

Mira shook her head, grinning as they walked. "I've made up my mind. I love it here, I really do, but it's time. I want to do something new. Something exciting…and something that's just for me."

The principal let out a long sigh that sounded dramatic even by her standards. "Whoever this boyfriend is, he better make *damn* good on whatever fairy tale he's selling you."

Mira flushed, warmth blooming in her cheeks like it always did when anyone brought him up. "Oh, he will. He always does. And I *will* send you postcards."

"You better, or I'm hunting you down."

They reached the front entrance, the afternoon sun bleeding through the glass, warm even on Mira's skin. Roberta's hand found her arm, squeezing gently, affection and farewell tangled together in the gesture.

"I'm going to miss you," Roberta said softly. "You've been the heart of this place. But...I'm happy for you. Really. It's like you finally found the thing you were missing."

Mira's throat caught for a moment, but she smiled. "I think I did."

"And just so you know, end-of-year farewell party is *mandatory*. No sneaking out early. And I expect to meet this mystery man of yours, even if he's some secret service spy or whatever."

Mira chuckled, but there was a flicker of awkwardness beneath it. "I'll be there. *He* might not. Crowds aren't really his thing."

Roberta rolled her eyes and groaned. "Fine. But if you ghost me? I *will* come find you and drag your glittering well sexed ass back here by the ponytail, do you understand me?"

"Crystal clear," Mira said, laughing now, heart light as they stepped outside into the golden hour glow.

But in that golden hour... A wind shifted. Soft. Sudden, and somewhere behind her as she heard the sound of Roberta's heels retreat away... A shadow...moved.

"Miss Mira Cassidy?"

The voice cut through the air like a wrong note.

Mira slowed, turning her head slightly toward the sound. Male. Older. Rough around the edges, like it had been dragged across gravel and never healed right.

"Yes?" she answered carefully. "That's me. How can I help you?"

There was a pause. Too long.

"Have you been hurt?"

Her brows pulled together. Instinctively, her fingers lifted to her sunglasses, nudging them higher on her nose as if grounding herself. "No," she said, confused now. "Why would I be hurt?"

"I know," the man said, voice tightening. There was something restrained in it, an anger barely leashed. "I know you've been lied to. But we won't let anything happen to you."

Cold slid down her spine. Mira shifted her weight, angling herself toward where she knew the sidewalk sloped toward the parking lot. Toward freedom. Toward familiar sounds. "I don't know what you're talking about," she said, keeping her voice even. "I need to leave. Someone's waiting for me."

Another voice joined in, female this time. Too calm. Too rehearsed. "You don't have to worry. They won't be able to hurt you anymore."

Her heart kicked hard against her ribs. "I think you've got the wrong person," Mira said quickly, already moving, cane tapping faster now. "Please-"

The man spoke again, closer now, far too close. "We're here to help you. You don't need to be scared."

Hands closed around her arms. Hard. Unyielding.

"Hey-no-let go of me!" she shouted, swinging her cane wildly, the hollow crack of it striking something solid once, then twice, before it was wrenched from her grip and tossed aside.

Her feet left the ground. Panic surged, white-hot and blinding. "Help! Someone, please!"

Something pressed against her mouth. Cloth, dipped in something chemical. Bitter and wrong. She thrashed, bit down, tried to scream, but the world tilted, her limbs suddenly heavy, uncooperative. Voices blurred together as she was shoved forward, the scrape of metal beneath her, a door slamming shut.

"Get her in," the man barked. "Now."

The engine roared. Tires screamed against pavement. Mira's vision, what little she perceived, just the shadows and sense of light, collapsed inward, darkness swallowing the edges first. Her thoughts scattered, slipping through her grasp like sand.

And in that final, fading moment, with fear clawing at her chest and the echo of his warmth still lingering in her bones...

She whispered his name.

"Garin..."

Then everything went empty, and her cane, left on the sidewalk as the only true witness to what occurred.

Chapter 23

The argument hits his ears before the steps do. Voices, sharp and low, clipped like blades striking stone.

Garin was already moving before he consciously registered them, boots carrying him down the steps into the foyer on instinct alone. The scent in the air was wrong, filled with stress, fear, anger. Leah's heels clicked sharply against marble. Beau's voice was restrained, Southern calm pulled too tight over something volatile.

"I told you," Leah hissed. "You don't get to decide that on your own, not about this."

"And I told *you*," Beau shot back quietly, "let me handle it."

Garin stepped fully into the light, and both of them went still. The silence that followed was heavy, pregnant with something unspoken. Garin's eyes flicked between them once…twice…

Then dropped. There, Leah's hand was clenched around something pale and familiar. Folded, and bent slightly at the grip. One end scuffed, scraped raw in a way it hadn't been that morning.

Mira's cane.

The world narrowed. His vision tunneled until there was nothing but that object in her hand.

"Where," Garin said, his voice frighteningly calm, "is Mira."

Leah's mouth opened instantly. Her chest rose with a sharp inhale.

Beau snapped, "Leah-"

"Don't," Garin warned softly.

Beau stepped forward, palms raised just a fraction. "Viking, listen. We don't know for sure-"

The word *know* never finished landing. That is the last mistake Beau Thorne ever makes with him. Garin moved. Not like a man, but like a force of nature. One moment Beau is standing, the next, Garin has him by the throat, slamming him into the stone pillar by the front door with such violence the entire manor shudders. Dust rains from the ceiling. A picture frame crashes to the floor.

Beau doesn't even have time to snarl before Garin's forearm pins him there, stone cracking beneath the pressure. A growl rips from Garin's chest, low, feral, ancient enough to make the walls themselves recoil.

"**WHERE**," he roars, fangs fully bared now, eyes blazing, "**IS. MY. MATE.**"

Leah freezes. Not in fear, but in recognition and she makes no move to stop him or plead now. Because this isn't posturing. This isn't rage. This is a Bloodborn who has lost his anchor.

Beau doesn't fight him. Doesn't even try.

He knows better.

Instead, his hands lift slowly, palms out, not in surrender, but truth.

"Garin," Beau says, voice steady but grave now, "listen to me."

His grip tightens. Stone groans as he shovs Beau harder into the pillar, so much so that it threatens to snap from the pressure.

"If you do not speak," Garin snarls, "I will tear this town apart stone by stone until I find her."

"Leah," Beau said tightly, eyes never leaving Garin's. "Tell him."

Leah swallowed hard. "We found the cane," she said quickly, voice shaking now. "Near the school. Parking lot. Snapped strap. Scuff marks. No blood, but signs of a struggle."

Garin's grip tightened involuntarily.

"And," Leah continued, forcing the words out, "Sheriff Schaffer just called. There were reports. Two men and a woman matching outsiders' descriptions seen near the campus. Witnesses thought it was some kind of...intervention after they caught some of the conversation. Bobby is trying to get the footage pulled from the school now."

Intervention.

The word detonated in Garin's skull. The LightBorne. His breath went still. Slowly, *slowly*, he released Beau, stepping back as the Southern king dropped to his feet, coughing once, hand braced on the pillar. The foyer was deathly quiet now. Garin stood rigid in the center of it, fists clenched so tightly the leather of his gloves creaked.

"They took her," he snarled, not a question. A verdict.

Beau straightened, jaw set hard. "Yes."

Leah stepped closer, holding the cane out to him with shaking hands. "They left it behind. Like a message. They wanted you to know they took her."

Garin took it. The moment his fingers closed around the familiar curve, something inside him fractured. Mira's laughter echoed in his mind. Her teasing. Her warmth curled against his chest. Her voice whispering his name as she fell asleep.

And the idea of her fear...*calling for him*...

The manor lights flickered. Somewhere deeper in the house, glass shattered. When Garin lifted his head, his eyes were no longer merely blue. They burned now, glowing like icy flames trapped inside.

"I want everyone down here, now." he said, voice iron-clad. "Rafe, the twins, *now*. Simon pulls every contact he has in this state to get that footage. I want to now who took my Mira."

Beau nodded once. "Already moving, son. But you need to let them work, you can't go around breaking down every door in the town."

Garin turned toward the doors. Leah reached for him. "Garin-"

He didn't stop walking.

"If they touched her," he said, each word measured, lethal, "I will end them."

The Viking of Thorne Manor did not rage blindly. No. He hunted, and the LightBorne had just declared war.

"If a single drop of her blood spills," he says, voice shaking the air itself, "I will end them. Every last LightBorne breathing will drown in their own blood until I am satisfied they have paid for every drop of hers."

Garin was not a man now. Not a lover. He was the Viking, a monster unleashed not by hunger, but by **love**. And his had been taken.

Beau didn't waste another second.

"Twins! Rafe! Asses here, now!" His voice cracked like a whip through the foyer.

The response was immediate, boots on stone, bodies converging. The twins came in first, Rua already smirking, Cian loose-limbed and cocky as always, Rafe right behind them, posture alert but relaxed.

That relaxed air died the moment they *saw* it. The cracked pillar. Stone dust still clinging to Beau's coat. Leah standing rigid, one hand pressed flat to her thigh like she was holding herself together by force alone.

And Garin. Still as a statue. Still as a grave marker.

Cian's grin vanished. "...what happened?" he asked quietly.

Beau didn't soften it. Didn't ease them in.

"Mira's been taken."

The words landed like a gunshot.

Rua's head snapped up. "What."

"LightBorne," Beau continued, already moving, already commanding. "Daylight abduction. Outside the middle school. We don't know how they learned about her yet, but they did. And they acted fast."

Cian swore under his breath, raw, vicious. "Those fuckers!"

"As soon as the sun sets," Beau went on, sharp and precise, "Rafe and Rua go to the school. Pick up the trail. I want *everything*, footprints, tire marks, residue, wards, whatever they left behind. You two sniff out those sons of bitches."

Rafe nodded once, all humor gone. "I'll find it."

Beau turned to Cian. "You're with Simon. I don't care if the school has cameras, backups, or some janitor's dusty laptop from 2009, you get the footage."

Cian's jaw set. "I'll peel the building apart if I have to."

"Good. Glamour whoever you need. Principals. Custodians. IT staff. I want faces, I want names. I'll deal with the after effects myself if I have to."

Beau pivoted then, slowly, back toward Garin. "We will find her," he said, voice steady, meant to anchor. "We've brought people back from worse."

Garin didn't answer. He was already moving. His eyes locked on Rua and Rafe.

"I'm coming."

Rafe hesitated, just for a breath. "Garin–"

"If there is a trail," Garin said, voice low and absolute, "I will follow it."

Rua glanced at Beau. "That wasn't a suggestion."

Beau studied Garin for a long moment. The Viking didn't look frantic. He looked *focused*. The kind of focus that leveled villages.

Finally, Beau nodded. "Fine. You go. But you follow *Rafe's* lead until contact is made. We can't risk exposin' more of us and give those bastards a reason to bring in more."

Garin gave a single, sharp nod.

Leah stepped forward then, her voice tight but fierce. "Bring her home."

Garin didn't look at her, but his fingers tightened around Mira's cane where it still rested in his hand.

"I will," he said.

Rua rolled his shoulders, expression turning feral. "LightBorne picked the wrong woman."

Cian's smile was gone now, replaced with something cold and vicious. "And the wrong Viking."

As the orders scattered the coven into motion, Garin turned toward the doors, already halfway gone in his mind, already tracking, already hunting. They had taken his peace. They had taken his little flame. And the world was about to remember what happened when Vikings went to war.

The motel squatted at the edge of Thorne Ridge like something that should've been condemned decades ago, paint peeling in sickly sheets, a flickering neon **VACANCY** sign buzzing like an insect on its last legs. The air smelled of damp carpet, old smoke, and rot. Even the floor creaked in protest as dusk settled over the Georgia mountains.

Mira fought.

She didn't stop moving even as the drug dragged at her limbs, even as the room tilted and her head swam. Hands hauled her across the room, rough fingers biting into her arms, and panic sharpened her instincts like nothing else ever had.

She kicked her foot out, trying to connect with anything.

Missed.

Swung again, this time connected with a shin. Someone cursed but whoever held her, tightened his grip. When they won't let go, when fear spiked hot and bright in her chest, she twisted her body hard and *bit*.

Her teeth sink deep into flesh, and she swore she tasted the hint of blood when she did.

A man yelped, high, startled, and his grip finally broke. Mira dropped, the impact knocking a breath from her lungs as she hit the carpet with a soft, pained groan. The fibers scratched her palms as she scrambled, still dizzy, still heavy, but alive and *angry*. She crawled quickly, fingers sweeping desperately for anything, a lamp cord, chair leg, broken glass, *anything* she can use to defend herself.

Boots shuffled around her, a door slammed and then, that voice spoke again. That older, rough, barely restrained tone from back at the school.

"You don't need to do this," the man mumbled, breath controlled, like he's calming a spooked animal. "You're safe here."

Mira froze, not because she believed him, but because her body needed the pause. Her heart hammered like drums in her ears. Her head lifted, chin trembling, trying to place where the sound came from.

"Don't lie to me," she spat, voice hoarse. "You drugged me. You dragged me. You *kidnapped* me."

A chair scraped softly. "I saved you," the man corrected. "From monsters."

Her laugh is sharp and broken. "You *are* monsters."

Silence.

Then footsteps, measured this time, not rushing. She felt the air shift as someone crouched a short distance in front of her.

"You've been deceived," he said, humor thick in his rough tone now. "Blood-drinkers are very good at that. They make you feel safe. Wanted. Loved."

Her hands curl into fists. "You don't know him," she snarled. "You don't know *anything*."

A sigh, heavy, almost disappointed. "We know exactly what he is," the man relied. "And what he was planning to do to you."

Mira's stomach dropped.

"Turn you," he continued. "Strip you of your humanity. Trap you in a cursed existence you didn't ask for."

Her breath stuttered, but her voice doesn't waver.

"I *did* ask," she snapped fiercely. "And you don't get to decide what ruins me."

There's movement behind her, some fabric shifting, someone circling. A softer voice now, female, tense. "She's more stubborn than the report said."

Mira lifted her chin higher, even as the room spins.

"You will not touch him," she said back, because she knew. She knew what was coming. "And you will not touch me again."

The man in front of her chuckled, cold, humorless. "Oh, Miss Cassidy," he murmurs. "You're already in it far deeper than you realize."

"Who are you?" Mira snapped, voice sharp despite the fog still clinging to her limbs. "Take me back. **Now.** Before this ends badly for every one of you."

Footsteps shuffled closer. Too close. She heard fabric move, felt a presence lean in, and then fingers brushed her hair, tucking a loose curl behind her ear as if the gesture is gentle. Familiar. Mira recoiled violently, shuffling back to put distance between them.

"**Don't touch me.**" Her voice cracked like a whip, raw and furious.

The air shifted, and the softness drained from the room.

"My name," the man said at last, voice hardening into something iron-cold, "is Alexander Weber. And I lead this sector of our organization. We are-."

Her laugh is bitter, breathless, cutting him off before he can spin any sort of lie. "You're not a sector. You're not heroes. I know what you are."

That earned a sound from him, sharp, humorless, and she knew that he was beginning to lose whatever mask he wore for her sake. "You know nothing."

"You're the monsters," Mira fired back. "You hunt people. You kill innocents and call it justice."

That's when it snapped.

Alexander's hand shot out and clamped around her face, tight, fingers biting into her jaw, forcing her head up. Not brutal, but controlled. Deliberate. The kind of grip meant to remind her who held the power.

His voice dropped, venomous. "We **save** people from those things."

Mira gasped, hands scrabbling at his wrist, fury blazing hotter than fear.

"We've buried wives. Children. Brothers," he continued, breath hot with rage now closer to her cheeks. "We've watched blood-drinkers tear families apart and call it love. So don't you dare-"

"Let go of me!" she snarled, twisting against him.

"-stand there and preach ignorance," he snapped back. "Just because you're blind doesn't mean you get to be *naïve*."

Her chest heaved, then she stilled, and when she spoke again, her voice was quiet this time, steady in a way that cut deeper than shouting ever could.

"Even blind," She hissed, teeth clenched, "I can see the truth."

Alexander faltered, just a fraction, and she could feel the hesitation in him now.

"You're afraid of him," she went on. "Of what you can't control. Of what you *can't* break." She yanked her face free from his grip, breath shaking but unbowed.

"And when my Viking finds me," she said now, voice low and lethal, "you'll finally understand what a real beast looks like."

Silence crashed down around them, and a soft grin split her face, because she knew Garin would find her, he would never let them take her. She knew...her Viking was on the move.

"The best part? He wont even say a word while he does it."

The door locked with a solid *click* after her warning, and somewhere, far away, through stone, forest, blood, and bond...

A Viking felt his world tear open.

~~~~~~~

The wooden floors groaned beneath Garin's weight as he descended the stairs, a war god reborn in the modern age. The gleam of steel clung to him like a second skin, twin blades strapped across his back, curved daggers on his hips, the fine leather harnesses wrapping over his thick frame like bindings for some long-awaited ritual.

And then there was the axe. Not just any axe.

His.

The one forged in a land that no longer bears its old name. The one that tasted shield and bone and war beneath a northern sky long before this manor ever stood. He ran his thumb along the haft once, reverent, then lifts it easily, muscle and memory answering without hesitation. Old as the grave. Etched with runes Mira could never see but had once run her fingers over like braille. The weapon was silent now, but in his grip... it felt alive again.

For centuries, Garin had refused to lift arms against mortals. He had walked away from battles, wars, and even threats when it came from the realm of men.

But this? This wasn't a man's doing. This was a mistake of fate, and Garin would make the world regret it.

Tonight breaks that vow.

At the base of the stairs, two figures waited. Rua, with that fire-red hair tied back for battle, had a small blade at his hip and a silver-braided blade across his back. The Irishman's knuckles were bloodless where they gripped the hilt.

Rafe, standing tall and quiet beside him, didn't smile. The Texan wolf wore black and ash-grey sweats, easy to remove and replace, a reminder that this wasn't a rescue. This was a reckoning. He had already shifted once to get her scent, and he'd found it.

"Are you ready?" Rafe asked, voice low, almost reverent. "If we do this, we gonna do this right. Start at the school, then I'll take us from there."

Garin didn't answer right away. His gaze shifted past the front doors, toward the horizon. The sun had finally disappeared, swallowed by the snow-laced Georgia mountains. Dusk gave way to full night.

And in that darkness, something primal stirred.

His fingers curled tighter around the axe handle as he growled low, voice scraped from the bottom of his soul.

"Lead me to my hugr," he said. "And I will tear apart every man who dared lay a hand on my wife."

Rua bared his fangs in savage agreement, and Rafe turned toward the door, eyes glowing faintly as the hunt ignited. The manor opened its jaws behind them, and somewhere in the dark, the men who took Mira Cassidy are about to learn what it meant to awaken something ancient, devoted, and utterly without mercy.

Chapter 24

They arrived just after dusk. The school loomed like a dead thing beneath the failing light, snow curling around its edges and blanketing the rusted playground with eerie stillness. The security lights above the side door flickered, casting long shadows that stretched toward the trio of hunters standing in the dark.

Garin stepped out of the SUV first, boots crunching over packed ice. He didn't speak. His axe remained sheathed for now, but the weight of it on his back was a promise. Behind him, Rua's long coat snapped in the wind as he exited next. His eyes flicked over the school grounds with sharp, deliberate disdain, red hair burning like a beacon in the snow.

Rafe crouched low near the side door. His nostrils flared, and hands grazed the ground, then the wall, then the ground where the discarded cane had been found abandoned in the frost.

"She dropped it here," he muttered, fingers brushing the snow-dusted concrete. "Right by the side entrance."

Garin's jaw clenched.

"Can you smell her?"

Rafe let out a slow breath, still crouched. "Barely. Lotta scent noise, some kids, staff, something sweet, maybe cafeteria crap. Hard to isolate her at first, but…" He trailed off, then reached into his coat pocket, pulling out one of Mira's scarves. "Leah had this in the car. Used it to hone in."

Rua, lounging against the wall now, rolled his eyes. "Real useful, mutt. How many playgrounds you gotta sniff to find a trail?"

Rafe didn't even look up, just flipped him off with one gloved finger. "You wanna smell around next time, Red, be my guest."

But Rua didn't smile. Not now. Because Rafe's head lifted sharply, his entire frame tensing.

"I got it." His voice dropped. "She didn't go to the parking lot. Her scent veers hard, over that fence, toward the back street." He pointed down the alley beside the gym. "Whoever took her, they didn't use the front. They came prepared."

He stood, brushing snow from his knees. "The trail ends at the road. Vehicle picked her up, it was fast. No struggle scent. No blood."

Silence fell like snowfall, and then Garin turned. His eyes, cold and merciless, locked onto Rua.

"Your turn." His voice was gravel and ice. "Rafe tracked her scent. Now you track what he can't. Their steps. Their blood. Find the trail they left for you."

Rua straightened. No more sarcasm now. No more fire.

Just fury.

"Aye," Rua said, eyes darkening as his hand fell to the silver hilt across his back. "Let's find the bastards."

Rua went quiet. Not his usual mouthy kind of quiet, no, this was the kind that came just before someone got torn apart.

The redhead stepped toward the edge of the curb, where snow had crusted into sheets of white and gray. His boots broke through the frost with slow precision, and Garin saw it. The shift. The change. That flicker behind Rua's green eyes that told him the blood was waking. That whatever human part of the Irishman still lingered was pulling back, making room for the thing that had learned to stalk prey through darkness, centuries ago.

Rua's irises gleamed now. Not with light, but with memory. With something that had once been hunted…and had chosen never to be prey again.

Garin stood still, his fists flexing at his sides. He didn't speak. Didn't move. Just watched as Rua tilted his head, sniffed once, not like Rafe did, but deeper. Hungrier. Like he was *feeling* for a thread left in the marrow of the earth.

He didn't need to ask Rua if he found it, because Garin could feel it. Something shifted in the air around them, subtle but sharp, like the crack of lightning before a storm split the sky. Rua's frame went rigid, his cocky posture gone. His eyes, once calm, now glowed like forest fire under moonlight, pulsing with unnatural light.

He stood near the patch of curb Rafe had pointed out, breathing deep again, but not like a wolf. No. This was something older. Rua didn't sniff the air, he *felt* it. The blood, the panic, the echo of fleeing hearts and hurried hands that had dared lay hold of *his* woman.

Garin didn't blink, didn't interrupt. He watched. Rua's hand hovered over the air, fingertips twitching as if pulling at invisible threads. And then…

A low growl escaped the redhead's throat. Not like Rafe's wild snarls, but something tighter. Controlled. The sound of rage wrapped in magic. His boots moved. Fast. Back to the SUV without a word.

Garin turned on instinct and followed, already knowing what was coming.

"Get your shaggy ass in the driver's seat, Wolf," Rua barked, flinging open the back door. "Now."

Rafe didn't argue. He saw it too, that Rua wasn't joking anymore. The flame had been lit, and it wasn't going out.

"You got it?" Rafe asked as he slid behind the wheel.

Rua slammed the door behind him. "Aye. I got it. They were messy. Sloppy." His voice was low and lethal, soaked in that thick Irish snarl now. "Their blood was screamin', hearts poundin' like drums. They didn't plan this proper. It was desperation. Maybe hunger. Maybe fear. But they took her, and they left a trail clear enough even *Beau's lazy ass* could've followed."

Garin's fists clenched as the SUV peeled out.

They should've been afraid.

Rua's eyes locked on the road ahead like a predator, glowing brighter as they gained speed.

"I can still feel it, Viking," Rua said without looking at him. "How her pulse jumped. How they rushed her. How she fought." His jaw ticked. "She didn't go easy, that's your girl."

Garin's voice, when it came, was low and cold enough to frost the windows.

"Good." Because neither would he.

He could feel the pressure rising in his chest, like battle drums building in his ribs. But it wasn't time yet. Not yet. Rua was still talking, directing Rafe turn by turn like he was reading fate off the road.

And Garin? He looked down at the cane in his lap, of course he had brought it with him, he needed to hold something of her, until he held her again, and he held it like a blade.

They would pay. He would make sure of it, and if Rua could feel the way their hearts had pounded in fear...Garin would make damn sure that by the time they found Mira, those hearts would be *the last thing to stop beating*.

The SUV tore through the night, tires screeching as Rua leaned forward between the front seats like a wolf uncaged.

"Left, *now*, Rafe! Jesus, do I need to drive it myself?"

Rafe grunted, hands tightening on the wheel. "Not unless you want a dent in your pretty face, Red."

"Feck off, next right, *bollocks*! That's the turn!"

Rua's curses spilled like blood on a blade, sharp and rapid, slipping between clipped English and snarled Irish.

"I can feel 'em, they're not far. Fucking gobshites left a trail a blind man could follow."

Garin didn't speak. He didn't need to. His silence was the pressure in the car, the storm behind every word Rua snapped, the weight in the air so thick even Rafe stopped cracking jokes. The Viking's hands rested on the axe laid across his knees, one he hadn't lifted in centuries.

But now?

Now, he plotted.

He should be wise. Should be *measured*, take prisoners, get answers, spare the ones who might have been misled. But the moment the SUV rounded the bend and that *building* came into view...

All reason shattered.

A decrepit roadside motel, sagging under the weight of rot and rain, windows boarded in places, others flickering with dying yellow light. The sign buzzed overhead with a missing "E," reading simply:

NO VACANCY - MOT_L

It wasn't a place for mercy. Not tonight.

The tires had barely skidded to a stop when Garin moved, out of the SUV, boots slamming the cracked pavement.

"Garin-wait!" Rafe called, but it was too late.

Two men exploded from the shadows ahead, both dressed head to toe in black. One had a rifle lifted, already aiming. The other? Twin blades. Like that would save him. Garin didn't hesitate. Didn't blink.

Didn't *breathe*.

He was *upon them* before their weapons had even leveled.

The one with the rifle fired. Too slow.

Garin caught the muzzle with one hand, *snapped* the barrel like dry twig. The man's scream was cut short as Garin's other hand slammed into his chest, sending him flying back through a fence, wood exploding on impact.

The second man swung both blades at once, slashing low and fast. Garin didn't move back. He *stepped in*.

The first blade kissed leather. The second barely brushed his ribs before the Viking twisted, letting the pain fuel him. His fist crushed the man's windpipe before the next swing could come, and the body dropped like stone, not even a scream before his life ended.

Behind him, Rua and Rafe approached, both falling into pace like wolves answering their alpha.

"Any chance we leave one alive?" Rafe muttered.

Garin's eyes burned like firelight. "If they're smart, they'll run if they want to live."

"They won't," Rua said grimly, already drawing one of his curved blades. "They took *her*, remember?"

And Garin did. He *always would*. They moved forward together, toward the motel's entrance, toward the woman the humans stole. And tonight? Garin would remind them why monsters feared the old gods.

Another one burst out from the crumbling motel office, frantic and loud.

"Delta-nine, we got contact, they're here!"

Gunshots cracked, too wild, too panicked. The muzzle flashed again and again as he shouted into the small comm on his shoulder, barking orders to whoever might be dumb enough to answer. But he was already dead and didn't know it. Garin moved like a storm unchained, boots pounding, eyes locked.

The bullet didn't matter. The shouting didn't matter. Only *Mira* mattered.

In one brutal surge, Garin's hand closed around the man's throat, cutting off both scream and comm chatter. The pistol clattered to the ground a second before Garin *slammed* him into the concrete. The man *cracked* against it like ice against stone, blood spurting from his mouth, eyes wild and limbs twitching.

Rua crouched beside him then, elegant and feral, fangs gleaming beneath a wicked grin. His voice was velvet edged in a growl, thick with his Irish lilt.

"C'mon now, be a good lad. Say the number. Give us the room, and maybe the big man won't turn you into paste, yeah?"

The man spasmed under their gaze, coughing hard, his voice wet and broken as he choked it out. "F-fourteen…r-room…fourteen…"

Garin let him go with a snarl of disgust, the man collapsing to the ground, gasping. Behind him, he heard Rafe's voice, low, calm, dangerous.

"Sheriff, it's Rafe. We got a situation. Motel out on highway seventeen, the run-down one with the busted neon sign. Yeah… that's the one." A pause. "Room fourteen. Bring backup. Might be some arrests… might be more body bags."

He tucked the phone away and turned back to Garin, who was already striding toward the row of rooms, his axe slung across his back, a short sword now in hand. Rua followed close, eyes burning green, his bloodlust matching the Viking stride for stride.

Room Fourteen.

It was near. Too near, and Garin could feel it. Something behind that door… something sacred and furious and *his*. She was close.

"Don't let anyone else touch her," Garin rumbled low, to both men behind him. "They laid hands on my wife. Only my hands will answer that crime."

And with that, he stalked forward, toward the door. Toward the reckoning.

~~~~~~~~~

She was thrown.

Not hard enough to break her, but hard enough to bruise hard enough to remind her that Alexander wasn't trying to play savior anymore. The mattress caught her back, but not her breath. It left her coughing, limbs aching, the dizzy edges of whatever they'd drugged her with still fogging her head. Her cane, her only weapon, was still gone.

But her fire wasn't.

Her hands gripped the bedding beneath her as she sat up slowly, breathing deep, trying to get her bearings through the chaos erupting around her.

But then…

Gunshots.

Close. Her head whipped toward the sound, heart hammering, and the room erupted into a flurry of motion. She heard the shift of boots, the shuffle of drawn weapons. A voice over a headset crackled and panicked. Another deeper voice, firm, calculating.

Alexander.

"Jonah, move your ass now! You flank the south end, hold the line. If they're here already, they're close. Don't let them breach this floor!"

A second voice, female, sharp and furious:

"Alexander, listen to me- we can't-"

Mira recognized her now. Abigail. She'd been the only one who hadn't handled her like cargo. The only one who'd spoken like Mira was still human.

"You said you wanted to help people," Abigail snapped, footsteps pacing across the tile. "But this one? He's too old. You didn't tell us she was *mated* to a Bloodborn, much less one as ancient as-"

SLAM.

Something cracked, a desk or a wall, beneath Alexander's fist.

"Then leave!" he roared. "You and your coward of a brother. You think this fight was ever meant for the weak? Go. Go run. You never should've been part of this!"

"You'd just throw us out!? Just like that?"

"Yes! I've trained dogs that listen better than the two of you! I never should've let you two children join this organization. You're no better to live than your coward parents!"

Silence. Cold... Suffocating.

Even blind, Mira could *feel* it, how the air changed.

The way neither Jonah nor Abigail moved. How one breath caught, one soul coiled in shame or fury, maybe both. Then came Abigail's voice. Low. Cut from steel.

"...Fine." A pause. Her next words were sharper than blades. "Then die alone." And just like that, Mira heard them leave. A door. A hiss of wind. Running steps.

But she didn't breathe easy. Because Alexander hadn't moved. She could *feel* him. Still standing. Still watching. Still ready to use her as bait. She shifted on the bed, hands clenched into fists, her voice low and vengeful.

"You're not ready for him." She turned her head toward where she could sense him, heart pounding. "You're not ready for the blood he'll spill. You're not ready for *my* Viking."

The wall behind them *shook*. A door slammed open with a force like thunder. A growl that sounded less like a man and more like a *god of war* echoed down the hall. He was here.

And the reckoning had finally come.

Alexander didn't hesitate. The second Abigail's footsteps vanished down the exterior walkway, his control finally snapped completely. Mira felt it in the way his grip changed, no longer calculated, no longer restrained. Just *desperate*.

His hands yanked her off the bed again, fingers digging into her upper arms hard enough to bruise.

"You hear that?" he snarled close to her ear. "That's your proof. They abandon each other. They always do. Monsters don't love, they *consume*. Just like your beast is doing to my men."

Mira twisted, pain flashing through her shoulder as she fought him, her voice sharp and unafraid.

"You're insane! You don't even know what you're doing!"

That made him laugh, a short, ugly, unhinged sound like made her shiver in disgust.

"No," he snapped, shaking her once. "I'm the only sane one here. You're a blind woman who doesn't know any better. You think that thing chose you out of love? He chose you because you're weak."

Her breath hitched, but not in fear.

In rage.

"Let me go," she hissed. "You don't get to decide what I am."

His grip tightened. "I'll fix it," Alexander said, voice trembling with zealotry. "I'll fix *you*. After I kill every last blood-sucking monster that comes through that door, you'll thank me. You'll see what loving a beast really costs. But I'll fix it."

But before he said anything else…The door didn't open.

It **exploded**.

Wood shattered outward in a deafening crack, metal screaming as hinges tore free. The pressure in the room dropped instantly, like winter crashing through the walls. Mira gasped as the air *changed*, cold slicing across her skin, goosebumps racing down her arms. And beneath the chaos, beneath the shouting, the alarms, the pounding boots, she felt it.

That presence. That vast, terrifying, familiar weight she had come to know better than her own breath.

Alexander froze. His grip slackened just enough for Mira to feel it. And that was when she grinned.

Grinned wide and slow, the cold wind kissing her cheeks, curling in her curls. Because she couldn't see the doorway, but she didn't need to.

The growl that answered her wasn't human. It wasn't even *vampiric*. It was the sound of a god who had found his mate bruised in another man's hands, and decided the world would pay for it.

Mira?

Mira relaxed into that cold, deadly air like she was finally home. She tilted her head toward the ruined doorway, where something ancient and furious now stood, and she said softly, almost kindly

"Oh… you're so fucked now."

Chapter 25

The world narrowed the moment he crossed the threshold. Wood splinters crunched beneath his boots, the door nothing more than wreckage at his back, and the room smelled wrong, filled with fear, gunpowder, sweat, cheap detergent, human panic. It all blurred into white noise the instant his eyes land on **her**.

Mira. In *his* arms. No… in another man's hands.

The mortal is older. Salted grey in his hair. Eyes bright with zealotry and madness, veins standing out in his neck as if rage alone keeps him upright. His fingers are dug into her arms, hard enough that even from across the room Garin can see the marks already blooming there.

Handprints.

On her.

Something inside Garin **broke**.

Not snapped, *breaks*, like an ancient glacier splitting apart after centuries of pressure. His fist clenched so hard the bones of his hand creaked. Muscles locked down his spine, his shoulders rolling forward like a war-beast bracing for impact. Power coiled in him, old and brutal and awake, and his vision sharpened until the world goes icy-bright.

Blue eyes ignite, not glowing prettily, not theatrically. They burn like a snowstorm summoned by angry gods. The man turned then, finally noticing him, mouth opening to speak, to threaten, to justify, to preach…

Garin never hears the words.

All he sees are the red marks on Mira's skin. All he feels is the **wrongness** of another's touch on what is *his*. His voice, when it comes, is not loud. It doesn't need to be. It rolls through the room low and vibrating, a sound that belongs on battlefields and funeral pyres, not motel rooms.

"Remove. Your hands."

The human laughed, actually laughed, high and frantic.

"You think I'm afraid of you?" the man snarls. "You monsters think you can live among us, take our women, corrupt an innocent, fragile-"

Garin moved. Not fast.

Inevitable.

In one step he is there, Mira gone from the man's grip as if the air itself reclaimed her. Garin's arm wrapped around her waist, hauling her against his chest, his body turning just enough to shield her completely.

So she felt the cold of him. The steel, and the promise of safety. And then Garin looked back at the man. Looked *down* at him.

"You touched my mate," he said quietly.

The word is not shouted. It is *declared*.

"I will take your hands first," Garin continued, voice flat, deadly calm. "Then your knees. Then I will decide how much of you I leave breathing for the law to collect."

The man stumbled back a step, suddenly pale, suddenly unsure, the reality of the thing in front of him finally cracking through his madness. Garin didn't give him time to recover. He shifted Mira fully behind him, one massive arm locking her safely to his back, and raised his axe.

Ancient steel catches the light, and somewhere behind him, through the chaos, the shouting, the thunder of boots, he hears Rua laughed softly.

The Viking's Harmony

"Oh," the Irishman murmured with grim delight. "He's dead."

The scent of fear hung in the air like rot. Garin didn't hesitate. The moment the human lunged for the table, reaching with trembling, calloused fingers toward the steel laid out like some pathetic altar, Garin moved first.

He was across the room in less than a blink, snatching the man by the collar and launching him like a ragdoll into the far wall. The crash thundered through the chamber, dust and drywall collapsing like snow from a brittle cliffside.

"Rua. Get her out. Now."

His voice cut through the rising chaos, ice-laced and absolute. Mira's voice followed, panicked, soft, *his*, calling out his name. But Garin didn't look at her.

He couldn't.

If he did, he might see the bruises. The red, blooming prints on her delicate arms where this *thing* had dared to touch her. He might see her trembling lip, her bare feet still pressed against the floor where she'd been dragged, her warmth…

And he would kill this man without honor. So instead, his voice came again, iron-willed and final.

"Go with him, Light. I will bring you home. Shortly."

She hesitated. Of course she did, because she knew what he meant by *shortly*, then, behind him, a groan.

A curse. A threat.

"You're not taking her home," the man growled, blood in his mouth. "You'll be destroying her."

The room pulsed with something *primeval*. Garin turned, slowly. His boots echoed against the wood as he crossed back to him. Then he moved again, a blur of fury, grabbing the man by the throat and hoisting him into the air like he weighed nothing. The old hunter clawed at his forearm, gasping, kicking…

But Garin didn't release.

Instead, his voice broke through the silence with all the devastation of a winter storm.

"You dare," Garin snarled, "believe my flame to be fragile?"

He slammed the man into the ground, boards cracking beneath the force, then hauled him up again.

"You *dare* touch what is stronger than your own pathetic will?"

Another throw, this time against the table itself, steel clattering and scattering like ants.

"You *dare* say you would destroy the only *song* I've ever known?"

The air thickened with frost, mist curling off Garin's shoulders, off his bared fists, the heat of his rage freezing the very breath from the room. His blue eyes glowed like the eye of a storm, ancient and endless.

And now?

He was only just beginning.

The man, desperate and terrified, fumbled in his pocket, pulling out a small knife. A pathetic thing, trembling between his fingers. Before he could even bring it up properly, he stabbed Garin in the arm. The blade sank into flesh. But nothing happened. No recoil, no pain. Not even a wince.

Garin didn't even blink.

With the hand that was still gripping the human by the throat, he ripped the blade out of his own arm as casually as one might pull a thorn free. A thin line of blood appeared, but it was already fading. Then, as though fueled by instinct older than memory and older than war itself, with deliberate, merciless strength, he shoved it straight into the human's shoulder.

The man immediately went rigid. A terrified gasp caught in his throat. Garin leaned in, cold and ancient in the way he moved now. His voice was an ice-laced thunder, deep, unmoved, and unyielding.

"You think to show *me* pain with that?" He spoke with the weight of centuries in every syllable. "You think you know how Vikings handled *men like you*?"

His blue eyes were like shards of glacial light in winter's heart. He began to speak, not to threaten, not to argue, but to **declare**.

The words were a ritual of dread.

"In my time...Men who dared lay hands on another's woman were shown precisely *how* our blades spoke. First, the one who betrayed trust Would be bound and made to kneel. Then..."

He paused, slow, savoring the terror in the man's wide eyes.

"...a blade would be placed *at* their throat. A blade no weaker than the courage they lacked. Then, we would force the man onto his stomach, where we take our blades, and carve into his back like it was nothing but meat for our dinner."

His voice was steady. Old. A force of nature that did not need to raise itself to break spirits. And as each word left his lips, his fangs grew. Longer. Sharper. Cold and inevitable. Like twin spears drawn for judgment.

"I would take my time with you, human." He snarled, voice never wavering, instead, Garin leaned down closer, and continued, "I would enjoy snapping your ribs one by one, each for every bruise I find on my mate. Then.." He gave a soft pause, only for his lips to bare in a grin that betrayed the true nature of his words, "I would rip your pathetic excuse for lungs from your fragile, broken body, and display them like the wings of a great bird. I would display you for all to see, for whoever dared come near what is *mine*."

The man beneath him did not scream. Not yet. He was *pale*. All color had fled, all the blood had drained from his face. All life seemed to have fled his posture. Only fear remained, raw, jagged, unmasked, and in Garin's gaze, the storm did not waver.

The man trembled beneath him, body pinned, blade still lodged in his shoulder, eyes wide and horrified, watching as Garin's fangs glinted like glacial death.

But…it stopped, because he heard them. Sirens. Wailing in the distance, drawing nearer with each ragged breath the mortal took, flashing lights casting red and blue through the thin, cracked motel curtains.

Bobby. The sheriff. And with him? The mortal law. Garin's lips curled, not into another smile, but into something crueler. Something colder. He leaned in even closer, his breath like the bite of winter air against the man's skin. His voice, a low and deadly rumble in the man's ear.

"You think I am a beast…" The man didn't breathe. Garin's hold tightened, not to crush, but to remind. "You think I'd tear your lungs from your ribs. Spill your entrails onto this filthy carpet. End you like the screaming coward you are, as I drain every ounce of blood from your body."

He paused, the vibrating snarl beneath his voice fading into something more composed. But it was no less terrifying.

"But I won't." He dropped the blade. Let it clatter to the floor. "You'll face judgment. Among *your* kind."

Garin slowly released his grip on the man's throat. Not out of mercy, but as a sentence.

"Let them see what you are. Let your own courts see what you've done. Let them stare at the monster they bred and trained, who kidnapped a woman from her place of work, and held her hostage."

And just before he stood to full height, just before Bobby and his deputies burst through the door, he bent down, one last time. Voice like ice over bone, eyes aflame with eternal snow.

"But if you *ever* come near my coven again... If you so much as *breathe* in the direction of my flame..." His lips brushed the edge of the man's ear like frostbite. "I will show you ways to die that will leave you *begging* for death."

He stood then, a monolith of judgment. His coat blood-flecked, his pale hair wild, his body towering as the door swung open, and Sheriff Bobby stepped in, weapon half-raised, freezing in his tracks at the sight. Garin said nothing. He only turned... and walked toward the hallway before the other human officers would find him there.

Because Mira was waiting, and his fire... still needed holding.

~~~~~~~~

Alexander's vision swam as the cold rushed back in.

The room felt wrong without the monster in it. Too small. Too quiet.

His fingers slipped on blood as a rough hand seized his arm, **hard**, unyielding, and wrenched him upright. Pain exploded through his shoulder where the knife still sat buried, and he snarled, thrashing as Sheriff Bobby hauled him back with a grunt.

"No-no, you don't understand," Alexander barked, voice hoarse, frantic. "He's still here. He went after her. You have to stop him, he's a monster, he'll hurt her, he *will*-"

"Easy!" Bobby snapped, shoving him back against the wall. "You're done. Calm yourself down before you make this worse."

Alexander laughed, it was sharp, broken, hysterical in a way that would unsettle anyone.

"Make it worse?" he spat. "You didn't see him. You didn't *see* what he is. Ancient. Vile. He slaughtered my men like animals!"

Bobby's jaw tightened. He reached up and spoke calmly into the walkie clipped to his shoulder.

"Yeah. We've got a live one. Male. Middle-aged. Delusional and violent. Claims multiple assailants, but he's the only one in the room."

Alexander went still.

"What?" His breath hitched. "No. No, there were others. There was a vampire. Tall. Black hair. Blue eyes like, l-l-like winter-"

The Sheriff looked at him then. Really looked. The room told a different story. No other bodies. No signs of a supernatural brawl. Just overturned furniture, blood, weapons scattered like a paranoid shrine, and one man spiraling apart.

"You're alone," Bobby said flatly. "Been alone this whole time."

Alexander *lost it*.

"No!" he screamed, thrashing as cuffs snapped shut around his wrists. "You're blind, you're all blind! They hide among you, poison your towns, take your women!" He strained against the cuffs, veins standing out in his neck as deputies moved in to help restrain him. "The Bloodborn will ruin you!" he shouted as they dragged him toward the door. "They'll take everything, your families, your children, she's already lost!"

Bobby jerked him forward hard. "That's enough. All units," the sheriff continued into the radio, calm and steady, "secure the building. We're taking Weber in."

Alexander's boots scraped as he's dragged forward, his words devolving into a near-scream, spit flying as panic and fury twist together in his chest.

"They're monsters!" he yelled. "They're hiding in this town, Bloodborn, wolves, all of them, this place is rotten, *they'll ruin you all!*"

He was hauled out into the cold mountain air, still shouting, still fighting, his words dissolving into incoherent rage and certainty twisted into obsession. Behind him, the motel room stood empty. No Viking. No monsters.

No proof.

And as Alexander Weber is shoved toward the waiting patrol car, his voice finally cracked not in rage, but something closer to terror.

"You don't understand," he gasped, straining one last time against the cuffs. "You don't understand what you're protecting."

The door slammed shut. The sirens drowned him out. Only the echo of terror... and the certainty that somewhere, out there, the thing he hated most had already won.

Alexander sat hunched in the back seat now, wrists cuffed tight, shoulder burning where the knife still throbbed. Red and blue lights smeared across the glass, the world outside stretching and warping as the car peeled away from the motel and wound down the mountain road.

The smell of blood hadn't left his nose. Neither had the cold.

They thought he was alone. That thought hit him all at once, and something in his chest *snapped*.

A sound crawled out of his throat before he could stop it. Low at first. Wet. Broken.

A laugh.

It startled even the deputy in the front seat, who glanced back through the divider with a frown. Alexander laughed harder. His head tipped back against the glass, breath fogging it as the sound built, ragged, unhinged, carrying the sharp edge of someone who had seen the truth and knew no one else believed it.

"Go ahead," he muttered, half to himself, half to the dark rolling past the windows. "Lock me up. Write me off. Call me delusional."

His laughter cracked again, almost joyful now.

"This isn't over," he whispered, words trembling with conviction. "Not even close."

Images burned behind his eyes, blue eyes like a killing winter, hands strong enough to shatter bone, a woman who smiled because she didn't understand what she'd chosen.

"They're out there," he hissed. "I *felt* them. I crossed the line and the air changed. You don't get rid of that kind of evil by pretending it doesn't exist."

The car took a sharp turn. His shoulder screamed. Alexander welcomed the pain. It grounded him. Reminded him he was still here. Still breathing. Still *right*.

"And it's not just them," he murmured, grin cutting sharp across his face. "Someone else is moving pieces. Someone who knows how to hide. Someone who wants this quiet."

The laughter came again, soft now, conspiratorial, recalling the woman who had come to him, the blonde hair, the pale lips…the anger in her own voice.

"But monsters always slip. And when they do…" His eyes gleamed in the flashing lights, fever-bright. "I'll be ready."

The patrol car disappeared down the road, carrying a man the world would soon forget, while the war he'd sworn himself to had only just begun.

Sheriff Bobby Schaffer stood just outside the motel, boots planted wide, hands braced on his hips as the patrol car disappeared down the mountain road. Red and blue lights bled into the trees before finally vanishing, taking Alexander Weber and his madness with them.

Bobby exhaled slowly. Not relief exactly, but the kind of breath you take when a gunfight ends and you're still counting fingers.

Behind him, deputies moved through the wreckage of the room. Weapons bagged. Blood photographed. Statements half-taken from men too shaken to make sense of what had happened. The motel itself creaked, settling back into its usual rot like it hadn't just witnessed something ancient and violent tear through it.

"Christ," he muttered under his breath. "What a mess."

Gunshots. Federal-looking lunatics. Kidnapping. And not a *single* body left behind that made any kind of sense on paper. The kind of scene that gave sheriffs ulcers and made paperwork grow teeth.

His phone buzzed.

Bobby didn't jump, but he didn't relax either. He pulled it free and answered without looking at the screen.

"Yeah."

Beau's voice rolled through the line, low and calm, like it always was when the world had nearly ended but *technically* hadn't.

"Tell me it's done."

Bobby exhaled slowly through his nose. "It's done. Weber's in custody. Fighting it, ranting about monsters, the whole nine yards. I'm already pushing for a psych plea, he's unstable enough it'll stick. His people scattered the second the cavalry showed."

He glanced back at the motel. Broken door. Blood that didn't quite tell a full story. Too clean in places it shouldn't have been.

"No sign of Garin," Bobby continued. "No sign of the Irishman either. Wolf shifted and vanished before we rolled in. Whatever happened in there… ain't on record."

A pause.

"And Leah?" Beau asked.

Bobby snorted softly. "She'll eat this case alive. Kidnapping a disabled teacher off school grounds? Jury won't even blink. Weber won't see daylight for a long damn time."

There was a faint sound on Beau's end, relief, maybe. Or just breath.

Bobby turned, eyes following the road again. The taillights were gone now. Just darkness and trees and the low hum of insects beginning to wake.

"Beau," he said, quieter.

"Yeah."

"Something about this don't sit right."

Silence stretched. Bobby shifted his weight, boots crunching on gravel. "Weber was unhinged, sure. But he was convinced. Not desperate. Not guessing. He thought he had help. Thought someone fed him just enough truth to point him in the right direction."

He lowered his voice, instinctively.

"And men like that don't just stumble onto things they shouldn't know, especially not the women y'all keep close."

Another pause, longer this time. "I'll keep my eyes open," Beau said finally.

"I know you will," Bobby replied. "Just...don't get comfortable. Storms don't always announce themselves before they hit."

He ended the call and slipped his phone back into his pocket. For a long moment, the sheriff just stood there, listening to the night settle back into place. The mountains were quiet again. Too quiet.

Somewhere out there, beyond the trees, beyond the road, beyond the reach of human sirens, something had learned where to look, and how to act against the Thorne Coven. Bobby squared his shoulders and turned back toward his deputies.

The war wasn't here anymore. But it sure as hell wasn't over.

Chapter 26

The wind howled around her ears, fierce and fast, and yet she didn't feel afraid. Mira clung to Rua, not out of fear, but instinct. She didn't need sight to understand just how fast they were moving. The sound of the ground beneath his feet seemed to vanish and reappear in bursts of unnatural speed. Her fingers gripped at his coat, pressed tight to his chest as the world whipped by, blurred and breathless. Her head tucked near his throat, heart racing with a different kind of panic.

Garin.

They'd left him behind.

She trusted Rua, he could feel the steadiness in him, the warmth of his chest, the protective strength that hummed through his arms like a promise. But her heart still twisted.

Was he okay? Were they hurting him?

Her voice was trapped in her throat, not because she didn't want to ask, but because she already knew the answer wouldn't soothe her. Then, slowly, the rush began to fade. The world stilled around them like a held breath finally exhaled.

Rua stopped. She felt the shift first in his posture, the gentle slowing of motion, then the solidness of the earth beneath his boots. When he lowered her carefully to the ground, his movements were gentle, almost exceedingly careful, as though she were something breakable, sacred.

"You alright, love?" he asked softly, the cadence of his Irish accent a balm.

"I think so," Mira whispered, adjusting to the stillness. Her legs felt like jelly beneath her, and her hands trembled faintly with the leftover adrenaline. "I don't even know if I have any bruises, but my body aches. I couldn't feel much, just…fear. Heat. Then darkness."

Rua crouched beside her. "Would you let me check?" he asked. "Only if you're comfortable."

She gave a small nod. "Okay. I… I trust you."

She lifted her arms slightly as he pushed her sleeve back with care. His fingers were deft but delicate as he traced over her skin, and then he hummed, a low sound, not displeased, but not entirely neutral.

"Few bruises here," he murmured. "Right where those bastards grabbed you. Their grip was too cruel for you."

"I fought them," she said suddenly, her voice firmer than she expected. "I didn't scream. I kicked and hit until… they drugged me. One of them shoved something in my mouth, it tasted terrible. I bit the other one. Hard. He wouldn't let go of me in the hotel until I did."

There was a pause. Then, Rua chuckled, low and rich. "That's the woman of Garin's I know. A fighter." His grin colored the air between them even without sight. "Just like us."

Mira's lips parted in surprise. Then a shy smile touched them. "You really think that?" she asked softly.

"Without a doubt. You don't need to see to know how to survive, love. You've got fire in you. And he sees it. I do too."

She blinked, a sudden prickle of tears threatening to rise, but she swallowed them back. The warmth of Rua's words settled over her like a shield, like sunlight trying to coax her from the ache. He helped her stand again, steadying her as he did, always gentle with her.

"You're safe now," he said quietly. "And Garin? He's not far. He's fighting for you."

"I know," she whispered. "I just… needed to hear it."

Rua nodded. "He's a good man. Quiet, aye, but you're the only sound that breaks through. So hold on to that, alright? We'll go back for him."

And she did. She held onto it like a lifeline. Like the promise of a silent warrior with hands carved for violence, and a heart that beat for her alone.

The crack in the snow sounded like a gunshot. Mira's breath caught, her whole body coiling tight, and then she heard it. A low laugh behind her.

"Speak of the Viking." Rua's voice was laced with satisfaction and something warmer, a relief.

Mira didn't wait. She turned, heart slamming into her ribs, and *ran*. Ran through the snow like it would never slow her again, ran on instinct, on hope, on the tether of something wordless and divine, and launched herself into a pair of arms she already knew would be waiting.

His arms.

Garin caught her like she was the only thing in this world worth catching. Her legs wrapped around his waist, arms locked around his neck, and his own arms crushed her close, his face buried deep into her hair like he was drowning and she was breath. She could feel the tremble in his chest. Could feel her own tears warm against the cold wind.

"Oh thank God," she whispered, and then again, "Thank God, thank the gods, yours or mine, I don't care. I don't care. You're okay. You're okay…"

Like she hadn't just been the one held hostage. Like she hadn't been the one bruised. She didn't care. Not when his hands were still solid, not when his arms still shook with fury that wasn't for her, ut for what could've happened.

Behind them, Rua's voice cut through the quiet snow.

"What happened to the human?"

There was a pause. Garin didn't lift his face from Mira's hair. His voice rumbled low, sharp as the winter air:

"I left him alive." A beat. "For the humans to deal with."

Then silence again, except for Mira's heart pounding in sync with his. Her Viking. Her peace. Her wrath. Her home, and the snow began to fall again like nothing had ever happened. Until the realization hit harder than anything else.

He left him alive.

Mira stilled in Garin's arms, head pressed against his chest as those words sank in.

Even Rua sounded stunned behind them. "You... *left* him?"

Mira slowly leaned back, her hands reaching upward, searching, and finding, the hard line of Garin's jaw, the sweep of his beard beneath her fingertips. She touched his face like it grounded her, like it was the only thing that kept the world steady.

"You left him alive?" she repeated, voice quieter now. "Garin... *why?* I didn't expect that."

She felt it before she heard it. A slight curve against her palm, the smallest hint of a grin.

"Would you rather I'd gutted the man, my flame?" The dry edge in his voice almost masked the violence beneath it. Almost.

Mira hesitated. Her throat bobbed. "No," she whispered. "But still..."

Rua moved closer behind them, voice curious but dark. "You're tellin' me the same man who hurt her, who laid a hand on your woman, gets to breathe easy tonight?"

Garin finally lifted his head, but kept Mira tucked against him. His voice rumbled low, deeper than before, like the Viking inside him still had blood on his tongue.

"He won't breathe easy." Another pause. "I left him alive because living with the knowledge that a *beast* spared his life...

will torment him more than anything I would've carved into him."

The silence after that wasn't empty. It was *full*, so full Mira couldn't hold it anymore. The tears broke loose, silent and warm down her cheeks as she pressed herself tighter to him, her voice muffled against the place over his heart.

"You're not a beast," she whispered. "You're my home."

And then, softer, breaking down after everything that had happened that day, after what they could've lost.

"Please, Garin. I want to go home."

His arms locked tighter around her, and the snow kept falling as her Viking leaned down, and pulled her into his arms with no hesitation. She didn't even feel the snow anymore. Just the strength of his arms curling beneath her, one at her back, the other beneath her legs as he lifted her like she weighed nothing at all. Her breath hitched, partly from the motion, partly from the overwhelming sense of safety that followed it.

She didn't need to see his face to know what it looked like.

Fury still lingered in him, she could feel it in the tension of his muscles, in the way his chest rose and fell like a slowed war drum, but when he spoke, it wasn't rage that coated his voice.

It was vow.

"I'll take you home, my goddess," he murmured, voice low and rough, like winter wind over steel. "I'll take you home…and I swear to you, nothing like this will *ever* happen again. Not while I still breathe."

Something in her broke further at that. Not out of fear. But release. Relief. She leaned her head into the crook of his neck, one hand clutching the collar of his coat, the other brushing over his chest like she could anchor herself to the thrum of him beneath.

"I know," she whispered, her voice almost too soft to be heard. "I know you won't let it."

And just like that, the fear began to ebb. Because she wasn't in a stranger's arms anymore. She was in her Viking's, and he was taking her home, to their family.

~~~~~~~~

Garin didn't set her down. Not once. Not when Rua stopped beside him to catch his breath. Not when they cleared the line of trees at the edge of the forest. Not even when the manor came into view, its gothic spires bathed in the soft hush of morning snow.

With every heavy-footed step through the woods, something in him began to settle, slow and reluctant, like a beast led back into its cage. The fury hadn't left him. It never would. But her, *her*, in his arms, breathing soft against his throat, had quieted it. He carried that silence up the long path to the gate, and when it opened, he saw them.

Beau Thorne, standing on the porch with that ever-unbothered posture of his, arms folded and gold-flecked eyes tracking Garin like a hawk. And Leah, phone to her ear, voice sharp, efficient, Southern steel on the line with Bobby no doubt, making sure that the Sheriff was handling everything according to plan to keep Alexander behind bars.

Garin's boots hit the porch steps heavy. Mira didn't stir. She was too wrapped around him, too trusting, like she knew the second she let go, it would all become real.

He wasn't letting that happen. Not yet.

Beau stepped down from the porch to meet them halfway. His eyes moved over Mira, then back to Garin. "Glad she's alright," the Southern vampire said low, his jaw tense. "You good? Everyone else okay?"

Garin gave a short nod, eyes flicking briefly toward the trees behind him. "Rua and Rafe did well," he said simply, voice like grinding gravel. "Led me to her without delay. I do not know where the wolf is now."

That's when a familiar, easy-breathing voice called out behind him, the Irishman piping up at last.

"Shifted the second the damn sirens hit," Rua said as he jogged up, brushing snow from his coat. "Didn't want to be caught half-dressed again by humans. Said something about not wanting to explain away a naked man with a tail to the police."

Beau huffed a sound that was half amusement, half exasperation. "Typical."

Garin didn't laugh. Couldn't. He only looked down to the woman in his arms, the woman who still hadn't let go of him, and he realized he wouldn't set her down until she asked him to. Because Mira was home now, he wasn't letting her be taken ever again.

He shifted Mira gently in his arms, adjusting her weight so her head could rest closer to his chest. He started forward again, eyes set on the manor's double doors, his focus absolute. Get her inside. Get her warm. Get her safe.

He had *one* priority. But Beau's voice cut across the space before he could cross the threshold.

"Garin."

The Viking stopped. Only barely. The muscles in his shoulders coiled tighter. His spine straightened like a drawn bow. Slowly, his head turned just enough to acknowledge the coven's Southern king standing behind him, boots creaking against the old porch wood.

Beau's tone was calm, but low, firm beneath the molasses smooth. "We'll need to talk to her. Later. There's things she might've heard. About the LightBorne. Could be useful."

Garin didn't turn fully. Didn't *have* to. His voice, when it came, was a quiet rumble of thunder in the throat. "Not now." A pause.

"Now, I tend to my mate." And without another word, without a glance backward, he pushed open the door with his shoulder and carried Mira inside. The manor greeted them with warmth and low candlelight, but Garin didn't stop in the foyer. He didn't wait for any more questions. He didn't ask for help. He took the stairs two at a time, silent save for the distant hum of Leah's voice still barking orders to the sheriff on the line outside. His boots echoed low across the floorboards, but the rage inside him was louder.

Not the kind that burned wildly anymore. This one simmered. A coiled, relentless ache. A wrath that had no place to land, because the man responsible still *breathed*, and Garin had *let* him.

But in his arms was something greater than vengeance. Mira.

His woman. His *light*. And with each step deeper into the manor, the weight of what *almost* happened, the shadow of what could've been lost, pressed harder against the cage of his ribs.

He held her tighter, and didn't stop walking until they reached their bedroom. Garin didn't speak as the bedroom door shut behind them. He only exhaled, slow and ragged, before crossing to the bed, *their* bed, and kneeling beside it with devotion.

He hadn't let her go once since he first took her into his arms in the snow. Not even now. But he lowered her, finally into the soft furs, her body so light in his grip it made the ache in his chest nearly unbearable. The rage hadn't left him. It never really did. But it had shifted, curled tighter, deeper. No longer roaring. Just *coiled*.

He moved with quiet care. *Too* quiet. Garin began to remove the wet fabric of her clothes, piece by piece, jaw tight as the snow-damp cotton peeled away from her skin. When the edge of a bruise came into view, faint, discolored fingerprints on her arms, her ribs, his fingers twitched, and for a heartbeat, his fangs bared behind a clenched jaw.

But he didn't speak. Didn't snarl.

Didn't let himself *snap*.

He only exhaled again, and draped the thick furs over her bare skin, tucking them around her form like a vow. He reached for another to layer overtop, anything to restore the warmth that had been stolen from her, but her fingers found his.

Small, soft, and always so steady when it came to her ouch of him. She caught his hand before he could pull away, and though she couldn't see the storm in his eyes…he knew she *felt* it.

Mira's voice was soft and certain.

"Garin… it's okay." He didn't move. "*I'm* okay," she whispered. "We're home now."

But his breath hitched again, too heavy for a man like him. And when he finally looked down at her, eyes searching her pale, freckled face, the quiet in him broke.

"I came too close to losing you tonight."

It came out hoarse. Gravel and grief mixed with the regret of bringing such a beautiful song into a terrifying world.

"I never wanted this for you. Not the fear. Not the pain. *Not this.*"

His voice trembled, not from weakness, but from a depth of love he couldn't always name. She was his softness. His only peace. And tonight, that peace had nearly been ripped from him.

But Mira, his flame, *wouldn't have it.* Even blind, kidnapped, drugged and terrified, she didn't falter. Her hands gripped his, then his shoulders, pulling him gently down until he followed her into the bed. He didn't resist. He *couldn't*. His body folded beside hers, head bowed, arms curling around her like a fortress reborn.

Her forehead found his, and her words met his soul. "We have eternity," she whispered. "All of it. I've never been more sure...that I want to spend forever with you."

The breath that left him then was sharp. Like a man just now realizing he was still alive. Still holding the most precious thing he'd ever been given, and tonight? He wasn't letting go, not for a lifetime.

They lay together in silence at first. Not for lack of words, but because some aches were only soothed by nearness, by skin against skin beneath the furs, by the weight of her hand tracing gently up his chest until it came to rest above his heart.

Still laced with fury. Still haunted by the memory of her *not being in his arms,* and Garin, who had faced gods and monsters, who had survived the centuries on blood and battle and silence, *spoke first.*

"Nothing will ever separate us again." His voice was low. Gravel-wrapped. Almost like a vow spoken at a burial site. Because it *had* felt like dying, when she'd vanished.

He turned his head, pressing his lips into the crown of her hair, his voice rough as frost behind his beard.

"I can't bear it, Mira. The thought of losing you. I can't. I *won't.*"

She didn't flinch. Didn't waver. Instead, his little flame *tightened her arms* around him like a vow returned.

"You will never lose me," she whispered, and her voice, soft as it was, carried more fire than any oath. "Not ever. No ignorant hunter, no mean old queen yelling at me, no curse, no cruelty, no madness..." She reached up then, tracing the line of his jaw, her blind gaze steady even if her eyes couldn't meet his, "...nothing is taking me from you."

And that, *that* shattered what was left of the walls inside him. Garin inhaled once, harsh and deep, and pulled her impossibly closer until her head fit perfectly beneath his chin and his arms circled her like steel.

"I love you," he breathed, at last. Not as a whisper. Not as a confession. But as something carved into bone. Something ancient, eternal.

"I love you, Mira. My flame. My peace. My purpose." His voice cracked at the end, but he didn't stop. "I would burn every kingdom. Drown every god. I would let the world fall to ash if it meant keeping you safe. *You're mine.* And I am yours. Until the end of all things."

And in the hush that followed, Mira only held him tighter. As if she'd *always known*. As if fate had simply been waiting for the moment Garin would speak those words aloud, and mean every damn one.

Chapter 27

Back downstairs, in the depths of the manor, the ache of the night still hadn't dampened within the study of the Frenchman. The door burst open with a crack against the wall within a moment's notice.

Simon didn't flinch, never did. He'd heard her coming.

Cian barely had time to pivot when Leah stormed into the study, all fire and fury, Rua at her back like a red-haired wraith of war. Her heels clicked hard against the wood floor, her gaze locked on the thick folder in Cian's hands like it had personally wronged her.

She snatched it without a word.

"Good evening to you too, Counselor," Simon murmured, smoothing down the sleeve of his shirt with a calmness he did *not* feel.

Leah flipped through the folder fast, her eyes scanning surveillance stills, images printed in grainy black and white. A man with salt-and-pepper hair. Average build. Walking too calmly down a school hallway. Entering a restricted wing. No child in sight. Then…a shot outside the building. A familiar vehicle. A plate.

Simon folded his hands behind his back. "It's him," he said quietly. "Matches the man Sheriff Schaffer took into custody at the motel."

Leah didn't look up. "The fucker who had Mira."

"Oui."

"And no sign of any of us in those frames?" she demanded, still flipping.

Cian shook his head. "No vamps, no wolves, no pissed off to hell Viking. Bobby was careful. Took Garin and Rua's names outta everything before he filed the report, avoided any of us bein' mentioned in them. Said he was prepping a full psych plea and sealing the arrest under mental delusion."

"Smart man," Rua muttered. "Knows how to play the long game."

Simon nodded once. "Which means you should have no trouble, Counselor Ricci. Kidnapping. Assault. Unlawful confinement of a vulnerable adult. All human charges. All provable. All without touching our world."

Leah stopped flipping. Her jaw was clenched, the muscles twitching. But her voice, when it came, was steady and cold.

"He's going to rot." She tucked the folder under her arm, and immediately whipped her phone back out, like it was a sword of her own. "Lee-Ann? Me again. Have Mary prep the statements. I want everything clean and filed by morning. We're keeping this bastard locked away without triggering *any* federal interest."

Rua gave a low whistle. "You're hot when you're terrifying."

"I know," she snapped, brushing past him toward the door. "Simon, Cian, thank you for the proof."

Simon inclined his head, but before she vanished, he spoke once more, quiet, but firm.

"Leah." She paused. "This was too close," he said simply. "Far too close. And I fear...it will not be the last time."

A breath, a moment, and then Leah, with a look over her shoulder that could slice steel, replied, "Then they better be ready. Because next time? I won't be building a case."

She left, and the study fell silent again. Simon looked down at the remaining copy of the stills, the grayscale print warping beneath his fingers as his grip tightened.

Cian glanced over, voice low. "Thinkin' what I'm thinkin', mate?"

"That this was orchestrated," Simon said. "Yes."

Cian's jaw set. "You think someone pointed that human our way?"

"I think someone *gave* him Mira's name, someone who knew far too much." And with that, Simon turned to the window, staring out at the snow-covered world beyond Thorne Manor's ancient walls. Because storms didn't always come howling through the trees. Some of them were already *inside*.

The moment he was sure they were alone, Simon exhaled, quiet but deliberate. A hand passed over his silver hair, fingers lingering at the back of his neck as if trying to press down the stress building there. He turned to the twins, already knowing how this would end.

"This was too close," he said, the words low and clipped. "Far too coordinated to be mere coincidence. The LightBorne should not have been able to come this close. Not here."

Cian stepped forward, the folder still in his hand. "Aye, I agree. When I glamoured the security guard, I saw it, Simon, they surrounded her, and they didn't treat her like a stranger. They spoke like they knew her. Like they *studied* her."

Rua's jaw tightened, the muscles ticking as he crossed his arms. "And it wasn't just that," he added. "They *knew* where to find her. That motel wasn't anywhere near the roads she usually takes. That was a calculated abduction."

Simon's eyes flickered between them, but didn't settle. He turned toward the window instead, toward the snow-lit trees beyond. "You both did well," he said at last. "You truly did...

But we need to restore the boundaries that kept us safe. Patrols. Curfews. Schedules. What we built worked for a long time-"

"No," Rua snapped, his voice low but unmistakably firm.

Cian was gentler, but no less resolute. "Simon, we're not saying throw out the rules, but you have to see where that thinking has gotten us. You locked us away to stay hidden, and they *still* came."

Simon's shoulders stiffened. Rua stepped forward again, eyes sharp with the weight of everything they'd seen.

"You called it safety. But it's a cage. And we're not fucking livestock."

"We're not *children* anymore," Cian added. "We saved Mira, we helped bring her home. And we'd do it again. So don't put us back in the dark like cattle waiting for slaughter."

Simon still didn't look at them. His hands were clasped behind his back now, the picture of control. But his voice, when it came, was quiet.

"I know you're not children," he said. "That's why this hurts more." And in the silence that followed, the war between fear and trust swelled, old wounds and new truths cracking like frost beneath their feet.

Simon turned slowly, just in time for Cian to close the distance between them, standing tall and unmoved, green eyes locked on the older vampire. "Don't look away this time," Cian said quietly, but there was nothing gentle in his tone. "Whatever happened to Mira, it wasn't because of us not being careful. Something else is going on. Something worse."

Simon opened his mouth to respond, but the words were already slipping from him like smoke. "You don't know that. We can't assume-"

"We can," Cian interrupted, heat rising behind every word. "And caging us won't stop it."

Simon's jaw tightened, hands still clasped behind his back, but his posture remained too composed. A scholar clinging to discipline. "This is not a cage," he tried.

But Cian stepped even closer, eyes burning now.

"*Is ea atá sé,*" he snapped in Irish. "*It is.* You've stopped being a teacher. Stopped being a father." His voice cracked with bitterness. "Now you're just our *keeper.*"

The words landed like a slap. Simon flinched, but only just. His expression didn't fracture, but something behind his gaze flickered. A wound reopened, ancient and buried deep, and still, he didn't raise his voice. "Everything I've done," he said slowly, "I've done to protect you. I always have."

A silence passed, just one beat too long, and then Rua spoke from where he leaned near the desk, arms crossed, fury brimming like stormwater against a dam.

"You can't protect us by locking us away, *da.* That's not protection. That's control. That's fear, and we are *not* your prisoners. We are not your beasts."

Simon's composure cracked just slightly at that, his eyes darting between them, lips parted as if to speak… but nothing came out, because in that moment, the study, so often a place of strategy, of safety, felt like a battlefield instead. Not of blood and blade, but of grief. Of boys who had become men, and a father who didn't know how to let go.

It was another heartbeat before Rua and Cian both moved as one, eyes drifting away from Simon as they took their leave…in silence. Simon stood alone now, in the wake of their silence. The study door clicked softly shut behind the twins, but their absence rang louder than any slammed door ever could. He didn't need to see their faces again to remember the look in their eyes, twin flames glowing with pain, rebellion, and something far heavier.

Betrayal.

He stood there a moment longer, the soft creak of the old manor settling around him like the weight of history. His jaw tightened, then loosened.

"*Putain de merde,*" he muttered sharply under his breath. A rare curse, ripped from a man who prized control above all else.

Fingers pinched the bridge of his nose. His eyes shut, and without another word, he turned from the room and stepped out into the icy air beyond the manor's front doors. Winter greeted him like an old adversary, cold, biting, sharp. He welcomed it, hoping the chill would clear his thoughts where reason had failed.

It didn't.

But something else did arrive with the wind. A faint *crunch* of snow.

Simon's head lifted, eyes narrowing as he scanned the white-washed tree line just beyond the courtyard, and there it was.

A wolf, massive, just slightly more than a natural beast. Its dark silver coat gleamed in the moonlight, tinged with brown around the muzzle. Wild and noble, regal and scarred. But Simon saw the truth in the creature's stance… and in its eyes.

Those eyes weren't wild. They were calculating. Familiar.

"Rafe," Simon greeted with the flat chill of a man unused to being surprised.

The beast didn't growl, didn't shift. Just stood still, and held Simon's gaze. In his jaws, he carried a black hoodie, torn and ruffled at the edge. Simon tilted his head slightly, arms folding across his chest.

"What's this, then? A token of tonight's chaos? Or perhaps a souvenir for the collection of clothing you destroy?" His voice was cutting, but not sharp enough to pierce the deeper emotion buried beneath. He knew what it meant. What Rafe had seen. What he had done. But still, Simon was tired of riddles.

The hoodie hit the snow with a *soft thump*, and Simon's eyes followed it, unreadable. Then came the sound he dreaded, not because it frightened him, but because it reminded him of things primal, of things even he had no power to master.

Bone cracked. Flesh tore. The sound of a beast unmaking itself echoed into the frozen dark.

Simon turned his face away. He didn't flinch, but he didn't watch either. Some things were sacred, and some things… were just unpleasant.

Then came the voice. That deep, gravel-lined drawl, drenched in Texas heat even in the dead of winter.

"Ha. Ha. This ain't no souvenir, Simon," Rafe mocked. "And I reckon you oughta stop playin' games before one of us stops bein' polite."

Simon exhaled slowly, eyes narrowing as he turned back. The wolf was gone, and in its place stood a man, tall, broad, muscled, his skin still streaked with snowmelt and blood. Rafe's hair hung damp around his shoulders, chest bare to the cold like it meant nothing to him. He was tugging on a pair of sweatpants with that same lazy confidence he always wore like armor.

Simon's voice cut sharp through the air. "What games, *exactement*, are you accusing me of now?" He didn't raise his voice. He didn't have to.

But Rafe just picked up the hoodie from where it lay and threw it straight into Simon's chest. The vampire caught it easily, reflexes always intact, even when his mind was frayed. The disheveled fabric hung from his fingers like an accusation. Rafe's eyes locked onto his, hard.

"Some scents," he said darkly, "don't need a shift to pick up." He stepped past him, boots crunching the snow. Shoulders bare, his movements sharp. "And that one?" he growled without turning back. "Smells like a betrayal you better deal with, professor. Instead of makin' jokes."

Then he was gone, leaving Simon alone beneath the stars again, with nothing but silence, suspicion…and the hoodie in his hands.

The useless clothing hung limp in Simon's hands, dark and damp with snow. For a moment, he scoffed, shoulders tense with the same disdain he always had for Rafe's dramatics.

"*Toujours théâtral*," he muttered under his breath. But as he lifted the garment to his nose, the motion casual at first… something in his posture shifted.

His breath caught. Stillness wrapped around him like frost, and then, his fangs slipped down. Slow. His pupils narrowed, the brown of his eyes darkening until near black, a flicker of something ancient behind them. Rage, not bloodlust. Not yet. Because the scent wasn't just familiar. It was *known*, intimately.

Undeniable.

And the fury it stirred in him wasn't for the human it originally belonged to. It was for what it meant. He lowered the hoodie with exquisite slowness, the fabric still curled in his pale hand like a noose waiting to tighten. The only mercy in this moment, the only thing Simon could be remotely grateful for, was that *Rafe* had brought it to *him*.

Not Beau, not Garin, nor the rest of the coven. Not yet. He would deal with this.

Quietly, and *personally*.

No one needed to know, not until he was ready to let them.

~~~

Simon didn't stop to put on civility.

Not when the scent still burned in his nose like smoke clinging to a battlefield. Not when his jaw was locked so tight he could hear the grind of his own teeth. Not when his hand clutched that black hoodie with enough force to leave creases in the fabric.

He moved like a man possessed. Not with madness, but with clarity.

Cold, clinical, *lethal* clarity.

Up the stairs. Past the portraits. Past the doors the others had long since shut for the night. Until he reached *hers*. The rooms Evangeline had been confined to since Garin's voice, his *growl*, had made it crystal clear that she would not come near Mira again. Not after her veiled threats. Not after that performance of control she tried to keep and failed.

Simon didn't knock. He didn't have to. He *owned* every corner of this manor, and she knew it. The door slammed open against the wall, cracking wood with the force of his entry. And there she was, seated on a chaise in the soft candlelight, feigning serenity, a book open in her lap. Evangeline barely had time to look up before Simon threw the hoodie down in front of her. It hit the floor with a *wet thud*.

The scent bloomed immediately in the warm air. A scent that didn't belong anywhere *near* her. Not that human. Not that man. And her eyes... oh, how they flickered. The faintest shift. Surprise, maybe. Guilt? He watched for it, *craved* it. But Evangeline had worn masks for centuries, and she didn't drop it easily.

So Simon dropped his voice instead. Low.

Dangerous if she dared provoke him.

"Would you like to explain to me," he said, each word a dagger gliding down her spine, "*why* Mira's kidnapper smells like you?"

Her lips parted, just slightly. He took a single step forward, and her book slid to the floor.

"I suggest you think carefully before you answer." His fangs still hadn't retracted. And they wouldn't, not until she gave him the *truth*.

Evangeline didn't rise. Didn't flinch. She simply arched one brow and gave a soft, practiced laugh. "You must be mistaken, mon cœur. Humans often wear heavy cologne, perhaps it lingered-"

"*Non.*"

Simon stepped forward once, and the air thickened. Not from volume. From power. From the coiled, ancient restraint of a man who had spent centuries mastering control, and who now held it by a *thread*. His fangs gleamed in the candlelight.

"The only reason you are still breathing," Simon said, his voice razor-sharp and quiet as snowfall on a coffin, "is because my heart still remembers what it once felt for you."

That shattered any pretense of warmth. The lie she'd tried to spin evaporated, her eyes narrowing just slightly. Simon's own gaze didn't waver. Not once.

"I will burn this," he said, lifting the hoodie between two fingers like a contaminated relic. "I will not tell Beau. I will not tell Mira. And you will not speak a single word about this to *anyone.*"

She opened her mouth. He cut her off.

"You will *never* come near Mira again. You will obey the rules I set forward, and there will never be another betrayal from you, Evangeline."

Evangeline stood now, her pride finally catching flame. Her long limbs moved with theatrical grace, chin lifting with that queenly air she so loved to wear. "You forget yourself, Simon. I am your mate. I have every right!"

"You have *no* rights," he said, so softly it hissed. His accent thickened, his pupils blown wide. And still, not a single raised volume. Just lethal precision. "You chose *me* over the Eternal King. Over Solas when you would have been sent to your death, again. You bound yourself to *my* will, *my* protection, *my* coven. And I will *not* tolerate defiance again."

The silence between them cracked like black ice. Her gaze burned with hatred now, no longer veiled. No longer adorned with false affection.

"You will obey." He repeated it, eyes narrowing down onto her, as if daring her to fight him again. "Or I will allow this coven to do to you, what Solas and his courts were about to order before I took you. Do I make myself clear?" Simon asked.

And slowly, lips curled like venom, Evangeline sneered, her own fangs flashing in the low light, almost as though she would curse him again, but she answered.

"Yes… mon maître."

There was no love in it. No devotion. Only a thread of submission. The last remains of a crumbling bond built between two beings who will continue this masquerade…

Simon left without another word, his back to her, the hoodie still smoldering in his grip. It would not survive the night, and Evangeline?

She was lucky that she would.

Chapter 28

She could still remember the crack of the frozen ground. The way the snow had shattered beneath her boots as she ran into his arms that night. The way her body had *known*, even before her mind could catch up, that Garin would be there. That he would always be there to catch her.

Of course he had been. He'd come for her like a storm of blood and fury, a Viking made flesh and myth, and ever since that night, he hadn't let her go. It had been months since that frozen night, the night her heart had almost stopped from fear, and his had nearly shattered. Since the day she'd made her choice to stay by his side not just for a season, but for all the centuries to come.

Still… he hadn't let her out of his sight. Not once. He held her as if the world might try to take her again, perhaps it would. But it wouldn't succeed. Not this time. They'd all been there, healing in different ways. Leah had stormed the courts like an Italian thunderhead, ensuring Alexander Weber would never touch fresh air again, forced to be locked in a mental facility outside Atlanta, hidden from sight, from the world. Garin had only nodded once when he heard the news. Quiet. Cold.

She'd never asked what he'd wanted for Alexander. She already knew. After that, he'd moved her in. Beau had opened the manor doors without a single question, giving his blessing like a king placing a crown, welcoming her into the home permanently.

Mira the blind mortal who would soon leave her humanity behind.

She hadn't stepped foot back in her little house on Route 19 since the day she'd been returned to Garin's arms. Not because she couldn't, but because Garin wouldn't let her out of his sight long enough to try. He never made her feel caged. But God, did he cling.

Even now, as she sat on the edge of their shared bed, sunlight pooling over her skin like a final offering from the mortal world, Mira could feel the depth of his fear, just beneath the surface of every look, every kiss, every fierce, silent promise.

She *loved* him for it.

He'd gotten the twins and Rafe to pack up everything she owned. Rua had labeled the boxes with sarcastic notes like *"Your thousand scarves, lass,"* while Cian had wrapped every one of her teaching books with gentle care. Rafe had carried everything without complaint, even the cracked flowerpot from her porch that still smelled like rosemary.

He didn't mind staying at the school, either. Didn't grumble when Garin assigned him the task of keeping watch from a distance.

He just parked that beat-up truck of his outside the middle school every morning with his boots up on the dash, and said, *"Mornin', sunshine. Seeing eye dog's on duty."*

It made her laugh every time. He drove her home with a quiet smile most days, grumbling about traffic or the weather or how the cafeteria tacos smelled like death. He'd even called himself her hero once, after she tripped on the curb and he caught her with one arm before she could fall.

"Don't worry, little mama," he'd drawled. *"I got eyes on you even when you don't."* And once, when he helped her into the truck, he'd added with a wink, *"Don't tell Garin, but I think your husband likes me."*

But now... Now the seasons had changed. The snow had melted. Spring had come and gone, and the Southern heat was rising thick in the air.

And Mira knew. This would be her last summer as a mortal. She sat there, fingers tangled in the hem of one of Garin's linen shirts, her cheek resting where his chest had been not long before. He'd gone to speak with Simon, but not before pressing a kiss to her temple like she was still breakable. Like he didn't know she was already braver than she'd ever been.

Today would be the beginning of the end, and the start of forever. She'd chosen him, she'd chosen eternity, and she wasn't afraid. Not of the change. Not of the pain. Not even of death. Because death had come for her once, and her Viking had ripped it away with his bare hands.

Now she would rise, not as a woman taken, but as one *reborn*. In love, in fire if need be. In fangs and freckled skin, with her song still strong in her chest. Her last breath as a mortal would not be filled with fear. It would be filled with *him*.

And gods help them both...

She was ready. She would say goodbye to her humanity, and be born again into the arms of the only man who had ever seen her fully, even in her darkness.

Into the eternity waiting in Garin's eyes.

The knock was soft, but Mira had already begun to recognize the unique rhythm of each presence in this house, each member of the coven announcing themselves not with sound, but essence. And this one... this one shimmered with calm.

"Come in," Mira called gently, her voice steady despite the weight in her chest.

The door creaked open, and the faint jingle of layered jewelry was all she needed to identify who had come. The subtle scent of dried herbs and crushed rose petals drifted in like memory on a summer breeze.

"Mave," Mira said with a soft smile, turning her head toward the footfalls now approaching the bed.

"I thought I might check on you, little one," the seer said, her warm voice laced with something ancient, yet still sounding so musical as she spoke. "How are you feeling?"

Mira let her hands rest against her lap, the hem of her sundress brushing her thighs as she answered honestly, "Nervous... but ready. I've been ready for a long time."

She felt the mattress dip as Mave sat beside her, the weight comforting, familiar, and then a touch, gentle fingers curling around her own, placing something warm and curved into her palms.

A mug.

"I brought you something," Mave said. "A brew I've developed over the years. It's made with herbs that help the body relax, make the transition easier, it will ease the pain, if only a little."

Mira lifted the mug toward her nose, inhaling instinctively... and paused.

"...Is this hot chocolate?"

Mave let out a low, melodic laugh. "Yes. Garin told me you loved it, and he thought there was no better way to begin forever than with the same drink you served him the night you first welcomed him into your home."

The emotion hit her fast, deep in her ribs, almost enough to spill over. Her throat tightened, and she exhaled softly before whispering, "He's so wonderful."

"Yes, he is," Mave said, brushing her fingers along Mira's knuckles.

And so, in the stillness of that moment, with the fading sunlight pooling in soft golden patches across the floor, Mira lifted the warm mug to her lips, took a sip of the rich sweetness, and let it anchor her. This was the last drink she would ever taste as a mortal, and it was comfort. It was memory, and it was love.

She closed her eyes and whispered to herself, *"I'm ready."*

~~~~~~~~

The sun had just begun to slip beneath the horizon, casting a deep amber glow through the windows of the study, warm light catching on old tomes and etched glass decanters lining the shelves. Garin stood in silence, massive hands wrapped around the small, worn leather journal Simon had placed in them. The Viking's calloused fingers looked almost too large, too brutal, for something so fragile. But he held it with reverence all the same.

Across from him, the Frenchman stood with his usual calm, one hand in his pocket, the other gesturing lightly as he finished his explanation.

"You must keep her calm," Simon said, his voice soft but firm. "That's what Mave is preparing her for now. Her mind must be at ease. Her body, as relaxed as possible. It will not stop the pain, but it will help her endure it."

Garin nodded once, his eyes unreadable beneath the heavy line of his brow.

Simon stepped closer then, his tone sharpening just enough to cut through the quiet. "And you, Viking, you must control yourself."

"I will not harm her," Garin said lowly, almost a growl.

Simon didn't flinch. "No. But you must understand, this is not battle rage. This is... hunger. You will feel her blood, and it will not feel like hers. Not to the part of you that takes. It will feel like warmth, like worship, like the answer to every ache you've ever had. You must drain her slowly, and listen."

He tapped two fingers lightly over his own heart.

"Listen to her. To the sound of it. When you hear her heart falter, when you hear the last beat rise, you must act.

Immediately. Slice your vein, and press it to her mouth. She must drink your blood before that final beat ends…or it will be too late."

Garin's jaw tensed, the veins in his neck pulsing beneath pale skin as he absorbed the gravity of it. "And if I fail?" he asked, voice like gravel and frost.

Simon shook his head. "You won't. Because you won't let yourself lose her. Not again. Not ever."

Garin's grip tightened on the journal. The silence stretched between them, heavy with ancient tension, but this wasn't a rivalry tonight. This was the passing of knowledge. One immortal to another.

"Merci," the Frenchman murmured at last.

But Garin only turned toward the door, eyes burning like the coals of an old forge, ready to step into forever.

"My light waits for me," he said, voice iron and reverence entwined. "And I will not be late."

Simon's voice broke the silence just before Garin reached the door. "Garin."

The Viking halted mid-step, broad shoulders stiffening beneath the weight of the moment. He didn't turn, no he didn't need to. The emotion in Simon's voice was clear.

"She's… remarkable," the Frenchman said. "But you know… this won't change her sight. The turn, our blood, it cannot give her what was taken. She will still never see you."

The room stilled. For a moment, the only sound was the faint whisper of wind curling against the windows, brushing past the manor as though the world itself paused to hear what the Viking would say.

Then…

"I have never wished to fix her." Garin's voice was quiet, but carved from granite, unshakable. "She sees with her heart," he continued, turning his head just slightly. "And I will be her eyes in this eternity... just as she is my harmony."

Simon didn't reply. He didn't need to, because Garin stepped forward without hesitation now, out of the study, through the long hallway lit by soft wall sconces, and toward the only future that mattered.

The one where Mira waited. The one where he would hold her through fire and blood, and into forever. Every step up the grand staircase echoed like the toll of a distant bell, each one carrying more weight than the last. Garin's hand gripped the wooden banister, not for balance, but as if grounding himself to the moment. His boots moved slow against the polished floors of Thorne Manor, each step toward the bedroom door a march into a new eternity.

He could feel it. The shift in the air, the hush of the house around him. The roar of his heart in his chest, and beneath it all, the ancient prayers rising on silent breath.

Let her rise.

Let her flame burn brighter.

Let her song carry.

He had never prayed for peace before. But now? Now he begged for it. When he reached the door, he stood still. Just for a moment. A breath caught in time. Then his large hand wrapped around the doorknob and turned it. The door creaked softly open...and there she was.

Mira.

Bathed in the soft amber light of the bedside lamps, her curls spilling like wildfire over her shoulders. Her freckles dotted across her pale skin like constellations, her lips curved into that gentle smile, **his** smile. And those green eyes, sightless, yes, but locked on him the moment he entered, like she felt his presence in her bones. Her smile grew, radiant and full of trust. Of love. In that instant, Garin knew.

His prayer had already been answered. She would rise. She **was** rising, and she would be his flame, his song, his home... for all of eternity.

He barely remembered crossing the room. One moment, she opened her arms to him, gentle, welcoming, certain, and the next, **he was there**, drawn like a moth to the only flame he had ever called home.

Garin sank into her embrace, wrapping his arms around her smaller form as if he could shield her from everything that had ever tried to take her. His mouth found hers in a kiss that stole the breath from his lungs and gave it to her instead, desperate and reverent, a vow sealed with lips and longing.

She melted into him, as she always did. As she always would. He broke the kiss only to whisper against her mouth, his voice low and thick with emotion.

"Are you ready, light of mine?"

Mira didn't hesitate. She never had when it came to him. Her hands found his face, fingers warm against the roughness of his beard, and she smiled with a kind of love that shattered everything in him.

"Yes," she breathed. "Always yes."

And with that, Garin laid her down gently onto the fur-covered bed, the place that had known their first laughter, their first shared dreams, and now... would witness the first heartbeat of their forever.

His breath trembled as he hovered above her. His lips had worshiped every inch of her face, kissed away the nerves and traced promises into her skin. But now, they lingered at the hollow of her throat, where her pulse fluttered beneath pale, freckled skin like the beat of a drum leading him into battle.

This was no battle.

It was a surrender. A gift.

His fangs descended with a quiet sound, a deadly grace only she could make beautiful. And for one final moment... he paused. But her hand found him, fingers weaving into the braid at the back of his head, grounding him as only she could. Her voice was soft, a breath against the shell of his ear.

"I'm ready, my love. Go ahead."

A low growl rumbled in his chest, primal and aching. And then he sank his fangs into her throat. The moment Mira gasped, his entire body tightened. Not from restraint. But from the way her blood ignited his senses. It was not like anything he'd ever known.

Not just fire. Not just life. It was sweet, like the memory of hot chocolate on her lips. It was vibrant, like her laughter in the dark. It was music. Her heartbeat the rhythm. Her soul the melody.

It was her. And for the first time in centuries, Garin felt himself tremble, not from hunger, not from rage... but from the overwhelming knowledge that this woman, this song, this flame, had chosen to become his for eternity.

As he drank though, Garin's grip on the world narrowed to three things...

Her heartbeat, his control, and the sacred flame of what was about to begin.

He drank slowly, as Simon had instructed, each pull a test of restraint against the deepest instincts roaring through his blood. Her taste was divine, enough to unravel him, but it wasn't the hunger he fought.

It was the way she moved beneath him. Her body arched into his, trembling not in pain, but in overwhelming sensation as his venom began to flood her veins. It awakened every nerve, made her gasp, whimper, cling to him, desperate for something more, something he couldn't give. **Not yet.**

A growl rumbled in his chest as her hips shifted against him, and it took every ounce of discipline he had to pin himself in place, to stay focused. He braced a hand beside her head, forehead pressed to hers, eyes closed tight as he whispered rough, broken promises in Old Norse, prayers to the gods, to the fates, to whatever force had led her to him.

"Hold on, light of mine… almost…"

And he listened. Past the rush of blood. Past the echo of her moans. Past the fire in his own veins.

He listened.

There it was, faint, slowing, fragile. **Her heartbeat.** Still steady… but weaker now. Each thump, a dying drum, a countdown to the edge of the abyss. Garin's jaw flexed. He tasted the end coming.

Soon, it would be time.

Then… She begged. Her voice cracked, hoarse and trembling, "Please…Garin…more…", but her hands were already slipping from his shoulders, her pulse softening beneath his tongue like the final flutter of a flame gasping for air.

He felt it. The shift. The moment her mortal body began to give way, that was when *Garin moved*. He tore his mouth from her throat, not with violence, but with urgency, and in the next breath, sank his fangs into his own wrist, teeth piercing flesh as hot blood welled fast and bright. A growl rumbled from deep in his chest as the pain cut through him, but he welcomed it. Welcomed the sacrifice.

Then he pressed his bleeding wrist to her lips and cupped the back of her head in his other hand, guiding her, urging her.

"*Drink, Mira,*" he whispered fiercely. "*Now. Quickly.*"

Her lips parted instinctively, weak and trembling, but she obeyed. As his blood touched her tongue, her body shivered, violently, and Garin's free hand cradled her head, holding her steady, his voice lowering into a reverent whisper. Nothing else mattered. Not the sun now set outside. Not the world beyond their door. Only this.

Only **her.**

"Take it. Take all you need. Come back to me…"

And as the first drop of his blood passed her lips, Garin closed his eyes, held her close, and **waited to meet her again in forever.**

Epilogue

The world was unraveling.

Inside Mira's body, chaos reigned, raw and consuming. She couldn't move, couldn't breathe. Her lungs refused to work. Her limbs jerked in spasms she couldn't control, and her throat...

Was she screaming? Or was that just the sound tearing through her mind?

She didn't know. The only thing she did know was pain. Agonizing. Unrelenting. Every cell of her burned and froze all at once, as though her skin had been peeled away to expose her soul to both flame and ice. The fire licked beneath her ribs. The chill settled into her bones.

It was something else too, there was his blood. Still on her tongue, sliding down her throat like something sacred and wrong. But not metallic. Not coppery or bitter. No, Garin's blood was something else. Like the hush of firelight. Like hot chocolate in winter. Like the first note of a love song she hadn't known was written for her.

But it filled her lungs like water. She felt herself drowning in it, in him, like her body was no longer a vessel, but a war zone for transformation. Her fingers twisted in the furs beneath her. Her legs trembled violently.

Her heart...

It wasn't beating anymore. Panic tried to rise. But breath wouldn't come. She gasped. It hurt. It all hurt. Her back arched, a cry ripping from her lips that she couldn't hear, only feel, vibrating out into the ether. Her nerves burned so brightly that the edges of the world began to blur and darken and spin. But then...

Music.

So faint at first, she thought it might be her mind fracturing. But then it swelled. That same haunting melody. The one from her dream all those months ago. The one that called her to the forest. The one that brought him.

Garin. Her Viking.

It was not the sound of instruments, but of soul, of harmony pulled from a place between life and death. Of a voice that knew her name before she ever spoke it. Mira clung to it. Through the pain. Through the cold. Through the fire. Because if she was burning, then that melody would be the wind that fanned her flame. If she was dying, then that sound...was her resurrection. And through the silence of a stilled heart, Mira whispered, not aloud, but from somewhere deeper.

I hear you... my love. I'm coming back.

The melody had become a symphony now. Not of instruments, not of notes, but of soul, a song stitched from memory and marrow, stitched from him. It wrapped around her like sunlight through stained glass, like warmth after a storm. And it pulled her. Called her.

Rise, little flame... rise.

She didn't know how long she had been gone. There had been pain. There had been cold. There had been everything. Now? Nothing.

A gasp tore through her lips, sharp and alive. Her body jerked upward, desperate to claim this breath, this rebirth, but strong arms caught her. His arms. And the song? The song was his voice now.

"Mira..."

Her name cracked from her mouth like lightning, raw and broken, but it was hers. Then, she felt them. Her fangs. Sharp. Heavy. Real. Sliding low behind her lips like they had always been meant to live there.

A breathless laugh escaped her, full of wonder, full of heat, and Garin, her Viking, her husband, her eternity, was already leaning in, his hand at her cheek, his lips brushing hers in a kiss that was not of this world.

"Welcome back," he murmured against her mouth, voice thick with emotion and awe. "My wife."

It was welcome, worship. It was home. In that moment, Mira Cassidy, no longer mortal, no longer fragile, knew only this:

She felt the world differently now. The quiet thrum beneath it. The harmony woven through shadow and flame, and somewhere deep within her chest, where her heart once beat, the song began again. Not loud nor frantic. No, it was steady. Endless. Two voices, finally in tune. Two souls, lost in a darkness, now joined together in the symphony of forever.

And wrapped in his arms, with eternity stretching open before her like the first note of a symphony yet to be played…

Mira couldn't wait.

www.ingramcontent.com/pod-product-compliance
Lightning Source LLC
LaVergne TN
LVHW091621070526
838199LV00044B/892